To Robin

# Crash into Me

"You're a good woman to have around," he said.

"I won't be here long."

Sonny knew by his reaction that she'd said the wrong thing. She'd meant the words as a polite brush-off, but he wasn't the least bit deterred. Instead of defusing the tension, her vague time line had ratcheted it up.

Now he wanted her immediately.

Oops.

She knew it was time to walk away, but when Ben pulled her against him, he was so deliciously warm she almost wept. Letting the full length of her body press into his, she turned her head, resting it against his chest. She felt the cotton of his sweatshirt across her face, the tattoo of his heartbeat beneath her cheek. As she inhaled the scent of his soap, and the sexy, masculine smell of him, her hands snuck under his T-shirt, by their own volition, and splayed over his smooth, sleekly muscled back.

He sucked in a tortured breath.

She dug her nails into his skin, trying unsuccessfully to stifle a moan. If she got this hot from a simple touch, how could she keep her professional objective in sight?

"Summer—"

It was the name that brought her to her senses. The wrong name.

She jerked her hands away, pushing at his chest. His fingers were linked together across the small of her back, holding her in place. As she felt his response to her touch, an old familiar panic welled within her. That, as much as duty, made her say "I have to go."

"Stay."

"Don't make me struggle," she whispered.

He let her go, clenching his hands into fists as she slipped away.

# CRASH INTO ME

### Jill Sorenson

BANTAM BOOKS

CRASH INTO ME
A Bantam Book / February 2009

Published by
Bantam Dell
A Division of Random House, Inc.
New York, New York

This is a work of fiction. Names, characters, places, and
incidents either are the product of the author's imagination or
are used fictitiously. Any resemblance to actual persons, living
or dead, events, or locales is entirely coincidental.

Bantam Books and the rooster colophon are registered trade-
marks of Random House, Inc.

ISBN 978-0-553-59201-6

Printed in the United States of America
Published simultaneously in Canada

www.bantamdell.com

OPM 10 9 8 7 6 5 4 3 2 1

# ACKNOWLEDGMENTS

Writing is such a solitary exercise that I think we tend to forget how many people helped us along the way.

I'd like to thank the members of surfingsandiego .com and the surfers I interviewed at Windansea Beach. Everyone I communicated with was gracious in answering my questions and generous with their time.

Thanks to Larsen-Pomada Literary Agents, especially Laurie McLean. Your input on this project was integral and your support unswerving.

To Shauna Summers and Jessica Sebor of Bantam Dell, thank you so much for helping me make this story better, and for taking a chance on a new author. The experience has been amazing.

Thanks to my two best friends, Jennifer and Celeste, for always being the first to read my books (and praise them!) no matter how busy they are. And special thanks to the members of the San Diego chapter of the Romance Writers of America. We are a wonderful group.

Mom, you're the best. Thanks for always being there for me, and for my girls. We love you!

Last but definitely not least, thanks to Chris. You are proud of me, and it shows. You mean the world to me.

Any factual errors I made or liberties I took are completely my own.

# Crash into Me

# CHAPTER 1

FBI Training Center. Quantico, Virginia.

Special Agent Colby Mitchell was about to drop Special Agent Sonny Vasquez.

He pivoted, leading with his right elbow, intent on driving it home and ending a sparring match that had gone on far too long.

Vasquez was a legend, a chimera, a fantastical figure the cadets had heard about but seldom seen, so their attention was rapt. Then again, they probably would have enjoyed watching anyone get the better of Mitchell, who ran a grueling two-week training session. Although most of the trainees were in good shape, they valued the cerebral over the physical, and called Mitchell a meathead behind his well-muscled back.

Legend or no, Vasquez was the underdog, or had been before this impromptu demonstration started. Despite the considerable differences between them in height and weight, which should have tipped the scales in Mitchell's favor, he was the one dripping sweat and grunting with exertion, while Vasquez remained as cool and elusive as a goddamned ghost.

Mitchell added the energy of desperation to his blow. He did not want to lose to this particular opponent. His colleagues would never let him live it down, and Vasquez, too superior to gloat, would merely study him calmly, assessing his weaknesses, making it apparent to all that he wasn't up to snuff.

So he said a mental prayer as he swung his arm around, visualizing success, anticipating the winning impact of his triceps against Vasquez's smooth, perfectly shaped jaw.

But as his powerful body turned, he knew he'd miscalculated. Vasquez *was* a ghost, and Mitchell's prayer went unanswered. Instead of being in position to receive the blow, Vasquez had ducked under and down. In leading with his elbow, Mitchell made another fatal mistake: leaving open the vulnerable expanse between his armpit and waist.

Of course, Vasquez struck with the swiftness and ferocity of a mythical creature. The jabs to Mitchell's side were startlingly painful—how Vasquez wrung that amount of strength from those scrawny arms was an elliptical mystery.

Sucking in a sharp breath, Mitchell dropped his arm to protect his burning midsection, focusing only on preventing Vasquez's bladelike fists from striking into his sore ribs. Then he saw a premonition of his own defeat in those strange, light eyes, and Mitchell didn't have time to blink before Vasquez dropped *him,* with a blow to the temple so well placed it was almost a caress.

An excruciating, debilitating caress.

From the ground, Mitchell looked up at his nemesis in wonder, fighting nausea and gasping for breath, his eyes stinging with sweat and tears. The circle around them clapped and cheered, oblivious to his torture, or perhaps excited by it.

Bloodthirsty little guppies.

Vasquez's head gave a slight shake, indicating to the group that celebration was unnecessary. Mitchell groaned, letting his head fall back against the mat while Vasquez made a sanctimonious little speech about never underestimating a smaller opponent. After the crowd dispersed, Mitchell focused his eyes long enough to see Vasquez standing over him, neither smiling nor smug, offering a hand to help him to his feet.

At the sight of that hand, so slender and deceptively innocuous-looking, the same that had dealt his ego, not to mention his temple, a crushing blow, Mitchell snapped. He took the proffered hand and yanked on it, bringing the victor down to his level, and in a split second, Sonora Vasquez was on her back, with Colby Mitchell on top of her.

"How'd that sex change operation go, Vasquez?"

He grinned as beads of sweat from his forehead fell on her face. She needed to be reminded she was a woman, and if he wasn't man enough to do it on the mat, he was more than willing to have a go at her on the mattress.

More amused than insulted, Vasquez wiped away the offending drops of sweat like she was swatting at flies. "It's called sexual reassignment surgery, Mitchell. Don't they teach you anything in sensitivity training?"

"Yeah. I'm feeling real sensitive right now." He was aware of her breasts crushed against his chest and the soft apex of her thighs, an inviting warmth beneath him. She might not fight like a woman, but she felt like one, and although he willed his body not to, it began to respond to hers. He was enjoying dominating her a little too much. Still, he feared for his manhood. Vasquez would go ballistic if he got hard.

But she didn't go ballistic—she laughed. "The doctor said if I wanted to live my life as a man, I'd have to be happy with three inches, so I told him to forget it. I couldn't bear to look like you."

Mitchell grunted. "Keep wiggling, Vasquez. Those three inches will turn into six."

For a moment, she looked startled, as if she'd only just realized he'd been flirting with her. Before she could shield the reaction, her unusual eyes betrayed her panic, and Mitchell experienced an intense surge of satisfaction. Vasquez couldn't dislodge him, because she sucked at wrestling, and now he'd found her secret vulnerability: she was afraid of men. The vindictive side of him wanted to press her further, but he rolled away, because he was a meathead, not a jerk, and the last thing he needed was a sexual harassment charge.

"You're such a Neanderthal, Mitchell," she said, recovering.

"Ooga booga," he replied with a smile. "Want to go back to my cave?"

"No," she said, using the serious tone women affected when scolding a child, making it embarrassingly clear that she did not encourage his advances.

He shrugged, feeling amiable. Vasquez may have beaten him in front of everyone, but now he had her number. Good agents knew that most warfare was psychological, and Colby Mitchell was a very good agent. He was also smart enough to do damage control, and sensitive enough to treat Vasquez with respect, albeit belatedly.

"I was just fooling around," he said. "No hard feelings?"

The tension in her face faded. "Whatever, Mitchell." She brushed invisible lint from her jogging pants. "Next time you want to rub your wiener on someone, ask Stacy."

"Really?" Like most young, single males on the prowl, his attention was easily diverted. Vasquez was hot, but Stacy League was...built. His eyes roved over Special Agent League's very pleasing form as she sparred with another female trainee. She wasn't half as good on the mat as Vasquez, but who wanted an assassin in the sack? "She likes me?"

"You didn't hear it from me," she said, pulling herself to her feet. This time, he let her help him up.

"Thanks for the tip, cutie." He knocked her lightly on the chin.

She wrinkled her nose. "Don't push it."

"Do you want to know who likes you?" He scanned the room for a man who wasn't more afraid of her than attracted to her.

"No."

"Why not?" He smirked. "Oh, I get it." He took her by the shoulders and turned her toward the openly gay female cadet Stacy was sparring with. "Is she more your style?"

"You wish," she said, shrugging away from him. "Do I need to kick your ass twice?"

"Yeah. Show me how to do that temple thing."

She shook her head. "You're too strong to use it for immobilization. You can only do it with lethal intent."

He rubbed his hands together. "Goody."

Sonny took a deep breath before she entered Grant's office.

Although the summons ordered her to come right away, she'd taken the time to shower and make herself presentable. Contrary to popular belief, Sonora Vasquez was a woman, and sometimes she liked to look like one.

She knew her appearance added to her formidable reputation, so she usually didn't bother to accentuate her femininity. Her features were too strong to be called pretty, her eyes too fierce to put a man at ease, her mouth more appropriate for biting than kissing. For a blue-eyed blonde, her complexion was dark, giving her the unusual appearance of a dusky waif or a washed-out gypsy, and her hair was an unremarkable champagne motley. It was thick and unruly, so she kept it cropped short, which pleased her, not any man she'd ever met.

She'd always been a tomboy—by chance, if not choice, having been forced to wear her brother's hand-me-downs throughout childhood. She still couldn't afford designer clothes, expensive makeup, or sexy shoes, but she worked well with what she had: good bone structure, great instincts, and a killer bod.

The pride she took in her figure was mostly professional. She was a lean, mean, fighting machine, and few men wanted to tangle with her, in or out of the bedroom.

Special Agent in Charge Leland Grant was the only man, besides her brother, she'd ever trusted enough to get close to, but there were no sparks between them. Perhaps because he was happily married, and old enough to be the father she'd never had.

She knocked on the frosted glass office door before she entered, just to be polite, knowing he could see her more clearly than she him. Grant was on the phone, raising a "just another minute" finger in her direction, a gesture that had been annoying people for decades and didn't fail to elicit the same reaction in her.

Sonny slumped into a chair across from his desk, going for a posture somewhere between apathetic and insolent.

His lips curved as he watched her, and she knew she'd succeeded only in amusing him, so she let out the breath she was holding and sat up straight. This was her boss, not her best friend, and it would behoove her to act that way.

"Going somewhere?" he asked as he replaced the receiver.

She looked down at the slim-fitting jeans, high-heeled half boots, and snug sweater she was wearing. Why did everyone have to comment when she wasn't dressed like a slob? "The movies," she decided.

"With Mitchell?"

She frowned. "Hell, no."

"I saw you two training."

She wasn't surprised. The gym had a two-way mirror, which intimidated the cadets to no end, because they never knew when superiors were spying on them. It had been awhile since anyone had judged Sonny's performance, however. She'd been active for more than five years, and proven herself resourceful and adept on many occasions.

"For a second there, you froze."

Her spine stiffened, and she had to force herself to relax. "I didn't freeze, I considered. He's cute." Crossing her arms over her chest, she dared him to dispute her.

Grant didn't bother to. "It can't happen in the field."

She knew what he meant. He didn't give a damn if she screwed every agent on the payroll as long as she didn't turn into a helpless female at an inopportune moment. His concern was not for her safety, although such a mistake could cost her her life, but for the success of the team he led. He wanted to catch bad guys, and if she panicked during physical contact, she was more of a liability than an asset.

She gave him a cold stare that had withered lesser men.

Undaunted, he leaned back in his chair. "I have an assignment for you."

Her mood shifted. "Yeah?"

"It's a mother."

"Don't tease me."

"I'm not." He handed her a slick three-ring binder containing pages of glossy photos behind clear page protectors.

The man in the pictures was the most recognizable professional surfer on the planet. "Ben Fortune? You've got to be joking."

Grant was on the phone again, so he didn't answer her. She flipped through the file, studying a copy of Fortune's driver's license and memorizing much of his personal information at a glance. With his dark good looks and tall, muscular physique, the man was very easy on the eyes. In the not-so-distant past, his likeness had been used to sell everything from deodorant to men's sportswear. The candid shots, featuring him in a body-hugging wetsuit, low-slung boardshorts, or just plain old jeans and a T-shirt, ran like an Abercrombie & Fitch catalog.

There was one full-length photo, obviously taken from a distance, that was particularly striking. Fortune was standing alone on a rock-strewn beach, looking out at the ocean, surfboard wedged under one arm. It must have been taken in the early morning, because the picture had a grainy, grayish cast, like a fine coat of mist coated its surface.

Sonny associated surfing with crowded beaches and fun in the sun, but neither element was present here. The sky was overcast and the mood somber, even solitary.

This was not a picture that would have sold toothpaste.

After she finished perusing the file, with more attention to detail than was probably necessary, Grant handed her another, holding the phone to his ear with his shoulder.

It contained pictures of women. Like Fortune's, their faces were familiar, but not for world-class surfing or lucrative corporate sponsorships. They were victims of a serial killer who had been hunting off the coast of Southern California for the past two years. The bodies had been found along a relatively small stretch of land north of San Diego, in a ritzy, bohemian community known as Torrey Pines.

Sonny knew the area and its people well. Before attending the FBI Academy and accepting a job at VICAP, the most prestigious criminal apprehension program in the country, she used to live there.

Torrey Pines was a prime section of real estate, encompassing a couple of beachside neighborhoods just outside of San Diego's busy metropolis. La Jolla, the jewel, boasted a breathtaking coastline, shallow tide pools, and some of the best surfing beaches in California. In contrast, Torrey Harbor was quiet and low-key. It purported to be a quaint fishing village, although these days more of its residents made their living as artisans than on the sea.

Both communities had lost one of its local girls to a killer.

Hanging up the phone, Grant leaned back in his chair and folded his arms across his chest, awaiting her reaction.

"You think the SoCal Strangler is a surfer?"

He gave a noncommittal shrug. "It's a lead."

"Based on what?"

"Trace evidence." Picking up a list from the top of his desk, he read, "Titanium, neoprene, petroleum jelly, and sand." At her puzzled expression, he went on to explain. "Most wetsuits are made of neoprene, a synthetic, water-resistant material. The water is cold in California, and many surfers wear them year-round."

"Sand is obvious enough, but petroleum jelly?"

"Hardcore surfers get contact dermatitis from wearing a wetsuit all day. They put Vaseline around their necks, where the fabric tends to rub."

"What about titanium?"

"A component of high-quality wetsuits. The kind you buy when money is no object. They keep you warm in the winter, but rub the hell out of your neck."

"Are you saying that he was wearing a wetsuit when he perpetrated the killings?"

"Perhaps. A wetsuit would inhibit movement, but it would also be good protection against defensive injuries."

She frowned down at the photo in her lap, finding

the idea difficult to wrap her mind around. Ben Fortune was the stuff dreams were made of, and she wasn't just considering female fantasies. Boys of all ages aspired to be like him. "Surfers are a dime a dozen in Torrey Pines," she argued. "La Jolla is crawling with trust fund babies who have nothing better to do than ride waves all day. What links Fortune to these crimes?"

Grant deliberated for a moment. "There are some unusual circumstances surrounding his wife's death."

Sonny remembered the incident well. Before the culprit was arrested, Fortune had gone through a lengthy, much-publicized interrogation. Since then, he'd all but disappeared, shunning the contest circuit and retreating from the limelight. "She was murdered by a drifter," she recalled. "Darrius O'Shea. He made a full confession."

"Which he recanted."

"When?"

"Yesterday," Grant said, sliding a sheet of paper across his desk, "in his suicide note."

She picked up the copy of the note. It was poorly spelled but painstakingly executed, stating only that he hadn't killed Olivia Fortune, and in his final moment of clarity, wished to leave this world unencumbered.

People rarely lied in suicide notes. If anything, they used the opportunity to come clean. Even so, cynicism had her asking, "Does he have family?"

Grant smiled. "Not a soul. O'Shea was a veteran

and a loner. His parents, estranged wife, and brother are all dead."

"Hmm." Not much reason to prevaricate, with no surviving relatives. "Why would he confess to a crime he didn't commit?"

He leaned back in his chair again. "Who knows? Mental illness. Unresolved guilt over a separate incident. The lure of a warm bed and three square meals a day."

It wasn't unheard of for interviewees, especially the young and weak-minded, to make a false confession under duress. "He had the murder weapon," she pointed out.

"That he did," Grant agreed. "Fortune's wife was strangled with electrical cord, just like the recent victims. And although the incidents could be unrelated, there are enough similarities to warrant further investigation."

"Was Fortune considered a suspect before O'Shea was arrested?"

"Yes, but due to lack of evidence...or because of his family's connections with local law enforcement, he was never formally charged."

"What connections?"

"Mr. Fortune, senior, is a retired criminal court judge, and a very powerful man. He could have called in a few favors."

She closed the files in her lap, satisfied. "Where do I come in?"

Grant removed his glasses and massaged his tired eyes. "I want you to go undercover. Hang around, make yourself visible. Some of the victims were beach bunnies, surf groupies, and you're from the area."

She quirked a brow. "I'm from the other side of the tracks. Last Chance Trailer Park is not La Jolla Cove."

"An undercover assignment implies playing a role, Sonny."

"Grant, I'm twenty-eight. The eldest victim was twenty-two."

He studied her appearance. "You could look younger, if you wanted to. And wear sunglasses. Your eyes give you away."

Sonny shifted in her chair, bothered by the notion that anyone could see through her. "Why are you sending me?"

On this point, he leveled with her. "I need an attractive female whose looks garner attention, and you fit the bill. You're also familiar with the area, the laid-back attitude. I can't send a surveillance team with you, so you'd be on your own, for the most part, but I know you can handle yourself."

She crossed her arms over her chest. Grant was flattering her, and more importantly, enticing her with a challenging, high-profile assignment. Getting close to Fortune wouldn't be easy, and having free reign, with little or no interference, also sounded appealing. Of course, there were drawbacks. She was no sexpot beach bunny.

He read her mind. "I can offer you a limited wardrobe budget."

She smiled. "I'll take it."

"Fine," he said, replacing his glasses. "You'll go tomorrow."

Sonny rearranged the files on her lap, her mind on getting into character for a peach assignment. Returning to Torrey Pines would almost be like going back to high school, with new clothes, ten years of life experience, and the security of knowing she could kick the ass of anyone who got in her way.

# CHAPTER 2

After a week of observation, Sonny knew Grant's plan for her to infiltrate the ranks of a very close-knit society would fail.

She'd been set up in a small but costly coastal apartment less than a block from Windansea Beach in southern La Jolla. The location was choice for wave-, babe-, or boy-watching, all of which Sonny had been doing her fair share.

Ben Fortune was spectacular eye candy.

Fortune no longer competed professionally, but he was still on top of his game and in peak physical condition. He did things on the water other men only dreamed about. Sonny spent entire afternoons in wide-eyed amazement as he cut his board through curls of wave as sleek as glass, glided on the edge of breakers the size of thunderheads, and emerged from the pipe in a gusty mist, as if the ocean had breathed him in, and finding him worthy to ride another day, exhaled him back out.

The sport was so varied in its execution that she could pick Ben out from a crowd of dark wetsuits and light-colored surfboards. Each surfer was unique, in the way he held himself, almost crouching, or standing fully upright; in the movement of his arms, reaching out to touch the curl, fingers splayed, or hands clenched tight, as if he could grasp each exhilarating moment and hang on to it like a fistful of sand.

Fortune, in particular, had a style that was just plain beautiful to behold. At times he was electric, all sharp edges, quick drop-offs, and wicked cutbacks. He could also make his movements appear effortless, fluid, organic, as if his surfboard were an extension of his body, a living, breathing thing. Watching him was like communing with God; his easy grace was nothing less than transcendent.

As assignments went, it was tops. Sonny fell in love with the Pacific all over again, and could have observed wave after unadorned wave break upon the sandy beach, delighting only in the joy of indefatigable Mother Nature. Studying handsome athletes in their prime, perfectly muscled bodies encased in slick black wetsuits that left little to the imagination—perhaps it wasn't exactly a spiritual pursuit, but it was a great perk.

The problem was neither spiritual nor physical, but professional: the subject did nothing but surf. He didn't sign autographs, give interviews, or pose for photos, even with hardcore fans, and he certainly didn't condescend to acknowledge novice surfers. He might nod to his comrades or exchange a combination of words only they could understand, but even this level of communication was rare.

If still waters ran deep, Ben Fortune went fathoms.

His rejection of tourists, newcomers, and inexperienced surfers was rude, but his general attitude toward women was downright weird. Bikini girls were as assiduously avoided as the dank, lice-infested piles of seaweed that frequently washed ashore.

It was odd, for he was a man who had a reputation with the ladies. To hear it told, Fortune's second-favorite sport, once upon a time, had been scoring with chicks, and his success in this endeavor had been almost as prolific. He'd fathered a child out of wedlock when barely of legal age to do so, and after seven years of sowing his wild oats on the contest circuit, he'd finally married the baby's mama. Since then he'd been a good boy, faithful to his wife, by most accounts, even in the three years since her death.

Sonny's original strategy to approach him in a tiny bikini and trip all over herself asking for his autograph appeared to need some rethinking.

Perhaps Fortune was making amends for his misspent youth with this self-imposed stint of abstinence. Or he had a secret girlfriend (or boyfriend, one never knew). Or maybe, in an act of God befitting a surfing philanderer, an Aussie tiger had made off with his willy, as well as a piece of his surfboard, during that much-publicized shark attack along the Gold Coast.

If anything was going on with parts seemingly whole and certainly well-defined beneath his wetsuit, Sonny wasn't privy to it, and neither were her colleagues. All reports claimed Fortune lived like a monk, surfed like a madman, and had only one woman in his life.

His sixteen-year-old daughter, Carly.

Sonny crouched behind the group of rocks below the stone steps leading from the street down to Windansea Beach. She'd been following Carly Fortune since the teenager snuck out of her multimillion-dollar La Jolla residence a few minutes ago.

The house wasn't as ostentatious as it sounded. Snugly sandwiched between other family homes of similar price, it was moderately sized and favorably situated, with the nonexistent yard space and spectacular oceanfront views typical to the area.

Fortune probably could have bought the entire block, but for a guy who lived and breathed to ride waves, being able to count less than a hundred steps from your back door to the best surfing beach in San Diego probably meant more to him than marble flooring and suburban sprawl.

Fortune got up at 5:00 A.M. every day to (what else?) surf. He was an early-to-bed, early-to-rise type, allowing his daughter a certain amount of leeway for mischief.

Sonny didn't underestimate the cunning of the average sixteen-year-old girl, but she was an expert at ghosting, and could have kept up with Carly Fortune in her sleep. Needing little concentration for the task, she placed a call to Grant on her cell, having been given specific instructions to check in with him at 11:00 P.M., her time.

It was late in Virginia, but Grant kept odd hours. For all she knew, he'd been at a charity fund-raiser this evening.

"Grant," he answered in a terse voice.

"Vasquez."

"What have you got?"

"I haven't got jack."

"Then why are you whispering?"

"I'm following someone."

Carly Fortune, much to Sonny's surprise, wasn't meeting a boyfriend to smooch with or a friend to sneak a joint. She was walking out into the surf like a virgin sacrifice!

"Gotta go," she said, closing the cell phone and scrambling to the top of the tallest rock in the vicinity, no longer concerned with being seen. Carly was wading into the 50-degree Pacific, fully dressed. Not only that, Sonny thought, studying the play of moonlight across the surface of the water, she'd chosen a spot with a killer rip current.

Sonny wasn't the type to begrudge a teenage girl her high jinks, but Carly was in the worst possible location for a polar plunge. Even if the girl stayed calm and let the current take her out, or remembered to swim at an angle instead of spinning her wheels trying to get back to the beach, she'd be in for a grueling workout.

If she lived.

Sonny wasted a couple of seconds stowing her gun between rocks. Placing the 911 call, she ran down the uneven slope of sand toward the water, yelling out to the girl as she listened for the operator. "Carly!"

The surf was heavy, pounding—it was difficult to hear the voice on the phone right next to her ear. Either Carly couldn't hear her, or didn't want to. While Sonny watched, her dark head dipped underwater.

"Nine-one-one. What's your emergency?"

Sonny kicked off her sneakers and shucked out of her jeans, resting the phone on the crook of her neck. "There's a girl drowning at Windansea Beach. Carly Fortune, 561 Neptune. At the base of the stone steps. Hurry!"

By that time the icy surf was swirling around her thighs. Sonny threw her cell phone behind her, hoping to hit the sand, and pulled her sweater over her head, letting it fall into the water. She dove, ducking under the waves breaking against the sandbar. As soon as she started swimming, her strokes strong and sure, she felt the pull of the undertow, taking her out to sea.

The water was shockingly cold and the current surprisingly powerful. It occurred to her that she was in danger, despite her excellent health and extensive training. Riptides were deadly in summer, in warmer water and broad daylight, with lifeguards and other swimmers all around.

Under these conditions, the risk was tenfold.

In the few seconds she'd been submerged, the cold was already turning her muscles into jelly, and her lungs were fighting to contract and release every breath.

Sonny considered saving her strength for the swim back to shore. It was difficult to maneuver inside the current, and she wasn't sure she could locate Carly no matter what she did. Then she saw the girl's head bobbing up, mere inches in front of her. Putting every negative emotion behind her, she kicked furiously, reaching out...

...and coming up with an awesome handful of Carly Fortune's inky black hair.

She jerked, pulling the girl's chin above the surface and shoving her forearm underneath it. Positioning their bodies so they both faced the shore, she concentrated on keeping Carly's head above water long enough to give her a few instructions.

"If you want to live, you've got to help."

Carly nodded, clearly conscious and possibly not even hysterical.

"It's too cold to ride this out. We swim to the left, on three."

She nodded again, spitting out a mouthful of water, and gasped, "Okay."

Sonny almost laughed with relief. Drowning people were notoriously difficult to handle. She was lucky to find Carly Fortune in such an amenable state of mind.

"On three," she repeated, summoning strength. "One, two, three, go!"

They pumped their legs in a wild burst of energy

that defied the cold and used panic to its benefit. Carly kicked Sonny in the shins a few times in her fervor, but Sonny's limbs were so numb she barely felt it. Just when it seemed their efforts were all for naught, that the mighty Pacific was intent on crushing them in her icy grip, they broke free of the current and floated like buoys in calmer waters, drifting up and down on a lull between waves.

Sonny released her. "You did good, kid. Can you swim?"

Carly treaded water experimentally. "Yeah."

Never letting the girl out of her sight, or her reach, Sonny swam alongside her until their feet hit sand. If not for the biting cold, and a fatigue that went bone-deep, the going would have been easy, as the waves practically carried them back to shore.

Sonny lay there several minutes, red-faced, chest heaving, before the chills started. Carly quietly vomited seawater beside her, a good sign, in that the girl was both alive and purging her body of a substance it was better off without.

By the time the paramedics arrived, both of them were more in need of a hot bath and warm clothes than medical attention. This was California, not Antarctica. A five-minute dunk in 50-degree water was uncomfortable, not life-threatening.

Sonny was grateful for the rescue blanket the paramedics offered her, because she was cold and wet. Not having had the opportunity to retrieve her jeans, she was also naked but for a bra and panties. While she stood there shivering, Ben Fortune stormed the beach parking lot like a militant paratrooper, barefoot, like she was, but dressed in dry jeans and a soft-looking T-shirt that she envied.

"What the fuck is going on?" he asked of no one in particular.

Carly was in the back of the ambulance, huddled under a blanket, having her blood pressure taken. "Dad?"

Her voice sounded so raw that Sonny reevaluated the girl's motives for a late-night romp. Perhaps this had been a suicide attempt.

Carly let the blanket slip from her shoulders and threw herself into Ben's arms, the blood pressure gauge hanging loose, forgotten. Under the light of the street lamp, and the fluorescent glow from the back of the ambulance, his handsome face looked pale and his dark eyes hollow. He accepted the embrace woodenly, the way fathers did with daughters they no longer recognized nor understood.

Sonny's heart broke for both of them because they made a hug look as awkward as it could be.

"What happened?" he asked, his demeanor changing from bewildered to scolding in a split second. Sonny wanted to groan aloud at the uncanny ability of the male species to ruin a tender moment. "Do you have any idea what went through my mind? When the police called I thought you were—"

It wasn't her place to, but Sonny stepped in. "She's fine," she said, placing a hand on his shoulder. His gaze cut to hers and the corner of his lip curled up, as if he couldn't fathom why a strange woman would not only interrupt him but deign to *touch* him.

Sonny removed her hand, although his shoulder

was warm and masculine and felt very nice, because she was afraid of losing it.

Carly came to her defense. "She rescued me, Dad. I fell in the water."

He looked from one wet, bedraggled female to the other. "You *fell* in?"

Sonny had to hand it to him: even in a crisis situation he was savvy enough to question the incongruity of that statement. Windansea Beach had some jumbo rocks, but it was a flat stretch of land, not exactly the cliffs of Dover.

"Okay, so I jumped in, but there was a rip current, and it took me out..." As she trailed off, her lower lip trembled.

If it was an act, it was a damned good one. Ben seemed to forget about Sonny's presence entirely. "Why?" he asked quietly.

"I don't know," she wailed, covering her face with her hands. "I don't know."

He pulled her head to his chest and held her there, murmuring words of comfort and stroking her wet hair. The action was so rare to her that Sonny stared at them in wonder, awestruck by the simple gesture. She'd had a rough childhood, a worse adolescence, and in response to that, an often lonely adult life, over the course of which never had another person touched her so compassionately.

Over the top of Carly's head, his eyes met hers. "I am indebted to you," he said, his gaze raking down her body, making her more aware than ever she was barefoot and nearly naked underneath the blanket.

Sonny only shook her head, for her throat was closed, and she was unable to speak.

"Where are your clothes?" he asked.

She scanned the dark expanse of sea and sand. "On the beach somewhere," she said, finding her voice. "I took them off before I went in after her."

He nodded. A man who spent as much time as he did in the water knew how dangerous, and restrictive, wet clothing could be.

The paramedics donated the blanket and left to take another emergency call, finding nothing wrong, physically, with Carly Fortune. Sonny had refused treatment, so their asses were covered.

"Where do you live?" he asked.

"Around here," she said vaguely.

"How far?" he pressed.

"A mile," she lied, not meeting his eyes. He was very intense close-up, and although she was an expert manipulator, the situation unsettled her.

He unsettled her.

"We live right here," he said, indicating the back door with a jerk of his head. "The least I can do is invite you in to warm up."

She shrugged her assent, teeth chattering, and followed them up the stone steps, staring at his back as he held his daughter close. They passed through an unlocked gate, walked across a dark patio, and stepped over the threshold into the kitchen.

Just like that, Sonny was in.

Surrounded by the comforts of her own home, Carly reverted back into a normal teenaged girl—prickly, insensitive, and self-absorbed. "I've *got* to get out of these wet clothes," she said with a shudder. As Ben led Sonny from the kitchen to the living room, Carly dashed up the stairs, her shoes making squishy sounds on the hardwood flooring.

"Carly," Ben called after her, "why don't you bring something for, uh"—he didn't know Sonny's name, and she didn't offer it—"her to wear?"

At the top of the steps, Carly's pretty face puckered. "She won't fit into anything of mine," she said, studying Sonny's blanket-clad form with a critical eye. "You get her something." With that, she tossed her wet mane over her shoulder and flounced away.

Ben wore a pained expression. "Sorry," he said. "She's—" He broke off, finding no words to describe his daughter's disposition.

"It's fine," Sonny replied, admiring the interior of the house. The living room was spacious, inviting, and blessedly warm. A couple of overstuffed chairs and a leather couch faced a fireplace rather than a television set, and a live Christmas tree was set up in one corner, bedecked with a ragtag collection of ornaments that had obviously been made by a child.

Her heart melted at the sight.

"I like your tree," she said. "No one puts up lights around here anymore. I'd forgotten it was Christmas."

"We're all environmentalists," he explained. "Conserving energy."

"Is that it? I was afraid that acknowledging the change of seasons, in such a warm climate, had become passé."

He arched a brow. "Where are you from?"

"Out of town," she said, looking away. A fire crackled in the hearth. Sonny wanted to crawl inside it and curl up there to sleep, to stare into its depths until it reached out to eat her, to open up her blanket and let the flames lick at her body.

"You're too small to wear my clothes," he said with a frown. "But I suppose I can find you something."

And then he left her there, standing by the fire.

She felt a strange lassitude, a reluctance to benefit from this emotionally charged circumstance, and a disdain for the inherent ugliness of undercover work. Ben Fortune's love for his daughter was genuine and his gratitude was sincere. Sonny Vasquez would have accepted his thanks and walked away. Summer Moore was obligated to milk it for all it was worth.

He returned with a couple of neat, folded items. "These are mine. Carly may have been right about her clothes not fitting you. I don't understand how she fits into some of them herself." He shrugged, smiling, immensely appealing as a clueless single dad.

Her stomach fluttered in awareness.

Ben Fortune had the kind of face that photographers, sponsors, and advertisers loved, a natural charisma that leapt off the pages of magazines. His features were strong and rugged, not perfect enough to be boring, and his smile was becomingly off-center.

On paper, he was tall, dark, and handsome. In person, he was irresistible.

And how trusting he was, to allow a complete

stranger in his home. It certainly didn't gel with his standoffish public image.

She didn't smile back at him. Instead, she accepted his clothing, changed in his bathroom, and with a derelict disregard for duty, curled up in his chair and fell asleep, alone, in front of his fire.

"Who is she?" he whispered.

"How should I know?" Carly whispered back.

"She saved your life."

"I didn't catch her name while we were drowning."

"Maybe she's your guardian angel."

Her response was an unladylike snort, her apathy so honed to perfection that he almost bought it.

"Why did you go out there? Really? Were you thinking about—"

"No! God, why does everyone think I'm freaking out over Mom? I'm not."

"Carly?"

"Yeah?" She rolled her eyes, feigning annoyance.

"I love you."

For a moment, he had her, the old Carly, the girl who smiled at him radiantly, hugged him spontaneously, and loved him unconditionally. Then her eyes became shuttered, and that girl was gone. "I know," she said carefully, as if his love hurt her.

He turned his attention back to the stranger, for this Carly would retreat if pressed, and he couldn't bear to see her slip any further away from him than she was right now. "Should we wake her up?"

"Hell, yes. I won't be able to sleep with some random person in the house."

"Why do you think she's random?" he asked, adopting Carly's word for strange. He was irritated by her lack of gratitude, but he was also curious, and the woman was unusual.

"Just look at her."

In repose, she looked cute and cuddly, like a fuzzy kit fox or a wolverine cub, the kind that would mulch your arm into shreds if you reached out to pet it. He didn't know how he knew she was ferocious, but he did, and for some reason it endeared her to him. She also must be strong for her size; pulling a person out of the undertow isn't easy. Before she'd changed, he couldn't really tell what she had going on underneath that scratchy blanket, but he'd caught a few glimpses of something...curvy. Now her body was swallowed up by his loose jeans and oversized sweatshirt.

His gaze wandered back to her face.

Ben wasn't the type of man who noted the color of a woman's eyes, unless he was looking into them, and only then if he was trying to get her into bed. Hers were so striking he remembered them with perfect clarity. So light they should have appeared colorless, but didn't. They were strange, ice blue, electric. Hot and cold at the same time.

And her skin was warm. Especially now, in front of the fire. Her hair was drying in straggles around her face, hair the color of warm honey, like her skin. And her lips—

"Dad."

"What?"

"Are you retarded? You're staring."

He dragged his attention from the sleeping sylph. "What would have happened to you if she hadn't been there?"

Carly didn't want to answer, so she shoved at the stranger's shoulder, waking her abruptly. "Here's some tea," she said, pushing a cup into her hand.

Something dangerous flashed in the woman's light eyes, and for a second, Ben thought Carly was going to get a well-deserved faceful of Earl Grey. Then it was gone, as if he'd imagined it, and she accepted the tea with a tentative smile.

"We'd give you something stronger, but Dad's an alcoholic, so we don't keep any hard stuff around." When he glared at her, she blinked innocently. "Well, it's true."

"What's your name?" he asked.

"Summer," she replied.

"How old are you?"

"Dad!"

Summer laughed. "Old enough to know better."

"Know better than what?" Carly asked.

"Than to fall asleep in a stranger's home," she said, casting Ben an amused glance. When their gazes locked, a warmth passed between them, as though they'd shared a secret.

Taking a sip of tea, she turned to Carly. "How are you feeling?"

"Me? I'm fine." She studied her sock-covered feet, probably ashamed she had refused clothing to the person who had saved her life.

"Thanks for the tea."

"Dad made it," Carly allowed.

Summer's eyes met his again, over the rim of the cup, and his pulse thickened. "It was my pleasure," he said with a slow smile.

Carly jumped to her feet. "He thinks you're pretty," she blurted.

Summer sat up very straight, running a hand through her disheveled hair. It had dried in clumpy locks that were sticking up in some places and smashed flat in others. "I'm not," she said ruefully.

Carly nodded, almost impolite enough to verbalize her agreement.

They were both blind, Ben decided.

Summer peered down into her empty teacup, as if she might find some leaves down there to chart her future course. "I should go," she said.

"No," he protested, too loudly, rising to his feet.

Carly's sleek black eyebrows drew together.

"I mean, you're . . . you don't even have any shoes on," he said.

She shrugged. "I'll find them on the beach."

"I'll drive you," he offered, desperate to extend the visit. There was something about her. He didn't believe in angels, but he was unnerved by her, and it had been so long since he'd felt . . . anything.

"No," she said. "It was nice meeting you—Carly." She tasted the name on her lips, smiling as if she liked it. Then she looked at him expectantly.

"Ben."

He stared at her mouth, waiting for her to test his

name out the same way. "Good-bye," she said instead, glancing at Carly.

"Bye," Carly said, offering a tight smile.

"I'll walk you out," he said, willing Carly into silence with a pointed glare. Amazingly, she complied.

Behind Summer's back, he mouthed "Thank you" to his daughter.

She said *You're welcome* by flipping him off.


The tide was going out, not coming in, so her jeans, shoes, and cell phone were all where she'd left them on the beach. Ben looked out across the water, a grim expression on his face. To his trained eye, the undertow couldn't have been more apparent.

"Does your daughter know about currents?" she asked.

"Of course."

"A lot of people can't discern them from the shore."

Ben let out a heavy sigh. For him, and most surfers, all of the elements of the ocean were discernable at a glance. Not seeing a rip current would be like ignoring the water, or being unaware of the sand. "I think I'll lock her in her room until she's thirty."

Sonny smiled, because he sounded serious. "I'll give you back your pants, but I need to borrow your sweater, if you don't mind. Mine got swept away."

"Keep it," he replied absently.

Since his sweatshirt covered her to midthigh, and he wasn't looking anyway, Sonny dropped trou right there on the beach, stepping out of his jeans and into her own. By the time she zipped up, he was looking. She folded his jeans and returned them, still warm from her body, finding something unbearably intimate about the gesture.

They stared at each other for a long, awkward moment, the pounding of the surf the only sound in the dead of night. Then her cell phone rang, breaking the mood, and she was so flustered that she almost said, "Vasquez," ruining her cover.

"Hello?" she answered instead.

"Sonny?"

"Yeah, it's Summer," she said, in case Ben had radar hearing, and tipping Grant off she wasn't alone.

"What the hell were you doing? I was worried."

"I'll call you later," she said, clicking her phone shut and pocketing it.

"Who was that? Your boyfriend?"

"My boss," she said, surprised by the invasive question. "He can be a nuisance."

"Want me to take care of him for you?" he teased.

She studied his broad shoulders, his athletic musculature. She could take him down in less than three seconds. "I can take care of myself."

The hint wasn't subtle, so he would have no trouble picking it up. Still, he made no closing remark.

She stuck out her hand.

He accepted it, but instead of giving her a polite handshake, he held on to her, as if he wanted to keep her. "Let me take you out to dinner. To thank you properly."

She pulled on her hand, but he held fast. "Are you asking me out?"

"Yes."

"No."

He frowned, giving her the impression he was unaccustomed to rejection, and found it less palatable than he'd imagined. "What if Carly comes along? She loves to enumerate my flaws. You'll be in no danger of liking me."

She doubted it, but considered the invitation, if only to get her hand back. He radiated warmth, and at his touch, her body felt alive from the roots of her hair to the tips of her toes. She'd underestimated him, mistaken his laid-back attitude for congeniality. In the water, his movements were so graceful as to appear effortless. On land, he was just as smooth.

If he were any more intent on seduction, she'd be flat on her back.

Sonny would have to tread lightly. Grant wanted her to spy on Ben, not moon over him like a silly schoolgirl. He'd also be furious if she refused to foster this acquaintance.

"Someplace casual?" she asked.

He smiled, taking that as a yes. "What's your address? I'll pick you up."

"No, I'll walk over."

He let her have that one. "Five-ish? We eat early."

She nodded, and he released her hand.

"Tomorrow night, then."

Sitting down on the sand, she put on her shoes, waiting until he was out of sight to retrieve her SIG.

It wasn't until she was safely ensconced in her

apartment across the street that she placed a hand over her racing heart. It was beating fast and hard beneath her palm. Swallowing dryly, she closed her eyes and rested her back against the door, breathless with anticipation.

# CHAPTER 3

Ben met John Thomas Carver at the rock wall on the south side of Windansea Beach.

"Merry Christmas," he muttered, tossing him half a joint.

JT caught it midair. He'd always had quick reflexes. "Whoa-ho," he said, opening his palm. "What's this?"

"A little holiday cheer."

Ben's former drinking buddy and longtime surfing companion brought the partially smoked joint up to his nose and inhaled. JT was Ben's age and he looked it, with his suntanned face and the lines bracketing his mouth. Sometime over the past twenty years, Ben had blinked, and his skinny, sleepy-eyed friend had grown into a man.

JT had filled out considerably since his teens, and shorn his sun-streaked locks to a more conservative style, but he hadn't exactly sold out. He still cared more for waves than work, preferred bad girls to good, and couldn't say no to a recreational high.

Smiling, JT tucked the joint behind his ear. "You off the wagon?"

Ben leaned against the side of the wall, looking out at the mash of water. Choppy form, one-to-two-foot swells, nothing but foam soup and a crappy onshore flow. "Nah," he said, dragging his gaze back to land. "I took it away from Carly over the weekend. Last night, she threw herself into the Neptune rip."

That wiped the grin off JT's face. "Is she okay?"

Ben didn't know how to answer that. Feeling the hot press of tears behind his eyes, he took a moment to gather his thoughts. "Physically, she seems fine," he said, hearing the strain in his voice. "A stranger went in after her. A woman."

JT just stared at him, waiting for him to finish.

"I was inside, asleep. The cops called and woke me up, saying she'd been in an accident."

JT let out a low whistle. "That girl could drive a saint to drink."

"Yeah, well. I never claimed to be that."

"What are you going to do?"

Ben shrugged, shoving his hands deep into the pockets of his jeans. JT was more of a good-time guy than an intimate confidant, and having had few responsibilities in his devil-may-care life, he was hardly an expert on parenting.

The person he really needed to talk to was Olivia.

"Smoke that, would you?" Ben said, feeling

maudlin. "I want to make sure it's just pot she's messing with."

JT plucked the joint from behind his ear and moistened his lips, glad to be of service. "With pleasure."

Ben took a lighter out of his pocket, leaning forward to offer the flame while JT cupped his hands around his face, blocking out the wind. It took him a few tries to get the joint started. When it lit up, JT's eyes widened and he sucked in a lungful of smoke. "Tastes all right," he croaked, holding his breath.

Grunting, Ben pocketed the lighter and glanced around to make sure no one was looking, although he'd smoked pot on this beach a thousand times and never been caught.

JT took another few hits for good measure and doused the cherry with his wet fingertips. Then he split open the paper and studied its contents.

"Well?"

"Give it a few minutes to kick in, bro. Maybe it's creeper."

Ben laughed a little, touching the bridge of his nose, as close to hysteria as he'd been to tears a moment ago. If memory served, the term meant that the high snuck up on you.

"Looks like regular shit to me," JT added, pocketing what was left of the joint. "No black tar or white residue. No funny taste."

Ben nodded, trying to feel relieved.

"Are you really that worried about her smoking dope, man? We did a lot worse when we were her age."

"Maybe I don't want her to end up like me."

JT squinted at him, shading his eyes from the sun. He opened his mouth to respond, then got distracted by a pretty girl walking by and lost his train of thought.

Ben watched him with growing impatience.

JT waved a hand in the air, remembering what he was going to say. "Carly's a great kid. With a face like hers, you're lucky she's not out running wild with boys."

It made Ben uncomfortable that JT had noticed his daughter's good looks, but the truth was that everyone did. Like Olivia, Carly drew stares wherever she went, and someday soon her beauty would surely be Ben's agony.

It was no less than he deserved, for all the womanizing he'd done in his youth.

JT's face brightened with another idea. "Your dad never stopped riding you when you were growing up. That's why you took off, right?"

Ben's mouth twisted. "Yeah."

"So just be cool, and she'll turn out fine."

Ben thrust a hand through his hair, hoping JT was right. To say his father had raised him with an iron hand was putting it mildly. He'd demanded nothing less than excellence in every subject, every sport. Buckling under that constant pressure, Ben had dropped out of school and left home. He'd traveled around the world, in pursuit of pleasure and the perfect wave, molding himself into the kind of man his father disapproved of.

JT's parents, in contrast to Ben's, had been incredibly lax. His mother was a B-movie actress who couldn't be bothered with a young son on a movie set. She'd shipped him off to live with his dad, an aging rock star who'd been resting on his laurels since having a string of hits in the late seventies. He died of a drug overdose when JT was eighteen.

Ben wanted better for his daughter than what he and JT'd had. Every day he struggled to achieve a middle ground with her, but he never knew when to lay into her and when to lay off. Carly was a master manipulator, playing on his insecurities, and she'd had him wrapped around her little finger since birth.

Olivia had always hated him for making her be the only disciplinarian.

Ben pushed that thought aside and looked out at the cold blue Pacific, wishing it was pounding out something worthier, something more punishing.

Sonny didn't know why she was so nervous about her date. Her instincts told her that Ben Fortune as a murder suspect was just another dead end.

As a hot boyfriend, if she were free to treat him as such, he was a good start.

She spent too long getting ready, trying on and discarding several outfits. Although she'd bought a few new items with Grant's highly exaggerated wardrobe budget, she knew the last thing Ben would be interested in was another cookie-cutter beach bimbo.

She finally decided on the jeans, half boots, and sweater she'd worn to Grant's office. It was casual, unpretentious, and demure enough to keep him guessing.

To impress Carly, she added a Kate Spade clutch, a flashy little bronze number only large enough to hold her cell phone and a few essentials.

She left her SIG at home.

Sonny knocked on Ben's door, his borrowed sweatshirt in hand, noting the perfectly manicured landscaping around the front entrance. Juniper trees were interspersed with beach pebbles and colorful, decorative shells. Judging by their massive size, the shells were treasures from foreign shores.

When he opened the door, she shoved the sweatshirt into his arms in a lame attempt to deflect his attention from her appearance.

It worked, at first. "Cool," he said, as if he'd been looking around for a jacket or something similar to wear in deference to the winter chill.

As he raised his arms to pull the garment over his head, his T-shirt rode up above the low waistband of his jeans, exposing a few inches of flat stomach, outrageously sexy hip bones, and an intriguing line of silky dark hair leading down from his navel.

A sensual image came to mind, one of her falling to her knees and rubbing her cheek across that smooth expanse.

Her heart began to beat a pagan rhythm. Oh man, oh baby, oh... *yes*.

Oblivious to her lustful paralysis, he ran a hand over his hair, straightening the sweater's hem and cuffs. "How do I look?"

She had to laugh. "Good."

His eyes roamed over her, and he wasn't shy about

zeroing in on her breasts. "So do you. Better than good. Delicious."

Her stomach muscles clenched. "I look...delicious?"

"Yeah. Buttery and syrupy, like waffles. Or maybe I'm just hungry." He looked up the stairs. "Carly!"

Carly Fortune swept down the stairs, throwing her long hair over one shoulder, outdoing them both with a spectacular, slinky black dress. It was long-sleeved and high-necked, with a short skirt that showed off legs most women would kill for.

"I said casual," he complained.

"Daddy, you're wearing *shoes*. That's formal." She kissed his dark cheek in a Lolita-like greeting, solely for Sonny's benefit. Judging by the hard set of his jaw, he was not amused.

Carly summed her up coolly. "Are you a lesbian?"

Sonny almost choked. "Uh..."

"Carly!"

"What, Dad? Look at her hair."

"I'm sorry." He clamped his hand around Carly's forearm, applying enough pressure to silence her. "My daughter is obsessed with sexuality."

Carly's jaw dropped. "I am not."

"Then don't ask rude questions."

In a midnight blue Lincoln Navigator worth more than Sonny's annual salary, there was an argument over where they would eat. Ben still had a hankering for pancakes.

"I am not going to IHOP in this dress," Carly wailed. "How about Veracruz?"

Ben looked to Sonny for confirmation. "Sounds

lovely," she said, hoping she would live through the meal.

Veracruz was an upscale steak and seafood house where no one blinked an eye at their mixed attire. The maître d' called Ben by name, told Carly she looked stunning, and seated them at the best table in the house.

Sonny ordered a steak, hoping she wasn't showing her trailer park heritage by having it cooked thoroughly. Most snobs turned their noses up at anything but medium rare. As it turned out, the faux pas was much worse. Just when Sonny was cutting into her steak, thinking she'd dodged a bullet, Carly announced, "Dad's a vegetarian."

Her knife clattered against the plate.

"Don't you think that's wimpy?"

Sonny looked carefully, but she couldn't find anything unmanly about him. "No."

"Carly's exaggerating," Ben said, giving his daughter a quelling stare. "Enjoy your meal. Please."

"I'm not exaggerating," Carly insisted. "You don't eat red meat. It's totally gay."

His mouth tightened at the slur, but he let it slide. Sonny supposed he had to pick his battles. When Carly turned to her for a reaction, Sonny lifted her fork and took a big bite, wanting no part of the conversation.

Ben also polished off a good amount of his meal, not letting his daughter's surly mood bother him. For a gay man, he was giving off some pretty strong hetero vibes, and Sonny had to admit that under his gaze she'd never felt less like a lesbian. Every time their eyes met the air between them crackled with electricity.

"I have better things to do than watch you two stare at each other," Carly said acidly.

"Like what?" Ben asked, his patience worn thin. "Smoke weed in your room?"

Carly narrowed her catlike eyes at him. "When are you going to get over that?"

"It was five days ago."

"Oh, please. You've smoked a mountain of pot in your lifetime."

"That doesn't mean you can."

"You don't let me do anything!"

Ben nodded, agreeing that this was the best course of action.

"He doesn't even let me drive," she complained to Sonny. "I've had my learner's permit for six months."

Sonny tried not to shudder at the idea of Carly Fortune behind the wheel of an automobile.

"I'm going to the ladies'," Carly announced, squaring her shoulders.

"If you throw up, I'm taking the bill out of your allowance," he warned.

Sonny almost choked on her vegetables. What would be next? Hari-kari over dessert? Carly Fortune was a walking, talking teenage nightmare. "I'll go with you," she said quickly, putting her napkin on the table.

"He's only joking. I never puke."

Ben gave his head a slight shake, indicating that Carly was lying. Sonny couldn't conceive of a man who would be so nonchalant about his daughter's eating disorder, but when she studied him closely, she realized he was at the end of his rope. As she rose to follow Carly, he leaned forward, closing his eyes and pinching the bridge of his nose in a way that was positively heartbreaking.

No wonder he didn't go out. Carly sapped the energy from the room like a tsunami, sucking up everything in its wake.

"You may as well forget it," the girl said moments later as she emerged from a stall.

"Forget what?"

"Bagging the bachelor," she replied, performing a mini-toilette at the sink. "My dad isn't interested."

"Who said I was?"

Carly's eyes met hers in the restroom mirror. "Give it up. He's hot."

Sonny conceded the point with a nod. "Don't you want him to be happy?"

"He is happy. He has surfing and me."

"What about you? Don't you want a boyfriend?"

"No," Carly said, lifting her chin. "I'm going to be an independent woman."

Sonny smiled. "Okay."

"Okay what?"

"I'll leave him alone, if it means that much to you."

Carly looked suspicious. She wanted an argument, not an agreement. "Fine," she said anyway, whipping her long black hair over one shoulder.


"I'm sorry about Carly," Ben said again, leaning back against the seawall at the crux of some craggy rock formations at Windansea Beach.

"Don't be. You aren't responsible for her every action."

He looked out at the water, his expression somber. "Now you're thinking you should have let her take her chances out there, right?"

The Pacific was as stormy and unpredictable as it had been the previous evening, a formidable hash of blue and white, like the soapy surface of a giant washing machine sloshing back and forth. Sonny got a disturbing image of Carly's lifeless form, laying facedown on the foam-specked surface, dark hair floating around her head.

"I was a teenager once. Not too long ago," she added, in deference to the role she was supposed to be playing. Ben was awfully young for a man with a sixteen-year-old daughter, but she knew he wouldn't be interested in an immature girl, fueled by hormones and emotion. He had more than enough drama with Carly.

"Were you? I have trouble picturing you giggling or throwing tantrums."

"No. I misbehaved in other ways."

"Let me guess. You got into fights."

Her pulse accelerated. "What makes you say that?"

His dark eyes flicked over her. "There's something about you, a violence, lying just below the surface. I wouldn't turn my back on you."

"Jesus," she said with a shaky laugh, running her fingers through her hair. "Don't romanticize it. Just say what you think."

He shrugged easily. "If I'm wrong, tell me. I don't

mean to insult you. Perhaps violence isn't the right word. Maybe it's strength, or passion."

She didn't bother to tell him that he'd been right the first time. Nor did she need a diagram to understand his interest in her. "I don't want to be your next challenge, Ben. Like some big wave for you to conquer. Another cheap thrill."

He was silent for a moment, weighing her words. "I didn't think you knew—"

"Who you were? Why, because I didn't fall all over myself to go out with you? Not every girl is impressed by the size of your wallet, or your stick, surfer boy." She poked at his chest, and was rewarded when annoyance flashed across his face. "By the way, you're wrong. I didn't fight. I was promiscuous."

There. Let him chew on that.

"I don't believe you," he said after a pause. "Tell me some dirty stories, to prove it." He tried for a sly smile, but his eyes were heavy and intense.

She looked away. "I'm sure yours would put mine to shame."

He only nodded, guilty as charged. "Carly always rakes me over the coals for getting her mother pregnant when we were seventeen. I can't believe she'll be that age soon. God forbid she follows in my footsteps. Or attempts to outdo me in debauchery, which would be a challenge."

Sonny took pity on him. "She told me she wasn't looking for a boyfriend."

He brightened. "Really? That may be true, for now. But she does flirt with my friends."

She shook her head, not envying his position. "Maybe you *should* lock her away until she's thirty."

"I know I've indulged her too often," he said with a sigh. "She's always been difficult, and I've usually been . . . gone."

Sonny looked out at the dark, stormy Pacific. The evening had turned blustery, and it was time for her to go. "I told her I would leave you alone."

"What do you mean?"

"She's not ready to share you."

"Let me worry about Carly. She's important to me—hell, she's everything to me, but I can't let her dictate my life forever. I'll take you out again, just us."

"No."

"Fuck."

His frustration was matched by her own. She'd never felt this drawn to someone. They had nothing in common, besides an obvious mutual attraction and a history of youthful indiscretions, which had most certainly taken a greater toll on her than him. It had been her experience that a man could engage in any number of illicit encounters and walk away with a clear conscience and a spring in his step.

Even if she could pursue an emotional relationship with him, professional ethics decreed that she maintain a physical distance. Getting close to a subject was one thing, hopping into bed with him another.

She cursed Grant for putting her in this precarious situation. "Ben, it's not Carly. I can't get involved with anyone right now."

He looked perturbed, and impatient. "Is it because of that guy on the phone? Your boss?"

"Kind of."

His eyes narrowed. "Are you in love with him?"

"Of course not," she said with a scowl. Grant was like family to her, and there had never been anything romantic between them.

He smiled, more confident now that he would have her. "If you aren't involved with him, why's he calling you at midnight?"

Like Carly, he had a habit of asking impertinent questions. Sonny wrapped her arms around herself to ward off the chill. "I work with search-and-rescue squads. Troubleshooting, helping teams work together efficiently. Sometimes he needs to reach me at odd hours."

"Search and rescue?" He sounded impressed. "No wonder you went in after Carly."

"I've had some pretty extensive water training," she said. That, at least, was true.

"You're a good woman to have around," he said.

"I won't be here long."

Sonny knew by his reaction that she'd said the wrong thing. She'd meant the words as a polite brush-off, but he wasn't the least bit deterred. Instead of defusing the tension, her vague time line had ratcheted it up.

Now he wanted her immediately.

Oops.

She knew it was time to walk away, but when Ben pulled her against him, he was so deliciously warm she almost wept. Letting the full length of her body press into his, she turned her head, resting it against his chest. She felt the cotton of his sweatshirt across her face, the tattoo of his heartbeat beneath her cheek. As she inhaled the scent of his soap, and the sexy, masculine smell of him, her hands snuck under his T-shirt, by their own volition, and splayed over his smooth, sleekly muscled back.

He sucked in a tortured breath.

She dug her nails into his skin, trying unsuccessfully to stifle a moan. If she got this hot from a simple touch, how could she keep her professional objective in sight?

"Summer—"

It was the name that brought her to her senses. The wrong name.

She jerked her hands away, pushing at his chest. His fingers were linked together across the small of her back, holding her in place. As she felt his response to her touch, an old familiar panic welled within her. That, as much as duty, made her say "I have to go."

"Stay."

"Don't make me struggle," she whispered.

He let her go, clenching his hands into fists as she slipped away.

# CHAPTER 4

As soon as she returned to her apartment, still reeling from her date with Ben, Sonny went straight to the bedroom and took the case files out of the closet.

She needed to be reminded that Ben Fortune was a suspect, no matter what her instincts—or her body—told her. So what if he was ridiculously handsome? Serial killers were often charming, intelligent, and attractive. Some were accomplished liars, and experts at putting their victims at ease. On the surface they looked like anyone else, the average Joe or the boy next door, with no hint of the beast beneath.

Sonny spread the crime scene photos out on the surface of the bed, thinking that Ben was no more a killer than she was. Even so, she allowed for the remote possibility that her attraction to him was interfering with her professional objectivity. What an inopportune time to find out she wasn't immune to lust.

The images of death weren't any easier to look at the tenth, or even the hundredth, time around, but she forced herself to do another close examination.

Victim one, April Ramirez, was a brown-eyed brunette, very young, and very pretty. Daughter of cruise ship mogul Juan "Bailamos" Ramirez, she was found in Torrey Harbor at the base of Sunset Cliffs. She'd been raped and brutalized, her clothes torn from her body, and her wrists tied with her own bra. The marks on her neck, and the whites of her sightless eyes, spotted with aneurysms, told a terrifying tale.

The second victim was Sarah Knox, a free-loving, earth-saving blonde. She'd been a dedicated student and amateur drug dealer, cultivating hydroponic marijuana and a 4.0 GPA at SDSU. She was found nude, facedown on the beach near La Jolla Cove. Like April Ramirez, she'd been raped, and strangled with some type of cord.

Their killer knew better than to leave behind DNA, but there had been enough trace evidence at both scenes, namely wetsuit fibers, to link the murders together.

Was there also a connection to Olivia Fortune's death?

Sonny had obtained a copy of Olivia's file from the local police department, and there were many dissimilarities between Olivia's murder and the more recent attacks. Ben's wife had been killed in her own home, and this scenario suggested some degree of forethought or familiarity. There was also no indication of rape; the only genetic material present belonged to Ben.

There were more discrepancies in execution. Olivia had been strangled by a length of electrical cord, of the same size and circumference as the implement used in the later murders, but the marks on her neck looked very different from the marks on the other victims. They were multiple, for one, and tentative, for another. They were the kind of marks a fledgling killer would make, as though he wasn't sure how much pressure to apply.

Or as if he was entertaining second thoughts.

Troubled by the idea, Sonny shuffled through the file folder, looking for more information about Darrius O'Shea.

A decorated veteran of the Vietnam War, O'Shea had suffered a head injury during his final tour of duty. His marriage had dissolved soon after his return to San Diego, and in the following years he had few personal ties and no permanent address.

If not for the disability check he'd collected in person each month, one would have never known he was alive.

Less than forty-eight hours after Olivia Fortune's body was found, the police arrested O'Shea for vagrancy. Upon finding a monogrammed towel with Mrs. Fortune's initials stitched in gold thread, along with the infamous murder weapon, mixed in with his personal effects, two homicide detectives interrogated him.

O'Shea confessed to the crime eventually. Tests on

the items in his possession left no room for error. And yet, he had no motive, no history of violent attacks. In addition to the towel, only a small piece of jewelry had gone missing from the Fortune household. Olivia's wedding ring, which boasted a sizable rock, hadn't been touched, and Ben's money clip had been in plain sight, not far from the point of the attack.

O'Shea had been mentally evaluated and declared competent. The homeless vet was a man of few words, apparently, but his statement of guilt had been unequivocal. He spent the next three years in a maximum security prison. News of his death had been widely reported, although the specific details hadn't been made public.

Sonny reorganized the files and pushed them aside, lying back on the bed and staring up at the ceiling, collecting her thoughts. For the first time in her life, she was having difficulty separating her emotions from the case.

It wasn't like she'd never handled a rape/murder before. With her personal history, they were the most difficult, but she refused to let the past overwhelm her.

At least, not at work.

Tomorrow, instead of drooling over Ben Fortune, she would visit the prison where O'Shea had spent his last days. In order to move forward with the investigation, she had to delve deeper into the mind of the man who may or may not have killed Ben's wife.

• • •

Once her dad fell asleep, Carly snuck away from the house, needing ultimate privacy for the ritual she was about to perform. He'd removed all the locks to her room, even the one to her bathroom, so there was no longer a place at home where she felt safe from discovery.

Now she was hidden amidst a cluster of rocks at the northern tip of Windansea Beach. It was dark, and late, and she was alone. This time she made sure no one followed her.

She sat down on the damp sand with her back against a flat rock, casting one last look around before she removed the washcloth from the pocket of her jeans. She unfolded it gingerly, careful not to cut her fingers on the razor blade it concealed, and pulled her shirt over her head. Placing the washcloth against the lacy cup of her bra so blood wouldn't seep into the pristine white fabric, she lifted her elbow slightly, poised to draw the edge of the blade across a patch of smooth, unblemished flesh.

She inhaled sharply, savoring the moment, anticipating the quick flash of pain, the slick red trickle, and most important, the exquisite emotional release, as sweet and tender as a sigh.

Carly didn't have an eating disorder, but it was easier to pretend she did at the group therapy sessions her dad made her attend. Several months ago, he'd caught her hunched over the toilet, vomiting her guts out after her first attempt at cutting. Lots of the girls at her school were bulimic or anorexic; like drug and alcohol addiction, it was a designer disorder. Nobody sweated you for puking in the john after lunch—the only trouble was elbowing past the other Barbie dolls to get your turn.

She couldn't blame them, now that she'd seen their faces in group, had heard their stories, their confessions. Purging was the same as cutting, in a way. A fast tension reliever, an easy, purely physical liberation, a quick release of blood or food, in the place of emotions that were too strong or awful or dirty to be dealt with.

Carly understood the other girls, and commiserated with them.

She did feel bad about deceiving her dad. In group, the counselors droned on and on about honesty and open lines of communication, until the refrain repeated in her head like a drill.

But hadn't he let her down a thousand times?

Fuck group, she decided viciously, willing her hand to let the blade descend upon her flesh. Every time she went to therapy and hung with those losers, it got harder to make the first cut, and after she came down from the high it gave her, she felt twice as guilty.

"Don't do it." The low voice came from the rocky outcrop above her.

Carly let out a strangled squeak, almost slashing herself accidentally as she jumped. With horror, she realized that the voice was male, so she dropped the blade into the sand and brought her shirt up to cover her chest.

When he leaned forward, out of the shadows and into the moonlight, she took an unsteady breath. He was just a boy, her age, and therefore unthreatening.

"It's none of my business, of course, but it seems a shame to put scars on such beautiful skin." He leapt off the rock he was crouched on and dropped down to sit beside her.

Clutching her shirt to her chest, she began to scoot backward, reassessing him as a possible menace. She was tall, but he was taller, certainly heavier, and he moved quick. Plus, he'd been skulking around in the dark, watching her.

He plucked the razor from the sand and held it up to catch the meager light, showing her his intentions before he stashed it. "As a man, I'd say a mark or two doesn't hurt. But I've never known a woman who wanted to ugly herself up. Especially at such a pretty place."

In spite of herself, she smiled. He was probably just a smooth-talking juvenile delinquent, but she liked being thought of as a woman. "You're not a man," she said.

"Sure I am. Enough so that I was enjoying the peep show."

"Then why'd you stop me?"

"And let you mar perfection? Not a chance."

"I've done it before," she bragged, flattered by his compliments.

"I know. I've seen you."

Carly was disconcerted by the idea of being watched in a private moment. "My dad's going to kick your ass when I tell him you've been spying on me."

He eyed her shrewdly, or perhaps he was only trying to get another glimpse of what was under her shirt. "Go ahead and tell him," he said, calling her bluff. "I've got your razor blade, and I'll bet you have some old marks, scabs and stuff, under that lacy little scrap you call a bra. Yeah, bring him out here. I'd like to talk to him about what you've been doing."

"You're a freak," she said shrilly, worried now.

Carly was just about to run when the clouds shifted and a fortuitous ray of moonlight struck his face. She couldn't discern the exact color of his eyes or hair, although she assumed both were dark, but could make out his well-arranged features, and they were familiar.

"I know you," she said. "I remember you from junior high. You were a year ahead of me. What's your name?"

"James."

"James what?"

"James Matthews."

Despite the tension, or perhaps because of it, she laughed.

"What's so funny?"

"Your name. It's like two first names."

"Okay, *Carly,*" he said, with more sarcasm than was necessary to make his point.

She felt a flutter in her belly, like the tension she sometimes got before a big test. "You remember me?"

"Yeah."

"Where've you been? I mean, I haven't seen you at Shores."

"You go there?"

She rolled her eyes, nodding. "It sucks."

"I thought you went to private school, rich girl."

"No," she said glumly, letting the slight pass. "Dad's into social justice."

"What's that?"

"I don't know. Where do you go?"

"Nowhere. I have homeschool."

Her heart made a funny little twist. Only religious wackos and lowlife dropouts had homeschooling. "How is it?"

"Sucks."

They understood each other perfectly, for a moment, before a strange glint in his eyes made her remember that she wasn't wearing a shirt. James was cute, dangerous, and a little scary. It was an appealing combination, but she wasn't ready for what his eyes said she'd get if she lingered here. "I've gotta jet." She stood, careful to keep her shirt from slipping.

He jerked his chin up in a gesture boys used as *hello, good-bye, who cares,* and *whatever.* "Don't come back here, rich girl."

She looked over her shoulder, aware that the pose was provocative, considering her mostly naked back. "Why not?"

"This is my place."

Carly started to argue, then rephrased the negative comment into a question, like they'd taught her in group. "What do you do here? Besides peep at girls?"

His eyes licked down her back then went far away, across the ocean. "Same thing you do. I hide."

●   ●   ●

Ben heard Carly come in through the back door, but he didn't go downstairs to confront her. Instead he waited, listening for the sound of her footsteps, his pulse pounding with adrenaline. All of the fear and anxiety he'd experienced over the past few frantic moments upon finding her bed empty, transformed into rage.

She tiptoed up the stairs, making very little noise, for she'd had the foresight to remove her shoes in the hallway. Once inside the safety of her own room, she let out a deep breath and pulled the door closed behind her.

He reached out to click on her bedside lamp.

She blinked at the sudden light, her eyes huge with guilt and wide with surprise.

"Where the fuck have you been?" he asked. His voice was clipped, his enunciation carefully controlled.

She moistened her lips, eyes darting around the room.

"Don't lie," he warned, forcing himself to remain seated. He'd never hit her, never even spanked her as a child, but he was mad enough to make up for that oversight right now.

"I was with my boyfriend," she said, lifting her chin in defiance. "What's the big deal?"

He searched her face for signs of deception. Carly was a poor liar, despite having plenty of practice, but he couldn't always tell. "Summer told me you didn't have a boyfriend."

Her forehead wrinkled. "What does she know? You guys, like, discussed me?"

"What's his name, then?"

"James Matthews."

"You made that up."

"Did not."

Ben believed her, and it did nothing to assuage his anger. He hated the idea of some teenaged dirtbag taking advantage of his daughter's precarious emotional state. The last thing she needed right now was more turmoil.

Grabbing the makeup bag he'd found in her bathroom, he upended it on the bed, spilling its contents over the snowy white duvet cover.

Her pretty face paled. "You went through my stuff?"

He rose to his feet, eliminating the space between them in two angry strides. "Is this what your boyfriend taught you?" he yelled, gesturing to the bloody washcloths and razor blades on the bed. "To cut drugs and wipe up cokehead nosebleeds?"

When she didn't answer, he took her by the upper arms and shook her, trying to scare the truth out of her.

"It's not what you think," she stuttered.

"What is it, then?"

She stared down at the carpet, refusing to answer.

He released her, trying to maintain a semblance of control. It was impossible to describe the way he'd felt while searching her room. The scenarios he'd imagined and memories he'd relived. "When did it get so difficult for you to look me in the eye?" he asked quietly. "I tell you that I love you, and you act like it kills you. What the hell is going on with you, Carly?"

Closing her eyes, she leaned back against the door. "It's not what you think," she repeated in a whisper.

"We're not leaving this room until you tell me."

"Lisette and I were trying to give each other tattoos," she said in a rush of inspiration. "In Cultural Studies, we learned about this tribe in New Zealand, and figured we could do the same thing they did, with pen ink and razor blades."

"Bullshit," was his succinct response.

"If I was into coke, don't you think you'd find some white powder on that stuff?"

He glanced at the jagged pile of razors and stained washcloths. "That's a lot of blood for amateur tattoos."

"Yeah, well, we fucked up. It didn't work."

His eyes cruised over her warily. "Show me."

"Show you what?"

"This tattoo shit."

Trembling, she crossed her arms over her chest. "No."

"Why not?"

"It's on my chest."

"So?"

"It's on my boob, Dad."

He wasn't deterred by her display of modesty. "Show me now, or I'll call Lisette's parents and tell them what you just told me. At the very least, they can hear about the joints you two were toking Saturday."

"Fine," Carly grated, pulling her shirt up and the top of her bra down quickly, revealing a flash of crisscrossed scabs.

It was enough to send him over the edge.

Grabbing her by the arms again, he pushed aside the fabric, exposing a dozen raw-looking red lines. Some were partially healed, others fresh and ugly.

In an instant, he was murderous. "Lisette did this to you?"

She shook her head in denial, covering herself with her hands.

"This Matthew-Mark punk? I'll fucking tear him apart."

"No, Daddy," she said, her eyes filling with tears. "I did it. To myself."

For a moment, he was so stunned he couldn't breathe. He'd heard about self-mutilation before, but he'd never suspected his own daughter would resort to such measures. How could he not have known? And what else had she been doing while he'd had his head buried in the sand?

He sat down on her bed, shocked to the core. "You told me—no, you *promised* me—that you weren't suicidal," he said when he trusted himself to speak.

She began to cry in earnest. "I don't want to kill myself. Not really. I just get these feelings, and I can't get rid of them, so I cut myself, and they go away."

"I thought you were getting better," he said, wrapping his hand around her thin wrist and pulling gently, urging her to sit down next to him. "You said group therapy was helping."

"It is helping," she said in a choked voice. "I'm just crazy."

"You're not crazy, Carly," he said with the conviction of someone who loved her more than life itself.

He put his arm around her. "But if you're getting better, why are you cutting yourself?"

"I don't know." She wiped the tears from her face with the hem of her hooded sweatshirt. "It's easier than feeling all tied up in knots."

So was drinking, he knew from experience, and felt an ugly stab of guilt. He wracked his brain for some of the tenets of AA. "When you want to cut yourself, will you talk to me instead? I promise not to get mad. Maybe I can help you through it."

"Maybe," she replied with a noncommittal shrug.

"And you can work on that old rust-bucket in the garage. If you get it running, I suppose I'll have to let you drive it around sometimes." He cringed as soon as he made the statement, but she perked up visibly, so he couldn't retract it. Carly was obsessed with sports cars—and wouldn't you know it, he could afford whichever one she wanted. About a year ago she'd talked him into buying her an antique Corvette Stingray, a fixer-upper.

Determined to make it roadworthy, she'd taken two semesters of Auto Mechanics since then, and she was a whiz at it. Carly might be moody and spoiled, but she could also rebuild a carburetor like nobody's business.

He could only imagine how dangerous she would be in the driver's seat. His daughter was wild and reckless, just like Olivia. Just like him.

With parents like these, who needed enemies? Taking risks was in Carly's genes.

She looked up at him through dark, wet-lashed eyes, the picture of her mother, achingly beautiful in the lamplight. Ben almost couldn't bear the resemblance. Most of the time, the pain of losing Olivia was like a dull throb, an ache that receded more every year. Other times, like now, when they really needed her, it was so damned sharp...

Carly must have felt the same way, because she ducked her head, hiding the fresh tears that were swimming in her eyes.

He put a finger under her chin, tipping it up. "We'll be okay. We'll get through this. We can get through anything."

"Yeah," she said, trying on a wobbly smile.

He pulled her close, all but crushing her in a fierce embrace, then just held her for a long time as she cried.


"Did you find one yet?"

His dad's sly, cantankerous voice rang out, startling James as he shut the door behind him. When he saw the dark thing in the corner of the living room, the hairs on the back of his neck stood up.

Arlen Matthews was sitting back in his recliner, smoking. The cigarette smell and its glowing tip were the only indications of his presence.

"Maybe," James mumbled, clenching the keys in his fist. For the millionth time, he wished he had the balls to stand up to his old man.

"What's she look like? Big titties, I hope."

"Nah," he said, studying the dingy white shoelaces on his black canvas tennis shoes. "I mean, I couldn't really tell." Now, that was a blatant lie.

His eyes had eaten up Carly Fortune's lace-covered breasts like they were candy, and he knew their size and shape well enough to sculpt them from memory.

In fact, he'd probably be doing some inadvertent pillow-sculpting tonight, tossing and turning until he fell into a fitful sleep.

"Blond or brunette? Tall or short?"

"Blond," he said, warming up to the idea of lying. He'd never bring Carly back here anyway, so the deception was a petty rebellion, a last-ditch form of self-preservation. The old man had a heavy hand and ready fists, but he couldn't abuse everything. He couldn't read James' mind, or steal his dreams. "Not very tall. Short hair, too," he added, thinking of the long, silky black strands hanging down Carly's slender back. Yowza.

"Short hair?" Arlen let out a derisive laugh. "Are you sure it was a female? Hell, boy, you're so stupid, you wouldn't know the difference. Half-queer, as it is."

James didn't bother to respond to this familiar charge; his mind went carefully blank. He wanted to be alone with his thoughts, to replay his conversation with Carly, to fantasize about what might have been and what could never be. He'd keep every detail about her private. Cherish it, maybe. God knew he had precious little else to hold close to the vest: his dad controlled every shitty moment of James' fucked-up life.

James sighed, wishing he were somewhere else. Someone else.

"Did you get me that bottle?"

"Yessir." He pulled the pint from his jacket

pocket, relieved to have moved on to topics mundane. He stepped forward in the gloom, handing it in the direction of the winking cigarette and hoping for a quick getaway.

"Not so fast." A strong hand clamped on to his shoulder, forcing him down on the couch next to the recliner. "Take a load off."

He heard the familiar sounds of his father unscrewing the cap, the unmistakable *glug-glug* of potable liquid, the hiss of hot breath after a good chug.

"Drink?"

It wasn't really open for debate, so James took the bottle and brought it to his lips, pretending to take a healthy swig. His dad always got drunk faster, and passed out quicker, when he had a little company to help him along.

# CHAPTER 5

Ben wouldn't have forced the issue, but Carly insisted on going to school the next morning. It was the last day before Christmas vacation and she had finals. If nothing else, Carly was a conscientious student, and Ben never had to remind her to study or complete her homework.

When he was her age, he dropped out of school, much to his parents' dismay. After he brought home more earnings the following year than his dad, a well-respected (and well-paid) judge, they'd stopped complaining.

Or he'd stopped listening. By the time he turned seventeen, he'd owned a pricey bachelor pad in Pacific Beach, a swank upper-floor condo where there were no rules, no curfews, and the party never ended.

Finances aside, Ben counted it as a mistake. In

those formative years, he'd had too much money, too much success, and too many greedy people telling him he was God's gift to surfing. He'd thought he was indestructible, and on the water, he was. It was on land, with those earthly delights, that he'd run into trouble.

In his mid-twenties, after he'd cleaned up his act, he'd gotten a GED and gone on to college. By then, he was no longer a drunk, but he was still an obnoxious ass, overdue for a rude awakening. His professors didn't give a shit about surfing and weren't impressed by the size of his bank account. Sure, he could make money, but did he have any idea how to calculate his quarterly interest?

As it turned out, spending all your free time partying and sleeping around didn't make you a genius. Who'd have thought?

Ben drove Carly to school in silence, wondering if it was his faulty wiring and addictive genes that made her who she was. It was easy, but not particularly productive, to blame himself for her problems.

"I'm picking you up, too," he said as she stepped out at La Jolla Shores High School. Ben guessed it wasn't fashionable to wear a backpack anymore, because Carly always carried a small stack of books and a tiny, outrageously expensive designer handbag.

"Lisette's staying over tonight," she reminded him, tucking a wisp of hair behind her ear.

"Hell, no, she isn't."

"Dad. Her parents are going to Big Bear. I asked you a month ago."

He swore sulkily, remembering that Lisette's mom had called and made the plans herself because Lisette couldn't be trusted home alone. She was even more of a wild child than Carly. The last time the Bruebakers had left her in charge, she'd thrown a ten-keg rager on the west lawn. "Fine," he muttered, rubbing a hand over his tired face. "But you're still grounded, so you two aren't going anywhere. And no pot!"

Carly rolled her eyes as she slammed the door, a good sign she was feeling more like herself. Any other morning, Ben would have spent several hours in the ocean already. Carly was so self-reliant that she usually made breakfast, got ready, and went to school under her own steam. He thought he was being cool, letting her have her independence. Now he could see that he'd given her freedom when what she'd really needed was his attention.

He stretched his neck, trying to relieve the ache brought on by several nights of too much stress and too little sleep. On impulse, he took out his cell phone and dialed the number for Scripps Hospital as he drove away.

A crisp-voiced operator asked how she could direct his call.

"I'm trying to solve a mystery," he said in a conspiratorial tone, trying to lay on the charm. It sounded pretty rusty. "A woman saved my daughter from drowning the other night and I'd like to thank her."

The operator made a mew of sympathy.

"In the chaos, I didn't catch her full name," he continued, "and I'd like to send her a token of my appreciation. Is there any way you can take a peek at the emergency report and see if it lists her address?"

"Oh, sir, I'd love to give you that information, but—"

"Ben," he interrupted helpfully, keeping his fingers crossed. "My name is Ben Fortune."

She hesitated. "Ben...Fortune?"

"Yes."

Clearing her throat, she said, "Well, I think we can make an exception, just this once..."

Sonny was getting out of the shower when a loud, warbled sound alerted her. She wrapped a towel around herself and listened for a few seconds before she realized that the strange, off-key melody was her front doorbell.

Curious, she peered through the peephole. Ben Fortune's image was distorted by the warped glass. Interesting. How had he found out where she was staying?

When a shiver of awareness traveled down her spine, she didn't lie to herself and call it unease. Having a suspect invade her turf should have made her feel apprehensive, not excited, but she'd always been a little twisted.

He raised his hand to depress the buzzer again, so she opened the door. "Don't do it. I can't tolerate that particular combination of sounds this early in the morning." She smiled, pleased with her precaffeine wit.

He didn't smile back. "Can I come in?"

"Sure," she said, studying his face. He was a damned fine-looking man, even with bloodshot eyes and a hard, tense mouth.

She stepped aside, inclining her hand in invitation.

Her apartment had come furnished with thrift-store rejects and bargain buys. The brown wool couch, with its scratchy cushions and sharp, rectangular shape, looked like a throwback from the seventies. It was so uncomfortable people must have been avoiding it for decades, because it was still in good condition.

A lacquered oak coffee table and green vinyl armchair, also genuinely retro, and undeniably ugly, were the only other points of interest.

"Like what I've done with the place?"

"No," he said, not bothering with diplomacy.

She frowned. "Do you want to sit down?"

"Not really." His eyes moved from her breasts to the tops of her thighs, lingering everywhere skin met terry cloth.

Discomfited by his perusal, she did a slow sweep of his body, proving that two could play at ogling the opposite sex. He was wearing a sky blue T-shirt that clung to the muscles of his chest and faded jeans that hung loosely on his hips. Instead of shoes, he had on a pair of ancient brown flip-flops, the kind only men with good-looking feet could pull off, and only then if they were near a beach. His were long, narrow, and tanned, like his hands.

He couldn't have appeared more casual, but she could tell by his rigid stance, his fists clenched at his sides, that he was far from relaxed.

"Coffee?" she offered, making one last attempt at hospitality. She didn't have much, but she did have a coffeemaker, and fresh brew.

"No."

Dare she ask? "What do you want?"

When she moistened her lips in anticipation, something dark flashed in his eyes. Almost unconsciously, she retreated, not aware of what she was doing until she felt the wall at her back. Stepping forward, he braced his left hand against the wall, beside her head. He had an interesting mouth, she thought, fixating on it. There was a small scar just above his upper lip, on the right side—a thin line, like a fingernail crescent.

He leaned in, putting his face very close to hers. "You lied."

She was so hypnotized by his mouth that the words coming out of it didn't immediately register. "I did?"

"You said you lived a mile away. My house is right across the street."

"I—" She broke off, feeling breathless. "I was disoriented."

"I called Scripps Hospital for your address, and they told me the emergency report says you gave Carly's name when you called nine-one-one. You knew who she was. At my house, you pretended not to."

Comprehension dawned. "Is that why you think I went in after her? To cozy up to you? Squeeze you for some cash?"

"Maybe."

Indignation burned through her. "Screw you."

"Okay." His response was flat, almost nonchalant, but she knew he was serious. "How do you want it? Because I'm in the mood for hard and fast."

It was probably the least romantic proposition she'd ever heard. And the most tempting. Ben Fortune was a very dangerous man if he could insult her and titillate her in the same breath. In her mind she told him to go to hell, but her throat closed up around the words.

His gaze locked on the curve of her lips and he hesitated, as if not quite certain how to proceed. Ironically it was she who leaned into him, pushing away from the wall and tilting her head back in brazen invitation.

And when he took her up on that sensual offer, closing the final distance between them, it was also she who panicked. She felt the full length of his hard body against hers, and just like always, she panicked. Before he had a chance to kiss her, she hooked her foot behind his ankle and shoved at his chest with enough force to send him crashing to the floor.

For a moment, he just stared at her, a stunned look on his face. Then he scanned the room for other assailants, as if she'd attacked him as part of a nefarious plot. Seeing no imminent threat, he raised himself up on his elbows. "Why did you do that?" he asked, truly bewildered.

Sonny crossed her arms over her chest and looked down at her bare toes, feeling heat creep into her cheeks. "You were crowding me."

"I wasn't going to force myself on you."

Her head jerked up. "I know," she replied. Strangely enough, her reaction had nothing to do with his status as a suspect. It was more about her past than about him.

For a moment there, she hadn't been thinking about the case at all.

Warily, he motioned for her to stay back. "I'm going to get up and go now. No sudden moves, okay?"

"I apologize," she said, wanting to kick herself for making such an obvious blunder. Grant would have a conniption fit if he knew she'd broken character. "Please don't leave. Sit down for a minute. Did I hurt you?"

He laughed with more derision than mirth. "Only my pride."

As he staggered over to her living room couch, her gaze dropped to the seat of his jeans. They fit loose, but the muscles underneath appeared very firm indeed. "Is that where you keep it?" she murmured. "In your back pocket?"

Recovering his composure with remarkable ease, he made himself comfortable on her outdated couch, taking up as much space as humanly possible. "Why don't you check and see?" he suggested, flashing her that signature, off-center grin.

Of course, her attention was drawn to his front pockets, and the well-worn fly of his jeans. Annoyed with herself for looking, and for liking what she saw, she went behind the kitchen counter to pour a cup of coffee.

"Why are you afraid of men?"

"Why are you afraid of women?" she shot back at him.

"Who says I am?"

She could hardly admit she'd been investigating him, or that she'd seen his evade-and-retreat routine all over the beach. But she needed him to reveal something about himself, to deflect the attention away from her. "Carly told me you don't date."

"Carly," he choked, running a hand through his hair. "I don't want to talk about Carly."

"Fair enough," she said, taking a sip from her cup. "Sure you don't want some?"

"I don't drink coffee."

"You're a regular goody two-shoes, aren't you?"

He narrowed his eyes at the provocative remark. "I'm not afraid of women," he said, studying her face. "Except maybe you."

"You avoid them, don't you?" She waited for his answer, sipping coffee.

When he hesitated, she wondered if he was thinking about his wife. He looked almost guilty, as if he'd just betrayed her memory. Perhaps he wasn't as unflappable, or as innocent, as he pretended to be. "I've had a lot of them come on to me, on tour, at contests," he said, staring down at his hands. "I got tired of it."

"Tired of adoring women? That would be a first."

"Sometimes it was more than adoring."

"Really? Do tell," she cooed.

"Don't patronize me," he replied, having no trouble reading her flippancy. "I'm not the one whose overreactions border on assault and battery."

"You're right. Forget I asked."

Her casual dismissal of the subject irked him, as was her intention. "If I tell you, will you show me what you've got underneath that towel?"

"Not today," she said.

His eyes roved over her body with undisguised interest. "On a publicity tour in Japan, a girl grabbed me and wouldn't let go."

"Grabbed you where?"

He gave her a pointed look. "Where do you think?"

She hid a smile behind her coffee cup.

"I'm kind of big over there, no pun intended, and until that day, I didn't realize how popular I was. The crowd got a little wild, she got a good hold, some bodyguard pulled me the other way, and—" He saw her expression. "What? You think this is funny?"

She gave up trying to hold in her laughter. "Sorry. It's not. It's really not."

"You're damned right it's not. I was out of commission for weeks."

"No surfing?"

"I could still surf."

"Oh."

"Yeah." He paused, considering. "Something like that happened to you?"

"My story isn't as cute as yours."

He shrugged, leaning back to listen anyway.

Feeling a mild panic, she glanced at the clock on the coffeemaker. "You're sweet, but I've got to be somewhere in an hour."

His eyes widened with disbelief. Obviously, he wasn't accustomed to being summarily dismissed. She was willing to bet no woman had ever told him he was sweet, or called him a goody two-shoes, or laid him out on the ground like a pile of bricks, either.

To his credit, he was persistent. But then, a man didn't become a world champion by heading in when the surf got rough. "Sure you don't want to drop that towel?"

"I'm naked underneath this towel."

"I know."

Keeping it carefully closed and firmly in place, she showed him to the door. On his way out he gave her a hungry look, the kind designed to melt a woman's resolve. It took every ounce of strength she possessed to act unaffected.

Sonny didn't exhale until she shut the door behind him. Willing her pulse to stop racing, she wondered how long it would take him to realize she hadn't answered his question.

She never told him how she knew Carly's name.

•    •    •

Otay Mesa Prison, where Darrius O'Shea had been an inmate, was the only maximum security prison in San Diego County. It was a sprawling expanse of concrete buildings and sun-baked earth, located near the depressingly dusty and appropriately named Brown Field, within a stone's throw of the border.

Freedom beckoned from beyond heavy chain-link fences and snarling curls of razor wire, so close the prisoners could almost taste it.

Sonny was asked to turn in her service revolver and sign a release form before she went inside, a process she was familiar with, having visited jails before.

Her brother, Rigo, had been incarcerated for most of his adult life.

She didn't care to be stripped of her weapon, especially considering the facility's "enter at your own risk" policy. Like the U.S. government, Otay Mesa Prison refused to negotiate for hostages.

"I'd rather hold on to my SIG," she said to a bored-looking guard.

"It could be taken from you," he explained unnecessarily.

She studied the gun belt at his slim waist, thinking about how easy it would be to give him a swift, efficient demonstration of her skill. "Whatever," she said instead, removing the holster at her hip and handing it over.

"Deputy Duncan will accompany you."

She nodded at the other guard, who stood tall and alert. Military training, she noted as she preceded him down the hall.

Not that she needed backup.

Men who had been in prison for a long time had predictable reactions to visitors, especially females, so officials knew better than to parade her about. The tall guard led Sonny down a deserted walkway to a private interview room and waited quietly while the inmate she'd come to see was brought in for questioning.

Andrew Leeds had been convicted of armed robbery and aggravated assault more than five years ago. He'd occupied the cell next to Darrius O'Shea's for the duration of his incarceration, and had reported his suicide.

Although Leeds was a young man, in his late twenties at the most, he was also a hardened criminal who resembled a typical long-timer in many ways. His head was shaved clean and his reddish blond facial hair, trimmed in an odd, intricate design. Webs of tattoos adorned his thick neck and snaked down the length of his brawny arms.

She kept her eyes on his face as she extended her hand. "Mr. Leeds? I'm Special Agent Vasquez."

Leeds didn't return the favor, dropping his gaze to give her body a thorough examination, but he did return her handshake.

Clearing her throat, she added, "Thank you for agreeing to speak with me."

"My pleasure," he murmured, taking a seat at the same time she did. The guard who'd escorted him stood sentry outside the door. When she inclined her head, Deputy Duncan joined him there. Leeds raised his brows and studied her anew, seeming impressed by her lack of concern at being left alone in a room with him.

She got right down to business. "What can you tell me about Darrius O'Shea?"

His eyes narrowed. "What do you want to know?"

"Did he talk about the murder?"

Leeds shifted back in his chair, bracing his hands on the edge of the table between them. A cocky-looking woodpecker twitched on the middle of his forearm. "Maybe."

Sonny didn't have any bargaining chips. Hopefully, the novelty of her presence here would be enough to keep him talking. "Did he ever claim to be innocent?"

"Sure," he said with a smirk. "We all are."

"Did you believe him?"

He shrugged. "Guys with clear consciences don't usually hang themselves."

Good point. "Do you think he was mentally disturbed?"

"We all are," he repeated, not smiling this time.

"What was his state of mind in the days before the suicide?" she pressed. "Did he seem disturbed? Was he sleeping, eating, acting strange?"

Leeds considered this question more carefully than the others. "He had nightmares," he admitted. " 'Nam stuff. They got worse and worse. During the day, he hardly ever talked, but in his sleep he wouldn't shut up." He ran a hand over his smooth head. "Drove me batshit."

"What did he say?"

"Nothing that made much sense. Soldier's orders. Sometimes he would mumble that he didn't do it. Others, he'd say he was sorry. Over and over again, 'I'm sorry.'" Leeds rolled his big shoulders, as if his muscles were tense.

"Was he speaking to his war comrades?"

"I don't know."

"Did you ever ask him?"

"No," he said shortly, his eyes blazing with scorn. Men, in or out of prison, rarely questioned each other about personal issues.

"Is there another inmate he confided in?" she continued, glancing at his tattooed forearm. Leeds was obviously a member of the Peckerwoods, a dangerous all-white gang. "A group he was affiliated with?"

"Not really," he said, cracking his knuckles. "He kept to himself."

Sonny felt a wash of frustration. Leeds wasn't exactly a fountain of information. "Did you notice anything different about him, that final night?"

"Yeah," Leeds said, his voice flat. "He was quiet."

She left the prison feeling conflicted. Last week after studying O'Shea's file, she'd spoken to the detectives who had . . . facilitated his confession. The interrogation tactics they'd used were hardly cruel or unusual, and if they hadn't delved too deeply into O'Shea's motives, it was because they hadn't needed to.

The electrical cord yielding his fingerprints was better than a smoking gun.

Even so, Sonny found herself doubting the veracity of O'Shea's sworn statement. Despite her profession, she had very little confidence in the criminal justice system. It wasn't beyond her scope to believe Darrius O'Shea had been framed, coerced, or manipulated.

The person she cared about most—her brother, Rigo—was in prison, and his situation colored her worldview. He was guilty, of course, but that fact didn't make her love him any less.

Sighing, she drove back to La Jolla, navigating freeway traffic with absentminded ease. On a whim, she passed Neptune Street and continued on to Shores Beach, where O'Shea had been arrested. She parked in a pay lot and got out of her rental car, crossing her arms over her chest as she walked across the sand.

An affluent area like Torrey Pines didn't have a large homeless population. The beaches were well patrolled, the sidewalks clean, and the boutiques upscale. The cost of living here was too high for most street people. Fast food, inexpensive clothing, and cheap liquor weren't readily available.

She looked down the beach, past the cliffs leading toward San Diego Harbor. Closer to the busy metropolis, there were always vagrants, some of whom wandered along the coast, drawn by the lure of soft sand and a comfortable sleep.

Wind whipping at her short hair, she cupped a hand over her eyes and considered the opposite direction. Windansea Beach, where Ben lived, was only a few miles to the north.

Nibbling at her lower lip, she pulled her attention back to her immediate surroundings. The small parking lot was about half full. She didn't see any bearded men or overloaded shopping carts, but it was broad daylight, and there were some nooks and crannies to hide in at the base of the cliffs.

Out on the water, there were only surfers, black wetsuits gleaming in the sun.

# CHAPTER 6

Lisette Bruebaker was in love.

Carly's dad was so freaking *hot*. Every time she got close to him she thought she might go up in flames. She'd been practicing her sex kitten expressions in the mirror all week, along with the "Oops! I dropped something" ruse she employed at school. Boys never failed to sneak a peek down her top, or up her skirt, when she wanted them to.

Ben Fortune had never looked at her that way, but she hadn't targeted him for seduction before. He'd be a hell of a notch in her bedpost. The man was a catch and a half.

On the flip side, Carly had been a total drag lately. She'd been grounded since her dad caught them getting stoned in her bedroom last weekend, so they couldn't go anywhere, and Carly wouldn't even consider smoking weed again. Every time Lisette brought it up, Carly made a pouty face and said it made her "freak out."

If Lisette's parents hadn't made plans to go out of town, Ben probably wouldn't have let her come over. He was *way* too strict. Carly wasn't allowed to have friends in her room when she was on restriction, and he'd been really steamed about the pot. He'd actually grabbed Lisette's wrist and taken the joint right out of her hand. It was the only time she could remember him touching her.

He'd been so ... forceful. Mmm.

Drag or not, Carly was a good friend to have. Half the boys at school were in love with her. Or in love with her dad, which amounted to the same. Lisette might have been jealous if she hadn't benefited from the association. Carly was a perfect partner in crime. Guys were always approaching Lisette to get to her.

Carly didn't put out, but Lisette did, so it was a win-win.

Unfortunately, things had been going sour between them for weeks. Carly had been acting weird since way before the pot incident, and Lisette had the feeling this sleepover was going to be their last. Carly just couldn't keep up with Lisette's wild ways.

If Lisette was going to make a move on Ben, it would have to be tonight. This might be her only chance.

After dinner, Ben cleared off the kitchen table and the three of them pasted together a family scrapbook, like the frickin' Brady bunch. It was totally lame, except there were a couple of hunky photos of Ben without his shirt on. Carly's mom had also been super-sexy. Dark-haired and sultry. Like Carly, only with bigger boobs.

Lisette liked to fool around with girls, too, just for fun. It sure got the boys to take notice, and it was kinky. She'd even talked Carly into kissing her once, but Carly had giggled like a dork the whole time and totally ruined the mood.

Lisette hoped Ben Fortune was kinky. He'd have to be, to do it with her, wouldn't he?

Getting into the spirit of the evening, she let a pencil roll off the table. Oops! "I'll get that," she said breathlessly, making sure her cleavage was on full display as she bent down.

It turned out to be a total waste. He didn't even notice.

Later, Ben took her and Carly to the video store to rent DVDs. He always let them get whatever they wanted, and although Lisette had requested *Cabin Fever,* Carly picked some dumb movie about racing cars: *The Fast and the Furious.*

Ben didn't watch with them, but he did check in a few times, to Lisette's delight. To her disappointment, he didn't look her way when she flashed her panties at him.

Lisette wished they'd rented scary movies instead. She loved scary movies. They were always full of horny teenagers, and the screaming and stuff made her hot.

Hours later, when Carly finally fell asleep, Lisette was struck by inspiration. She knew one thing she could do, something she was damned good at, and it never failed to hold a man's attention.

• • •

Ben was having the most realistic erotic dream of his life. Summer had not only dropped her towel, she'd dropped to her knees in front of him, and was taking him into her mouth, drawing him deep, practically eating him alive.

He was reaching down to tell her to take it easy, they had all night, when he came up with a tangle of long, curly hair.

Oh, *shit*.

Coming fully awake, he jumped out of bed, stumbling, his feet still wrapped up in the sheets. Light from the hallway illuminated the room enough for him to confirm that the woman in his bed wasn't Summer.

It wasn't a woman at all, but a sixteen-year-old girl.

His daughter's best friend, Lisette.

"Don't you want me to finish?"

Following her gaze down his body, he realized he was fully aroused, and she was responsible for it. This wasn't an erotic dream. It was a fucking *nightmare*.

He jerked his boxer shorts up with shaking hands. "Get out," he said through gritted teeth, feeling totally violated.

She pouted prettily.

"Get the fuck out, now!" He looked around the room in a panic, as if the pedophile police were about to burst in on them. "I'm going to call your mom and tell her about this, you little—" He bit off the word he was about to say, reminding himself that Lisette was just a confused girl, not much different from Carly, and he would go apeshit if some unfeeling bastard called his daughter names.

Her face crumpled. "But I love you!"

"Oh, Christ," he muttered, turning away from the sight of her naked body.

Like Carly's cutting herself, this was a situation he couldn't have anticipated. He knew Lisette was a problem child and a bad influence, that she wore too much makeup and too few clothes. Her parents let her run wild, and he'd always felt kind of sorry for her. Never once had he imagined she would try to climb into bed with him.

He should have locked his door.

"Just get out of my room, Lisette," he said over his shoulder. "I'm not interested in little girls. Don't ever do this again."

"I'm not a little girl, you asshole, I'm a woman!"

He felt the pillow hit his back, and was infuriated to think that Carly might wander in on this insanity. He couldn't make Lisette leave, short of physically removing her, and he wasn't going anywhere near her. Spine stiff with fury, he walked out of the room.

Downstairs, as he dialed her mother's cell phone number with stabbing fingers, it occurred to him that Lisette would have a very different story to tell about tonight's debacle, one that could get him into a considerable amount of trouble.

If he kept his mouth shut, she probably would, too.

Then again, silence implied guilt.

Before he could rethink his actions, Lisette's mother answered. Her voice was low and throaty, as distinctive as always. From the background noise, it sounded like she was at a party.

"Sheila. This is Ben Fortune."

If the name caused her any distress, her voice didn't reflect it. "Ben. What can I do you for?" She laughed lustily at her own joke.

"You know Lisette is staying over here with Carly, right?"

That got her attention. "Right. Oh, right. Is everything okay?"

"Not really. They're fine, but—"

"What? You're breaking up."

"I said—"

Static interrupted him, and it was the last he heard from her. After a few minutes, he gave up trying to reach her, and when he ascended the stairs again, he found his bed empty. Breathing a sigh of relief, he locked the door to his bedroom for the first time since Olivia died.

He was exhausted, but sleep eluded him until just before dawn.


On the south side of Windansea, he waited, crouched in the shadows. He'd seen the girl before and considered taking her. What he'd just witnessed through the ocean-facing window of Ben Fortune's bedroom had clinched it for him.

He prided himself in being calculated in his selections. Only when he disassociated himself from the act, and the victim, did he feel satisfied by the out-come. He'd learned to release his twisted needs with strangers after that initial, near-fatal mistake.

Choosing a woman he knew, even in passing, was risky; choosing one with a connection to Ben, even more so. Emotions were tricky, sticky things that sullied this dark business. He liked to kill clean.

He took several deep breaths, trying to calm the beast that lurked within him. It wanted to grab the girl and tear out her throat. Hold her down while she struggled to break free. Wipe the taste of Ben from her lips as she took her last breath.

In the chill of predawn, he was far from cold. He was sweating, panting, raging. Bloodlust burned inside him, hot and bright.

After that first, grievous error, which had almost precipitated his downfall, he'd been afraid to strike again. A year had gone by. He'd planned, deliberated, waited. And finally, when the perfect opportunity presented itself, he'd leapt upon the female offender and wrung the life from her malformed body.

The memory made his mouth water.

She'd been nothing to him, nothing to anyone. She was just another pretty face, little more than a sexual plaything, and that had infuriated him. God, how he hated her kind, and relished making one pay for the transgressions of all.

A nameless sacrifice would be a better candidate than the girl who had just left Ben's bedroom, eyes flashing with anger, curly hair flying around her tearstained face.

But she was right there in front of him and he couldn't deny himself the pleasure.

Just before dusk, Carly went to look for James at the same place she'd seen him last.

Across Windansea Beach, the sun dipped low into the Pacific, casting shimmering gold over that tumultuous expanse. The waves were choppy, no good for surfing, so her dad had settled into his leather chair with one of his boring philosophy books. He was such a nerd.

He let her go out under the pretext of jogging, a sport she used to enjoy. She was going to take it up again, she decided, putting in a good sprint to get there. She'd have to sprint back if she wanted to arrive home in time to avoid suspicion.

While she waited, leaning back against the dark gray stone, she sifted sand through her fingers, letting her mind drift back to the last time she was here, and what she'd been doing. Or about to do. Moaning in frustration, she closed her eyes, wishing she could make a tiny little cut, just a swift, sweet nick, to take the edge off.

"I thought I told you not to come here."

Her eyes popped open. Again, she'd neither seen nor heard his approach. In the shadow of the rocks at sunset, there was enough light to see that she hadn't exaggerated his appeal in her mental picture of him. He was tall, but not gangly enough to be an awkward jumble of knees and elbows like some boys his age. In the last rays of the sun, his brown hair glinted like bronze, and she saw that his eyes were a striking dark blue.

"You don't own the beach," she replied sulkily, wondering why her heart was doing double-time.

"I don't want your blood on my sand."

"Do I look like I'm bleeding?" She raised her hands to show him that they were empty, not realizing until then that she held fistfuls of sand. "You're just disappointed that I haven't taken off my shirt."

"No," he said, drawing out the word. "I don't like seeing you hurt yourself."

"Why do you care?"

"I don't know," he replied, looking out at the last sliver of sun.

"I can't do it anymore anyway. My dad found out."

"Good."

She squinted up at him. "Whose side are you on?"

"Mine. Why are you here?"

She brushed sand from her hands. "I need your help."

That got his attention. He sank down beside her, intrigued. "With what?"

She felt her face grow warm and was glad for the approaching darkness. "I told my dad you were my boyfriend."

His blue eyes narrowed. "Why would you do that?"

"I needed an excuse for sneaking out the other night."

"Jesus," he said, running a hand through his hair.

It was short, but kind of thick and wild, as if he cut it himself. "Is he going to kill me?"

"I don't think so. I told him your name and stuff, so I wanted to know if you'd go along with it."

"Go along with what?"

"With pretending to be my boyfriend," she said, exasperated.

"Why?"

Carly had pictured him jumping at the chance to play her knight in shining armor, not asking twenty questions. "Why should you help me, you mean?"

"No. Why do you think you need a pretend boy-friend?"

"Oh. Um, I guess I don't want to get caught in a lie. Not that cutting yourself is any better than lying, but I just feel so lame for making that up. Besides, I want my dad to quit treating me like a little girl."

"You think having a pretend boyfriend is the best way to assert your independence?"

"I guess not," she said, because he had a point.

"You could get a real boyfriend."

"Not one with your name."

"Say we broke up."

Embarrassed, she stared down at the sand. "I want him to think I'm mature, not a slut with a new boyfriend every day."

"Like Lisette?"

Her head jerked up. "You know her?"

He smirked. "Doesn't everyone?"

"All the boys do," she admitted cattily. "We're not friends anymore."

"Why not?"

"We just aren't." She examined his expression with suspicion. "You're not screwing her, are you?"

He was quiet for a moment. Then he smiled again, going from handsome boy to teen-dream heart-breaker in a split second. "I'm not even your fake boyfriend yet, and you're already jealous. I like it, rich girl."

Carly punched him on the arm, using a little more force than was playful.

With amazingly quick reflexes, he grabbed her fist before she could retract it and squeezed hard enough to startle her. "Don't do that again," he warned.

She felt a shiver of awareness, for his hand was large enough to cover her fist, and felt strong. "Touchy, aren't you?"

The glaze in his eyes cleared, and he slowly released her. "What duties am I to perform, as your boyfriend?" he asked, after a pause.

His voice was low, teasing, cutting through the tension that had cropped up between them. This was the behavior she'd expected of him, but she found herself too shy to flirt back. "You'd have to meet my dad."

"Oh, God," he groaned.

"And maybe, um, take me to the movies."

He insulted her by mulling it over. Then he had the nerve to bargain with her. "On one condition."

"What?"

Staring at her mouth, he said, "If you want people to think we're dating, we should act natural with each other."

"So?"

"So, you should kiss me."

Her stomach fluttered. "Kiss you?"

"Yeah."

"That's your only condition?"

He appeared to consider adding a few more, but was smart enough not to push his luck.

"All right, then." She leaned in to place a very sweet, very chaste kiss on his lips.

When she pulled back, his eyes were strange, as if her innocent touch had disturbed him deeply. "I meant a real kiss," he said, clearing his throat.

"Oh." Feeling self-conscious, she moistened her lips, leaned in some more, and waited.

Nothing happened.

When she opened her eyes, he had the gall to laugh.

"You're not doing this right," she complained.

"Neither are you."

She bristled. "I've kissed boys before."

"I know."

"What do you mean?"

"I saw you at Lisette's thirteenth birthday party," he said. "We played seven minutes in heaven. You went in the closet with Mark Mahalo."

She smiled at the memory. "Who did you go in with?"

He shrugged, throwing away a shard of driftwood he'd sifted from the sand. "I was in ninth grade then, too old for a junior high school gig, but I went anyway, because I didn't get invited to any other rich girl parties. That same year, my dad would send me to buy him a pack of cigarettes every night. If he let me keep the change, I'd make about twenty-five cents a trip, and it took me a whole year to save ten dollars." His gaze reconnected with hers. "I would've given every penny to go into that closet with you."

The blunt admission was almost beyond Carly's comprehension. She'd spent a thousand dollars in one afternoon, easily. Ten dollars was nothing to her. A tip for her hairdresser. But from the look on his face, she knew he was sincere, and his intensity excited her. "Now's your chance," she breathed, putting her mouth up to his again.

He leaned back. "This isn't Lisette Bruebaker's closet."

She didn't understand his hesitation. "You don't want to kiss me anymore?"

"Yeah, but I don't want to go at it like thirteen-year-olds."

"Is that what I'm doing?"

"Yes."

She retreated, hugely offended. "Fuck off, then. You're the one that wanted to do this." She stood, preparing to walk away in a huff.

Laughing again, he pulled her back down to sit by him. "And you're the one who needs a fake boyfriend. Do you want me to help you out or not?"

"Not."

"Fine," he said, calling her bluff. "Have a nice life."

Her mouth made a thin, determined line. "What do you want me to do?"

James couldn't believe she was naïve enough to let him dictate the particulars of their kiss. His heart started pounding with excitement, but he tried to play it cool. "First of all, you have to get closer," he suggested, glad he'd taken the time to clean up a little before coming out to look for her. "You're going to hurt yourself, craning your neck like that."

Determined to prove herself, she crawled into his lap, put her arms around his neck, and pressed her breasts against his chest. "How's this?"

"Better," he said, gritting his teeth. "But you don't want a guy to think you're easy." He put his hands on her hips and scooted her back a few inches, out of the danger zone, so she couldn't feel just how affected he was by her proximity.

At his neck, she clenched her hands into fists.

"Simmer down, rich girl. I'm just telling it like it is."

"Now what?" she growled.

"Now relax. You're all tense."

Closing her eyes, she took a deep breath. The movement caused her breasts to brush up against his chest again, and he almost groaned aloud. To cover, he cleared his throat and continued the lesson. "You have to work up to it. Maybe you could, uh, kiss my neck."

Concentrating on the task, as if he were a Chemistry test that she wanted to ace, she bent her head to him and licked his skin, just above the collar of his T-shirt. "You taste salty," she murmured. Her warm breath caressed his neck, cooling the wet mark her mouth had made.

He couldn't hold back a low moan.

"What's wrong?" she asked.

"Nothing. You're doing well." Too well. "I think we can move on."

She closed her eyes and put her lips on his. Again, he didn't take over for her. "Open your mouth," she said, blinking up at him.

"Make me. Use a little finesse."

She frowned in confusion, and he had to smother a laugh. He was pleased by her lack of experience, and not above taking advantage of it thoroughly. "Like this." Very slowly, he traced the fullness of her lower lip with his tongue. When she sighed in delighted understanding, he pulled back. "See?"

"Uh-huh." She stared intently at his mouth. "Let me try."

She mimicked his actions so skillfully it required a monumental effort to keep his hands where they were at her waist. In seconds, she'd eclipsed his meager talent. Needing no further instruction, she slipped her tongue into his mouth and threaded her fingers through his hair.

He leaned back and let her have her way with him, forgetting that he'd orchestrated this scene and abandoning his earlier resolve to keep her away from the danger zone. When she deepened the kiss, wriggling in his lap, he couldn't stop himself from cupping her cute little ass and drawing her closer, letting her feel what she was doing to him.

She gasped against his mouth then melted against him, acquiescing. In the blink of an eye, he was stretched out on top of her, kissing her like a madman and giving his hands free reign over her lithe body.

He must have been too rough, because when he slid his hand beneath her sweatshirt, she cried out.

James froze. "Sorry," he said, rolling off her. He'd never meant to take it this far. "Carly—God, I'm sorry. Are you okay?"

She sat up, running a hand through her disheveled hair. "Of course I'm okay. Sorry for what?"

His mouth dropped open. "For losing control, I guess. Hurting you."

"You didn't hurt me."

"I didn't? You made a noise."

She blushed. "It wasn't that kind of noise."

"Oh." He groaned in understanding, and pain. "I don't think this boyfriend-girlfriend thing is going to work out."

"Why not?" She stood, shaking sand from her clothes.

*Because I can't trust myself around you,* he wanted to shout. Instead, he walked down the beach a few steps and shoved his shaking hands into the front pockets of his jeans.

"Come over tomorrow, for dinner. Around six."

Pretending to be Carly's boyfriend in front of her dad didn't hold the same appeal as making out with her on the sand. And if *his* dad found out . . .

"You can't back out," she warned. "You've already collected your fee. And if everything goes well, maybe I'll let you kiss me again."

With that, she flashed him a grin and took off, sprinting down the beach, her hair wild and loose down her back. James watched until she disappeared in the twilight, knowing he would keep his end of the bargain.

Because although he'd pretended it hadn't been enough, her first kiss had been perfection, charming in its innocence, devoid of all artifice, and the least ugly moment of his entire, bottom-dwelling life.

# CHAPTER 7

"Can you come over?" he said without preamble. They'd never spoken on the phone before, but it didn't occur to Sonny to ask who it was, even to be coy.

"What's up?" she asked, caution warring with pleasure.

"Carly invited her boyfriend to dinner." He would have said the devil was coming in the same tone.

"I thought she didn't have one."

"Yeah," he said with a sigh. "I knew it couldn't last."

Her lips twitched. "And you need me as, what? A buffer?"

"I suppose. Carly recommended that I invite some other people, probably to take the heat off her guest. She thinks I'm going to grill him."

"Are you?"

"I don't know. I feel sick."

Sonny had no trouble imagining the effect of young, overactive male hormones on Carly's already troubled psyche. "Does she know you're inviting me?"

"It was her idea."

"Ah." Now she was a distraction, evidently more useful than as a rival for Ben's affections. "Who else is coming?"

"My mom, my brother, maybe one of his boyfriends."

"Boyfriends?"

"Yeah. He goes through them like I used to go through surf groupies. I hope Carly doesn't take after either of us."

She felt a flutter of panic at the thought of meeting his family, especially under an assumed identity. What a coil!

Although her gut feeling told her Ben Fortune was innocent, she still had a job to do, evidence to collect, and information to gather. If Olivia Fortune had been the SoCal Strangler's first victim, Sonny had to find out why the killer had chosen her.

Perhaps he'd known her. And Ben.

Surrendering to duty, curiosity, and an overwhelming desire to see him again, she let out a deep breath and asked, "What time?"

Just before six, Sonny walked across Neptune Street, toward Ben's front door. A teenaged boy was pacing the curb a few doors down, head tilted to one side, his body language suggesting he was practicing introduction scenarios. Hiding a smile, she approached him, deciding to offer her assistance.

"Hey," she said, startling him with her presence.

When he turned around, her first impression, based solely on appearance, was that Carly Fortune had good taste. Her second, based on what was going on behind those pretty blue eyes, was that Carly was playing with fire.

Physically, he wasn't threatening. Neither large nor impressively muscled, he had a lean, hungry look that made his cheekbones stand out in his face. Despite those sharp edges, he was handsome, and if one didn't stray beyond the surface, he appeared nothing more than a better-than-average-looking boy. His dark blue sweater was of good quality, mended haphazardly in a couple of places with black thread, indicating that he'd done it himself. His jeans were faded from too many washings, and his shoes, a scuffed brown leather that must have been quite expensive when new, were worn but clean.

It was amazing what kind of deals you could get in Torrey Pines, shopping secondhand.

The particulars of his clothing were telling, but the flash she'd seen in his eyes upon her surprise approach concerned her more than his socioeconomic status. His defensive, fight-or-flight reaction reminded her more than a little of herself.

In the next instant, he erased the hostile expression and relaxed his stance, regarding her with mild curiosity.

"You must be Carly's boyfriend. I'm Summer." She stuck out her hand in greeting, telling herself the kid was sketchy, not necessarily evil.

"James." His handshake was firm and calloused. Interesting.

"You want some tips?"

"Tips?"

He looked so hopeful that Sonny breathed a sigh of relief. There was nothing sinister about a skinny boy with a puppy-dog crush. "Carly's dad is a nice guy," she said. "Be polite, and you'll go far. And he's kind of..." she paused, searching for one word to convey laid-back, health-conscious, environmentally aware, and liberal, "...a hippie, so don't try to pull any tough-guy bullshit. It won't impress him."

He nodded, filing the information away. "No sports talk, then?"

The kid was quick. "I'm not sure if he likes anything but surfing." Although he was too young to be a suspect, she gave him another quick once-over. "You surf?"

"Nah," he said glumly. His eyes lit up. "I fish, though."

Sonny smiled. "Then you know about the ocean. Currents, wind, waves."

"I know some stuff."

"Okay, but don't go spouting off. The more you talk, the more likely you are to do or say something stupid."

Taking no offense, he smiled back at her. "Who are you?"

"I'm a friend of Ben's." Sonny knew exactly how her words translated in the mind of a boy his age, so she cut him off, midthought. "Ready?"

"Yes," he said, eyeing the Fortune residence with trepidation.

"Oh, and I think Carly's uncle is gay, so don't freak out."

"Why would I freak out?"

Why, indeed? "You're okay, kid."


Before they could knock, Carly yanked open the door, her black eyes sparkling with mischief. She looked James over, not bothering to simper or flirt, and gave Sonny a similar perusal. "You two need major help," she decided.

Taking James by the hand, she dragged him upstairs, motioning for Sonny to follow. In her bedroom, she turned her critical eye on James first. She must have seen the warning in his expression, because she said, "You look good. But can I put some gel in your hair?"

He shrugged, scanning her bedroom, more interested in her private domain than the state of his hair. He appeared to be surveying the windows for break-in potential, when he caught Sonny watching him. Embarrassed, he turned his attention back to Carly.

Predictably, his gaze dropped to her breasts, which jiggled as she worked gel into his hair. His shoulders stiffened, and his cheekbones acquired a dull red stain.

Sonny hid a smile. Oh, to be a teenaged boy, in a constant state of sexual frustration.

When she was finished driving James crazy, Carly stepped back and nodded her approval. Then she faced Sonny. "You, on the other hand, need a lot more attention." She made a gesture that indicated imperfection, from head to toe.

Pleased that someone besides himself was under scrutiny, the corner of James' mouth quirked up. Out of loyalty to Sonny, for the tips, he said, "I think she looks okay."

Carly sizzled him with a glance. "Go make nice with my dad. He's in the kitchen."

He paled. "Without you?"

"Yes. Offer to set the table."

Muttering something about being crazy for agreeing to come, he wandered out to meet his nemesis.

Carly started fussing with Sonny's hair, rubbing gel into it with her hands. She paused, testing its texture between her fingertips. "Your hair is so thick," she mused. "It feels just like James'." She tilted her chin up smugly. "So, what do you think of him?"

Sonny thought Carly had met her match. James was probably as unstable emotionally as she was. Ben had better be prepared for his daughter to grow up fast. "Are you ready for a steady relationship?"

"It's not serious," she said offhand.

"Just playing with his heart?"

Carly frowned. "No. I mean, I don't think so. That sounds complicated."

"Love usually is."

She gave a trilling little laugh. "We're not in love."

"And three days ago, you didn't want a boyfriend."

Carly dismissed the idea that things were moving too fast, youthfully secure in her own judgment, despite the fact that it had already been proven faulty a number of times. She stepped back to study her handiwork. "Oh, wow. Your hair looks hot."

Sonny glanced in the mirror. Carly was right, and she had a clever hand with styling. Instead of thick, unruly locks, her short hair fell back from her face in soft, sexy waves. "How'd you do that?"

Ignoring her, Carly rifled through her makeup drawer, coming up with a few items that suited Sonny's coloring. "Your eyes are great," she allowed, "but they overwhelm your face. You need to balance it out, soften your cheekbones, accentuate your lips." Carly waved a brush like a magic wand over Sonny's face, then applied a sunset-colored lip gloss.

Sonny had to admit the extra touches became her. When she smiled at her own reflection, Carly giggled in delight. Sonny couldn't believe this was the same sullen girl from the restaurant. Her moods were indeed mercurial.

"We need to sex you up."

"What?"

"Unbutton a little. You look all stuffy."

"No way! Your grandmother is down there."

Carly rolled her eyes. "She's wearing a more daring outfit than this, believe me."

Sonny looked down at her navy blue shirtwaist dress. Made of a stretchy cotton blend that molded to her figure, it wasn't as stodgy as Carly made it sound.

"Oh, all right," Sonny said, unfastening enough buttons to show a hint of cleavage.

"You aren't Jewish, are you?"

"No, why?"

Carly took a delicate silver chain out of her jewelry box and put it around Sonny's neck. It had a tiny cross that twinkled in the light, drawing the eye just where Carly wanted it to go. "There. Perfect."

Sonny covered the cross with her hand. "Is your dad religious?"

"Not really. But he did go to Catholic school, and you look like a naughty nun. He'll love it."

Ben hated Carly's boyfriend.

James Matthews had shaken his hand with more strength than necessary, called him sir like Ben was an old man, and looked him straight in the eye while he did it.

He was a punk, Ben decided, with a chip on his shoulder the size of Catalina Island.

James relegated the task of setting the table to Carly by pretending he didn't know how it was done. She took over for him with a sweet smile, all the feminist training Ben had instilled in her down the drain in the blink of an eye. Then she offered to make a salad, and proceeded to do so with proficiency, James at her side. The two had been giving each other smoldering looks ever since.

You'd think chopping tomatoes was some kind of aphrodisiac.

Speaking of aphrodisiacs, Summer was looking tasty enough to gobble up. Ben couldn't glance at her without feeling a sharp tug in his chest, and an equally troubling sensation lower. It was rude of him, but he'd decided to ignore her in order to stay focused on the task of hating James.

They went outside to eat, in a space warmed by standing heaters, lit by Chinese lanterns, and blessed with the gorgeous sights and sounds of the Pacific. In the background, the waters of an edgeless pool sparkled, and the Jacuzzi churned and bubbled, as hot and restless as Ben's mood.

"What's this?" a man called out from the other side of the patio. "Having a party without me?"

His friend JT was standing at the gate leading down to the beach. With the moon at his back, he was little more than an outline of broad shoulders and a glint of white teeth. Ben recognized him by his voice, which was low and distinctive, as raspy as rough-grained sand.

Ben muttered a curse under his breath. He didn't want JT around tonight. He was too distracted to keep him away from Summer.

"I knew I smelled good things cooking," JT said, not bothering to wait for anyone to invite him in. "You have room for one more?"

"Would you leave if I said no?" Ben asked, scowling.

"Hey, Mrs. Fortune," JT called out, brushing past Ben and moving on to easier targets. "You get prettier every year," he vowed, bringing her hand to his lips.

"Oh, you," Grace said, pulling her hand from his with a smile.

When JT zeroed in on Summer, Ben felt his shoulders stiffen with apprehension. *"Bonita señorita,"* he singsonged. "Where've you been all my life?"

Summer laughed at JT's Paulie Shore imitation, as amused by him as all women were. JT had always had a way with the ladies. In their wilder days, the two of them had frequently competed over the same girl in addition to the same wave. Ben's professional success had often worked in his favor, but JT had been granted access to just about any bed on finesse alone. Once there, he was easily bored, never staying with one woman long enough to make a real connection.

"Are you Nathan's boyfriend?" she asked.

Ben choked back a laugh.

JT placed a hand over his heart, where the barb had struck. "Cruelty, thy name is woman," he groaned.

Summer darted a glance at Ben, not sure where she'd gone wrong.

"Frailty," Ben corrected.

JT frowned at him. "Huh?"

" 'Frailty, thy name is woman.' It's Shakespeare." Once again, his gaze roved over Summer's sinuous physique. "And not really applicable, in my opinion."

JT jerked his thumb in Ben's direction. "Lose this buzzkill and run away with me. I'll never correct you when you misquote."

Although he knew JT was only joking, Ben had to stifle the urge to put him in a headlock. "JT is a friend of mine, not Nathan's," he explained. "My brother would never date such a poor specimen."

"Too true," JT admitted wryly.

"Sorry," Summer said. "I didn't mean to offend."

"No harm done." JT lowered his voice to a whisper. "We won't tell Nathan."

Summer laughed again.

Ben clamped his hand around the back of JT's neck, exerting a painful amount of pressure. "Make yourself useful," he said, leading him away, "and man the grill."

The evening went downhill from there. JT undercooked the vegetables and overcooked the fish. Nathan showed up solo, for once, with a bottle of outrageously expensive wine that Ben couldn't sample.

And Carly held James' hand under the table the whole time.

His mother was lovely, as usual, but clueless. Grace considered it wonderful news that Carly had a boyfriend. Ben and his younger brother had been born relatively late in her life, and Carly was her only grandchild, much to her dismay. Nathan wasn't going to produce any, and Ben hadn't been inclined to date, much less procreate, in years.

If he was lucky, she wouldn't mention greatgrandchildren until after dessert.

Nathan wasn't helping, either. He seemed to find James fascinating, but he'd always had a weakness for a pretty face.

"Where's Peter?" Ben asked when he remembered his brother's latest lover's name.

Nathan arched a brow at his surly tone. "He's flying in tomorrow. Should I bring him over for Christmas, Mom?"

Grace smiled serenely. "If you want a quiet, peaceful day, you won't."

"Dad still living in the Stone Age?"

"We could always celebrate here," Ben offered, in no mood to deal with his father's bigotry on top of everything else.

"Yes," Carly exclaimed, liking the idea. "Let's have a pool party. Grandpa's such an old grump. And I like Peter."

"Darling, you've never met Peter," Nathan said.

"Oh. Who was that one guy?"

"Emilio?"

"No, no. After that."

"Greg."

"Yeah, Greg. He was cute."

Nathan sighed wistfully. "He was, wasn't he? Too bad."

"What happened to him?"

"You know, I don't really remember. I think we just drifted apart."

Ben coughed back a sound of sarcasm. Nathan had a notoriously short attention span with men, and Carly was forever romanticizing his fickle ways.

"Summer's a lesbian," she announced.

JT straightened immediately, delighted by the news.

"Carly—" Ben warned.

"I mean, she's still deciding," she amended.

Too polite to call Carly out for lying, Summer stared down at her plate, probably wishing she'd never met any of them.

Nathan's brown eyes twinkled with amusement. "I've never known Ben to date a lesbian before. Then again, he hasn't dated anyone besides himself in so long, I wasn't sure he was still interested in women. Switching teams, brother?"

"Yeah," he replied stonily. "Tell Peter I'm available."

Grace patted Summer on the shoulder. "Just look to God to help you find your answer. I find that consulting the Bible on matters of the heart is always useful."

Summer fingered the chain at her neck. Ben's gaze was drawn, inexorably, to the valley between her breasts. "I'm not really looking for an answer, to that, ah, particular question."

"She's not a lesbian, Mom," Nathan explained.

"Oh? And Ben isn't going to date Peter, is he?"

Feeling all eyes on him, Ben dragged his gaze away from Summer's chest.

"Not in this lifetime," JT said with a smile.

"I can't keep up with the crazy jokes you young people tell," Grace complained.

In a blatant attempt to redirect the conversation, Summer turned to Carly and James. "Do you two take classes together?"

"No," James replied. "I have homeschool." When this answer was met with uneasy silence, he added, "I'd rather go to Shores, but I work during the day."

"You work?" Ben asked.

"Yeah. On my dad's fishing boat."

"Every day?"

"Monday through Saturday."

"All day?" He was insultingly skeptical. "Is that even legal?"

James shrugged. "It's legal to work eight hours a

day, or more, once you're sixteen. I know because my dad looked it up. He took me out of school to work part-time when I was fourteen, and he looked that up, too. Now we put in ten-hour days, pretty regular."

"Is that how old you are? Sixteen?"

"No, sir, I'm seventeen. I'll be eighteen in March."

Ben groaned, covering his face with his hands. His life was over.

"My dad's an alcoholic," Carly said in a rush, trying to reestablish control over the situation.

"So's mine," James admitted.

Ben lifted his head, seizing the opportunity to find something else to dislike about his daughter's boyfriend. "Do you drink, too?"

"No, sir," James said carefully, squinting at him. He might be a dropout, but he wasn't stupid. "And maybe if you'd sober up once in a while, Carly wouldn't go down to the beach to cut herself with razor blades."

Ben felt his face go white, because James had scored a direct hit. Of course he felt responsible for Carly's actions. Any parent would. And although he hadn't had a drink in ages, he knew his alcoholism would have a lifetime effect on her.

Carly's wail of outrage broke the silence. "James! My dad's a *recovering* alcoholic. He's been sober for years. And how could you tell everyone I cut myself? Oh my God, I could just die!" She threw her napkin down and fled.

A shocked hush fell over the table.

"I'm sorry," James said, rising from his chair. "I

never met an alcoholic who didn't drink anymore. I'll just . . . go apologize to Carly."

"I should leave," Summer said. "It was a pleasure to meet you all."

"No," Ben said, snapping out of his self-pitying stupor. "You're not going anywhere." He stood, towering over James. "Neither are you," he said.

Summer arched a dark blond brow and crossed her arms over her chest. Her cool expression indicated that he was in for a tongue-lashing later, and not the kind he would enjoy. James was easier to intimidate. He gulped. And sat.

"Carly is going to come down here and we will all enjoy a pleasant meal together. Even if it kills us!" Ben stormed away, intent on making everyone else suffer through the remainder of the evening, just as he would.

Sonny survived the rest of the night by a thread. After Carly returned, puffy-eyed and sniffling, James sat in uncomfortable silence, JT made inconsequential conversation, Ben brooded, and Sonny fumed.

Nathan drank wine and enjoyed himself, too contrary not to have a good time.

Before everyone left, they made plans for a Christmas pool party, discussing the finer points of the weather forecast, which Ben seemed to either know instinctively or have memorized by rote. According to him, it was supposed to be sunny and 75 on December 25, an average winter day in San Diego, if a little warmer than it had been lately.

Carly said good-bye to James and went up to her room, sighing dreamily.

Although Sonny stayed behind to help Ben clean up, what she really wanted to do was tell Grant to shove this assignment, rescind her promise to attend the Christmas pool party, and walk away from the Fortune family, never to look back.

Ben wouldn't let her. Taking her by the hand, he led her outside to stand on his beautiful, heated patio, look out at his expensive, oceanfront view, and cajole her into staying in his too charmed, too complicated life. "You're going to dump me, aren't you?"

Startled, she jerked her hand from his. "We're not even dating."

"Yes we are."

She turned away from him, leaning her elbows against the top of the rock wall that separated his patio from the beach and wondering what she was doing here. Ben Fortune wasn't a killer, and she had no business pursuing this angle of the investigation. She was playing him, and herself, by continuing their association.

But if Ben hadn't killed Olivia, who had? Sonny was becoming increasingly convinced that Darrius O'Shea was innocent. There were too many similarities between the recent murders and Olivia's untimely death.

When a victim was attacked in her own home, the search always began from the inside out. Ben was a natural suspect. So was his friend JT. The husky-voiced surfer was a smooth operator, no doubt about that, but Sonny couldn't picture him planning anything more nefarious than a lazy seduction. Besides, he'd been ruled out already. According to the case file, he'd been surfing with Ben the morning Olivia was murdered. Several witnesses recalled seeing Ben go inside, while JT stayed in the water.

Sonny felt a flutter of nerves as Ben came up behind her. Until Grant gave her the go-ahead, stringing him along was her job. So when he put his arm around her, she let him. And, as always, the thrill she experienced at his touch had nothing to do with his status as a suspect, and everything to do with her awareness of him as a man.

"I'm sorry."

She pulled back to study his expression. "You are?"

"No," he admitted. "I'm too pissed off to be sorry. But I know I shouldn't have ordered you around like that in front of my family."

"An honest admission is better than an insincere apology."

"Well, you got both."

"Lucky me."

He worked his fingers through his dark hair in frustration. It was too long, and had a tendency to curl at the ends. In the water, it looked as smooth and sleek as an otter's pelt. She wanted to run her fingers through it, then down, over his chest, and lower, where that silky line of hair disappeared into the waistband of his jeans.

"I'm jealous."

She raised her eyes to his face. "What?"

"I'm jealous of Carly's boyfriend. Can you believe that?"

She smiled. "Of course. It's plain to see."

"I don't want her to grow up. I don't want her to get hurt. But even more, I can't help but feel she shouldn't need anyone but me. If I were giving her enough positive male attention, she wouldn't have to look elsewhere."

"Ah. Does it work the same way for you?"

"What do you mean?"

"Why am I here, if Carly fulfills all of your emotional needs?"

"I have . . . other needs."

"And she isn't allowed to have sexual needs? Why, because she's a girl?"

"Yes, damn it! I don't want to know about her sexual needs. She's my daughter."

Sonny threw back her head and laughed. "You're going to know about them. And you'd better start talking to her about sex."

"I've talked to her about sex," he replied defensively.

"What did you say?"

" 'Don't do it.' "

"Ben," she scolded. "You need to make sure that she respects herself. That she understands the repercussions of her actions."

His expression grew pained. "I always thought Olivia would do this."

At the mention of his former wife, Sonny felt a twist of pain inside her chest. Maybe it was the way he spoke her name, or the tortured look on his face, but it was obvious he was still in love with her. Never mind the case, or that she was here under an assumed name, playing a role. Forget Summer Moore; Sonny Vasquez was crushed.

"What do you want from me?" she asked in a whisper.

Ben understood the question. The subjects of conversation might have changed, but not the topic. Slipping his arms around her waist, he dipped his head low, putting his lips very close to her ear. "Sex," he breathed, making the word a caress.

The laconic statement wasn't meant to be insulting, but he was surprised when she didn't pull away. Instead, she looked up at him with those amazing blue eyes, and he saw his own ache mirrored there, along with hesitation, and a hint of fear.

Ben wasn't sure why it sent him over the edge. Her reluctance was a novelty, and he certainly wasn't accustomed to women being afraid of him. He knew he should be afraid of her, too. The threat she posed to him was much more than physical.

He'd never had a strong sense of self-preservation, so he went ahead and kissed her. She must have been suffering from the same malady, because she kissed him back.

His movements were stiff and awkward from lack of practice, but she didn't seem to notice. When he tasted the seam of her lips, she parted them with a moan, twining her fingers through his hair. Pulse pounding with desire, he pressed closer, touching his tongue to hers, letting his hands roam over her lower back.

She went very still.

He lifted his mouth from hers. "You're not going to hurt me again, are you?"

She laughed a little, tilting her head back to expose the silky column of her throat. Tantalized by the sight of that honeyed skin, he placed an openmouthed kiss there, following the delicate silver chain down her neck.

She clutched his hair. "I have to be in control."

A wave of heat washed over him. On board with whatever kinky game she wanted to play, he raised his head and held his hands out to her, palms up. "Where do you want them?"

She put them on her breasts. "How about here?"

He groaned in agreement, backing her up against the rock wall and taking her mouth under his once again. Instinct had him pinning her in place with his body, his erection swelling against her belly, her nipples hardening at the brush of his thumbs. Frustrated with all the fabric between them, he unbuttoned her dress to the waist and released the front clasp of her bra.

"Wait," she panted.

He stared down at her naked breasts. Her nipples were like pale brown sugar, beautiful, delicate, and unexpected. With a tremendous effort, he brought his eyes back to her face. "Why?"

"You're going *way* too fast."

"Oh. Fine." He retreated, sitting in a cushioned patio chair, waiting for his heart to stop pumping blood to his groin.

She didn't give it a chance. She straddled his lap, giving him a spectacular view of well-toned thighs and sheer white panties. His throat worked convulsively, his erection throbbed, and his fingers itched to touch her.

Clutching the underside of the armless chair, he closed his eyes and tried to regulate his breathing, but he hadn't been with a woman for so long...

"Okay," she said, looking down at his face.

He couldn't keep up with her thought processes. "Okay what?"

"You can touch me now."

"Where?" he asked reverently.

Impatient with him, she pressed her delightful breasts to his face. "Here."

Wrapping his arms around her, he took one sweet, caramel-colored nipple into his mouth, hearing her sharp intake of breath and feeling her shiver of excitement. Greedily, his fingers slipped under her skirt, past the flimsy barrier of her panties, between her legs.

She was slick and hot and... crushing his trachea with her forearm.

"Stop," she warned, applying pressure by holding one arm behind his neck, another in front. It was a damned effective headlock.

His hands fell away from her. Hell, in a minute he might pass out if she kept squeezing.

When she released him, he coughed and sputtered, covering his aching throat with one hand. "Goddamn," he said in a strangled voice. "I'll have to tie you up to have sex with you. No man is safe around you."

She moved off his lap, closed the clasp of her bra

with shaking hands, and pulled her skirt down over her legs.

"Where are you going?" he asked.

"Home," she said, buttoning the front of her dress.

He rose to his feet and went to her, taking her by the hand. "Wait. I didn't mean it. I won't tie you up. Hell, you can tie me up. Stay."

She let out a slow breath. "No. You're right. I'm a menace."

"I don't care. I like it."

Shaking her head, she pulled away. "You're not a masochist."

"Sure I am. Whip me, beat me, make me sorry. Just don't leave me like this."

His insinuation that she owed him something for getting him worked up did not go over well. "Hey. I never said I was going to sleep with you."

He still wasn't thinking with his brain. "Are you serious?"

"Yeah, I am. Bye."

He held on to her arm, detaining her. Her eyes flashed a violent promise, a warning that he recklessly ignored.

It was a mistake.

In an instant, the arm holding hers was wrenched up between his shoulder blades and he was flat on the ground, face pressed into the stone patio. "Please," he wheezed, short of breath and instantly contrite. "Feel free to leave, whenever you like."

"You're damned right I'll leave." She pressed her knee into his back, punishing him a little.

"Will you please let me up?" he asked, resisting the urge to struggle. He didn't doubt she could hurt him some more if she wanted to. How she'd incapacitated him so easily, he couldn't fathom. He had at least fifty pounds on her, all of it muscle.

When she relaxed her grip and moved away, he breathed a sigh of relief. Wincing at the blow to his ego, not to mention the pain in his shoulder, he pushed himself up off the ground, hoping he wouldn't be too sore for surfing tomorrow.

"I'm sorry," he said slowly. "Nathan was right. I have been dating myself way too long. There hasn't been anyone since Olivia." He studied her from beneath lowered lashes, anticipating her response.

For a moment, he was sure she was going to walk out on him. Then she cocked her head to one side and said, "If you treat yourself as badly as you have me, I don't suppose you ever get lucky at the end of the evening."

Burying his hands in his jeans pockets, he shrugged his shoulders sheepishly. "Actually, I'm a pretty cheap date."

Her lips twitched. "I'll just bet you are."

He liked her, he realized. Not just her face and her body and her sadistic sexual quirks, but her sense of humor, her personality, and her kindness. "Where did you learn those moves?"

"Self-defense classes."

"Oh, yeah? Will you teach me?"

"No."

He supposed he deserved that. "Will you teach Carly?"

She considered. "Maybe."

"Want to come over tomorrow?"

"Definitely not."

He thought fast. "Carly and I go to Tijuana every Christmas Eve for midnight mass. Come with us. I promise not to make any insulting overtures." He smiled ruefully. "At least, not in front of her grandparents."

She regarded him with suspicion. "If all you want from me is sex, why are you inviting me to family gatherings?"

He didn't have a good answer for that question. Neither did he want her to read too much into his invitations. "At this time of year, it's all I have to offer," he said finally. His game was way off, he knew. He used to be able to tell women what they wanted to hear.

She smiled at his honesty. "I'll think about it."

"The sex?"

"The midnight mass."

# CHAPTER 8

"Rise and shine, sailor." The smell of whisky pervaded the room.

James opened his eyes with great reluctance. He'd been dreaming of Carly, of taking her on a trip around the bay, just the two of them. When he dropped anchor, finding a romantic cove where they could while away the day, he'd seen something swimming in the water, a dark shape, shimmering just below the surface...

"What?" he grumbled, rubbing his eyes. "It's Christmas Eve. We aren't working today."

"Yes we are. Piss away that hard-on and make me breakfast."

Groaning, James threw back the pile of wool blankets and stumbled into the bathroom. The cold, more than anything else, brought his constantly raging hormones under control. Arlen Matthews didn't believe in wasting money on central heating.

James pulled on his clothes and headed toward the kitchen. With only the basic food items available, the morning meal was never a grand affair. James made do with cold cereal, as usual, after mixing a disgusting concoction of raw eggs, hot sauce, orange juice, and milk for Arlen. He was supposed to add a little hair of the dog, but judging by his dad's breath, he didn't need any more alcohol.

James sighed. He'd be captain *and* first mate today.

He drove, navigating Arlen's old blue pickup truck through light traffic to Stephen's place downtown. His brother must not have been expecting to work either, because he wasn't waiting on the front steps of the run-down duplex as usual.

"Goddamn druggie," Arlen mumbled, taking a swig from a flask.

James turned off the engine. "I'll go in."

Arlen shrugged and settled into the passenger seat, pulling his trucker cap down over his bloodshot eyes.

The door wasn't locked, and James didn't bother knocking. It was an informal kind of place. Inside, two guys he knew by face, if not name, were playing video games in the predawn light. Drug paraphernalia littered the coffee table. They barely glanced at him as he passed by.

At the open bedroom door, he paused, knowing from experience to keep his eyes averted. His brother's girlfriend was an exhibitionist. "Stephen?"

"James," Rhoda murmured. "Come in, honey."

A little voice in his head told him not to look. He

should have listened to it. Rhoda was on the bed, her nude limbs entwined with someone else's. James blinked, thinking he was seeing an optical illusion, for he counted more breasts than should have been present. Then he realized that Rhoda was with another woman.

"Want to join us?" she asked, sliding her hand over the curve of her partner's belly.

The other woman was passed out cold.

James pulled the door shut and continued down the hall, shuddering with revulsion. He couldn't believe his brother crawled into bed with that. Rhoda was a dizzy blonde, overdyed, overused, and worn out. Drugs had sucked up all of her feminine curves, but it was her personality, more than anything else, that made her unattractive.

Stephen was in the back room, shirtless, barefoot, doing a line. It was probably 60 degrees in the room. The Matthews men weren't big on cranking up thermostats.

When he noticed James standing there, he jumped to his feet, wiping powder from his nose. "Motherfucker! I thought you were the cops."

James rubbed a hand over his face. If Stephen was worried about getting busted, why did he leave the doors open, have strangers coming and going at all hours, and keep glass pipes out everywhere? "Dad wants to work."

Stephen didn't consider saying no. "Shit. Let me get ready."

An hour later, on the water, the early-morning sun broke over the horizon. It was going to be one of those spectacular winter days, crisp and clear, with miles of visibility and hardly any churned-up surf marring the smooth blue blanket of ocean. A good day for fishing, although James would rather be anywhere else.

When they pulled in the net, it was heavy with catch. James normally didn't care for his brother's company when he was wired, but today he was thankful for it. Arlen was snoring at the helm, dead to the world, and it took the strength of three men to pull in the net, even with the motorized spool. Stephen was so hyped up he had the energy of two, and James had more muscle than meat on his bones, so they were able to bring the net up to the surface together.

"Feels like a thresher," Stephen said, indicating the extra weight.

"Merry Christmas," James replied with a grin, wiping sweat from his forehead. A large shark would be a good catch, more than enough to call it a day.

But it wasn't a thresher. Two bluefin were tangled in the net, still squirming, not enough to warrant an early dock.

The weighty portion of the catch was a different species altogether.

A woman.


The surf was up at Windansea Beach. Waves like glass had been breaking in picture-perfect sets since dawn.

Ben had promised to make Carly blueberry pancakes for breakfast, so he dragged himself out of the water midmorning for a break. After hosing down his gear, and himself, he dressed in jeans and a T-shirt and made his way to the kitchen, whistling, his mind on six- to ten-foot swells and a killer offshore flow.

"You have to take me shopping," Carly announced. She was flipping pancakes, having given up on waiting for him to do it.

He grabbed a plate and helped himself. "On Christmas Eve? I'd rather not."

"Please, Dad? I don't have anything for James. Did you see the sweater he had on last night? He's awfully poor."

"So what?"

She changed tactics. "Did you buy a gift for Summer?"

"No," he admitted, gazing out the window with longing. "I don't need to," he decided.

"Dad, you can't invite her to our Christmas party and not give her anything. It's totally rude."

"What do you care? On Thursday you told her to take a hike."

Carly turned off the burner. "I like her now." She fixed herself a plate and sat across from him. "You want her to be your girlfriend, right?"

He took a huge bite. "Wrong," he said out of the corner of his mouth.

"Oh," she said, arranging a napkin over her lap self-importantly. "I see. You're just using her for sex."

He didn't bother to deny it. Maybe Carly could learn a few things from him about the male brain. "I'm an adult. I can do whatever I want."

"That doesn't make it right, Dad. What if James was using me for sex?"

"Is he?" Ben asked, putting his fork down angrily.

"No. Don't you get it? Summer is somebody's daughter, too."

Yes, but she wasn't *his* daughter. "Summer is old enough to make her own decisions," he said dismissively. "You aren't. James isn't."

"James is the same age you were when you got Mom pregnant."

He closed his eyes against the pain, having never seen the knife before she slid it between his ribs. "Carly, the last thing I want is for you to go through that same heartache."

"You're lucky she took you back," she said after a moment.

He couldn't deny that. The unlucky one, in all of it, had been Olivia. If she hadn't forgiven him for all those years of drunken abandonment and flagrant infidelity, maybe she'd be alive today.

Pushing aside the guilt, before it suffocated him, he studied his daughter's beautiful face. She looked exactly like Olivia had when she was seventeen. "Are you thinking about having sex?"

Carly blushed. "No."

"Come on."

"I'm not! Not right now anyway. I'm not ready."

She started to get up, to clear away the plates, but he detained her, holding her wrist. "What if he wants to, and you don't? What will you say?"

"I'll say no, Dad. He won't pressure me. He's not like that."

"All boys are like that, Carly." Some grown men were, too. Ones old enough to know better, and dumb enough to do it anyway. "They say they're in pain. They say all the girls do it, and you're a tease if you won't. They say they'll find another girlfriend who will. What if James says those things? Are you ready for it?"

She met his eyes. "Yeah. If he says anything like that, we're over."

"Okay." He thought of another thing boys did when they wanted something a girl wouldn't give. "What if you say stop, and he doesn't?"

"I'll kick him in the balls, Dad. But don't worry. James stops when I tell him to."

He felt like he'd been sucker-punched. "He does?"

"Yeah. We were kissing, the day before yesterday, and he tried to, um—" Carly broke off, wondering how to phrase it.

"What?" he growled.

"Dad, if you're going to get all mad, I'm not going to tell you this stuff."

Ben much preferred being in the dark. "Tell me," he said anyway, clenching his hand into a fist beneath the table.

"He touched my, um"—she made a sweeping gesture over her chest—"you know. I made a noise, and he thought he hurt me, so he stopped. It wasn't that kind of a noise, I said, but—"

Ben held up a hand, having heard more than enough. "I get the idea. Don't you think you guys are moving a little fast? How long has he been your boyfriend?"

"Not very long. But I'm not a little girl anymore. I can decide when I'm ready."

Ben and his daughter were close, but he was far from comfortable with this topic of conversation. His parents had never said a word to him about sex, and at St. Mary's, the private school where he'd suffered through adolescence, sexual education was limited to receiving penance for confessing to impure thoughts.

Maybe that was why he'd been so intent on educating himself with every willing female he could find when he was Carly's age.

He didn't want to encourage her to take the same path he had, yet he couldn't bear to treat sex like a sin. "When you're ready, will you use protection?" he asked finally, wondering if he sounded too permissive.

"Of course. I'm not as stupid as you and Mom were." She took the plates to the sink. "Do you want to know? I mean, if I decide to do it?"

He didn't want to know anything more, ever again, but if she needed to talk to someone, he had to be there for her. It was his job. "Yes. You can tell me anything." As she rinsed the plates and put them in the dishwasher, he said, "Carly?"

"Yeah, Dad?"

"You know I love you, right?"

Her hands, busy wiping down the granite countertop, stilled. "Yeah."

She never said it back to him anymore, like she used to. That was normal for a teenager, he supposed, but it still hurt. "Okay. I just wanted to make sure that you weren't thinking I was ignoring you, or feeling like I didn't care. That I'd rather go surfing than spend time with you."

"Well, that last one is true."

"No. It isn't."

"Don't get all mushy, Dad. Just take me shopping."


"Cut her loose."

Stephen couldn't tear his gaze from the girl's ravaged face. Her hair hung like lank seaweed, curling around her throat. Scavenger marks riddled her naked body, and her skin was tinged greenish black.

"Did you hear? Take out your blade and cut her loose. She's tangled up."

James staggered to the side of the boat and lost his breakfast over the edge. A motley mess that had once been Fruit Loops floated on the surface. Tiny surfperch made jerking, stabbing motions at it while he groaned with nausea.

"Do it," Arlen said, motioning at Stephen with his knife.

"No way. They'll know if I touch her. Don't you watch those police shows?"

"They won't know jack shit. Her skin's sloughing off all over the place."

Stephen grimaced, glad he was still jacked up enough to feel numb. At the helm, James started dry-heaving.

"Quit your bellyachin', boy," Arlen yelled over his shoulder, "or I'll throw you in with her."

"Maybe we should call the Coast Guard," Stephen suggested.

Arlen squinted at him. "We're on the preserve," he said, as if that were reason enough to throw a dead girl back into the sea like undersized catch. It was illegal to drop a net in protected waters, and the penalty for breaking that particular environmental sanction was a $500 fine. "Besides, don't you recognize her?"

Stephen glanced down at the body and shuddered. "No."

Arlen eyeballed him derisively. "Drugs done fried your brain, son. It's that little neighborhood whore. Don't look like she'll be putting out no more."

Shaking his head, Stephen turned away from the gruesome sight.

In the end, Arlen did the job himself, muttering about lazy boys and loose women, shaking the body from the net instead of cutting her free, to save the time and hassle of having to mend it later.

The rest of the day passed in taut silence.

After work, Stephen took his daily wage without a complaint. When James asked if he could spend the night at Stephen's, Arlen grunted his permission. His truck was squealing around the corner before they got to the front door.

Stephen sat on the stoop, pulling out his pack of cigarettes and a wad of cash. "Here," he said, counting out half his pay. He knew their dad never gave James a dime. Living expenses, Arlen claimed, ate up every cent of his little brother's paycheck. "Merry Christmas."

"Thanks," James said, pocketing the cash and taking a seat next to him.

Stephen lit up a smoke and waited for James to

speak, although he dreaded the conversation. He was coming down hard, his brain like mush, his body ready to crash. Times like this he hated being an addict. The higher the high, the lower the low.

"Did Dad ever bring home whores, when you used to live with us?"

Stephen took another drag. "You know he did."

"Yeah. Yeah, I remember." James came around to the real question he wanted to ask. "Did he try to make you do stuff with them?"

Stephen inhaled deeply, wishing it was dope. "Yep."

James looked away, his mouth drawn. "I can't do it."

"You don't have to," Stephen replied. "Don't let him bully you into it."

"He rapes them," James said. "Whether he pays or not. Whether they tell anyone or not. That's what it is."

Stephen nodded, thinking that what he and Rhoda did behind closed doors wasn't much different. Hell, he was so screwed up that he'd begun to think pain and depravity were normal. No better than he deserved. No worse.

"I never want to have a girl like that. If she's willing, you don't have to pay her."

"Don't think about it," Stephen said, giving the only advice he could. "Don't worry about what he does." Reaching out, he wrapped his fingers around James' upper arm. "You'll be eighteen soon. You'll get out." His voice shook with intensity. "Promise me you'll get out."

James squirmed in Stephen's grip. "What will you do?"

"Don't think about that," he repeated. "Don't think about anything. Just go. Go and never look back."

"What about Mom?"

Stephen released him with a sigh, returning the cigarette to his mouth. His stomach was hurting now, and he longed to go inside, to heat the glass until the smoke rose up, to inhale over and over again. He wanted to forget about the day, forget himself, assuage his ache.

That query went unanswered, so James asked another. "You think he killed that girl?"

Stephen didn't look at him. Couldn't look at him. The next logical question, the one about their mother, remained unspoken.

Carly didn't have any trouble choosing Christmas presents for James.

With Ben's help, she selected a handsome diver's watch, the same kind he used, of such stellar quality it boasted a lifetime guarantee even under the brutal wear and tear of salt water. She also chose a midnight blue cable-knit sweater, claiming it matched James' eyes.

Ben rolled his.

Carly would have bought out the whole store if he hadn't stepped in. He didn't care about the money, but he had to draw the line somewhere. "You'll embarrass him, Carly. He doesn't want to be thought of as a charity case."

"I guess you're right," she sighed. "What should we get for Summer?"

Ben shrugged.

"Jewelry?"

He pictured the tiny silver cross she'd had around her neck last night. "No. Too personal. We don't know each other that well."

"What does she like?"

"I'm not sure."

"Don't you ask her about herself?"

"No."

"You are so clueless."

Actually, he wasn't. He knew better than to encourage a woman into thinking they were embarking upon a long-term relationship.

"Lingerie, then?" she teased.

"Even I'm not that obvious."

"Good. Perfume?"

"She doesn't wear it."

"How do you know?"

He knew because he'd smelled and touched and tasted her skin at most of the places women put perfume. Although he could think of a few more spots he'd like to introduce himself to. "I just do."

They came back to jewelry, having exhausted all other options. Carly found an unusual pale blue stone pendant, hanging from a platinum chain. It was smoky and ethereal, like Summer's eyes.

"Why don't you say it's from you?" he asked

when Carly insisted that he buy it. It was too expensive, too lovely, and too fitting to be an offhand gift.

"You have major issues," she sighed, but agreed.

In the car, on the way home, she said, "She's been dead a long time. When will you let her go?"

Never, he thought.

He couldn't let her go any more than he could forgive himself for killing her.

As usual, Sonny had difficulty deciding on an outfit to match her assumed role and the occasion. She finally settled on a calf-length skirt and soft leather boots, both vintage, and her own. The black cashmere sweater was new, bought with federal funding, and it had a neckline low enough to show off Carly's silver cross.

She figured she may as well wear it again, especially since it was Christmas Eve.

Sonny Vasquez wasn't fond of religious accoutrements. Summer Moore, she decided, could wear one without overanalyzing its symbolism. Besides, the necklace drew the eye to her cleavage, and although she wasn't planning on letting Ben round second base again, she wasn't above making him wish he could.

When he opened the door, he didn't say anything about her appearance. Gone was the simple charmer who'd told her she looked delicious.

"Come in," he said, very formally.

He was wearing gray suit pants and a white dress shirt. A black-and-gray-striped silk tie hung loose at his neck, and his toes were covered by black socks. He had sexy feet, she recalled, missing the sight of them bare.

"Do you know how to do a Windsor?"

"Yes," she said, following him upstairs. Sonny had knotted ties for her brother every time he'd gone to court, so she'd had a lot of practice.

While he sat to put on his shoes, she studied the room. On the wall to her left, a framed portrait of a nude Hawaiian girl stood against a backdrop of brilliant green palm fronds. A strategically placed hibiscus—giant, luscious, and gorgeously red—made the full-length picture more artistic than erotic.

The rest of the room was austere in comparison. White walls, sand-colored carpet, and white crown molding. The bed was huge, but low to the ground, its white down comforter and fluffy white pillows blending in with the surroundings rather than dominating the room. A black mahogany dresser had a pair of cuff links on top, nothing else. Across from the bed, there was a fireplace, its hearth cold and unlit.

Beyond a half-wall partition, a pale green love seat and matching chair faced a smart-looking plasma screen TV. The weather channel was on mute. Mahogany bookshelves, filled with scholarly-looking volumes, completed the room.

The space was visually striking, modern, and sterile. The shock of red hibiscus in the framed photo and the green leaves in the background, a motif that was repeated on the designer couch as well as the floor-to-ceiling curtains, were the only splashes of color.

The focal point, however, was not the floating bed, flat screen TV, or naked island nymph. It was the view. The west-facing wall was all glass, with windows so tall and wide Sonny felt as though she could step right out into the Pacific.

She shivered, wrapping her arms around herself tightly.

Ben ducked into the master bath, probably to make himself even more devastatingly handsome, so she browsed his book collection while she waited. Jean-Paul Sartre. Karl Marx. Dostoyevsky. Immanuel Kant.

He liked philosophy. Ew.

"You read this stuff?" she asked, raising her voice.

He reentered the bedroom, crossing it to stand in front of his dresser drawers.

"Uh, yeah. Some of it."

She pulled a book off the shelf. Sigmund Freud: *Civilization and Its Discontents*. "You believe in this crap?"

"What crap?"

"Penis envy."

He glanced at the book she held and fastened his cuff links. "That one's not about penis envy. But no, I'm not a fan of that particular theory."

"Oh? Explain why."

"Well, oversimplified—"

"By all means, oversimplify. Otherwise, my penis-deprived brain will explode."

He laughed. "I've never met a woman who wasn't delighted with what she had. Are we in agreement?"

"Yes," she said, replacing the book, disappointed that she hadn't been able to start an argument.

"Are you going to knot this tie for me?"

She walked up to him, looking into his deep brown eyes. He was so controlled today, so reserved. It made her want to mess up his hair and unbutton his shirt. Instead, she formed a nice Windsor knot, taking longer than was necessary, standing closer than she had to, smoothing the tie down over his sternum and her hands across the impressive breadth of his shoulders when she was finished. "Done," she whispered, pressing her stocking-covered knee to his thigh.

"Thanks," he said tersely, stepping away from her.

"I didn't know this was such a formal affair. I would have worn my ball gown."

His eyes raked over her, lingering on the swells of her breasts. "You look fine," he said in a low voice, then lifted his gaze to the doorway.

Sonny didn't have to look over her shoulder to know Carly was standing there, eavesdropping. In over five years as an agent, and a lifetime of hyper-awareness, she'd never been snuck up on.

Nor had she ever lost herself so completely in a role.

Sonny bit her lower lip, on the cusp of madness. Here she was, old enough to know better, dumb enough to do it anyway, in danger of falling for a man who wasn't even bothering to pretend he was interested in a real relationship. On the job, no less.

She turned toward Carly, vowing to stay focused on her assignment, not Ben Fortune's bedroom eyes, for the remainder of the evening.

Before crossing the border from San Diego to Tijuana, Ben explained that Carly's grandparents had been married on Christmas Eve fifty years before. They'd hired a professional photographer to mark the occasion, and invited Ben and Carly to be part of the family photo, hence the more formal attire.

Over a hundred friends and family members were in attendance, also decked out in their finest, most of whom didn't speak a word of English. While Ben and Carly posed for the photo, Sonny sat out the festivities at a long table in the banquet hall.

When Ben found her again, she was chatting with several other revelers and enjoying some delicious holiday fare.

"I didn't know you spoke Spanish," he said.

"You don't know much about me."

He couldn't argue that. "What are you?"

She finished off her tamale with a smile. "A woman. What are you? A space alien?"

"You know what I mean."

"My mother is Guatemalan."

He raised an eyebrow in surprise, and Sonny reacted defensively, having encountered this reaction many times. Her mother was of Spanish descent, but the majority of Guatemalans were native Mayans, marginalized to coffee plantations in their homeland, often used as farmhands in the United States. In San Diego, Guatemalan heritage was synonymous with cheap labor and dark skin.

"There are light-skinned Hispanics in Guatemala, just like any other Latin-American country," she explained.

He held his hands up, claiming innocence. "I didn't say there weren't. I've just never met a blue-eyed Guatemalan."

"And how many Guatemalans do you know?"

He smiled. "One. My gardener."

"You have a gardener? You don't even have a yard."

"What I do have, he's done an excellent job with."

She smiled back at him, shaking her head at the extravagancies of the disgustingly wealthy.

"You take after your mom?"

"No. People tell me I look like her, but I don't see it. She's very pretty."

"So are you."

She just shrugged, not bothering to disagree. In her experience, when she tried to deflect a compliment, it was assumed that she was fishing for more. "She and my brother have dark hair. When I was a kid, everyone called me *guera*."

"What does that mean?"

She couldn't believe he didn't know. Several of Carly's relatives had been calling him the masculine equivalent of the word all evening. "It means light hair or skin. Or, in your case," she added, for his hair was dark and his skin sun-browned, "white boy."

"Oh. I wondered about that."

"Why didn't you ask Carly?"

"I don't trust her translations."

"That's probably wise. She told her grandmother I was your fiancée."

He rubbed a hand over his eyes. "I knew it."

"She's made quite the turnaround. Was it less than a week ago she was warning me away from you?"

He glanced at his daughter, smiling and beautiful, posing for photographs with her grandparents. "Just wait. When she has her first fight with James, she'll be cursing you to hell and lighting herself on fire."

"You have a morbid sense of humor."

"I'm not joking."

"Maybe James is good for her. She looks happy."

"He's a fucking martyr," he said sullenly. "If he were just some dumb jock, or a spoiled rich kid, like she is, I wouldn't worry half as much."

"You may be right. I think he cares about her, though."

He didn't dispute her. Instead, he brought her back to his original question. "So where'd you get the blue eyes, my little Guatemalan princess?"

"My dad, I guess."

"You don't know?"

"I don't even know his name."

"Isn't it Moore?"

"No. That's my stepdad." She felt a twinge of guilt for deceiving him with the phony name, but she was telling the truth. Everett Moore had been her stepfather, and the thought of him made a darkness pass over her, like a cloud occluding the sun.

Ben must have seen it on her face. "Is he the guy?"

She didn't have to ask what he meant, but she did. "The guy who what?"

"Who made you afraid."

"He was one of them."

Ben's mouth made a thin, hard line. "Where is he now?"

"Why? So you can find him and beat him up?" She laughed, shaking her head.

"I feel protective of you, and you think it's funny?"

"No. What's funny is that you assume I need a protector. That tough-guy avenger crap is more about you than me, and it's insulting. You want to make him pay for ruining your good-girl fantasy, for turning me into a real person with a lot of sexual hang-ups."

He was silent for a moment. "So where is he?"

Her jaw dropped. "Did you hear anything I just said?"

"Yes."

"So?"

"So, I think it's bullshit. I've known you had hangups from the beginning. Who doesn't? I still have nightmares about the Japanese girl with the Kung Fu grip. I've always thought of you as a real person—you saved my daughter from drowning, for Christ's sake. And believe it or not, in my fantasies, you're a bad girl." His eyes flicked over her. "A very, *very* bad girl," he emphasized. "Nothing has changed, except that now I want to kill your stepfather."

"My brother beat you to it," she said. "He'll be paying for that mistake the rest of his life." Upset with herself for giving too much personal information away, she made a nervous gesture from him to her, indicating their relationship. "Last night you told me this was about sex. No emotional involvement."

He leaned back in his chair. "Sex continues to be my primary objective," he said with a lazy smile, looking out at the open floor. "Let's dance."

She cast him a skeptical glance. The music had just started, and several other couples were already dancing. "You cumbia?"

"Does it involve a lot of thrusting and grinding against each other?"

She smiled back at him, amused in spite of herself. "No."

He sighed in mock disappointment. "Let's do it anyway."

James borrowed some clothes and a duffel bag from his brother and left. He couldn't face the idea of fighting off Rhoda, or anyone else, tonight. Stephen didn't know it, because he'd been more interested in drugs than sex for years, but James had already been with some of the party girls who drifted in and out of his brother's house.

On James' seventeenth birthday, Arlen gave him a shot of whisky and a punch in the eye, saying that anyone who was still a virgin at his age was either queer or retarded. James was just a teenager, all hormones and attitude, with a lot of anxieties and even more to prove, so he set out to prove he wasn't queer with the first girl he laid eyes on, in an awkward but consensual grapple against Stephen's bathroom sink.

It wasn't a shining moment of his life, but it was a breakthrough.

He'd known he wasn't queer, but he hadn't been sure he could have sex like a normal person after all he'd seen and done. James discovered that not only could he do it, he could enjoy it, with an empty heart and a blissfully blank mind.

His performances hadn't been memorable, but neither had the girls, and at least he didn't need money or violence to get off. Still, it had deepened rather than filled the void inside him, so he'd stopped going over to Stephen's house looking to break up the monotony of his miserable existence by getting laid.

When Lisette Bruebaker showed up a few weeks ago, James hadn't approached her with anything particular in mind. They'd laughed about playing seven minutes in heaven at her thirteenth birthday party. She was so pretty, so full of life, so much different than the intoxicated, hollow-eyed girls he usually saw at Stephen's.

And she reminded him of Carly.

So when Lisette took him into Stephen's closet, he followed her, and when she dropped to her knees to give him her own little version of heaven, he didn't tell her not to. He just threaded his fingers through her hair and pretended she was Carly.

He hadn't lasted anywhere near seven minutes.

James groaned aloud at the memory, feeling sick to his stomach. If Carly ever found out about that, she'd never talk to him again. He knew very little about sex, and even less about girls, but he knew when to keep his mouth shut. Carly wouldn't like to hear that he'd been in a closet with her friend.

Her dead friend.

As he walked by Carly's house, he looked around, checking it out, making sure everything was safe. If someone could brutalize Lisette and dump her in the water, what was to stop them from doing it to Carly?

His gut clenched at the thought.

Stashing his bag between rocks at Windansea, he walked down to the 24-hour mini-mart to make the call. He knew better than to dial 911. Instead he looked up a phone number for a homicide detective.

"Staff Sergeant Paula DeGrassi, Homicide Division," one of the listings read. It sounded pretty official, and for a moment, he wavered. This could get him in some really deep shit.

Then he thought of Carly, her pretty face. Her slim body tangled in a net.

So he dialed, palms sweaty, heart pounding, blood pumping to his ear where it was pressed against the receiver. Thank God for voice mail. James left a short message, giving Lisette's name and a pair of memorized GPS coordinates.

When he returned to Windansea, he stayed awake for a long time, staring at black waves crashing against a bone-white beach.

He was dead-tired, too freaked out to sleep.

# CHAPTER 9

The following day, Ben rang Sonny's drunken song-bird doorbell several hours before the pool party was scheduled to begin. When she opened the door, he smiled, and her heart did a funny little flip-flop in her chest.

"I know you work out," he said, like that was a greeting.

"How?"

"You're in great shape."

Smiling back at him, she leaned against her door-jamb. "Is that a challenge?"

"I'm not allowed to surf on Christmas. Family rules. Carly wants to run on the beach, and I'm dying to get some exercise."

So was she. "You go stir-crazy after only one day without surfing?"

"Yeah. I get the shakes."

Sonny tried to wipe the silly grin off her face, but it was Christmas, and she had nothing pressing on her schedule. Grant wouldn't even expect her to check in. Her boss would be spending time with his *real* family, unavailable for the entire day. "I'll meet you in a few minutes," she decided. "Prepare to get whipped."

Before the run, Sonny gave Carly her first self-defense lesson as a warm-up. The girl was lithe and limber, and would have been a good student if she'd taken the subject seriously. But she was a typical teenager, naïve and optimistic, confident in the assumption that she would always be safe.

Ben, on the other hand, was a very quick study. He was able to flip her over, off her feet, after less than five minutes of training. It unsettled her, but she reminded herself that he was a world-class athlete, a powerful man in top condition.

She cut the lesson short before he got too cocky.

Carly was a better runner than a grappler, having natural grace, legs like a gazelle, and energy to burn. She lacked drive and endurance, however, so she tired more quickly than Sonny or Ben. After a couple of miles, she let them go on ahead, taking a break to sit on the sand.

Sonny gave it her all, but Ben beat her easily. In a contest of self-defense, he was no match for her. In one of raw athleticism, she was the loser.

Gasping for breath, she collapsed on the sand, totally spent, conceding her defeat. She hadn't pushed herself so hard in a while, and it felt good, although winning would have felt better. Gloating, he sat down beside her, pulling his T-shirt over his head and using it to wipe his face.

"Oh my God," she said, when she saw his chest.

He looked down, running the T-shirt over himself absently, mopping his sweaty abs. "What?"

"Your body," was all she could manage.

"What about it?"

In a wetsuit, he was spectacular. In jeans and a T-shirt, a suit, or a sweater, he was gorgeous. But bare-chested, he was ... wow.

"It's hideous," she said, smiling.

He smiled back at her. The sexy, off-center smile, the well-toned body ... it was like a double whammy. "I've been told that before."

"I'm sure you have. Put your shirt back on. You're scaring little children."

He laughed.

She rested on her side, facing him, one hand against her cheek, bent elbow supporting the weight of her head. The other arm, draped across her stomach, made slow, lazy circles in the sand. "How often do you jog?" she asked.

"I don't."

She sat up in disbelief, no longer relaxed. "How could you beat me, then?"

"Surfing, swimming, paddling out. It keeps you in shape."

Her eyes wandered over his chest. "I can see that. You must lift weights."

"Nah."

"Sit-ups?"

He clenched his stomach muscles self-consciously. "Never."

"You are such a liar," she accused, insanely jealous.

"What do you do?" he asked, giving her body a similar examination.

"Me? I do everything."

His eyes darkened.

"I mean, I do cardio and strength training. I have to work so hard to maintain what little muscle tone I have." She flexed her own bicep, feeling it, comparing it to his. He didn't have that overworked, overstylized look some men spend hours every day in the gym to achieve. He was just tight and hard and perfectly toned.

Her hands itched to test every inch of him for firmness. "I can't believe you get all that from surfing."

He shrugged, making those gorgeous muscles dance in the morning light. "I have to work to keep my muscle mass lower, actually. It's better to be quick and light on the water."

"Is that why you're so health-conscious? To keep from bulking up?"

"Yes. Nobody thinks it's strange when an Olympian has a strict diet regimen, but because I'm a surfer, I'm supposed to live on burgers and French fries. It's a stereotype."

"You make a pretty good-looking poster boy for clean living," she decided, letting her eyes fall over his flat stomach, down to the silky line of hair that dipped into the waistband of his shorts.

"You're embarrassing me."

Her gaze returned to his face. "Am I?" She grinned,

enjoying his discomfort. "Sorry, I forgot. Being worshipped by women is tiresome. You're so over it."

"I'm going to throw you in the ocean," he growled.

"Go ahead and try," she said, delighted with the suggestion.

And he did. Or she let him. By the time they came out of the icy surf, laughing, dripping, soaked to the skin, and covered with sand, neither was sure who had gotten the better of whom.

When Carly caught up with them, she was horrified by their childish behavior. "I am not walking down Windansea with a couple of wet dorks," she said. True to her word, she kept her distance, trailing a hundred feet behind them the entire way back to the house.


In contrast to the playful, easy ambience of the morning jog, Christmas with the Fortunes was a tense, quietly antagonistic celebration.

Ben's father was a physically imposing man, tall and distinguished-looking, decades older than his wife. A retired criminal court judge, he was also loud, supercilious, and critical.

Ben's brother, Nathan, brought a vintage bottle of burgundy, a friendly smile, and his boyfriend, Peter. Judge, as everyone called him, drank the wine, ignored his younger son, and flat-out refused to acknowledge Peter's existence.

Ben, on the other hand, was treated as though everything he touched turned to gold. It was strange, as he'd done nothing to earn his father's approval, from what Sonny could ascertain. He'd chosen surfing over football, crushing his father's greatest vicarious dream. He also dropped out of school to follow the endless summer, a move that had been even less popular with his folks. And when he finally went to college, he majored in Philosophy instead of Prelaw.

Despite these disappointments, Judge gave Ben his deference, and his respect.

Nathan was the one who'd followed in his father's footsteps at Harvard Law. Having done a background check on him already, Sonny knew Nathan was a public defender, and he'd also played college ball. Lacking Ben's size and natural athleticism, he'd gone far on guts, pride, and the steely determination of a second son desperate to prove he was good enough.

He wasn't, and he never would be.

In the courtroom, Judge wouldn't have discriminated against a person based on race, religion, or sexual orientation. It was a shame he couldn't allow his son the same courtesy.

The Fortunes had their differences, but one thing was clear: they all adored Carly. When she wanted to be, the girl was like a ray of light.

Sonny figured they would use the holiday as an excuse to spoil her rotten. She was wrong. For a family of considerable wealth, the gift exchange was completed with very little fanfare, the items more thoughtful than lavish. Carly, for instance, gave Ben a philosophy book, and he presented her with a set of crescent wrenches that sent her into raptures.

Sonny accepted a gift with surprise, reading the card aloud. "To Summer. Love, Ben," was written in dramatic, feminine script. She put a hand over her heart, as if deeply touched. "I didn't know you felt this way," she teased, much to Carly's delight. When she opened the package, the smile fell from her face. "It's beautiful," she said, lifting the necklace up to see the stone in the sunlight. It was the most elegant piece of jewelry she'd ever seen. "Thank you."

"Carly picked it," he said brusquely.

It was no less than she'd suspected, but hearing him say it out loud, in front of everyone, made her chest tighten and her throat close up.

Throughout the remainder of the day, Sonny analyzed Nathan through an investigator's eyes. He had a lot of jealousy issues with Ben, but he wasn't into surfing, and it was a stretch to think he'd planted trace evidence in an attempt to frame his hotshot older brother.

JT Carver was a surfer, but another unlikely suspect. He'd been out catching waves with Ben the morning Olivia was murdered, and was actually his alibi. JT had a few marks on his record, minor charges involving drugs and alcohol, but there was something about his Jeff Spicoli routine Sonny didn't buy. Perhaps it was merely an indication that he knew he wasn't living up to his full potential, because although she found him clever, at times his joviality seemed forced.

Unfortunately, he'd flaked out on the party, so she couldn't study his handsome countenance for signs of deception.

By late afternoon, Grace and Judge left, and soon after, Nathan and Peter made their excuses. James showed up just in time to frolic with Carly in the heated pool. The two of them substituted a lot of playful wrestling for sex, just as Sonny and Ben had done on the beach that morning. When the pair got a little too frisky, they were relegated indoors to watch DVDs.

Sonny wasn't sure which situation was more dangerous: Carly and James hanging all over each other, half-naked, underwater, or sitting together, clothed but unsupervised, on the living room couch.

Ben kept glancing toward the sliding glass door uneasily.

"Let's go in the Jacuzzi," Sonny said, stretching her arms over her head. After this morning's workout, her muscles would love it.

His eyes wandered over her, then drifted back to the house, but he nodded.

It was easy to understand his reluctance. With Carly and James nearby, he couldn't seduce her, and that put a damper on his plans for the evening.

Ben was already wearing blue-and-white boardshorts, so he removed his T-shirt and tossed it on the patio table. Sitting down on the coping at the edge of the Jacuzzi, he waited for her to undress with undisguised interest.

Following his lead, she took off her jeans and tank top right there, stripping down to her black string-bikini. She was glad James was indoors, because it was very brief, and she drew the line at revving up teenaged boys.

Ben gaped at her, devouring her body with his eyes.

Frowning, she checked her swimsuit, making sure everything important was covered. "What do you think?" she asked, because he was still ogling her.

"I think I need a cold shower."

She laughed. "I was afraid I had a peekaboo nipple."

He lowered himself into the water with a groan.

Sonny took a seat beside him, enjoying his discomfort immensely. Leaning back and closing her eyes, she let the hot water massage away her tension.

"So," he began after a while, "how are we going to get over your, uh, phobia?"

"I suppose you have a few ideas," she commented dryly.

"You could tie my hands behind my back with your bikini top."

She smiled at the suggestion, which would leave her upper half conveniently bare. "No."

"Okay, then. Your bikini bottoms."

Laughing, she shook her head.

He was silent for a moment. "I would never hurt you."

She looked over at him. "I know."

"Then let me prove it to you."

Getting into the Jacuzzi with him had been a mistake, she realized. Lengthening shadows stretched across the patio, cloaking the pool in darkness. No one could see them. "What about Carly?" she asked anyway, her eyes darting toward the house.

"I'm not suggesting anything . . . X-rated."

Sonny worried at her lower lip, considering. It was so easy to pretend she really was Summer Moore, that Grant didn't exist, that the situation was natural, unplanned, spontaneous.

It was so tempting to give in to what Ben wanted. What she wanted.

"Okay," she said. "But you have to promise you won't touch me."

He nodded slowly and she knew he would keep his word. In effect, it was the same offer he'd made earlier, sans bikini top, but she didn't want to have to tie him up to trust him.

"What do you want me to do?"

A thrill raced through her at his words. She did like a man who was eager to please. "Um...sit up there again." She pointed at the coping around the edge of the pool. "And keep your arms at your sides."

Resting his palms on the coping, he raised himself up, drawing her eye to his rock-hard triceps and strong forearms. Warm water ran in rivulets down his torso, into the low waistband of his shorts. The fabric clung to his thighs, covering him almost to the knee. Studying the way his body hair was plastered to his calves, she fantasized about rubbing her smooth legs against his rough ones, delighting in the differences between them.

Taking a deep breath, she brought her eyes back to his face.

"Now what?" he asked.

She moved closer, placing her hand on his knee and situating herself between his spread thighs. The position was provocative, considering that it brought her breasts level with his lap, but it was kind of awkward for kissing.

It was getting too hot in the Jacuzzi anyway, she decided, boosting herself up out of the water. Wrapping her arms around his neck, she perched her bottom on one well-muscled thigh, carefully avoiding the erection that was already tenting the front of his shorts.

His white-knuckled hands gripped the edge of the coping, but he didn't move. Holding himself stock-still, he waited, his mouth as tense as his body.

At dusk, the temperature was no longer balmy, but she didn't feel the chill. Her heart was racing, drumming a wild beat at the base of her throat. Her nipples peaked with arousal, pushing against the wet fabric of her bathing suit.

Lifting a trembling hand to his face, she traced his lips with her fingertip, as if to make sure they were real. They felt real, and warm, if not exactly pliant. Leaning in, she kissed the crescent-shaped scar above his mouth.

He inhaled a sharp breath.

Taking the plunge, she threaded her fingers through his hair and flattened her breasts against his chest, kissing him like she meant it. His mouth was hot and open, eager for her tongue, and she gave it to him, tasting him deeply.

It was incredibly, unbearably exciting. Pleasure spread through her, pulsing between her thighs. After a few more kisses, she was rubbing herself along the length of his erection, feeling him harden even more, hearing him groan.

Then he broke his promise not to touch her. Putting his hands on her hips, he pushed her back gently, ending the contact and the kiss.

Panting, she blinked up at him in confusion.

"This is going further than I thought."

Remembering Carly, she experienced a sharp stab of disappointment. It wasn't every day Sonny got this comfortable with a man. Never, in fact. Even with Grant she was careful to maintain a safe distance, and their relationship was platonic.

She laughed softly, moistening her throbbing lips. "Too X-rated for you?"

At her hips, his fingers clenched. "Let me get rid of James."

Ducking her head, she pulled away from him, away from temptation. "Sorry. The window to my capitulation just closed for the evening."

He muttered several inventive curses, all directed at his daughter's boyfriend. As it turned out, Ben's animosity was justified, and after he helped her climb out of the Jacuzzi, he was awarded an immediate outlet for his frustration.

Inside the house, on the living room couch, James and Carly were engaging in some inappropriate behavior of their own.

When Ben saw James with his hands all over his daughter, he snapped. Striding forward with a furious growl, he lifted James off Carly and threw him on the ground. It might have ended there if James' instinctive reaction hadn't been to come up swinging.

"Leave her alone," James yelled, launching himself at Ben.

Having little experience with the cycle of abuse, Ben didn't realize that James was only protecting himself—and Carly. Sonny, however, recognized the feral gleam in the boy's eyes all too well. James only understood what he knew, and he'd been taught that when a man put his hands on you, he intended to inflict pain.

Sonny was forced to intervene. Subduing two overwrought males at the same time was tricky, in that there were twice as many flying fists and elbows. James was smaller, but he was scrappy, agile, and combative, not an unworthy opponent. She went for Ben, for having instigated the fight, he deserved it more.

Jumping on his back, she slid her arms up under his and laced her fingers behind his neck, rendering his upper body motionless. It was a good way to get her teeth knocked out by a bucking head, so she kept her face close to his neck. "He's just a kid," she said into his ear, trying to appeal to reason.

"Goddamn it," Ben grated, struggling against her, his chest heaving.

Sonny held tight. Carly was wailing, begging for him to stop, and James, lost in the haze of violence, broke loose with a right hook so well placed that Ben's head rocked back, hitting Sonny's lower lip so hard she saw stars.

Carly switched sides in a split second. "Don't hit my dad, you asshole!" She dove toward James, tackling him, and they landed in a tangle of arms and legs.

Sonny almost couldn't bear to watch the impending disaster. If Carly hit James, James would hit her back, Ben would beat James senseless, and in the end, someone would be dead, badly injured, or in jail.

It didn't happen. Carly drew her arm back to strike, but James caught her wrist midair, stilling her hand. Blinking rapidly, like a just-awakened dreamer, he scanned the mayhem in the room. Carly was crying, tears streaming down her pretty face. Ben was rubbing his jaw and glaring, daring him to feel lucky.

Sonny felt blood trickle from her lower lip. When James saw it, his face paled.

"Shit," he said, letting his head fall back against the hardwood floor. Still sobbing, Carly crawled away from him, into her father's arms.

Without another word, James got to his feet, walked to the door, and left.

# CHAPTER 10

James awoke at the coldest hour of the day, just before dawn. He was curled up in the fetal position, in a damp, uncomfortable crevice between rocks, at what he'd come to think of as his own personal hideaway on Windansea Beach.

He was warm in some places, freezing where his body touched the sand. A hand was shoved down the front of his pants, for heat, he supposed, or comfort. He awoke this way almost every morning and it never failed to embarrass him.

Wiping grains of sand from his face, he realized that he wasn't alone. And the hand down his pants wasn't his.

"Carly," he whispered, cranking his head around to see her, snuggled up behind him. "Wake up."

She mumbled something unintelligible and shifted, pushing her hand down farther, seeking warmth.

He groaned, wondering if it was too cold for him to get hard. Nope.

"James?" she asked, feeling his reaction.

"Take your hand out of my pants."

Sleepily, she complied, moving away from the danger zone. "It's so cold," she said, sliding her palms over his clenched stomach muscles. "Make me warm." She put her mouth against his neck and did that thing she knew he liked.

"Carly, don't," he protested weakly. "Don't touch me right now."

"Why?"

He turned to face her, and she initiated a frontal attack, throwing one of her legs over his hip and slipping her arms around his neck. Arching her back, she put all of her soft parts against his hard ones. "Touch me," she said against his ear. "I'm so cold."

She didn't feel cold. She felt hot, all over. Her mouth, when it met his. Her hands, in his hair, under his shirt. Her stomach, silky and smooth, when he splayed his fingers over it.

"Yes, James," she moaned, tracing his lips with her tongue. "Make me warm."

How could he deny her? He couldn't remember why he'd tried. Instead, he slid his tongue into her mouth and his hands underneath her sweatshirt, covering her naked breasts.

The simple act of touching her, with no barriers between them, was so exciting that he stilled for a moment, reveling in the feel of her. Beneath his fingertips, there were lines, marks she'd made with the razor, but they were rough with healing, not tender and new. A wave of pride and protectiveness washed over him, so strong he wanted to place his mouth there, to worship every inch of her skin and tell her how lovely she was. Because he was afraid she might misinterpret the gesture or push him away, he didn't raise her shirt. Instead, he brushed his thumbs over her nipples, over and over again until he thought he would surely embarrass himself if he continued.

The sounds she was making were driving him crazy.

Breathing hard, he moved his hands over her back, pulling her tight against him. She was wearing the same jogging pants he'd seen her in before, the ones that said JUICY across the butt. He traced the letters with his fingertips then slipped his hands beneath the fabric, finding nothing but soft skin and a lacy thong.

James' heart thudded painfully. Any blood left in his head rushed south.

He took his hands out of her pants slowly, afraid to move too fast. The danger zone was on red alert. "Turn around."

Her eyes flew open in surprise.

He smiled at her reaction. "Your butt is like ice. Turn around, and I'll warm you up."

Smiling back at him, she turned around and snuggled into him. He opened his jacket and enveloped her in warmth, experiencing an intense satisfaction when she murmured her pleasure.

"Do you think I'm too skinny?" she asked, after a few minutes.

"No," he said, clenching his teeth against the renewed urge to take her hips in his hands and surge forward, testing those slender proportions.

"Really? How about these?" She brought his hands up to her breasts. "Too small?"

He gave them an exploratory squeeze. "You're perfect," he said in all honesty, hoping they'd laid the subject to rest.

She wasn't quite satisfied. "Then why don't you want this?" she asked, putting his hand between her legs and covering it with her own.

"Carly," he said in a tortured whisper. "I want it so bad I'm shaking."

That, he knew she could feel. And the other evidence, prodding her backside.

"Then why aren't you trying to convince me to do it?" she asked.

He tried to calm himself with slow, even breaths. "Because we've only been going out three days. For pretend." Even so, he couldn't stop himself from stroking her through the thin material of her jogging pants, feeling her heat.

"I don't care," she moaned, tilting her hips up and pressing the tips of his fingers against her, harder. "I want to."

"No," he said, denying himself, as well as her. Putting some very necessary distance between them, he rolled away from her and sat up, resting his forearms on his bent knees. "You shouldn't let me touch you."

She cozied up beside him and put her head on his shoulder, slipping one arm under his. "I like it when you touch me."

"Your dad doesn't."

"So? What do you think he and Summer were doing in the Jacuzzi?"

He thought of the blood on Summer's face. "Is she okay?"

"She's fine. Why did you freak out like that?"

He didn't answer. "You should go back home before you get grounded again."

"Where will you go?"

He rubbed his hands over his eyes. He'd had barely four hours of sleep in two days. "I'm supposed to be staying with my brother, but his house is kind of hectic."

She frowned. "Holiday visitors?"

He laughed at the very idea. "Yeah. Oh, yeah. Holiday visitors, having a merry fucking Christmas."

Impatient with his obscure humor, she said, "So why can't you go to your dad's? Are you afraid he's going to hit you?"

He jerked away from her. "Shut up."

"Fuck you," she returned. "Do you think I'm stupid? I've seen your bruises."

He stood, ready to leave her there. Then he remembered Lisette and reconsidered. "Come on. I'll take you home."

She lifted her stubborn jaw. "I can get home by myself."

He paled at the thought of her wandering around in the dark last night, looking for him. "You shouldn't be out at night on your own. It's dangerous."

"Why is it dangerous for me, but not you? You can sleep on the beach, but I can't walk down it by myself? That is total bullshit."

He couldn't tell her why he knew she had to be extra-careful. "What's that?" he asked instead, seeing the blue sweater she'd left lying on the sand.

"It's your Christmas present, you stupid jerk." She picked up another box and threw it at him. "Here's another one."

He gathered up the stuff and followed her as she stormed down the beach. The first rays of dawn were beginning to peek over the horizon, painting streaks of pink across the sky. "I have a present for you, too."

She stopped, tucking a flyaway strand of hair behind her ear. "You do?"

Reaching into his pocket, he pulled out a tiny package wrapped in plain white paper. "Here."

She opened it carefully.

"It's nothing new or expensive," he mumbled. "I just wanted to give you something, to show you..."

She watched his face, waited for him to continue.

Doing it right, he took her hand in his. "I wanted to ask you to be my real girlfriend."

"All right," she said with a shy smile. Studying the ring in the early-morning light, she saw that it was antique, silver, and engraved with a swirling design. "Where did you get it?"

He smiled back at her. "Out of a shark's belly."

Her jaw dropped. "No!"

"Yes. See if it fits."

It did.

•   •   •

*Sonny was back in the Jacuzzi with Ben. Steam was rising up from the hot water, and they were exploring each other languidly, touching, caressing, kissing...*

*Then a warning bell sounded in her mind, and he pulled away from her, leaving her cold. She tried to follow him, but her legs were like jelly. She couldn't move. Rubbing at her eyes, she tried to focus on his wavering form, but the fog was too thick. She couldn't see.*

*Then the silver blade of a knife flashed, slashing down, into her stomach.*

Gasping, she lurched up in bed, holding a hand to her belly.

A dream, she realized with relief. Just a dream. Her cell phone, the trigger of her nightmare, was ringing. With a shaking hand, she reached out to pick it up from the pile of clothes beside the bed. "Vasquez," she growled, annoyed with Grant for interrupting what could have been a perfectly good sex dream.

"Brass is at your boyfriend's right now."

She kicked the blankets off her legs, stumbling over to look through the already bent vertical blinds. Sure enough, a police cruiser was parked in front of Ben's house. "Why?"

"Anonymous caller reported a floater. Allegedly, it's Lisette Bruebaker. Carly Fortune's best friend."

Her heart dropped. "No."

"The body hasn't been found, but Mrs. Bruebaker confirms that the girl's been missing. She didn't file a report, because Lisette isn't that reliable as far as checking in. Mom figured she was just partying."

"Nice."

"Yeah. Guess who she was supposed to be staying with."

Sonny wrestled her legs into sweatpants, shoved her feet into shoes. "Who?"

"Carly and Ben Fortune."

Swearing, she hung up the phone and ran out the door. To her relief, the uniform was messing around inside his patrol car, playing with the radio. He wasn't a detective, she noted. Just some beat cop collecting information.

Ben opened the door, taking in her frazzled appearance with a lazy smile. "Can't wait to see me again?"

She smiled back at him self-consciously, wishing she'd had time to brush her teeth and fix her hair. "Actually, I was going to ask Carly if she wanted to go for a jog."

Hearing the magic word (her own name) Carly came up behind Ben and put her hand on his shoulder. "Why is there a police car out front?" she asked, sipping something warm and fragrant from an earthenware mug.

Sonny managed a careless shrug.

"Have you had breakfast?" he asked, studying her bruised lower lip.

She resisted the urge to run her tongue over the split. "Not yet," she said, glancing at Carly. "Is that coffee?"

"It is," Carly replied. "Some of us real humans need caffeine in the morning. Do you like banana nut muffins?"

"I love them," she said. "Did I mention I was going for a jog?"

"Yeah, I'm up for it." Stretching one arm over her head, Carly gestured for Sonny to follow her back to the kitchen. "Are you going to show me some more of that karate stuff? It was so cool how you held back Dad last night."

Sonny had polished off a cup of coffee and a muffin before the cop finally made it to the front door. When the doorbell rang, she excused herself, because she really did have to pee, but she also wanted a chance to eavesdrop for a moment upon her return.

After a quick trip to the bathroom, she skulked her way down the hall, surprised to hear that the policeman was inside. This wasn't a doorstep interview. She stopped, back pressed against the wall, listening as the deputy continued questioning.

"Did Lisette say where she was going, or tell you what her plans were?"

Carly's response was vague. "I never knew what Lisette was planning to do next. She was kind of unpredictable."

"Did she have a boyfriend?"

"Sure. The whole senior class."

"Anyone special?"

"No. She liked to date around. Did something happen to her?"

"Her mom hasn't seen her for a while. It's just routine."

The officer's statement seemed to put Carly at ease. That was a mistake, from an interviewer's standpoint. "She's always like that. When school is in session, she goes to class. On breaks, she's like, all over the place."

Sonny heard the sound of the deputy flipping paper on a wire-bound notebook. "You said you last saw her Friday night. Not Saturday morning?"

"No," Carly answered quickly. "When I woke up, she was already gone."

"Mr. Fortune?"

"I went surfing pretty early. I didn't check on them first."

"Is it possible that Lisette left in the middle of the night? Snuck out?" There was an awkward silence, during which no one answered verbally. Instead of taking advantage of it, letting it draw out, the cop forged ahead. "Is that typical behavior for her, to leave early, without saying good-bye?"

"No," Carly admitted. "Usually she hangs out longer."

"Did anything out of the ordinary occur while she was here?"

Neither Ben nor Carly responded, but Sonny could practically feel the room ignite with tension. She had to see their faces now, so she entered the room and sat down, trying to be as unobtrusive as possible.

"You can tell him, Dad," Carly prompted.

Ben did not have the countenance of an innocent man. Sonny felt something snap inside her, unleashing an emotion she didn't know she could feel, didn't realize she was capable of. She pushed it back, denied it, focused only on his face.

His handsome, perfect, lying goddamned face.

"Tell him what?" he asked, darting a glance Sonny's way.

*You son of a bitch,* Sonny responded with her eyes.

"About the pot." Carly tilted her head toward the officer, as if preparing to divulge all. "He caught us smoking a joint in my room. Totally freaked out about it, of course. I'm still grounded."

The officer looked to Ben for confirmation.

"Teenagers," he said with a charming shrug that may or may not have been an admission.

To his credit, the cop wasn't fooled. "Mr. Fortune, a girl is missing. If you have some information to share, I would recommend you do it now."

Ben's eyes narrowed, but he didn't say anything more. Sonny realized that he hadn't answered a single question directly, and that he knew exactly what he was doing. He'd been through an exhausting round of interrogations in the days after his wife's death, an experience that must have had a profound effect on him. He was now a man who guarded his family, his privacy, and his words. He also understood the system. After all, his father was a retired criminal court judge, and his brother a public defender.

"Did you confiscate the marijuana?" the officer continued.

"There wasn't much left to confiscate, but yeah."

"What did you do with it?"

"I got rid of it," Ben said in a defensive tone.

Carly leaned back and crossed her arms over her

chest, adopting Ben's uncooperative attitude and presenting a united front.

The cop gave up on the drug angle. In Torrey Pines, smoking weed was more of a revered local pastime than a crime. "Tell me what she said or did last. Her attitude before she left. Anything that might help us find her."

"I don't remember anything but falling asleep," Carly said, twirling a lock of hair around her slender finger. "We were, like, totally stoned, you know?"

"Mr. Fortune, did it ever occur to you to notify Lisette's parents that she left early?"

"No." He glanced at his daughter. "Carly didn't mention that she was missing."

Carly tossed her hair back with dramatic flourish. "I didn't know she was, like, *missing* missing. I thought she was just out having a good time. Maybe trying to dodge getting put on restriction."

She was laying on the Valley Girl routine a little too thick, but the cop only nodded, as if he also suspected Lisette Bruebaker would turn up on her own. Before he left, he focused his attention on Sonny, surprising her. "By the way, ma'am, can I ask how you got that busted lip?"

Behind his back, Carly's eyes widened with panic, and she shook her head pleadingly.

Sonny pasted a smile on her face, hoping it wouldn't crack under the strain. There was no time to consider her decision, so she just went with it, upping the total of liars in the room from two to three. "Carly did it. Kitchen cabinet." She made a motion with her hand, like a door hitting her in the mouth. "An accident."

He tapped his pen against the notebook in his hands. "Well, thank you for your time."

After the door closed behind him, the three of them stared at one another. Ben broke the silence. "I should call Lisette's mom. See if she needs anything."

As he left the room, Sonny crossed her arms over her chest, waiting for Carly to do some serious explaining.

"Thanks for not mentioning James."

"Is he in trouble?"

Carly didn't meet her eyes. "Not that I know of. But he's kind of weird about us, won't tell his dad and stuff. If the cops showed up at his house, his dad might freak out on him."

Sonny nodded, flexing her hands. She had a plan now, and it didn't include a morning jog. Although a physical release, in lieu of beating Ben senseless, might be in order. "You still want to run?"

Carly nodded. "Yeah. But I think I'll go on my own, if you don't mind. Sometimes I just need to get out, go fast, be free. You know?"

She knew.


In the kitchen, Ben hung up the phone quietly, his back to her. Carly could be seen from the west-facing window, already halfway down the beach, her hair flying out behind her like a wild Arabian's.

"They're organizing a search party," he said.

"Some of the other parents are meeting over there at noon."

His expression was severe, the perfect portrait of a concerned father with his own teenaged daughter to worry about. Underneath all of that was guilt. Even if Sonny could pretend nothing was amiss for the sake of the investigation, it wouldn't ring true to her character. Summer Moore may not be a hard-eyed cynic like Sonora Vasquez, but she was nobody's fool. "What did you do?"

He smoothed his hand over the black granite countertop, looking down at it, instead of at her. "Nothing."

"Don't lie to me." She moved closer, forcing him to face her. "Please don't lie."

He met her eyes. "What are you asking me?"

Sonny considered that question carefully. "If you slept with her."

He started to speak, then appeared to think better of it, and remained silent.

It hurt, so much more than she thought it would. So much more than she should have allowed it to. Because she'd known the instant he'd gone along with Carly's story that the lie had been one of omission. He'd caught Lisette and Carly smoking pot two Saturdays ago, not last Friday.

So what had actually happened when Lisette spent the night? She gave herself three guesses, and the first two didn't count.

"I'm going surfing," he said, walking outside. He may as well have added, "Fuck you."

Shaking with fury, Sonny followed him to the

poolroom. It was as posh as the rest of the house, with its designer shower stalls, custom surfing gear, and built-in sauna. When she came through the open door, he was tugging on his state-of-the-art, titanium-lined wetsuit. It fit him like a second skin.

She had to take a moment to calm down before she was able to speak. "You told me you hadn't been with anyone since Olivia."

He pulled a surfboard down from the rack, his movements swift with anger. "Don't ever"—his eyes were intense, his tone vehement—"talk about my wife."

Sonny didn't bother to heed that warning, although it cut through her deeper than the phantom blade from her nightmare. "What did she do when you cheated on her, Ben? Look the other way?"

A muscle in his jaw ticked. "Don't compare yourself to her. Do you think I owe you my loyalty because I've tried to fuck you a few times?"

She felt the color drain from her face. "You owe me an explanation."

"I don't owe you a fucking thing." He brushed by her, crossing the patio and making his way down the winding steps to the beach.

She wanted to shout obscenities at him, to push him down the stairs and pummel him with her fists, to scream and yell and smash his handsome, arrogant face.

Instead, she turned her back on him.

In his tumultuous emotional state, Ben hadn't bothered to lock his door or engage the security system, and she was going to take full advantage of it. Don't get mad, she reminded herself. Get evidence.

Hands trembling, imagination running overdrive, Sonny returned to the kitchen and threw open drawers until she found what she needed. Ziploc bags. Hopefully his bed would have the same sheets from Friday, the night Lisette stayed over.

Sprinting up the steps, taking two at a time, she entered Ben's room, bypassing the bed and going straight to the master bath. The trash can was empty. Neat freak, she cursed silently. Storming out, she raided the nightstand by the bed, looking for condoms. There was one box, brand new, unopened.

"Thought you were going to get lucky with me, didn't you? Arrogant bastard."

Moving quickly, she looked through every drawer, rifling through silk ties and cotton boxer shorts, running her fingertips over stacks of T-shirts and neatly folded jeans. She slid her hands underneath the mattress, got down on her hands and knees to look under furniture, stood on tiptoe in his walk-in closet.

There was nothing. Not even a speck of dust.

She picked up the remote for the plasma screen TV and did a quick channel search. Nothing more titillating than HBO. Sonny wasn't a tech whiz, but she knew how to find out if he'd ordered any pay-per-view movies or kept DVDs on file.

There was only one title; the date, September 17th. She played it.

"Jesus," she muttered, sitting down on the edge of the bed. She suffered through the wedding video only long enough to acknowledge that Olivia had been her polar opposite. Tall, dark-haired, and gorgeous, she was lushly feminine, a more womanly version of Carly. The only thing more painful to witness was the look on Ben's face as she walked down the aisle.

Perhaps he was a pathetic cliché, the sainted widower who watched his wife instead of porn.

Then again, lonely people often acted in desperation.

Sonny flipped off the TV with a twist of her wrist, wanting to throw the remote through the damned screen. Returning to the bathroom, she searched the medicine cabinet for tweezers. Finding a new pair, she ripped it out of the package, then stripped the blanket and top sheet off the bed.

There were no stains, but the expensive white cotton appeared wrinkled, comfortable, slept in. Apparently, he wasn't so fastidious that he changed sheets more than once a week. Or even after entertaining a female guest.

There was one long, curly hair, obviously a woman's, probably Lisette's. The sight of it made her heart sink.

He wasn't a saint after all, was he?

"You fucked up, Ben," she said under her breath, collecting the hair meticulously before she began to go over every inch of the sheets for more trace.

## CHAPTER 11

Ben wasted a perfectly good session, too distracted to keep his mind on waves. The sport required a Zen-like concentration, and he didn't have it. He was pissed off at Summer, pissed off at himself, and extremely pissed off at the decent-looking break that kept crumbling to mush every time he got into position.

"Fuck!" he yelled as he resurfaced, startling a couple of regulars who were communing with the surf gods in companionable silence.

Ben gave up. Flipping his wet hair off his forehead, he waded out of the ocean, shoving his surfboard under one arm and storming across the beach.

He couldn't believe Summer thought he'd slept with Lisette. The girl was young enough to be his daughter, for Christ's sake. The very idea turned his stomach.

Her interrogation wasn't just insulting, it also brought back a lot of unpleasant memories for him. Olivia had constantly bombarded him with accusations. Usually, her suspicions were correct, and she had every right to be jealous. While she'd stayed home taking care of Carly, he'd been traveling from one beach to the next, hopping from party to party and bed to bed.

Olivia hadn't put up with his antics for long. She broke off their relationship just before Carly's second birthday, issuing the ultimatum that he give up drugs, alcohol, and other women. It took him five years to honor her request.

He regretted every one of them.

After he got clean, he hadn't so much as looked at another woman, but Olivia had never really trusted him because he'd lied to her so many times in the past.

Ben didn't need Summer giving him the third degree, thinking the worst of him, reminding him of his myriad failures as a husband and a man.

He did a good enough job of that on his own.

Scowling, he ascended the wooden steps leading to his back patio, assuring himself he was only sorry he hadn't been able to get her into bed. He knew he was lying, and that he'd handled things badly with her this morning, but damned if he would apologize to her, when she was the one who'd accused him of statutory rape!

Muttering a string of curses, he showered off in the poolroom and pulled on some clothes before he headed inside the house. Carly was sitting at the kitchen table with a pensive expression on her face and dark sunglasses covering her eyes.

Ben cleared his throat. "Ready?"

"Yeah."

He drove them to the Bruebaker residence in silence. As he parked inside the gated entrance, he noted that the media was out in full force. Although he would have used his notoriety to draw attention to Lisette's disappearance, her parents hadn't asked him to, and for that he was grateful.

After Olivia's murder, the press had hounded him mercilessly. The police had treated him like a criminal. While he'd been in shock, unable to process what was happening, they'd ripped his reputation to shreds and thrown it to the sharks.

The furor died down eventually, but in that first month, the media hadn't had the decency to leave him, or Carly, alone. They'd made a circus of Olivia's funeral.

Two weeks ago they started calling again, clamoring for his response to Darrius O'Shea's death. He had no comment. Countless times, over the past three years, he'd dreamt of tearing the man apart with his bare hands.

Now that O'Shea was dead, Ben felt nothing. Not even relief.

If the media saw him here, they would probably rehash every detail of his wife's murder, turning his devastation into a tasty news bite once again.

Ben found a pair of sunglasses in the glove compartment and pulled the hood of his sweatshirt over his head.

"You look like the Unabomber," Carly said.

He gave her similar perusal, seeing solemn eyes behind dark lenses. "Why did you lie to that police officer?"

Her mouth made a thin line. Instead of answering, she glanced away.

The aftermath of Olivia's death had scarred his daughter in ways he could only imagine. At a time when they needed each other more than anything else, the police had kept them apart, questioning them separately, trying to pit Carly against him. Trying to break them down.

He despised them for putting her through that.

Carly might have lied to the police just to be uncooperative. Or maybe she was hiding something. Maybe she knew Lisette had been in his room that night.

His gut clenched at the thought. "Do you know where Lisette is?"

She gave him a disgusted look. "No."

He decided she was telling the truth, and hoped he wasn't fooling himself, believing what he wanted to believe. "How are you doing...with the cutting?"

"Fine," she said, crossing her arms over her chest.

"You haven't—"

"No."

Floundering, he careened from one difficult topic to the next. "Are you still seeing James?"

Her sleek brows drew together. "Yes. Why?"

"He seems kind of volatile."

"You attacked *him*, Dad."

He sighed, leaning his head back against the seat. "I guess that was uncalled for."

"You think?" She drummed her fingertips against the sleeve of her sweatshirt, glancing out at the media vans with trepidation.

The movement drew his attention to a ring on her finger. "Where'd you get that?" he asked, catching her hand to study the antique silver band.

"James gave it to me."

"When?"

"Yesterday," she said, pulling her hand away quickly. "It's nothing."

Ben's vision narrowed. He knew damned well she hadn't been wearing that ring on her finger last night. "Have you been sneaking out again?"

"No, I—"

"Don't you know what happens to girls who wander around by themselves at night?" he interrupted, stress coursing through him. "They get raped and murdered! You, of all people, should know that!"

She recoiled. "Do you think that's what happened to Lisette?"

His throat went dry. Lisette was probably up to no good, on drugs or in trouble, but dead? "No," he said softly, praying it was true.

Getting past the reporters unnoticed wasn't as hard as he'd thought. There were dozens of teenagers milling about, and the crowd was focused on Tom and Sheila Bruebaker, who were poised to make a statement.

Feeling a little ridiculous, Ben removed his hood but kept on his sunglasses. As he stood next to Carly, near the front entrance of the house, there was only one person who appeared to recognize him: Tom Bruebaker.

He was standing beside his wife, his hand at the small of her back. In a pin-striped shirt and dark slacks, a diamond-encrusted watch at his thick wrist, and the morning sun glinting off his silver hair, Tom cut a striking figure. His jaw clenched when their eyes met, and the older man looked away. At Tom's side, Sheila appeared fragile and elegant in a Chanel suit. She was holding on to his shoulder, as if she wasn't quite steady on her feet. Her fingers sparkled with jewelry and her eyes glittered with unshed tears.

The press conference lasted only a short time. Tom did most of the talking, asking for anyone with information about his daughter to come forward, and offering a considerable reward. Too overwhelmed to speak, Sheila wept prettily into a lace handkerchief.

Ben had known the Bruebakers for ages. He used to be able to call Tom a friend. Now the man was the closest thing to an enemy Ben had.

After the Bruebakers spoke with the press, everyone was ushered inside by a female officer who was in charge of organizing the search. Watching her reminded Ben that Summer worked with law enforcement. The way she'd looked at him this morning, her blue eyes cold as ice, was disturbing on many different levels.

Torturing himself, he replayed their conversation in his mind. He had to admit that by allowing his daughter to lie to the police, he'd given her reason to be suspicious. And when Summer had confronted

him about sleeping with Lisette, he'd been too proud
to deny it.

Then he'd insulted her by suggesting she meant
nothing to him, and wasn't worthy of speaking his
wife's name.

Ben stifled a groan, rubbing a hand over his face.
How ironic that he'd gotten himself tangled up with
a woman who challenged him at least as much as
Olivia had.

Sonny adjusted the fit of the Harbor Police uniform
before she stepped out of the women's locker room.
The black polyester pants were too snug and the
white shirt molded over her breasts, so it was perfect.
A navy cap and dark sunglasses completed the disguise. She didn't want to call too much attention to
her face.

Lamont Rousseau, a real member of the Coast
Guard, and her counterpart for the afternoon, was
ready and waiting for her at America's Cup Harbor.

They worked the docks for more than an hour,
trolling for sailors known to frequent the restricted
waters of the La Jolla Underwater Park and Eco-
logical Reserve, where Lisette's body had allegedly
been sighted. Most of San Diego's small vessel fishermen were second- or third-generation Portuguese or
Italian, with salt water flowing through their veins
and flippers for feet. They were a tight-lipped crew,
protective of their own, but one name in particular
kept cropping up, a man with no family ties in the
area. Unpopular with sellers and buyers alike, he was

rumored to employ several questionable tactics, including using nonregulation nets, scouting the reserve, and weighting his catch with filler.

His name was Arlen Matthews.

Sonny didn't recognize the name, having never heard it from James, so she was surprised to see Carly's boyfriend aboard a beat-up old boat named *Destiny*, with a young man who looked too much like James to be anything but his brother. As Sonny and Lamont approached, the boys' father emerged from the galley, wearing dirty blue jeans and a green trucker cap.

Sonny put a hand on Lamont's arm. "I know him. The youngest."

"Do you want me to go alone?"

She hesitated, considering. It was too important. And too much of a coincidence. "No. Just follow my lead."

Sonny approached the boat. "Good afternoon, gentlemen," she said with a smile, modulating the pitch of her voice. "Sloppy weather, isn't it?"

The fisherman's lingo she'd picked up didn't seem to put the Matthews men at ease.

"Sloppier than a TJ whore," Arlen Matthews agreed, pulling his hat low on his forehead. Mirrored sunglasses hid his eyes, and he had a cigarette clenched between his teeth. Like his sons, he had the lean, whipcord build of a lifelong sailor. While James and his brother had thick brown hair, Mr. Matthews' was all tarnished gold. The two older men were scruffier than James, less clean-cut, but they were all handsome. And wary.

Sonny wasn't amused by Arlen's off-color remark. "Good catch?"

"Fair," he grunted. "What can I do for you?"

"A couple of kayakers claim they saw the body of a drowned woman on the south side of the reserve. You all been out that way?"

Stephen and James made a busy show of swabbing the deck, their eyes downcast.

Arlen took a deep drag on his smoke. "Can't drop a net there. It's protected."

Sonny didn't say anything.

Arlen did a slow perusal of her body, insultingly obvious even though his eyes were covered. When he smiled, her blood ran cold. "Only dead bodies I've seen are these two," he said, jerking his thumb at his sons. "Get lazier every year."

Sonny glanced at James, wondering if he recognized her. She noted that his trembling hands were chafed and his arms sinewy with muscle. Both boys looked half-starved, but strong. She took a picture of Lisette out of her pocket and handed it to Arlen. "This is the girl we think may be out there. Do you know her?"

Arlen took the photo. "Nope," he said, barely glancing at it. He tried to hand it back, but she wouldn't take it.

"Maybe your sons do. She's more their age."

Arlen shrugged, but when he attempted to pass over the picture, it slipped from his hand and fluttered to the water. "Sorry," he said, making no move to retrieve it. In fact, he threw his cigarette butt right at it.

Lamont's nostrils flared with anger, but he maintained his silence.

"That's a filthy habit," she said, meaning smoking, littering, *and* disrespecting women.

"Ain't it just?" he replied with a smirk.

Wishing Arlen would remove his sunglasses, so she could see his eyes, she took a card from her pocket, fresh and hastily made, with a Harbor Police phone number and her assumed name. "If you boys see or hear anything, give me a call."

"Yes, ma'am," Arlen said, brushing his tobacco-stained fingers over hers. "We sure will."

At Harbor Police Headquarters, she picked up the phone to call her contact with local law enforcement, Staff Sergeant Paula DeGrassi. "Let me hear that message," Sonny requested. She listened to the boy's voice carefully, confirming her suspicions. "When did he leave it?"

"Christmas Eve. Late. I didn't get it until this morning. The body might be off the coast of Mexico by now."

Sonny thanked her and hung up. The hair she'd collected from Ben's bed was being processed at the crime lab. It could always be compared with hair taken from a brush at Lisette's house, or a DNA sample if one was available, in the event that her body was never recovered.

In most cases, no body meant no murder charge. James' phone call may have taken care of that technicality.

If the hair from Ben's bed belonged to Lisette, body or no body, Ben would be a prime suspect. Unless

Sonny could get something on Arlen Matthews, other than that he didn't report dead bodies because he was too cheap to pay a $500 fine.

Scumbag.

She was angry with Ben for lying to her, but she couldn't believe him a murderer. Arlen Matthews, on the other hand, was as shady as they came.

It was time to have a talk with James.

Sonny followed Carly down Windansea Beach, staying far enough behind that the girl wouldn't notice. Sure enough, Carly met James near a group of elephant-sized rocks, and the pair went behind them to engage in some hanky-panky.

When Carly emerged thirty minutes later, flushed and smiling, Sonny was too jaded to find it cute. Ben had better get ready to be a grandpa.

A hot, thirty-four-year-old grandpa.

Sonny waited for Carly to get out of earshot before she went in for James. The instant he saw her, he tried to run, proving he'd recognized her earlier at the docks. He was so fast he almost got out into the open, where she couldn't tackle him without taking the chance of being seen. He put up a hell of a fight, until he realized that while she wasn't exactly hurting him, neither could he break free from her hold.

"What do you want?" he asked, panting with exertion.

"Did you tell Carly you saw me today?"

"No."

Sonny breathed a sigh of relief. "I know you reported Lisette's body. I recognized your voice."

"Fuck," he muttered.

"You might as well keep talking."

"Are you crazy? You're a cop. I'm not telling you a fucking thing."

It was a pretty good impression of Ben, and it pissed her off. She twisted James' arm behind his back far enough to make it hurt. "Talk or cry."

She knew he was in pain, but he didn't make a sound. "You think you can do something to me that my dad hasn't already done?" he asked quietly.

She thought about it. "I can tell him about Carly."

He was silent for a moment. "Fine. Take your fucking hands off me, though. I'm not going to run."

She released him carefully, because she wasn't sure he wouldn't try to hit her, and he was stronger than he looked.

"You're wasting your time," he said in a cold voice. "I don't know shit. When we brought up the net, Lisette was in it. My dad shook her loose. That's it."

"Did he kill her?"

"How should I know?"

She found it telling that he didn't deny the notion out of hand. "What condition was her body in?"

James' skin took on an unhealthy pallor. "All messed up. Naked. Blue. Pieces missing."

"Cut out by a person?"

"No. Crabs will eat anything."

Sonny nodded, pleased with his sea expertise. "Could you tell how she died? Gunshot, stab wounds, marks on her neck?"

"I didn't look too long. But I didn't see anything like that."

"Did your dad know her?"

"Maybe not by name."

"Did he have sex with her?"

"I doubt it. She had *some* standards."

Sonny realized that James was either familiar with Lisette's reputation, or he knew her better than he let on. "What about your brother?"

"No. He didn't even recognize her."

"And you?"

His stricken face said it all.

"James, if it comes out later that you were with her, it will look bad. I need to know now, to protect you."

"I don't trust you not to tell Carly."

Ah, the single-mindedness of youth. His greatest fear wasn't going to jail or getting charged with murder, but being in the doghouse with his new girlfriend. "You keep my secret, I'll keep yours."

He sighed. "We didn't have sex, exactly. She sort of, um..." He made a quick gesture, indicating activity below the waist.

She understood what he meant. A no-strings blow job was hard to resist. Could Ben? "How long ago?"

"A few weeks. Before I started seeing Carly," he stressed.

"Okay," she said. "Tell me about your dad. What kind of man is he?"

"A psycho," he admitted. "But I can't say he's done anything violent. Other than rough up hookers. And me."

Sonny had suspected as much. "Will you be all right at home?"

"Not if he finds out I made that phone call."

A plan had already begun to form in her mind. "Here's what we're going to do..."

When James opened the door, it was clear he didn't recognize her. She'd dyed her hair black with a temporary rinse and covered her blue eyes with brown contacts.

Sonny wasn't sure the disguise was necessary. Even though she'd seen Arlen at the docks earlier, she doubted he would recognize her face. Or even look at it. She was wearing ratty jeans, a black tank top with no bra underneath, and way too much makeup.

She looked like a whore, all right.

"*Buenas noches,*" she said, scanning the room as would an FBI agent, or a money-grubbing hooker. "*Listos?*"

Arlen was sitting on the couch, cheap sunglasses shielding his eyes. He pulled at the brim of his cap lazily, not bothering to stand. "We don't speak Spanish here, señorita."

"I speak English, if you like."

"I like," he said. He had a whisky bottle in his hand, from which he took a slow, measured sip. "How much?"

"*Para los dos?*" She gestured, indicating both James and Arlen. "Two men?"

Arlen laughed, kicking James in the shin. Sonny

forced the smile to remain on her face. "He don't like women."

James' mouth thinned into a hard line, but he didn't bother to defend himself.

"*Pobrecito*," she said, reaching out to run her hand down James' cheek. "I like you, *papi*. You don't like me?"

As was her intention, Arlen immediately turned his anger toward her. He yanked her by the arm, bringing her atop his lap and spilling whisky all over the front of her shirt. "I'm the one paying you, bitch. You'll take care of me."

Suppressing the reflex to gag, Sonny murmured an apology as she explored the muscles in his shoulders. "I like you, too, señor. You are very strong."

When he tensed, she got the impression that he was just as uncomfortable with physical contact as she was. In a flash of intuition, she realized that his interest in women wasn't strictly sexual. He didn't want to touch her—he wanted to hurt her.

"You remind me of someone," he said, his gaze wandering over her face, the movement discernable through the dark lenses that hid his eyes. She wondered if the glasses were an affectation, a disguise, or if he was simply sensitive to light, after years on the ocean.

Sonny batted her lashes. "Sophia Loren?"

"No," he said, his mind far away, remembering, chasing, searching... "Anita."

Her stomach did a slow somersault.

"Anita Vasquez. You look just like her. Enough to be her daughter." Suffused with memories, he continued, "Damn, what a woman. Liked to get roughed up almost as much as she liked to fuck."

Sonny clenched her hand into a fist. She wanted to kick his ass into a blubbering mass of leathery skin and tobacco breath. Instead, she relaxed her fingers and raised them to his face. "*No entiendo,* señor. I am Juana, not Anita. Can I see your eyes?"

He grew instantly wary. "I don't kiss whores."

"No, no. Just look. You are very handsome."

He shrugged, liking the attention, probably intent on reliving some long-forgotten memories of her mother. If he only knew.

She lifted his sunglasses and stared into pale blue eyes, just like her own.

James stood over the prone body of their father. Arlen was sprawled on the dirty carpet, unconscious, covered with broken pieces of ceramic lamp. "What the hell? He didn't even do anything. You can't arrest him now."

Breathing hard, blood still pumping adrenaline, she looked up at James, wondering if he understood what had happened. Why she'd freaked out.

"What?" he asked, noticing her perusal.

She shook her head, trying to clear it. Sonny felt as though she'd just had her own brains knocked around. "Which way to his bedroom?"

James led her back to the master suite. It was a real shithole. Swastikas and Confederate flags hung on the walls, there were empty bottles all over the place, and hardcore pornography magazines littered every surface.

"Nice," she said, kicking a dingy pair of briefs out of the way.

James laughed, all but brimming with nervous energy. Then he got quiet. "He's not going to wake up, is he?"

"Probably not until morning. You might get a day off out of it, bud."

He stayed quiet while she rifled through Arlen's meager belongings. "I don't think I should be around tomorrow."

"That's probably wise," she said, cursing herself for losing control. Physically attacking a suspect before any evidence had been gathered was a grievous error. Not only had she put James in danger, she may have compromised the investigation.

What the hell was wrong with her lately? She'd never let her emotions get in the way of work before. "Does your dad keep mementoes?"

"Like what?"

"Jewelry, panties, women's stuff?"

James shrugged. "No. He always gives them a little something to remember him by, though."

"What's that?"

"Bruises."

Sonny thought about the trace evidence found on the victims. Like surfers, fishermen used durable, water-resistant fabric. "Do you guys wear titanium-lined gear on the water?"

James snorted. "Titanium's expensive. I'm lucky to get a pair of regular gloves."

She found of lot of disgusting things, some mildly illegal, none incriminating Arlen as the SoCal Strangler. He was an abuser of women and children, a racist, a cheat, and an evil man. But there was no evidence in his bedroom linking him to the murders.

Although she had no choice but to move on, Sonny was reluctant to leave James to his own devices. The kid was a disaster waiting to happen, and who could blame him? "Why don't you go to your brother's," she suggested. "Is it cool there?"

James nodded silently, and she knew he was shielding the truth behind his pretty blue eyes, the way she'd been doing most of her life. He reminded her so much of herself that she almost couldn't bear to look at him. Like her own reflection in the mirror, his angst was heart-wrenching to witness.

Together, they cleaned up the broken lamp and put Arlen to bed. Then she took James to Stephen's, because he had nowhere else to go. Several times on the drive over, she came very close to telling him who she was.

In the end, she remained silent, cursing her job, hating herself.

## CHAPTER 12

Ben couldn't sleep. What he'd said to Summer was killing him, keeping him awake, taking hold of his continence and ripping it to shreds.

Feeling like a bastard, and a fool, he dragged himself out of bed. After pulling on some clothes, he walked across the street to her apartment and knocked on her door. There was a light on inside, and he wondered if she was in there with another man. Her boss, maybe.

He gave himself a mental shake, knowing he had no cause to be jealous.

When she opened the door, she looked different. She let him in, her expression wary and her hair dark. Not a shiny, rich obsidian, like Carly's, but opaque black, sooty and lusterless.

"What did you do to your hair?" he asked, appalled.

She raised a hand to her head. "I dyed it."

"It looks terrible."

Her blue eyes narrowed. "Are you here to insult me?"

"No," he said, darting a glance around the room, more nervous than ever. Was he screwing this up on purpose? "I wanted to talk to you. To apologize."

"Just leave," she said, crossing her arms over her chest. "I don't want to hear it."

It hadn't occurred to him that she would shoot him down before he'd made his play. "I'll tell you what happened with Lisette," he said, unease welling up within him.

"I don't want to know, Ben. Don't you get it? It's too late. I don't care." She jerked her chin toward the door. "Now get out."

"She came into my room," he said, in a rush to convince her. "I was asleep. I didn't know what was going on—"

"Yeah, right," she said, her sarcastic tone belying the assertion that she didn't care.

"I was dreaming about you," he continued, following her as she stormed down the hall toward the back bedroom. "I'd been thinking about you all day."

"Oh, God," she cried, whirling to face him and thrusting her fingers into her coal-black hair. "You are so full of shit! Do you think I'll forgive you because you thought about me while you fucked her?"

"No. I mean, I didn't. When I realized she wasn't you, I pushed her away."

She paced the room a few times, considering his

words. Then she stopped and faced him. "I don't care," she repeated, crushing him with her apathy.

His stomach clenched with regret. He hadn't felt anything but a mild stirring for a woman since Olivia. The prospect of getting involved in a serious relationship terrified him, but he couldn't bear the thought of losing her like this.

"I care," he said, laying his cards on the table.

She stared at him in angry disbelief.

He fought against the urge to divulge all. His fear that Carly had something to do with Lisette's disappearance. The conflict he felt over his wife, whom he still wasn't ready to let go of. He'd never been able to do right by Olivia, and this new, insatiable lust for another woman seemed like an insult to her memory.

A memory that faded more every time he looked at Summer's face. Gazing upon her, blue eyes flashing with pique, her chest rising and falling with pent-up emotion, Ben had to admit he'd never felt so alive. While the woman he had vowed to protect with his own life was lying cold and dead, because of him.

"I shouldn't have said that I didn't owe you anything," he said, choosing his words carefully. "That all I wanted from you was sex."

"It's true, isn't it?"

"No."

"It doesn't matter," she said, leaning her head back against the wall. "I can't give you anything else. I can't even give you that."

He tried for humor. "Sure you can."

The corner of her mouth quirked up, but she closed her eyes, shutting him out.

"I never thought you were a quitter."

Her eyes flew open and her lips parted with astonishment.

"Or a coward," he added.

"Do you have a death wish?" she asked softly.

"Yes," he said, taking her by the upper arms. Maybe he was crazy, but he was dying for her to get physical with him. Anything was better than this lackluster rejection. He bent his head to kiss her, thinking it was better to go out with a bang than a whimper.

To his amazement, she didn't push him away. After a moment's pause, she laced her fingers through the hair at the nape of his neck and pulled him closer, kissing him back tentatively, curling her tongue around his.

Groaning, Ben lifted her against the wall, cupping her bottom in his hands and pressing himself against her. "I'll go slow," he promised, although every instinct was telling him to drop his pants and take her right here, right now, right up against the wall.

Grabbing fistfuls of his T-shirt, she brought his mouth back to hers. When that contact wasn't enough, she put her hands under the fabric and slid her palms over his chest.

"Did I say slow? I meant—"

"Take off your shirt," she interrupted.

He pulled it over his head, willing to do anything she asked.

"I have this fantasy," she began, tracing the line of hair above the waistband of his jeans with her fingernail, "about kissing you here."

For a moment, he forgot how to breathe. He could almost hear the blood rushing from his head to his groin. "I don't think—"

She put her other hand to his lips, shushing him. "I have another fantasy. It's that you do everything I say."

He was desperate to fulfill that one, and thoroughly, so when her mouth wandered down his chest, he held himself very still, trying to think about going slow.

Then she was on her knees in front of him, exploring the length of his erection with her hand and the skin of his belly with her tongue. When she began releasing the buttons on his fly, he had to stop her. "Wait. You can't...do that right now."

She touched her open mouth to his hip bone then blew gently on the wet spot she made. "Why not?"

Strangling a moan, he lifted her to her feet and maneuvered her to the bed, laying her down on the rumpled blankets and stretching out on top of her. "I have a fantasy, too, you know," he said, panting against her throat.

"Oh?" She arched her neck to give him better access. "What does this fantasy entail?"

"Kissing you until you scream," he said, dragging his teeth across her tender flesh and trying to touch every inch of her arching body.

"Kissing me where?"

"Everywhere." He slipped his hand between her legs. "Here."

"Wait," she gasped, pushing against his chest.

He stopped, forcing himself to relax. Go slower. "What?"

"I think this would feel better naked."

Agreeing wholeheartedly, he rolled away to watch her undress, feeling like a teenager with his first woman. He couldn't remember ever being this aroused. While he stared, she shucked out of her jeans and pulled her T-shirt over her head, leaving her in nothing but a tiny pair of black panties.

Damn, she looked good. Yesterday, he'd almost swallowed his tongue when he saw her in that skimpy bikini. She was all sleek muscles and honeyed skin. Her thighs looked like they could squeeze the life out of him.

And her breasts. Good God, they were perfect.

"You, too," she said, gesturing to his jeans.

His erection was straining against the denim, making him uncomfortable. With her gaze on him, hot and intent, he proceeded to unbutton his jeans and push them off. The cotton boxer shorts he was wearing did a poor job of concealing his excitement.

She nibbled on her lower lip. "Would you stay over there a minute?"

He nodded, more than happy to ogle her from afar.

Watching him with cautious eyes, she took off her panties and cast them aside, exposing herself to him completely.

He couldn't help but stare. The contrast between her midnight-black hair and the tawny curls between her legs was startling. Erotic. His mouth watered to taste her, and his cock pointed the direction it wanted to go. But she'd asked him to sit still, so he did.

They were at an impasse. He got an idea. "Why don't you tell me what to do to you? Your fantasy, like you said. You're in control."

"This is kind of scary for me," she said.

"For me, too. I haven't done this in three years."

"What are you afraid of?"

"That I'll come the second I get inside you. Or even before."

She smiled. "Would you be disappointed if I came too soon?"

"No," he said, very seriously. "That, I'm counting on."

Taking a deep breath, she faced her fears. "Let's do your fantasy, then."

"Let's do both. You tell me where to kiss, and I will."

"Until I scream?"

He smiled back at her. "It's a lofty goal, I know."

"Let's see if you can achieve it." She scooted toward him, putting her arms around his neck. "Start here." She touched her fingertip to her lips.

He traced them with his tongue, slipped it inside. Moaning, she dug her nails into his shoulders and wrapped her legs around him, urging him closer. He could feel the luscious weight of her breasts against his chest and the tempting heat of her sex through the fabric of his boxer shorts.

"Hang on," he said, tearing his mouth from hers. If he pushed a little harder, he'd be inside her, and last he heard, cotton was no good as contraception. He eased back slowly, feeling sweat break out on his forehead. "Now where?"

She blinked at him in confusion then seemed to remember what they were doing. "Here." She cupped her breasts, offered them up to his mouth.

He'd never seen more delicious nipples. He flicked his tongue over one stiff peak, then the other, and realized that his cock was not going to cooperate with going slow.

His hands wouldn't cooperate, either. When he slid his palm up her thigh, and his middle finger inside her, she gasped and shuddered, as close to the brink as he was.

With a moan, he lowered his head. Parting her with slick fingers, he tasted her. She whimpered, thrusting her hands in his hair and holding him there, as if she was afraid he'd stop. He didn't. Placing his open mouth over her clitoris, he stroked her with his tongue and worked her with his fingers until she screamed. And screamed. And screamed.

Goal achieved.

When it was over, he rolled away from her, chest heaving. He threw an arm over his face, shielding his eyes.

"I came," she said, as if she didn't quite believe it.

"So did I," he replied, not sure he believed it, either.

She sat up. "You did?"

He nodded, totally chagrined.

She pulled his arm away from his face. "You came just from—?"

"I think touching you was the final impetus." He

thought back. "Or licking your nipples. That might have done it."

She stared at him, awestruck. "Do you have any idea how sexy that is?"

"Give me a few minutes," he said, closing his eyes. "And I'll show you something a lot sexier."

While Ben was in the bathroom, her cell phone rang. Scrambling off the bed, she searched the clothes-littered floor, her pulse pounding with anxiety.

"Hello," she said when she found it, answering in a breathless whisper.

"You didn't check in," Grant said. "What the hell have you been doing?"

Her mind went blank. "Uh . . ."

"A body washed up in Coronado Bay," he continued. "A young, dark-haired female. Odds are good it's Lisette Bruebaker."

"Do you want me to go down there?"

"Yes."

Ben walked into her bedroom, stark naked, and her heart started banging a wild reveille. His body was dangerous. Staring at him for too long might scorch her eyeballs.

He stopped at the foot of the bed, waiting patiently for her to finish the call, his gaze on the still-tingling flesh at the apex of her thighs.

Grant was talking in her ear, but she was having trouble processing his words.

"What did you say?" she murmured, moistening

her lips. Ben wasn't fully aroused, not yet, but he was definitely...interested.

"I said I wanted you to supervise the retrieval and the autopsy," Grant replied, a frown in his voice. "Why do you sound so strange?"

Sonny tore her eyes away from Ben's groin, rolling over onto her tummy so she wouldn't be tempted to look at him again. "You woke me up," she said, trying not to pant. "I was having a bad dream."

Grant started rattling off contact names and exact locations, the kind of information Sonny would normally be able to memorize at the drop of a hat. But Ben had climbed behind her on the bed and was sliding his palm over her hip, touching his mouth to her bare shoulder...

"Just text me with that stuff," she said, ending the call and letting the credit-card-sized phone drop from her hand.

"Is it an emergency?" Ben murmured, kissing the nape of her neck.

Every nerve in her body responded. Her brain turned to mush. "It's, an, um..."

He insinuated his hands beneath her, molding them over her breasts, and she couldn't recall her assumed name, let alone what she'd said she did for a living. His body covered hers, his erection a hot brand against her bottom. Inside she was trembling, melting, not yet recovered from the orgasm he'd just given her.

When his fingertips played over her nipple, tugging gently, she twitched with sensation, and when he slid his hand down her belly, into the slippery curls between her thighs, she jerked and moaned and came again, her second orgasm rippling over her like a warm tide.

She must have lain there for several minutes, body limp, face buried in soft pillows, before she remembered what she was supposed to be doing.

Hugging the pillow to her chest, she turned to look at him.

His gaze was heated, self-satisfied, full of sexual promise.

"I have to go."

He straightened, looking from her apologetic face to the hand he'd just touched her with in bewilderment. "What?"

Sonny blushed. His fingertips were still wet with her and his arousal was searing her hip, raring to go again, ever so much more than merely interested. "I'm sorry. It *is* an emergency, actually. A recovery."

It took a moment for his indignant expression to fade. His color was high and his mouth flat, but she knew he understood her responsibility, even if he didn't appreciate the fact that she'd gotten her jollies twice before she told him to leave.

She cleared her throat. "I didn't mean to..."

"Come again?"

She forced her eyes to meet his. "Yes."

Groaning, he pushed away from her, dragging his heavy body off the bed. He pulled his jeans up lean hips, a muscle in his jaw ticking as he buttoned the fly. "We'll finish this later," he decided. "I shouldn't leave Carly at home alone anyway."

Sonny bit down on her lower lip, considering.

Maybe she was a fool, but she believed his explanation about Lisette. Now that she was thinking coherently, she also had to own up to her mistakes. Being with Ben this way was madness. Jumping into bed with him wasn't just a bad career choice for her, it could hurt him, too.

If she was taken off the case for inappropriate contact, who would clear his name?

Reading the indecision on her face, he wrapped his hands around her upper arms and lifted her off the bed, surprising her with his vehemence. "Come to me later," he said, lowering his mouth to hers. "I don't care what time it is."

She nodded, accepting his kiss and returning his ardor, making it last, making it count. Her heart was beating like a drum and tears of regret stung at her eyes, because she knew that when she came to him again, it wouldn't be for his pleasure.

Carly awoke with a start. Sitting up, she grabbed her pillow and held it out in front of her like a shield. Heart pounding, she stared across the dark expanse of her bedroom.

There was nothing more sinister than a CD case on the floor, its plastic surface gleaming like a mirror in the moonlight.

With an unsteady laugh, she ran a hand through her tangled hair. She'd been dreaming of the undertow again, of swimming frantically, fighting for air, straining toward the surface. Just above it, a dark shape lurked (not Summer! her mind cried) and a large hand reached out, not to help her, but to push her down, down, down.

*Scrape. Scrape.*

Carly froze, a new awareness washing over her. A shadow stretched along the floor of her room, bisecting the moonlight.

The CD case was cloaked in darkness, no longer visible.

She jumped from the bed, recognizing the scraping sound for what it was: the slide of rubber-soled shoes seeking purchase against the stucco wall outside her bedroom window. And there, in menacing outline, was the silhouette of a man's head, his short, dark hair haloed by moonlight, face pressed to the glass.

Every instinct told her to yell, to run, to move, to search the room for a weapon and assume a ready stance.

Her body would not comply.

She just stared, her pulse racing, at the black figure outside.

"Dad..." she croaked, placing a hand on her chest, for the cost of making that sound was searing pain. Her lungs drew enough breath for a good scream, and then—

*Tap. Tap. Tap.*

Wait a second. Did burglars knock? Exhaling in a huff, she opened the window. "You scared the crap out of me!"

James heaved himself through the small space. "Sorry," he panted. "I was hanging in the wind out there."

She glared at him. "What are you doing?"

He gulped air. "I was afraid you were going to sneak out and look for me again. So I came by to check in on you. Make sure you were here."

She crossed her arms over her chest. "Here I am. Safe and sound, except for the twenty years you just took off my life."

He frowned at her in confusion. "Why are you so mad?"

"Because I almost screamed bloody murder! What if my dad comes in?"

James contemplated that possibility with a shrug, quite accustomed to the constant threat of violence. "Carly, I'm about to drop. Can I sleep here with you?"

She put her hands around his throat and squeezed. "I'm going to kill you."

He covered her hands with his own, rubbing soothingly. "In the morning, if you don't mind."

James would have sprawled out in a chair, or on the floor, but Carly insisted the bed was big enough for both of them. He kept his clothes on, and his shoes, just like he did at Stephen's, because he never knew when he was going to have to bolt.

Just as he was drifting off, she said, "Tell me about the girls you've been with."

His eyes fluttered open. He felt like he hadn't slept in a week. "No."

"Why not?"

"They didn't mean anything," he mumbled.

"Then you shouldn't have any trouble talking about them."

He sighed, sliding his palm over the indentation of

her waist. There was something so comforting about her body. Maybe Carly was more girl than woman, but she had curves in all the right places, and he didn't mind staying awake to humor her. "Five questions, short answers," he conceded.

Pleased with her victory, she snuggled into him. "Have you ever been in love?"

"Yes," he answered, after a pause, glad she couldn't see his face. When she bristled, he had to smother a laugh.

"What was she like?"

"Beautiful. Spoiled." He smiled. "Inquisitive."

He could feel, as if by sixth sense, her brow furrow in concentration. "All that? I thought you said none of them meant anything."

"This one did," he said with an exaggerated sigh.

"What was her name?"

He lifted his head from the pillow. "I don't remember any of their *names*."

Her right elbow connected with his rib cage.

"Carly," he choked. "Her name was Carly."

She grew very still. "Do you mean it?"

"Yeah," he said, nuzzling the back of her neck. "Now go to sleep. You used up all your questions."

"Tell me again," she urged.

"I love you," he said, without regret, breathing in the scent of her hair, savoring the feel of her skin.

"Why?"

Of course she had to know why. She was Carly.

He moved away from her to lie on his back, needing some space for perspective. Putting his hands behind his head, he stared up at her bedroom ceiling, searching for the words to explain it to her. "My whole life, I've been like a stray dog, the kind you see next to a Dumpster. Either you feel sorry for it or you want to kick it out of the way, because you can't stand the sight of suffering. It's human nature."

She turned to face him, her beauty bathed in moonlight.

"I've been half in love with you since junior high, because you were everything I wasn't. You're the kind of person everyone wants to be around."

"Just because of my dad," she countered.

"Maybe that's part of it," he replied, "but you have this glow about you, something all your own. No one would ever kick you out of the way."

"Oh, James," she said, cupping her palm around his cheek.

He took her hand away and held it instead. "You're the only good thing I've ever had."

She pressed her face to his chest, sniffling.

"You make me feel like a man."

"You're not a man," she whispered.

"That's what you keep telling me. Maybe someday I'll prove you wrong."

# CHAPTER 13

Flexing his hands in frustration, Ben crossed a dark, deserted Neptune, the street lamp overhead contorting his shadow into an eerie Nosferatu.

All he wanted to do was fall into his bed and sleep for a week. He might not even wake up early to surf tomorrow.

He was physically exhausted, sexually unsatisfied, and emotionally . . . well, he wasn't sure where he was emotionally. He didn't want to dig too deep there.

Summer was driving him insane, running hot one moment, cold the next. Now that he wanted to hold on to her a little while longer, she kept slipping farther away. He realized it was part of her appeal. She was elusive, perhaps deliberately so, and he was infatuated.

If he wasn't careful, she'd be leading him around by his cock.

Although he was dead on his feet, he stopped by Carly's room to check on her before he went to bed. She was sound asleep, as sweet and innocent as an angel, warm and safe in the security of James' arms.

Rage and indignation burned through him. Ben couldn't believe the little son of a bitch would dare to get horizontal with his daughter in his own house. In her bedroom, no less, right down the hall from Ben's. Then he saw that while Carly was under the covers, James was on top of them, fully dressed. He was sleeping soundly, his arm across her waist, shoes hanging off the edge of the bed.

It was time for a man-to-man talk, Ben decided with a grimace, kicking James' foot.

James woke with a start, tightening his arm around Carly's waist protectively. Noticing Ben's presence, he narrowed his sleepy eyes. Of course he was expecting a fight.

With movements that showed utter exhaustion and a reluctant acceptance of defeat, he rose to his feet, preparing to do battle.

Or, at the very least, to be tossed out on his ear.

Downstairs, on the way to the front door, Ben detained him. "Wait," he said, putting a hand on the boy's shoulder. When the corner of James' lip curled up in a feral, visceral response, Ben removed his hand. He'd never known a person more aversive to touch.

Except maybe Summer. But they were working the kinks out of that phobia pretty nicely, he had to admit.

He gestured toward the living room couch. "You

can sleep here if you want. I can't have you in Carly's room."

James' expression revealed suspicion. "Why would you let me sleep here?"

Ben took a pillow and blanket out of the closet. "Kid, you look about to fall over. I don't know what you've been doing, or why, but I feel sorry for you."

James deliberated, looking from the door to the plush space in front of the fire.

"Trouble at home?" Ben asked.

James scowled at the question, shuffling his feet instead of answering.

Ben was fairly certain James had been knocked around at home, and that didn't sit well with him. It didn't bode well for his daughter, either. "I'm concerned for Carly. Can you understand why?"

"Sure. You think I'm like my dad. That I'm looking for someone smaller and weaker to pound on."

"No," Ben said. With Carly, James was like a dog guarding a bone. "I'm worried about other stuff."

James didn't need to hear more. "We're not having sex," he said.

Ben couldn't help but feel relieved. But how long would that last? "She's only sixteen," he lamented, for even the most heartfelt intentions of a teenaged boy were tenuous, at best.

"I know," James said, frowning. "I'm not even interested in that."

"You're not?"

"Okay, I am," James clarified, "but I'm not going to do anything about it. I know she's too good for me." His blue eyes darkened with anger. "Isn't that what you're trying to tell me? That I'm just some dirty wharf rat with a drunk asshole for a dad and a mom who didn't care enough to stick around?" He glanced down at his hands. They were riddled with scars and calluses, much more like a man's than a boy's. "I know I'm not fit to touch her. These hands are only good for pulling in nets." He clenched them into fists. "And fending off blows."

Ben wasn't about to disagree with James' estimation of himself, even though his conscience told him he should. "Where's your mom?"

To his amazement, tears filled James' eyes. "I don't know," he whispered. "She left a long time ago. I haven't heard from her."

"Okay," Ben said, totally uncomfortable handling a boy's emotions. Carly was often tearful, and never ashamed to use it to her advantage. This was uncharted territory.

He searched for common ground. "Are you hungry?"

"Starving," James admitted.

Ben smiled. "Want a sandwich?"


Staff Sergeant Paula DeGrassi was at the crime scene well before Sonny arrived. She stood on a concrete walkway near the base of a man-made jetty that skirted Coronado Bay, the security lighting raining down on her silvery blond hair and gunmetal gray suit.

DeGrassi didn't look happy to see her.

According to Grant, she was a territorial ball-buster who ate FBI agents for breakfast. Although

Sonny was here to supervise the retrieval, not make friends, she smoothed one hand down the front of her jacket and pasted a cool smile on her face as she approached.

"Staff Sergeant DeGrassi? I'm Special Agent Vasquez. We spoke on the phone."

DeGrassi accepted her handshake with a grunt of acknowledgment and got down to business. "We have a young, dark-haired female who appears to have been in the water for several days," she said, turning toward a small man in a yellow jacket that said COUNTY MEDICAL EXAMINER. "I think we all know she wasn't dumped here, so let's not waste any more time trying to preserve the integrity of the scene."

The ME nodded his agreement.

"Dr. Ramashad," he said, sticking out his hand to greet Sonny. "If we wait much longer, the tide will take her back out."

While Sonny and DeGrassi watched from a distance, the ME and two CSIs performed the unwieldy task of removing the body from the jagged rocks lining the side of the jetty. The tide was coming in, making their job more difficult, sloshing against the rocks and sending up spouts of seawater with each approaching wave.

At 2:00 A.M., the air was still and damp, a moderate 60 degrees. Sonny wasn't cold in her jeans and jacket, and even with the lack of wind and excess moisture, her eyes were bone-dry, unblinking despite her fatigue.

The night had been the most surreal of her life.

She'd met her miserable excuse for a father and knocked him unconscious. Found out she had two half-brothers she'd never known about. And almost slept with Ben.

Did oral sex count? Sonny pictured herself in front of the board at Internal Affairs, taking the Bill Clinton defense.

Pushing that thought aside, she tried to focus on the details of the case, considering the ways this crime scene differed from the others. First and foremost, none of the previous victims had been submerged. Except Olivia Fortune.

Sonny had read the police reports and seen the photos. Emergency personnel had found an unintelligible Ben with his wife's dead body. Both were soaked to the skin. He later admitted to removing her from the tub in an attempt to revive her.

Staring at the jumble of rocks pointing out into the midnight blue Pacific, Sonny wondered if tossing Lisette's body in the ocean, or dropping Olivia's into a tub of bathwater, were attempts at washing away evidence.

It was also inconceivable that Lisette had swept into Arlen Matthews' gill net by circumstance. Either Arlen had killed Lisette and done a poor job of getting rid of her body, or someone wanted to make it appear that way. Sonny hated to cut the disgusting piece of slime a break, but she had to admit a well-known abuser of prostitutes made a convenient fall guy.

Of course, dismissing Arlen as the culprit hardly exonerated Ben.

After the body on the rocks had been loaded into

the back of the crime lab van, Sonny asked for a closer look.

The space was tight in the van but the lighting was better. Dr. Ramashad unzipped the cadaver bag, exposing what once had been a face.

It hardly resembled the pictures Sonny had seen of Lisette Bruebaker. She'd been a very pretty girl with overstyled hair, too much eye makeup, and a full-lipped pout. In summer a body that had spent almost a week in the water wouldn't have much skin, but at this time of year, the effects of decomposition were less pronounced.

The cold water hadn't saved her from scavengers, however, and they always started with the soft tissues of the face.

"Let me see her neck," she requested, her voice grim.

The girl's long hair was tangled over her throat, strangling her for eternity. Dr. Ramashad lifted it away carefully with a pair of silver-handled forceps.

The deep black crease he exposed was much easier to recognize than her face, and there was nothing tentative about it. If anything, it was overkill. There was no doubt in Sonny's mind now that the victim was Lisette Bruebaker and the perpetrator was the SoCal Strangler.

Feeling numb, she followed Sergeant DeGrassi downtown and sat in on the autopsy, her mind reeling. When the girl's hair was matched to the sample Sonny had collected from Ben's bed, he would be taken in for questioning. Perhaps even booked for murder.

Sonny would be under obligation to arrest the

only man she'd ever been in danger of falling in love with. She was powerless to help him, cursed by her inability to trust, a victim of her own investigative fervor.

Deciding not to go down without a fight, Sonny went back to her apartment and took out her laptop, running another, more detailed search on Arlen Matthews. Incredibly, the guy had no official criminal record. In fact, he seemed to have dropped out of thin air sometime in the mid-eighties.

Before then, he'd had no driver's license, no credit report, no history.


The door was locked, but he didn't have any trouble getting in. He could be stealthy when he chose to be, slipping in and out of most places undetected.

The cheap hardware on the back door at the Matthews residence was no match for him. Because he wanted to make it look like an inside job, he left the lock intact, and would have to remember to reengage it after he left.

Matthews was a mean, canny son of a bitch, quick to anger and tough as an old boot. He was also a pass-out drunk who wouldn't be able to defend himself, much less fight back, so the intruder went to the boy's room first.

It was empty.

An unexpected complication, but no reason to turn around and go home. Unconcerned with getting caught, the man clicked on the bedroom light and studied the contents of the room. The paint was cracked, the ceiling had water damage, and the furniture was atrocious. Despite the dismal poverty reflected here and throughout the house, this room was spotless.

The bed was neatly made, boasting crisp sheets and a scratchy-looking wool blanket. There was a small dresser against one wall with a jagged shard of mirror above it. The hardwood floor was scuffed but clean. In a milk crate next to the dresser, there was a stack of workbooks and a jar filled with stubby pencils.

"What the fuck is this?" he mused aloud. "David Copperfield's room?"

Shaking his head, he clicked off the light and moved on, finding Arlen Matthews' personal quarters with no problem. The sour smell hit him two steps before he entered.

Arlen's sense of hygiene left a lot to be desired. There were scummy clothes and dirty dishes everywhere. Sticky-paged porn mags littered the stained carpet. The man behind the mess was facedown on the bed, snoring. A trickle of blood ran from his hairline into his ear.

Another complication. Wasn't life full of them?

Killing a man wasn't going to be any fun, especially a stinking drunk with a head injury. All right, so it wasn't going to be a challenge, and it wasn't going to be executed according to his plan, but it *was* going to be easy.

The boy's disappearance, however, created a problem. James was a sneaky little bastard, always moving silently across the beach, drifting from one rock formation to another like a fucking sand ghost. Arlen used his son to procure women. And why not? The kid was beautiful. A sweet, sinewy bit of flesh.

He'd seen James from afar many times, and although he'd been careful, the boy may have seen him, too. After too many close encounters, he'd hunted elsewhere, preferring a more upscale neighborhood and a younger, classier target than what Arlen could afford. Since then their paths had rarely crossed.

Still, James Matthews was a loose end, one he couldn't wait to tie into a neat bow.

Sighing, he turned his attention to the foul-smelling beast on the bed. He could put the gun in Arlen's hand, raise it to his temple, and pull the trigger, but what if forensics proved he'd never regained consciousness before death?

Modern science could be such a nuisance.

With his signature attention to detail, he brought the slim bracelet out of his pocket and held it in his gloved hands, watching diamonds twinkle in the meager light. The piece was his favorite and he hated to part with it. It didn't fit his wrist, but he liked to feel the cool metal against his skin and remember his first kill.

Tears sprang into his eyes, because he wanted to bring the shimmering band to his lips one last time and knew he couldn't. Blinking them away, he laid the bracelet on top of an open magazine, finding it fitting that the spread-eagled sexpot on the page resembled Olivia.

She was a slut, but most women were. Only he

saw their true natures. Only he had the power to free their flesh.

Men like Arlen Matthews gave him a bad name. By raping women indiscriminately and then allowing them to live, Matthews created a cycle of abuse. The whores Matthews brutalized sometimes became predators themselves. They became the kind of women who would tie up a young boy and toy with him. The same kind of women who had gravitated to the coked-out sex parties at his porn-queen mother's house.

The abused became the abusers, having found a preteen plaything.

He shut the past out of his mind and focused on Matthews, hating him for his lack of foresight, his failure to plan, and his general disorganization. But most of all, he hated him for letting his victims live.

Feeling melancholy, he gathered up a dingy pillow and shoved it under Arlen Matthews' face, gripping the back of his neck when his body began to convulse, holding him down and forever ending his miserable, misogynistic existence.


Anita Vasquez had been dreaming about Mexico. Though originally from Guatemala, her family had moved to Arizona when she was ten, and they often crossed the border to visit relatives in the Sonora Desert. Some of her most cherished memories were of that strange and barren land. Like Ocotillo Wells, the Sonora was endless and arid, isolated in its beauty, with dusty sand dunes the color of her daughter's hair.

When she looked into her child's eyes for the first time, she saw that lonely, desolate place, underneath a sky so immense she'd reached up to touch it, again and again, yearning toward something unattainable until her slender arms ached.

That was exactly how she felt about Sonny.

A thousand times, she'd reached out to her. And come up empty, every time. It was her own fault, she knew, drawing the blankets around her. She had never been good with women. Girls.

She'd had four older sisters growing up, all dark and heavy-featured, none pretty and delicate, like her. Their jealousy had made her turn away from other females, even her own mother, who was too worn and old from having seven children before the age of thirty to give her youngest daughter any attention.

Anita got all the attention she needed from men. A sway of her hips, and they were hers. Men were not always gentle, but they were easy. If they had quick fists, and so many of them did, they were also quick to apologize, to soothe, to kiss away the pain.

Men were easy. Daughters, complicated.

Giving up on sleep, Anita got out of bed and put on a pot of coffee. She stood in the kitchen, looking out the window, struck by the memory of her daughter at seven years old, pulling on her mother's skirts. Sonny had been wearing a blue cotton dress, one of the few she owned, and it showed her scabby knees. A tortoiseshell clip was stuck in her light hair, hair so thick and unruly that Anita fought a battle with it on a daily basis, and lost.

"I don't believe in God, Mama," she said.

Anita whirled around, wiping her wet hands on her apron and stepping away from the sink. "*Ave Maria Purísima,*" she cried, making the sign of the cross and dragging her daughter to kneel before *La Virgen.* "Pray, *mija.* Pray for forgiveness, right now."

Sonny crossed her arms over her chest defiantly. "No. Why should I pray to something I don't believe in?"

Her jaw dropped. "You will go to hell if you don't. You will be condemned to *perdición, para siempre.*"

Sonny shrugged. "I don't believe in hell. Can I go play instead?"

Perhaps she should have slapped her daughter's impertinent face. More often than not, Anita had shaken her head, sighed, and let Sonny do as she wished. For all her strangeness, the girl was intelligent, and she never got into trouble at school like her brother.

For Rigo, Anita had made allowances. But fighting was one thing, sacrilege another. She made Sonny kneel in front of the statue for three hours.

When Anita was convinced she'd taught her daughter a lesson, she went to her and helped her up. Sonny could no longer move her legs, having been still for so long in that cramped position. Tears had poured from her strange, ice-colored eyes, but she hadn't made a sound as Anita rubbed the feeling back into her knees.

"Why, *mija?* Why didn't you tell me you were in pain?"

"I was waiting, Mama."

"For what?"

"I was praying, like you said. For God to take the pain away."

Anita hugged her close. "Oh, baby, I'm sorry. God does not always answer our prayers."

"I know, Mama."

Anita was surprised. "Do you believe in Him again?" Hope surged within her. She'd never felt this close to a common understanding between them.

"Can you hate something you don't believe in?" her daughter asked, after a moment of intense contemplation.

"No," she replied cautiously.

Sonny's pale eyes met hers. "Then I believe."


Sonny was surprised to find her mother already awake. Not only awake, but weeping into a cup of coffee, her heavy bathrobe belted neatly at her slim waist.

She steeled herself against the sight. Her mother liked to drink, and she liked to cry. Sometimes she did both at the same time, and wiped down the already clean kitchen countertops while she did it.

If only she could wipe her conscience clean, Sonny thought ungraciously.

"Do you mind?" she asked, helping herself to a cup of coffee. The cream was out, in a stainless steel carafe, and a bowl of raw sugar sat atop the counter.

She sipped experimentally then sighed with reluctant admiration. Anita Vasquez made a damned fine cup of coffee.

"I met a man," she said.

Her mother's brows lifted with surprise. "Really?" She patted the couch beside her. "Tell me about him."

Sonny sat in a chair opposite the couch, instead. It was pokey and uncomfortable, but she stayed. "He lives in Torrey Pines. La Jolla, actually."

Anita smiled, knowing that meant he was rich. "Is he handsome?"

"Yes," she said. Too handsome for his own good. Or hers.

"What color eyes?"

Sonny looked down into her coffee cup, having seen the rich, dark color before she added cream. "Blue," she said, changing the tone of the conversation. Standing, she took the picture from her pocket. "Here he is. Take a look."

When her mother saw the photo of Arlen Matthews, she gasped.

Sonny sat back in her chair and drank more coffee. It was going to be a long day. "Why did you never tell me his name? Why would you keep that from me?"

Still reeling from shock, Anita remained silent.

"What did he do to you?" Sonny asked.

Anita looked out the window, across the flat expanse of land in the distance. In the eerie predawn light, the harsh surface of sand glowed gray-white, as ethereal as moondust. "Nothing that hasn't been done before. Or since."

"Was he the worst?"

"Yes," she said without hesitation.

"Why?"

Anita stood and washed her cup in the sink, drying it carefully before she set it aside. "You never understood. The men in my life have not been perfect, this I know. But they were not deliberately cruel."

Rage licked through Sonny's body, quick and hot, like a burst of flames. "Everett Moore wasn't cruel?"

Anita regarded her with sad eyes. "No. He was sick."

Sonny laughed, but the sound held no humor.

"Your father was cruel," she said.

A hard, cold ball settled in the pit of her stomach. "Oh?"

"Some men have wicked tempers," she continued. "Arlen did not. He would hit when he was in a good mood. He would just strike out, lightning fast, while he was watching a ball game, in midsentence. He would do terrible, unmentionable things, then light a cigarette and tell me to move out of his way, because I was blocking the TV."

Sonny believed every word of it. And felt herself go dead inside.

Anita covered her mouth with one hand, remembering. "One day I came home from work early. I found Rigo curled up in the closet." She choked back a sob. "Arlen had beaten and tortured him. He was only six years old."

Sonny's heart went out to her brother. He'd never told her. "What did you do?"

"I threatened to press charges if he didn't leave." Her expression was troubled, her mind far away. "After he was gone, I vowed to never mention him again."

Sonny couldn't help but stare. A new idea occurred to her, one more painful than her memories of Everett. "Is that why you hated me? Because of what my father did?"

Her mother's face wilted with sorrow. "I never hated you, *mija*. I always loved you. I love you still."

Sonny found those words impossible to refute. Yet how could she believe them when confronted with so much evidence to the contrary? Too many times, Anita had chosen a man over her own daughter. Too many times, she'd looked the other way.

Sonny rearranged her face to hide her emotions, something she'd become very good at. "What name was he going by then? Arlen what?"

"Diels," her mother said softly. "Arlen Diels."

## CHAPTER 14

James opened the door for her, his hair sticking up all over the place, a fleece blanket around his thin shoulders. He rubbed his eyes in a measured lack of concern to see her, returned to his comfy spot on the couch, and proceeded to snooze.

Sonny tiptoed upstairs to Ben's room. Finding the door unlocked, she entered quietly, determined not to wake him up. She was feeling too raw for sexual intimacy anyway, too emotional to look him in the eye.

But she needed something only he could give her.

After visiting her mother, she'd turned off her cell phone and disengaged the GPS. Grant couldn't call her and he couldn't track her. When he caught up with her, she'd be reprimanded, at the very least. Until then, she was going to treasure every stolen moment.

Ben slept like the dead, obviously. He was sprawled

out on his back, one arm flung across the bed, the other lying on top of his chest. The comforter hung off the side of the bed. One leg, dark and hairy against the white sheets, was completely exposed.

She unbuttoned her jeans and let them fall to the floor, then hesitated at the hem of her T-shirt. Would he expect something from her if she came to his bed naked? Mired in self-doubt, she stood there, legs shaking, until fatigue overcame her. Pulling the T-shirt over her head, she crawled across his bed, succumbing to it. And to the overwhelming desire to explore his body, while he was asleep and vulnerable.

Very carefully, she pushed aside the comforter.

Beneath the dark blue cotton of his boxer shorts, his penis lay soft and thick, clearly outlined, impressive even in repose. He stirred, kicked the comforter off the bed completely, and rolled over onto his stomach.

The man looked as good from the back as he did from the front. His shoulders seemed to span more than half the width of the bed, his deltoids were well defined, and his butt was the stuff female masturbatory fantasies were made of.

She knew that paddling and swimming kept his upper body tight and right. Obviously, maintaining balance on a surfboard also required well-developed lower body muscles, all working together in perfect harmony.

Sonny imagined some of those muscles working, with him on top of her.

Unable to resist, she pushed down his shorts and eyeballed his sculpted buttocks like a voyeur. Below the waist, his skin was a shade lighter than his sun-browned back, and that paleness endeared her even as it added an illicit thrill. Sliding her palm over that masculine curve, she snuggled against him and fell asleep.

When she awoke several hours later, she was still lying on her side, her face pressed against his smooth back.

His body was tense. He was awake.

Moving her hand over his hip and down the front of his shorts, she discovered that he was not only awake but fully aroused. He must have been having some very sexy dreams, because so was she. The points of her breasts tingled, and between her legs she was already warm and moist, pulsing with sensation.

Even in sleep they turned each other on.

Instead of letting her explore, he took her hand and placed it over his flat stomach, covering it with his, stroking her fingers. Making a sound of longing, she placed a soft, openmouthed kiss between his shoulder blades, and he turned to face her.

Feeling vulnerable, Sonny ran a hand through her disheveled hair. She wished she could smooth over her emotions the same way, rearrange her face to show confidence and allure.

His eyes were hot on her skin, her breasts, her belly. From the set of his mouth and the hunger in his expression, she knew that he'd been awake and wanting her for a while.

Too nervous to speak, she hooked her thumbs in her panties and pushed them off. Lying back against the pillows, she offered herself to him in a gesture that needed no interpretation.

He reached into the nightstand and came up with a single condom. Suddenly as awkward as she, he stared at the foil-wrapped package as if it were a totally foreign object he had no idea what to do with.

Sitting up, she took the wrapper from him, pressing her lips to the throbbing pulse point at the base of his throat. He closed his eyes, struggling with some inner demons, and she saw that he was shaking.

His uneasiness calmed her as nothing else could have. She stepped into the role of nurturer, soothing him as well as herself.

She motioned for him to take off his boxer shorts, which he did. Then she held out her arms, a silent invitation for him to come over her, and he did that, too. Neither of them saying a word, she rolled the condom down him in a slow caress, taking her time.

When he couldn't stand it any longer, he trapped her wandering hands. Put them over her head. Pinned them to the mattress.

She wouldn't have allowed another man to restrain her, but with Ben, she felt excited, not overpowered. She wanted him on top of her. Inside her.

Moaning, she wrapped her legs around his waist, squirming beneath him, all but begging for him to come into her. He was right there, so close she could feel the blunt head of his erection throbbing at her body's opening.

She lifted her hips, wanting to feel more.

With a strangled groan, he laced his fingers

through hers and he pushed forward, filling her with one perfect thrust.

She gasped.

Nothing had prepared her for that moment. Not the intimate scene in the Jacuzzi. Not the sweet rasp of his tongue the night before.

It was too much. He was too big, too thick, too heavy, too masculine. The sensation was too intense, too emotional. She was on the verge of tears, and orgasm, and he hadn't even touched the right spot.

Very deliberately, he released her hands.

Sobbing, she threw her arms around his neck and pressed her face to his throat, longing for the sweet torment to end, hoping it would go on forever.

Using the position to his advantage, he slid his hands underneath her, curling his fingers around her collarbone. With his body covering hers, he pulled back and thrust forward, burying himself to the hilt, again. And again.

She could feel every inch of him, stretching her, sliding into her, creating an impossibly arousing friction. She couldn't stop herself from coming any more than she could keep from crying out loud.

He covered his mouth with hers, swallowing the sound. When she quieted, he raised his head to look at her, his eyes so full of wonder that she burst into tears.

Undeterred by her emotionalism, he just kept moving inside her, slow and easy, in no hurry to finish even though she already had. He watched her face, gauging her reactions, and soon she forgot her tears because he drove himself deep and hard and at just the right angle, hitting just the right spot.

She came again, almost immediately.

This time it was too much for him. Shuddering, he buried his head in the crook of her neck and let her skin muffle his cry as she convulsed around him.

Then it was over, much too soon, and he was heavy, sweaty, and spent.

Refusing to let herself bask in the warmth of his embrace, she pushed at his chest. "Get off me. You must weigh a thousand pounds."

He lifted his head from her neck and smiled that sexy, crooked half smile of his. His eyes were still sleepy, his cheekbones flushed, and his hair was all messed up, damp at the edges. He'd never looked better.

And she could no longer deny what she'd known all along. She was in love with him. "Feeling smug, are you?"

That wiped the grin off his face. "Well, yes. I mean, I can do a lot better, actually. But you did come twice."

She rolled her eyes. "You're proud of that? I can do that in the shower."

Taking the hint, finally, that she needed some space, he heaved himself off her. His ego, among other things, much too large to be daunted by her insults, he whistled a snappy tune all the way to the bathroom while she curled up in a miserable ball, feeling sorry for herself.

So I'm in love with him, she told herself. So what?

He'll never love you back, an annoying little voice returned.

Groaning, she buried her face under a pillow, trying to stifle it. In the bathroom, she heard him turn on the shower faucet, still whistling.

He'll never love you back, once he knows...

Furious with herself, and with him, for being so goddamned cheerful, she got up, stormed into the bathroom, and wrenched open the shower door. She was going to put a stop to all this love bullshit right now. Nip it in the bud. Smother it in its infancy.

He was rinsing soap off himself, smiling lazily. "Need me again so soon?"

"My brother killed my stepfather for raping me."

He regarded her thoughtfully, as if what she'd just said was average postcoital conversation. "Why don't you come in here and tell me about it?"

Her body humming with determination, she stepped into the shower. "I was sixteen," she said, wetting her hair and lathering it furiously. "Rigo was twenty-two. He wanted to be a famous soccer player. It was his life." She leaned her head back, rinsing.

He handed her the conditioner.

"My mom was always working odd jobs. And shacking up with strange men." She closed her eyes, rinsed the conditioner from her hair. "Everett, my stepfather, wasn't the first one who...took a liking to me." She barely noticed when he handed her some masculine-smelling shower gel, was unaware that she scrubbed a little too vigorously.

"I think you're clean," he said, taking the soap out of her hands.

She stared down at the drain, waiting for the water to run clear. "Some of them liked Rigo, too," she murmured.

He shut off the faucet, wrapping a towel around his waist and another around her.

"We both grew up pretty fast. He looked out for me. I looked up to him." She stepped out of the shower stall. "If not for Rigo, what Everett did would have happened a lot sooner. But he couldn't be there to protect me every minute."

She snuck a glance at Ben, expecting to see pity. Or disgust. What she saw was fury.

"Go on," he said.

Sonny had told this part of the story many, many times. Social services and court officials had made her repeat it, again and again. Like always, she delivered the lines flatly, her voice free of emotion, mind carefully blank. "One day when I came home from school, Everett was waiting for me. Rigo had been going to the local community college, playing on their soccer team, and he had practice." She looked through Ben, not really seeing him. "Everett followed me into my room. We scuffled. He slapped me, and I fell against my dresser." Remembering the explosion of pain, she lifted her hand to the back of her head. "By the time he was finished, I was barely conscious."

A lot was left unsaid, but she couldn't bring herself to describe the fear, the helplessness, the shame of reliving that experience every time she gave herself to a nameless, faceless boy in hopes of dulling her senses.

When she raised her eyes to Ben, she saw that his

expression was fierce. "How did your brother kill him?" he asked. "You said he beat me to it."

"Rigo was doing thirty days for possession when he met up with Everett in LA County Jail. He's never admitted it, but I think he got arrested on purpose. He stabbed Everett thirteen times with a sharpened pencil."

"How long ago?"

"Ten years."

"And he's still in prison?"

Tears flooded her eyes. "He got a twenty-year sentence. They made an example of him. Called it a gang-style execution."

Ben ran his hand through his hair. "How old was he?"

"Twenty-four."

"Jesus. Jesus Christ. What the fuck is wrong with the world? Did he appeal?"

"Yes, but he already had a criminal record, so that didn't help. And Everett's history was inadmissible." She shivered, suddenly cold and very, very tired. "Sometimes I think what happened affected Rigo more than me. He blamed himself for not being there. Even before he got arrested, he wasn't the same. He never played soccer again."

Ben wrapped his arms around her, but her body was stiff and unyielding. "Tell me what you need from me."

She lifted her head to look at him. "Breakfast?"

He leaned down to kiss her.

"Don't."

"Why not?"

"I can't deal with pity right now, Ben."

"Good, because I'm not offering any."

"What are you doing, then?"

"The same thing I've always been doing. Trying to get you out of your towel."

She glanced away, gulped down her question. Then faced him and asked it anyway. "You still want me?"

He cupped her chin, ran his thumb alongside her jaw. "You amaze me. To have gone through all that, and come out like you did? I can't fault your brother for murdering your stepfather. But it kills me to see you cry for him instead of yourself."

She fought against his hold, tried to pull away. He wouldn't let her. "If not for me, Rigo wouldn't have gone after Everett," she whispered, voicing her secret guilt.

"No," he insisted, meeting her eyes. "None of it happened because of you."

She'd told herself the same thing a thousand times. The words didn't erase the pain, or the guilt, but they helped. Just having him listen helped. Knowing he still wanted her helped.

She studied him carefully. "Are you sure?"

"Of course I'm sure. You think that five-minute romp satisfied me? Like you said, you can do better by yourself." He placed a hand over his heart. "My pride as a man is at stake."

"I didn't mean what I said. It wasn't that bad."

He threw back his head and laughed. "You just laid down the gauntlet."

"Your ego knows no bounds," she said in wonder. He bent his knees to pick her up, lifting her as though she weighed nothing. He carried her to the bed and tossed her down on it, not trying to be gentle, not treating her like she was damaged goods, or an object that might break.

He stared at her for a moment, undecided, then turned to his chest of drawers and put on a pair of jeans and a fresh T-shirt.

"Where are you going?"

"To get your breakfast, princess."

Smiling, she stripped off her towel and dropped it over the edge of the bed, leaving it lying on the floor. "It's too clean around here," she said, stretching out on her stomach.

His eyes darkened. "Not always."

On the balcony, Summer polished off the waffles and fresh fruit all on her own. She was wearing his fluffy white bathrobe, the one he never used, and lounging in a cushioned deck chair, the breakfast tray he'd brought her balanced on her lap.

A smile played on his lips. She looked like a pampered hotel guest, and he was happy to be of service. Carly and James had gone to an early matinee, so he was quite literally at her disposal, ready to cater to her every whim.

Ben stared out at the ocean, inordinately pleased with himself. It was another one of those perfect winter days, vivid and bright. At high tide, the sun was hot overhead, surf crashed against the rocks below, and sea gulls bantered noisily, searching for tasty snacks in the crevices after each receding wave.

"Aren't you hungry?" she asked, looking down at her empty plate.

"Not for food," he returned, watching her lick a drop of syrup from her fingers. Even with her newly black, poorly dyed hair, she was stunning, and the sun loved her. It made her blue eyes brilliant and warmed her honeyed skin.

"You have a one-track mind," she commented.

He murmured a vague agreement, his eyes traveling down her body. "Open your robe."

"Out here?"

He glanced around. "No one's watching."

Smiling, she set her plate aside and rose to her feet. Leaning against the balcony's decorative handrail, she looked out at the Pacific, the wind fluttering the edge of her robe, teasing her short hair.

Ben measured the rise of the handrail with his eyes. It was sturdier than an ordinary metal handrail, with a cap wide enough to sit on, and slats below.

He went to her. "You aren't afraid of heights?" he asked, his mouth near her ear.

She turned, slipping her arms around his neck and letting him boost her up on the edge of the rail. "No."

His house was at the summit of the cliff, sitting taller than the rest, and the view from this vantage point was incredible. He exhaled a deep breath, unbelievably happy to be here with her. It was almost like...

Surfing.

He stilled, feeling a wave of panic rush over him.

"Are *you* afraid of heights?" she teased.

"No," he said, but his voice sounded strange, far

away. He couldn't compare a woman to surfing. He *loved* surfing.

Then she pressed her lips to his, and he forgot about surfing. He forgot about everything but her hot mouth and gorgeous body, splayed before him, ripe for the taking.

He kissed his way down her silken throat to the valley between her breasts, aware of the cool breeze in his hair and the sweet salt smell of the ocean mingled with the scent of her body. He kneeled and dipped his tongue inside her navel while she moaned, threading her fingers through his hair.

Then he went lower, sliding his palms up her thighs. "You're not going to fall, are you?"

It was a joke, but she made the mistake of looking over her shoulder. And clutched at his T-shirt, as if losing her balance.

He stood, securing his hands around her waist. It took several seconds for him to catch his breath. "Don't scare me like that."

"Like what?" Her voice was shaky.

"I thought you were going to fall." He studied the drop to the rocks below, his gut clenching with apprehension. It was a very long way down. "This is kind of dangerous, now that I think about it."

"How did your wife die?"

The question made him feel like he was about to tumble over the edge. "I'm trying to go down on you three stories up, and you want to talk about my wife?"

"Maybe this is the perfect time to talk about it," she countered.

"Oh, yeah. Perfect." He swallowed dryly, looking out at the dark blue Pacific. The waves weren't epic, but they were good enough for practicing some tricky technical maneuvers. If only he could make with a quick cutback right now, to get out of this situation.

"She was murdered by a drifter," he said evenly. "Strangled to death."

"Oh, Ben," she whispered, pressing her face to his shoulder.

"I found her," he blurted, unable to help himself. He'd never been able to describe the scene to another person, not even the detective who'd taken his statement. Maybe if he could get the words out now, he could honor Olivia's memory without being paralyzed by guilt. "She'd been drawing water for a bath, and it was the sound that first alerted me."

She tilted her head back to look at him, and he knew his face was bleak.

"I heard the water running, so I went to look. The tub was overflowing, soaking the carpet, and she was ... there."

Summer covered her mouth with one hand.

"I pulled her out," he muttered, still hating himself. "I didn't realize ... I was so stupid. I didn't even see the marks on her neck." He drew in a shuddering breath. "Later, they said she'd been alive when he left her. She had water in her lungs. He hadn't finished the job." A tide of emotion welled up, but he shook his head, refusing to let it overwhelm him. "I don't know how long I held her before I started CPR. By the time the ambulance arrived, I was out of my mind. The

EMTs had to physically restrain me. I broke two of her ribs."

"Ben," she said kindly, "accidental injury isn't unusual when performing CPR."

He knew that, but it didn't matter. He would never forgive himself. "If I'd been home, I could have protected her. But I wasn't home. I was out surfing." His mouth twisted bitterly. "The story of my fucking life."

She regarded him with sympathetic eyes, but didn't offer any platitudes.

"If I'd treated her right while she was alive, maybe I wouldn't feel so bad. But I didn't. I was a shit husband. And a shit father. Jesus, I didn't even marry her until Carly was in elementary school. I was never there when she needed me." He knew he was getting maudlin, but he couldn't stop. The words were like a poison inside him, and he couldn't keep them there any longer. "At least when I was drunk, I had an excuse. But giving up drugs and alcohol didn't make me a superhero. I was still a selfish, irresponsible ass."

He didn't expect her to argue with him, and she didn't. Maybe that was part of his attraction to her. Like Olivia, she didn't cut him any slack.

"Why didn't you marry her?" she asked. "Until later, I mean."

"I wanted to," he admitted. "I asked her before Carly was born, and every year after until she said yes."

"What made her give in?"

"I got sober. She wouldn't have me until I'd been a year sober, and celibate."

"Celibate, too?" Her tone was light. "This woman was a paragon."

He gave her a wry smile. "It's one of the recommendations of AA anyway. And I'd already fucked everything that moved, so it wasn't much of a sacrifice. Besides, she was the only one I wanted."

Easing herself off the edge, she slipped out of his arms. "I should go."

"Hey," he said softly, reaching out to grab her wrist. She turned her head, trying to hide her tears, but he saw them. "I didn't mean to make you sad." Then comprehension dawned. It wasn't the story about how his wife died that made her cry, it was his description of how much he'd loved Olivia. Still loved her.

What woman wanted to hear that the man she was about to go to bed with was in love with someone else?

"Fuck," he said, wanting to kick himself. "I didn't mean to make her sound perfect. She wasn't. She cursed at me in Spanish all the time, and laughed because I couldn't understand her. She was vain about her looks and that bugged the hell out of me." He searched for something worse, something convincingly bad. "And she cheated on me."

Wiping her cheeks with the sleeve of his robe, she said, "She didn't."

He smiled, knowing he had her. "Yes she did."

"With who?"

He shrugged, with some difficulty. "It didn't really matter, because it was a one-time deal, and it was my fault anyway. I left on a three-month tour the week after our honeymoon. Laird Hamilton backed out at the last minute, and when they asked me to go, I said yes without even thinking about her, much less asking her opinion. The next day I was in Tahiti, getting pounded by thirty-foot waves with a six-foot drop to the reef."

"You are an idiot."

He laughed harshly, agreeing with her.

"Did you cheat on her, too?"

"No," he said, sobering. Not liking the question, or the context under which she'd asked it before. "And I didn't go on any more surprise tours."

Sonny stared back at Ben, finding him devastatingly handsome and painfully sincere. Every time he opened up to her she fell in love with him a little bit more. It was so ironic that his devotion to his wife, the very reason he would never be able to commit to another woman, was what made him irresistible to her.

In her mind, she was stepping over the threshold of balcony doors, walking past the stark, soulless interior of his bedroom, and right out of his life. In reality, and a repetition of their short, tumultuous history together, he wouldn't let her go. And she allowed him to detain her, because she wanted to stay.

"I'm not going to lie to you," he said. "I loved her. She was the mother of my child, and I really loved her. Being with her was as comfortable as breathing. She drove me crazy sometimes, but it was never like this." He put her hand against the middle of his chest. "There's nothing comfortable about you."

He was a little off the mark, as far as compliments

went, but his heart was pounding and his eyes were hungry.

Maybe he didn't love her, but he wanted her.

He must have understood that she needed more convincing. "I've never wanted a woman the way I want you," he said, covering her mouth with his and proceeding to convince her with some very tantalizing movements of his tongue. He broke the kiss, breathing hard. "If you don't let me fuck you again, I'll die."

She laughed at his overstatement, but he took himself very seriously, and went about seducing her as if his life depended on it. He sank to a cushioned lounge chair, pulled her onto his lap, and had her all but purring in minutes.

He touched her and she shuddered. She unbuttoned his pants and touched him, too, stroking lightly until he took her hand away.

"Come here," he said, leaning back in the reclining chair. Sliding his body under hers, he urged her forward until she was straddling his chest, her belly level with his mouth. Her robe gaped open, baring her from the waist down.

She cast a worried glance for watchful neighbors, who would surely be able to guess what they were doing. Seeing none, she felt totally exposed, nonetheless.

And unbearably excited.

Bending his head to her, he traced the rim of her belly button with his tongue. When she sucked in a breath, he glanced up at her, the corner of his mouth quirking into a slight smile. Reaching underneath her robe, he cupped her bottom and brought her up to him.

She twisted her fingers through his hair, gasping as he slipped his tongue inside her.

With a helpless moan, she surrendered, moving her hips, pressing herself to his mouth. When his tongue found her clitoris, the whole world fell away. She came in a shuddering rush, collapsing against him, brilliant orange sunbursts and white-hot flashes dancing behind her eyes. She could literally hear the crescendo ringing in her ears.

Or maybe it was just waves, crashing on the rocks below.

She drifted back to earth, chest heaving, and realized she'd just screamed down the rooftops in broad daylight. She felt her cheeks burn with embarrassment.

"Sorry," she said, climbing off him.

"For what?"

She stared at his face. Her scent was probably all over him. "For mounting your head. Smothering you. Going crazy."

He laughed. "You think I didn't like it? My mission in life is to make you go crazy." He shifted uncomfortably. "You can mount any part of me, anytime."

She looked down. He was painfully erect, oozing with arousal. She bent her head to lick the pearly drop from the tip. When she took him fully into her mouth, he moaned, and a moment later, she had him quaking with pleasure. "Baby..."

Making a soothing sound, low in her throat, she stayed right where she was.

"No," he said. "I want to be inside you."

"Do you have a condom?" she asked, because he was breathing hard, struggling with himself.

"In my pocket," he ground out.

She pulled his jeans down his legs and searched the pockets, doing the honors once again. Letting the robe fall off her shoulders, she climbed astride, easing herself down on him. As soon as he was buried to the hilt, she leaned forward and kissed him very softly on the lips. "I like you here," she said, tracing the crescent-shaped scar above his hard, beautiful mouth. She could feel his stomach quivering, and every inch of him, thick and pulsing within.

"Don't move," he warned.

"Okay," she breathed, clenching her inner muscles.

Groaning, he took her hips in his hands and rode her on him, hard and fast, up and down, back and forth, his movements wild, uninhibited, uncontrolled.

Panting, she pushed him back against the cushions, bracing her palms on his chest and reestablishing control. Matching the pace he set, she rode him desperately, raking her nails down his torso and squeezing his pectoral muscles, slipping her fingers into his mouth for him to suck.

When he licked the pad of his own thumb and placed it against her clitoris, she was so wet and sensitive that one touch sent her skyrocketing.

Gripping her hips tightly, he came, too, a hoarse

cry wrenching from his throat in the moment of release.

For a long time, she lay sprawled across his chest, replete.

"I love you," she murmured against his neck. His body tensed under hers as those words penetrated the sensual fog surrounding them. She lifted her head, wide-eyed and suddenly alert. "I didn't mean that," she said quickly.

He brought her head down to his chest. "I know," he said, stroking her back. His words were almost swallowed by the sound of the surf pounding on the shore below, and the heavy thudding of his heartbeat, a frantic rhythm that matched her own.

## CHAPTER 15

"Somebody's here," she said, placing a hand on his hip.

"Just Carly and James," he murmured against the back of her neck, smoothing his palm over her stomach.

"No," she whispered, sidling away from him. "Two men. Coming upstairs." She cocked her head, listening. "Do you have a gun?"

He looked at her like she was crazy. "What?"

"Go in the bathroom," she ordered, jumping up from the bed. Not waiting to see if he complied, she searched the room for a ready weapon. Knowing she had only seconds to spare, she jerked one of the upper drawers from his dresser, shook its contents onto the floor, and stood beside the door, stark naked, ready to brain someone with it.

Ben gaped at her incredulously.

"Get out of the line of fire," she whispered, motioning him with her free hand. "You don't have a gun, but these guys do. I can tell by the way they're moving."

Instead of leaving her to her own devices, he planted his back against the wall beside her, and when Special Agent Colby Mitchell kicked in the door, Ben jumped.

Sonny didn't.

She swung the mahogany drawer up, hitting Mitchell under the forearms and causing him to discharge his weapon into the ceiling. A cloud of plaster rained down on them. Although she'd banked her strength as soon as she recognized him, the impact must have been excruciating, for Mitchell fell to his knees.

She was on his back, with control of his gun, in the blink of an eye.

"Drop it," a voice said from behind her.

A bead of cold sweat ran down her spine. She trained the weapon on the back of Mitchell's head and cast a glance over her shoulder.

Grant was pointing his service revolver at Ben.

Underneath her, Mitchell began to shift. She never should have looked back. In that moment of distraction, he gained the upper hand. He rolled over her, crushing her underneath him, knocking the air from her lungs and smashing the back of her head against the hardwood floor. Disconcerted, she tried to put the gun between them, but Mitchell plucked it from her hands like he was taking candy from a baby.

Damn. He'd been practicing.

She was down, but not out, so she managed to get

enough leverage to aim a hard right at his left eye. He moved at the last second, and her fist glanced off his cheek, opening up the skin. Facial wounds were gushers, and she was pleased to have drawn first blood, although a blow to the eye socket would have been more effective.

In retaliation, Mitchell backhanded her across the face so hard she saw dark flashes.

"Are you done?" he asked.

She bared her teeth. "Get off me, you ape."

At the open doorway, Grant lowered his weapon. "Are you Benjamin Lyndon Fortune?"

Ben placed a hand over his heart, as if to make sure it was still beating. "Yeah. Who the fuck are you?"

"I'm Special Agent in Charge Leland Grant and this is Special Agent Colby Mitchell. We need to take you in for questioning."

Sonny's eyes flicked over Grant. The sound of her voice last night must have tipped him off to her wanton behavior, but she'd never have guessed he would fly in on the next plane, or try to take Ben into custody by force.

"Call off your dog, Grant," she said wearily.

"Let her up," he said, gesturing to Ben. "Get him instead."

As Mitchell released her, Ben's eyes narrowed. "You know these guys?"

Her stomach churning with dread, she stared down at the floor, unable to meet his gaze. "Just do what they say, Ben."

"Can I put my pants on first?" His tone was surly and bewildered, an understandable reaction from a super-rich judge's son who had never expected to be manhandled by the police. Or betrayed by a woman.

Grant motioned his assent. "Please do. Let's all holster our weapons, so to speak, and proceed in a rational manner."

Ben took it all in and came to the natural conclusion. "You're a cop, aren't you?" He jerked his pants up, shooting her an angry glare. "You lying fucking bitch. You're a cop."

Mitchell forced a laugh. "Look how bent out of shape he is. You must be dynamite in the sack, Vasquez."

"Fuck you, Mitchell," she bit out, mad at herself for letting him get the best of her, although her pride was stinging more than her face.

"Anytime, baby."

Sonny dragged on her own clothes, aware that Mitchell was ogling her nude form and furious with Grant for allowing it.

She'd just been demoted, and this was part of her punishment.

"By the way, I like what you've got going on downstairs," Mitchell added, elbowing Ben in the ribs. "Don't see that every day, do you? Usually it's the other way around. Light on top, dark down below."

Ben wasn't much of a fighter, but there was only so much insult a man could take in his own home. With a low growl, he drew back his arm and sent his fist into Mitchell's stomach. Mitchell didn't even flinch. Ben shook out his hand, wincing, and Mitchell had him facedown on the carpet, hands cuffed behind his back, before he could say *Ouch*.

"You want to resist some more, motherfucker?" Mitchell panted.

Ben's response was muffled, but it sounded affirmative. Not amused by his attitude, Mitchell jerked Ben to his feet, handling him with deliberate roughness.

Grant turned his dispassionate gaze to Sonny. "Speaking of body hair, thanks for the sample, Special Agent Vasquez. We've got a positive match on Lisette Bruebaker, from above *and* below stairs." He gave her a pitying look. "I regret that you had to take such extreme measures to collect it from this bed."

Sonny began to pull on her socks and shoes in silence, clenching her jaw until her teeth ached. By implying that sleeping with Ben had been part of her official duty, Grant was protecting her, but she was too devastated to feel relieved.

Grant inclined his head at Ben. "You're a popular man, Mr. Fortune. Getting your money's worth out of that Egyptian cotton."

Sonny glanced at Ben, gauging his reaction. The expression on his face, when he realized she'd been deceiving him from the beginning, tore her apart. She watched every tender emotion he'd felt for her wither up and die.

"I want my lawyer," he said, eyes cold.

"Take him downstairs," Grant ordered, dismissing Mitchell and Ben with a wave of his hand. When they were out of earshot, he turned to Sonny, his steely gray eyes speculative. Her boss was a hard-ass, but he'd never been deliberately cruel. He was aware of her history with men and had always treated her with respect. The look he gave her now was more paternal than professional, but it still cut her to the quick.

Knowing he cared enough about her to be disappointed, she felt twice as ashamed of herself for letting him down.

"How long have you been here?" he asked.

She couldn't help but flush. "A few hours."

He squinted down at her, taking in her messy hair and casual attire. "Go make yourself presentable," he said. "I need you to work a crime scene."

Her stomach tightened. "Another victim? Who is it?"

"A local fisherman. Some guy named Arlen Matthews."


Carly wanted to pay for the movie, but James wouldn't let her. She had also suggested they skip the movie and go somewhere they could be alone together.

Honor demanded he refuse.

James took his promises very seriously, and he didn't want to screw up the unspoken trucc he and her dad had called over turkey-and-avocado sandwiches the night before. Ben had given James permission to take Carly to the theater, not anywhere else.

She sulked, but in a denim mini-skirt and black sheepskin boots, she looked damned good doing it. Her stretchy plum-colored knit sweater covered up what the top underneath didn't. This morning, she'd been taunting him with flashes of silky midriff.

James didn't argue with her choice of movie, even though it was an artsy flick, because he figured that on a date, ladies picked and gentlemen paid. He didn't get a chance to go to the theater very often, and when he did, he preferred mindless action over thought-provoking drama.

So did everyone else, from the looks of it. Due to either the early-bird show time or the heavy subject matter, the theater was empty.

It dawned on him that she'd chosen wisely. "You have great taste in movies," he said with a grin.

"Thanks," she replied glibly, finding a secluded corner in the back row.

The multiplex was the new kind, with comfortable bucket seats and adjustable armrests. He pushed the one between them all the way up.

"Wait," she said as he reached for her.

He looked around the empty theater. "Why?"

"The lights are still on. Someone might come in."

James settled back in his seat, watching concession advertisements float across the screen. "Want some popcorn?"

She shook her head.

"Coke?"

"No thanks."

The lights began to dim. Thank God.

"What do you want?" he whispered, putting his lips against the sweet curve of her neck.

"You," she said in his ear, making him shiver. Then she pushed him away. "But let's wait until the movie starts. Lots of people come in during the trailers."

He groaned and sat back in his seat, counting the moments until he could kiss her. There would be four or five previews, at four or five minutes each. A freaking eternity.

Long before that time was up, he noticed her fidgeting in her seat beside him. In the dark, he couldn't see what she was doing, but when she pressed a wadded-up ball of fabric in the palm of his hand and said, "Hold these for me," he figured it out.

His heart started pounding in his chest, blood rushed from his head to his groin, and he swallowed convulsively. Getting rid of the evidence, he shoved her panties into his pocket, afraid someone would shine a spotlight on him and arrest them both for lewd conduct. He'd been painfully eager to kiss her, to make out with her, maybe even feel her up a little bit, but she'd just taken his innocent fantasy right into porno territory. What was a man to do?

Without turning toward her, he placed his palm on her bare thigh, picturing in intense detail what she was wearing. And not wearing.

She took his hand away and put it on his knee, giving him a reassuring pat. "Wait until the movie starts," she repeated, and continued watching the previews with an incomprehensible serenity.

Sweat broke out on his forehead as he imagined pushing her back against the seat and climbing between her long, slender thighs. "I can't fuck you in the theater," he blurted out, loud enough for the first row to hear, if anyone had been sitting there.

Laughing, she covered his mouth with her hand. "Shh! Who asked you to?"

Her panties were burning a hole in his front pocket, and she was wondering where he got the idea?

"We don't have to do anything," she said, annoyed

by his reticence. "Give me back my panties, and we'll just watch the movie."

He shifted in his chair. "No way. I'm keeping them."

She wasn't getting her way, and she didn't like it, so she pouted for a few minutes. Then she said, "I'm going to get popcorn."

He held her arm. "No you aren't."

She shrugged, digging a twenty out of her pocket. "You go, then. I want a small popcorn, a large Coke, and some Red Hots."

"I can't," he grated.

"Why not?"

He brought her hand to his lap and let her feel why not.

"Oh," she said, giggling. "That would be noticeable at the concession stand."

In the end, she went herself, because even though he was too stubborn to return her panties, she was too proud to let him order her around. He seethed the whole time she was gone, imagining her flirting with the popcorn boy, whose tongue had already been hanging out when he'd watched her walk by on the way in.

If he only knew.

She got back, set the popcorn tub between her legs, and invited him to grab a handful. He declined.

James tried to pay attention to the movie, but it was a lost cause. Instead, he concentrated on stifling his overactive imagination.

Halfway through the movie, she asked, "What are you going to do with my panties?"

He turned to look at her beautiful face. In the

flickering light, her hair was as black and shiny as a raven's wing. "What do you think I'm going to do with them?"

"Try them on?" she guessed.

He couldn't help but laugh. Then consider. "No," he decided. "At least, not the way you mean."

She crinkled up her cute little nose, not following his train of thought. "You're not going to smell them, are you?"

He smiled at her ignorance. It was the least he was going to do. "You should have thought of that before you gave them to me."

She bit into her lower lip, concerned. "What if they smell like..."

"Like what?" he teased, looking down at her lap. "Popcorn?"

"No." She tucked a strand of hair behind her ear. "Like me."

"I hope they do," he replied honestly.

Her breath caught in her throat. "Give them back," she whispered.

"No," he said, standing firm. Or sitting firm anyway.

Unleashing the fury of a thousand warrior ancestors, Carly leapt on him and raided his pockets. Popcorn spilled all over the floor. She didn't find her underwear. What she did encounter gave her pause. "You've been hard this whole time?"

He wrestled with his conscience, gave up, and pulled her into his lap, sent over the edge by her touchy-feely version of the Spanish Inquisition. Shoving his hand between her pretty legs, he did what he'd been desperate to do since she'd taken off her panties. "You've been wet this whole time?"

She gasped. Then moaned, tilting her hips forward.

He froze, appalled by his own behavior. Turned on by hers.

They stared at each other for a long moment. Then she put her arms around his neck and pressed her lips to his fervently, wriggling on his lap.

James groaned, thrusting his tongue into her mouth and stroking her with his fingertips. He had never gotten a girl off before—at least, not on purpose. In the past, expediency had been key, not technique, tenderness, or generosity. With Carly, he wanted to give everything, ask nothing in return, so when he paid attention to what her body wanted, rather than his, he gave them both their first orgasm. Hers was the first she'd had with another person, and his, the first he'd granted someone else.

Afterward, she lay panting in his arms, her face pressed against his neck. "Do it again," she whispered.

"I'd love to, Carly, but I'm having some...technical difficulties." He took his hand out from underneath her skirt, moving slowly, trying to think unsexy thoughts. The danger zone was about to explode.

He set her away from him, very gingerly.

"What happened? Did I hurt you?"

"Give me that Coke," he ordered. When she did, instead of drinking it, he put it in his lap. Through the layers of denim (his own) and cotton (borrowed, after a hasty shower this morning in the poolroom), the cold didn't do much good.

"Oh, God! I did hurt you. I'm sorry." She knelt in front of him, trying to find out what was wrong. "Did I smash your . . . parts?"

"No, Carly," he groaned. "I'm about to come in my pants. And since I'm wearing your dad's underwear, that would be a bad, bad thing."

She clapped a hand over her mouth, muffling a burst of hysterical laughter.

He closed his eyes. "I'm glad one of us is having a good time."

She was still on her knees when the police found them.


Nathan was having a splendid afternoon on the deck of his sailboat with Peter. They were moored off the coast of Catalina Island, enjoying the cool breeze, a bottle of Sauvignon Blanc, and each other.

When his cell phone emitted a few notes of "Wipeout," the ring tone signaling a call from Ben, Nathan slipped his hand into his pocket. "I've got to take this," he said, dropping a kiss on the top of Peter's sun-warmed head.

Whistling cheerfully, he skipped down the steps leading to the galley, for privacy and to get out of the wind. The interruption couldn't have come at a better time. Peter was charming, handsome, successful, and . . . yawn. Tediously boring.

"Hello?" he said into the receiver as his eyes adjusted to the change of light.

"Nathan? Where are you?"

Ben seemed frantic. Nathan felt a smile quirk his

lips. "I'm out on the water. Must you always call when I'm otherwise engaged?"

"Sorry. I'm in jail."

"In jail?" Nathan placed a hand over his heart, no longer enjoying his brother's distress. "Whatever for?"

"Summer Moore is a cop." He muttered a string of inventive curses, the volume fluctuating as he shifted the phone to his other ear. "That's not even her real name. It's Vasquez or some shit. She's been investigating me the whole time."

Nathan was astounded by this news. He considered himself a good judge of character and he'd liked Summer. "Why?"

"I don't know. Now Carly's friend is missing and they seem to think I had something to do with it."

"Which friend?"

"Lisette."

His stomach sank. Lisette Bruebaker was trouble with a capital *T.* She'd had a crush on Ben for years, and although she'd been quite overt in showing her affections, he'd never noticed.

"Why would they think you're involved?" Nathan asked carefully.

Ben sighed. "She was last seen at my house, staying overnight with Carly. And the rest...the rest I shouldn't say over the phone."

Nathan gripped the phone in his hand until his knuckles turned white. His brother wouldn't have touched Lisette, or any other underage girl, with a ten-foot pole. So why did he sound so worried? "Okay," he said, checking his Rolex. "Hang tight. It will take me a few hours to get there." He paused, considering the next course of action. "Have you called Dad?"

"No," Ben said. And then, "Fuck, no."

Fair enough. "What about Carly?"

"She went to the movies with James. I haven't been able to reach her. You'll have to call her cell phone, tell her where I am."

"Do you think that's wise?"

"It's either that or let her freak out about the bullet hole in the ceiling when she comes home," he said, raising his voice.

"Jesus Christ, Ben! Were you resisting arrest?"

"Yes. No. I don't know. They broke into my room like gangbusters. I almost had a heart attack. I didn't know what the hell was going on." The connection crackled with interference. "Is it even legal, for them to barge in like that?"

"In some cases," Nathan admitted.

"Like what?"

"Murder investigations."

Ben was silent for a moment. "What should I do?" he asked quietly.

Nathan was taking the stairs up to the deck two at a time. "Try to stay calm," he said, motioning for Peter to pull anchor. They needed to get back to the mainland, pronto. "And whatever you do, don't say anything."


Before heading to the crime scene, Sonny went back to her apartment, took out her laptop, and ran Arlen Diels through VICAP, the FBI's main informational database for the apprehension of violent criminals.

Sure enough, he had a history that read like a Spanish-language telenovela.

As a teen, Arlen had spent some time at a boys' home, and the resident psychiatrist, a man by the name of Sparks, had written detailed notes.

Arlen had been born in Beaufort, North Carolina, to fifteen-year-old Cora Lee Diels. Cora Lee died of a drug overdose in San Francisco's Haight-Ashbury district during the Summer of Love. It wasn't a great loss for Arlen, who'd been raised by his grandparents and never known his real mother, but Grandma Lynelle took the news hard. She passed on soon after, leaving Arlen at the mercy of his grandfather, an Onslow Bay fisherman by the name of Max Diels.

Max taught Arlen everything he knew about fishing, fists, and force. Grandpa Max loved his daughter, Cora Lee, more than a father should, but he hated Arlen. Just as Arlen would do with his own son, in a sad, vicious cycle, Max varied between beating his grandson senseless and calling him queer.

After Max drowned, under suspicious circumstances, in the Albermarle Sound, Arlen was placed in protective custody. At Black River Home for Wayward Boys, he quickly obtained a reputation for brutality. He also spent a lot of time in psychotherapy with Dr. Sparks, who found Arlen an excellent subject for study. In the good doctor's opinion, Arlen Diels was a sadist—and a sociopath.

By the age of nineteen, two years before meeting Anita Vasquez, Arlen had killed a man during a bar fight in Sarasota, Florida. Instead of waiting for the police to sort things through, he fled to California, just like his mother had done so many years before.

The rest of the story Sonny had to fill in from what information she knew of Arlen since his hasty departure from the Southern seaboard.

In San Diego, after spending some time with Anita Vasquez and her young son, Arlen found work aboard a small fishing vessel called *Destiny*. It was destiny, all right, because when old man Matthews died he left the boat to his only daughter, Gabrielle, along with a quaint little two-bedroom house in Torrey Harbor.

Arlen proposed immediately.

Gabrielle was probably delighted that Arlen offered to take her last name. Stephen came along nine months later. Gabrielle stuck around long enough to get pregnant with James, and to raise both boys into elementary school.

Then she disappeared. When Stephen was sixteen and James just eleven, Gabrielle Matthews fell off the face of the earth, and no one had heard from her since.

Sonny closed her laptop and rose to her feet. She dressed with special care, focusing all of her energy on her outward appearance, because inside she was a mess. In an attempt to maintain a cool, professional façade, she opted for a sedate white blouse, black tailored trousers, and a matching jacket loose enough to hide her SIG.

By the time she arrived at James' house, Paula DeGrassi and a team of CSIs were already there. Sonny felt nauseous. She wasn't ready to face the monster who was her father again, even if he was stone cold dead, facedown on the bed.

She forced herself to study the man with detached interest, analyzing details like an automaton, unable to look Sergeant DeGrassi in the eye.

The corpse wasn't the most gruesome sight she'd seen, not by a long shot. It was the most horrifying, however, because Arlen Matthews didn't appear to have been strangled, shot, or stabbed. If anything, he'd been bludgeoned, and by her own hand.

She leaned forward, holding her breath against the smell of old booze and fresh death, trying to see if he'd sustained any other injuries. Had Arlen Matthews died in his sleep, minutes or hours after she bashed him over the head?

This was bad. Oh, so much worse than getting caught in bed with Ben.

"His son found the body," DeGrassi said, referring to her notes. "Stephen Matthews. He sounded just like the kid who reported Lisette Bruebaker."

Sonny cleared her throat. "Really?"

"Yeah. And this guy was a small vessel fisherman, so it fits. That's why I contacted your special agent in charge."

Of course. Sonny hadn't been checking in, so Grant had no idea that Arlen was connected to the SoCal murders. Neither had DeGrassi, until now.

"I asked this kid, Stephen, about the phone call and he acted like he didn't know what I meant. Then he said yes, he made the call." She shrugged. "He's got another brother, James Matthews, age seventeen, who lives here and has yet to be accounted for."

Sonny's mind raced with possibilities. If she didn't come clean right now, James or Stephen could be implicated in Arlen's death. Last night, she'd washed her drinking glass and worn gloves while searching for clues. Other than the broken lamp, which might go unnoticed in this heap, there would be no trace of her here.

Then again, James would surely tell everyone what she'd done when they found him. Sonny closed her eyes and clenched her hands into fists, visualizing the dregs of her career swirling down the toilet.

"What's that?" DeGrassi asked, nodding to one of the crime scene technicians.

A young man in a white jacket and latex gloves was lifting an expensive-looking bracelet from the top of an open magazine. He froze, letting the jewelry dangle from the tip of his forceps. "It's been photographed."

"Put it down. I want to look at it."

Sonny couldn't believe her eyes. That bracelet had not been here last night. Absolutely no way, not a chance. She'd searched every inch of the place.

DeGrassi stepped forward, adjusting her glasses and peering down at the pretty, custom-made piece. Sonny came up beside her to do the same.

It was a simple platinum disk on a delicate silver chain. On the surface of the disk, a handful of well-placed sparkles, aquamarine and diamonds by the looks of them, made the crest and swell of a tiny wave.

Sonny's breath caught in her throat.

"Hmm," DeGrassi said. "Turn it over."

On the back, so small as to be almost indiscernible,

there was a romantic dedication. The engraved words made a chill run down Sonny's spine.

To Olivia. Love, Ben. Forever.

Sonny had withheld a lot of information from DeGrassi, but as staff sergeant of the Homicide Division, she must have known Ben was a suspect in his wife's murder, and that he was at the station being interrogated by Grant right now. "Give the techs a few minutes to see what else turns up, and you can take this to your S.A.C."

Sonny managed a brusque nod.

DeGrassi's sharp gaze narrowed on Sonny from over the tops of her reading glasses, but she didn't say anything more. Instead, she gestured to the CSI, indicating that he continue collecting evidence, and bagged the item herself.

Needing a breath of fresh air, and a moment to recover her wits, Sonny walked out to the backyard. It was as cluttered with trash and debris as the rest of the house. She was amazed that James could show up anywhere looking clean; she felt dirty after only a few minutes inside the place.

Tapping the toe of her shoe against the concrete patio beneath her feet, she pondered the case, searching desperately for some answers. Unless Arlen had roused in the middle of the night and brought out the bracelet, or in her frantic state of mind she'd missed it, the piece of jewelry had been planted.

Perhaps Sonny hadn't killed him after all. But who had? James, after she dropped him off at Stephen's? Stephen, before he called to report the old man's death? Or Ben, sometime between the orgasms he gave her last night and the awesome sex they'd had this morning?

Flushing at the memory, she shook her head in frustration. She couldn't vouch for Stephen's moral character, or blame James for wanting to knock his father off, but she knew in her heart that Ben wasn't a murderer.

Arlen, on the other hand, had Lisette Bruebaker in his fishing net and Olivia Fortune's bracelet on top of his dresser. He'd left at least one man dead in Florida. He also had a murky past that included abused women, tortured children, and a misplaced wife.

Crossing her arms over her chest, Sonny frowned down at the cement slab she was standing on. In one corner, using a boy's irreverent scrawl, James had etched his name and a date.

She counted back the years to Gabrielle Matthews' disappearance.

"No," she said, feeling her stomach turn over once again. "Oh, no."

## CHAPTER 16

Ben was taken into the interrogation room against his will, handcuffed and belligerent, barely cooperating with walking. A uniformed officer removed his cuffs and he sat down across from Special Agent Grant, rubbing his wrists. "I did *not* agree to an interview."

"I'll be doing most of the talking," Grant said with a shrug. He was about ten years older than Ben, but no less intimidating for it. Steely-eyed and svelte, he radiated strength and authority.

Ben hated him with a passion. "I want my lawyer."

Ignoring him, Grant pushed a few autopsy photos across the surface of the table.

Ben refused to look.

"She was such was a beautiful girl, before. Stayed over at your house a lot, I heard." He smiled, but it didn't reach his eyes. "I have three daughters myself. Some of those slumber parties can get pretty wild."

Ben maintained his silence, knowing exactly where this was heading.

"Did Lisette and your daughter have pillow fights, Mr. Fortune? Did they tickle each other, play truth or dare, call boys on the phone? Did they sleep in their panties, side by side in the same bed?"

"Fuck you."

"Carly's a lovely young woman," Grant said, switching tactics. "Takes after her mother, doesn't she?"

Ben's spine stiffened. "My daughter is here?"

"In interrogation room four, with my associate Special Agent Mitchell."

Ben studied Grant's face avidly, marking spots where he'd like to land a few blows. "What do you want?"

"I want you to answer a few questions."

Ben glanced down at the autopsy photos, against his will. And saw nothing he ever wanted to see again. "Let me talk to Carly," he said, swallowing his bile.

"As soon as we're finished here," Grant replied.

Ben weighed his options. He felt confident that he could answer their questions without incriminating himself. Carly, on the other hand . . .

"Fine," he said, agreeing to the interview. "But if I find out one of your no-neck goons talked to my daughter without my permission, or harmed a single hair on her head, I will bring a lawsuit down on you faster than you can blink."

Grant raised his hands, claiming innocence. "Of course, Mr. Fortune. We're doing everything according to procedure."

Ben laughed harshly, rubbing a hand over his face. "Yeah? Did your special agent fuck me according to procedure, or was she allowed to improvise?" Seeing anger flare in Grant's gray eyes, Ben leaned forward, enjoying a feeling of power he knew would be fleeting. "Because if she was just following instructions, I salute your training." He made an okay sign with his thumb and forefinger. "She was Class A. Topnotch."

A muscle in his jaw ticked, but Grant didn't rise to the bait. Instead, he brought an evidence bag out from a drawer under the surface of the table. When Ben saw what lay inside, his entire body went numb.

"Where did you get that?" he asked. His voice sounded strange, far away.

"Do you recognize it?"

Ben couldn't think of any reason to lie. "It was my wife's. She never took it off."

"Where did you last see it?"

"On her wrist," he said, seized by a memory of Olivia raising her hand to her hair and laughing, the bracelet twinkling in the sun. "The morning she died."

Grant stared back at him in silence.

"Lisette had that?" he asked, feeling an absurd twist of anger. "I thought someone in the coroner's office lost it. I filed a report."

"Tell me about your relationship with Lisette."

Ben wanted to take the bracelet out of the bag and

cup it in his hands, to close his palm around the tiny metal disk and sink into the past. Instead, he had to deal with Grant, who was holding the last remnant of his wife hostage and asking stupid questions about Lisette.

Lisette, who was gone forever, like Olivia.

"You bastard," he said without heat. "I didn't have a relationship with Lisette."

"She was in your bed."

"Not by my invitation," he murmured, no longer concerned with implicating himself. He was too disillusioned to care.

"Did Carly know?"

Ben snapped to attention. "Did Carly know what?"

"That Lisette had been in your room, in your bed? What would she have thought about her friend snuggling up to Daddy ... wearing Mommy's bracelet?"

He felt the blood drain from his face. On some level, he knew that Grant was trying to manipulate him into saying too much, but his insinuation that Carly had a motivation for murdering Lisette shook him to the core. Ben would do anything to protect his daughter. Anything.

"I heard she's been experiencing some emotional turmoil lately," Grant continued, smooth as silk. "Throwing herself into a rip current. Experimenting with drugs."

Under the table, Ben clenched his hand into a fist.

"Special Agent Vasquez told me all about her new boyfriend. He seems like *such* a positive influence. The uniformed officer we sent to pick them up said he found Carly on her knees in front of him at the movie theater."

Ben amended his initial impression of Grant. The man wasn't trying to goad him into talking; he was trying to goad him into fighting. "You lie," he growled, seconds from exploding across the table.

When a quick, efficient knock sounded at the door, they both turned to look.

Nathan poked his head in. His dark hair was attractively windblown, his eyes smoldering with intensity. "What'd I miss?"

Carly didn't have a chance to get her panties back from James before the police officer escorted her from the theater, claiming there had been a family emergency.

Over her shoulder, she pleaded with James to follow them, but she wasn't sure he had. When he saw the man in uniform, he'd practically climbed the curtains in his haste to get away. He seemed surprised to discover the policeman was there for her, not him.

Now she was in a room with another cop, a hunky FBI agent named Mitchell. He wanted to know about all the kinky stuff Lisette had been into. Carly didn't care if he had awesome biceps, she wasn't saying shit.

"I want to call my dad," she said, affecting a bored tone. "You can't keep me here without his consent."

"You aren't being charged with anything, Carly," Mitchell said amiably. "It's perfectly legal for us to ask you a few questions. Lisette's parents would thank you for cooperating."

Carly rolled her eyes. "Look, I don't know where she is, okay? I haven't seen her in a week."

"Did she say where she was going when you talked to her last? Tell you she was meeting someone? A boyfriend, maybe?"

She counted off her responses on her fingertips. "No, no, and I don't know. She didn't really have boyfriends, she had targets."

His eyebrows lifted. "Targets?"

"That's what she called them. Boys she liked. She'd zero in on one, screw him for a while, and move on."

"Like a game? Did you play, too?"

She shot him a disgusted look. "No."

"She was your best friend, right?"

"Yeah. Was. Past tense."

"Why is that?"

Carly tugged on the frayed hem of her short skirt, uncomfortably aware that she was wearing nothing beneath it. She'd only meant to tease James, not go all Britney Spears in public. "I got tired of her sleazy ways, I guess."

"Did she target the wrong guy? Your boyfriend, maybe?"

She gave him a cold smile. "No."

"Your dad?"

Carly felt her face freeze.

"How long have they been sleeping together?"

She tossed her long hair over her shoulder. "They

aren't sleeping together, asshole. I want to call my uncle Nathan. He's a lawyer."

Mitchell leaned forward. "Carly, do you remember a bracelet your mother used to wear? It said, 'To Olivia. Love, Ben. Forever.' "

She shook her head, but her eyes filled up with telltale tears.

"We found Lisette this morning."

"Is she okay?" she whispered, dreading the answer.

"No. She's dead."

Her heart sank. "What happened to her?"

"That's what we're trying to find out."

She moistened her lips, her throat so dry she wasn't sure she could get the words out. "Did she have my mom's bracelet?"

Mitchell posed a question of his own. "Did your father give it to her?"

Her protective instinct took over. "He wouldn't have given her the time of day," she returned hotly. "If she had it, it's because she found it somehow, or stole it from his room that night—"

"She was in his room? The night she disappeared?"

Carly clamped her mouth shut. Wrapping her arms around her middle, she stared down at the surface of the table until her vision blurred.

"Did your father and Lisette have an argument, Carly? Did you hear any strange noises? Sounds of a struggle?"

She blinked away the tears, refusing to speak.

"What about your mom and dad? Did they argue a lot?"

Her jaw clenched and her voice went hard: "I'd rather die than say anything bad about my dad. He would never hurt my mom. Never." She glared at him from across the table, taking in a ragged breath. "I want to talk to my uncle. I know you can't keep me here. You can't make me say another word."

James waited for Carly in the lobby at the police station, drumming his fingertips against his jeans-clad thigh, too intimidated to ask anyone where she was.

As Arlen would say, he was as nervous as a long-tailed cat in a room full of rocking chairs. Any minute, he expected a uniform to slap on the cuffs, arresting him for having his girlfriend in a compromising position in a public place.

Or any number of other, unreported transgressions.

James had witnessed a thousand illegal activities at Stephen's house, and he was no lily-white innocent himself. He'd been stealing a pint of whisky for Arlen from the booze aisle at Neptune Grocery every Saturday night for the past five years. It was more than luck that he'd never been caught. It was a freaking miracle.

He started sweating. Hell, they probably had a poster with his face on it around here somewhere. They were definitely looking for the anonymous tipster who left a message about Lisette. What if Summer had already turned him in?

Surreptitiously, he rose to his feet, holding on to the armrest of the chair for balance. Putting one foot in front of the other, he counted the steps to the door, his ears ringing in anticipation of someone saying, *Hey you! Get back here.*

He was only inches from freedom when he heard a voice behind him. "James!"

It was Carly. He froze, weighing his options. Bolting outside was pretty tempting. But playing it cool in front of Carly outranked all.

He turned to see her beautiful, troubled face. A beefy cop had his hand clamped around her upper arm. Uh-oh.

She struggled against the unwanted restraint. "This is my boyfriend. Get off me."

The cop squinted at James, sizing him up and probably finding him lacking. James gulped under the examination.

The officer nodded and released her. "Ma'am," he said in a polite voice, and ambled away.

Carly looked around the lobby uneasily. She seemed as nervous around the law as he was, if such a thing were possible. "I have to talk to you outside," she said, grabbing his arm and leading him away.

"Thank God," he replied, hurrying along beside her.

Outside in the parking lot, she stopped him, her face pale, eyes wide with panic. "They think my dad killed Lisette."

His stomach dropped. "What?"

"Lisette's been missing since last Friday, when she

stayed over at my house. Now she's dead and my dad is in deep shit."

James thought of all the secrets he'd been keeping. Some had been building his entire life. Others had piled up more recently. Arlen's abuse of women and children. Lisette's body. Stephen's drugs. Summer's job. Seven minutes in heaven. A lifetime in hell.

"Fuck," he said, sitting down on the curb, putting his face in his hands. "Fuck," he repeated, knowing what he had to do.

Carly stamped her foot. "I need your support here, James. I need someone to be strong, because I'm feeling really weak."

James stood up immediately, taking her in his arms and shielding her with his body, protecting her. "I'm here. I'll make it better. I promise."

While they stood there together, drawing strength from each other, a scruffy-looking young man came out of the lobby. His T-shirt was faded and his jeans were torn. Barely glancing at them, he lit up a cigarette and took a deep drag, seeking as much solace in that lonely action as Carly and James had in their embrace.

"That's my brother," James said, hardly recognizing him in the surreal situation. Waving to get his attention, he watched Stephen come forward, a puzzled expression on his haggard face.

James was intensely aware of Carly's slender arms around his neck, the proximity of her body, the smell of her shampoo. He knew how it looked to Stephen, and felt a measure of regret that he hadn't trusted his brother enough to take him into his confidence.

In addition to confusion, Stephen's face registered a mixture of emotions James didn't understand. One was relief. "Damn, man, where have you been?" he asked, glancing at Carly. "You had me worried half to death."

James felt Carly's hands drop away from him.

Stephen gave him a canny look. "This your girlfriend?"

"I'm Carly," she said, flashing a thousand-watt smile.

Stephen blinked, momentarily blinded by her beauty. Then he recovered. "Stephen," he said, shaking her hand. "No wonder you've been hiding out," he added, arching a brow at James. "I would be, too, if I had such a pretty lady to hide out with."

James shuffled his feet, uncomfortable with the deception.

"I have to go back inside and wait for my dad," Carly said, affecting a sulky pout. She didn't seem very pleased that he hadn't mentioned her to Stephen.

"I'll be a few minutes," James replied. He needed to talk with his brother about things he didn't want Carly to overhear.

She turned to leave and then halted, moistening her lips. "James?"

"Yeah?"

"Can I have my panties back now?"

His face grew hot. He fumbled in his pocket, came up with them, and pressed the tiny purple bundle in her hand.

She smiled and gave him a quick kiss before she walked away. Both brothers watched her go, admiring her cute little backside all the more for knowing it was bare underneath a scant few inches of well-worn denim.

When she was out of hearing range, Stephen whistled long and low, clapping James on the back. "Oh my God, bro! How in the hell did you hook up with that?"

"I don't know," he said, for it was glaringly obvious she was way out of his league. "But it's not what you think. She's a nice girl."

Stephen took a deep drag on his cigarette. "Whatever you say, dude."

James was adamant. "I mean it. I don't want you to get the wrong idea about her."

Stephen studied Carly's retreating form speculatively. James knew he saw only what she wanted him to see, a sultry façade, but Stephen shrugged, not really caring one way or another. Even before Rhoda and drugs screwed him up, Stephen had been wary of women. He liked looking at them, but that was about it.

"And whatever you do, don't say anything to Dad."

Stephen sobered, seeming to understand the reason for James' secrecy. "Well, James, that's what I've got to talk to you about," he said, dark blue eyes glinting in the sun. "Dad's dead."

When Carly emerged from the ladies' room, Ben was waiting for her. He clamped his hand around her upper arm, using more pressure than was necessary.

"You're in big trouble, young lady," he grated, leading her out the double glass doors.

"Why? I didn't tell them anything."

He paused, appalled that his sixteen-year-old daughter had lied to the police. Or, just as he had, simply withheld information. "You talked to them?"

Her perfectly arched brows drew together. "Not really. They asked about Mom's bracelet."

Anxiety coursed through him. Why had he believed that motherfucker Grant? Of course they were happy to release Carly—after they were finished grilling her.

She worried at her lower lip. "I said maybe Lisette stole it from your room."

"Why would you say that?"

Her pretty face crumpled. "I don't know!"

"You knew she came into my room that night?"

Carly covered her ears with her hands. "No! I don't want to know, okay?"

Ben looked around the parking lot uneasily. James and an older boy were standing by a tree-lined median, and for once, Carly's boyfriend was a welcome distraction. "We have to talk about this, but now is not the time. And here is definitely not the place." He nodded toward James. "What's up with them?"

"That's James' brother, Stephen," she said miserably. "I guess they're having a family crisis of their own."

Ben grunted, feeling less than generous toward James. "Say good-bye. We're leaving." When she started to comply, dragging her feet, he added, "And tell James you won't be seeing him for a while. You're grounded."

She whirled around. "What for?"

"For what you got caught doing in the movie theater."

Carly's face flushed pink. "They're fucking liars, Dad."

"Yeah, right. Tell your boyfriend bye-bye."

She crossed her arms over her chest. "No."

Ben saw red. "No?"

"I wasn't doing anything! Especially compared to what you did upstairs with Summer." Her voice lowered to a hiss. "And Lisette!"

Fueled by a dangerous mix of fury and shame, Ben dragged Carly over to where James and Stephen were talking quietly underneath a gorgeously blooming jacaranda. "What were you doing to my daughter in the movie theater, you ballsy little white-trash bastard?"

James blanched against the sudden onslaught. He looked from Ben to Carly. "Why don't you take your hands off her? Can't you see you're hurting her?"

Ben released her abruptly. The red marks on her skin were a testament to his loss of control, and having a boy half his age call him on it did not improve his mood. He stepped up to James, towering over him. "Start talking, before I put my hands on you."

Stephen inched closer, trying to play mediator. "Sir, my brother was just telling me what a nice girl your daughter is—"

"Shut up!" James and Ben said in unison.

Carly covered her face with her hands and wailed.

"I'm not a bastard," James said. "I might be trash, but I'm not a bastard. My parents were married. Unlike you and Carly's mother when she was born."

The cigarette fell, forgotten, from Stephen's be-whiskered mouth.

Ben felt the heat of rage suffuse his face. "Are you calling my daughter a bastard?" he asked in a low voice.

James sent Carly an apology with his eyes. "No, sir. I'm just letting you know I don't care for that label."

"Let me tell you what I don't care for, James. Last night you said you had good intentions. Today, some asshole cop tells me my sixteen-year-old daughter was going down on you in the movie theater!"

It was James' turn to flush. "No. That didn't happen. She's never done anything like that."

"I told you, Dad."

Ben looked from one solemn young face to the other. Carly had lied to him on numerous occasions, and he trusted James about as far as he could throw him, which was probably at least ten feet, in his current state of mind.

"We were just kissing," James said. "She was sitting on my lap, and I told her to get up because I was getting...uncomfortable. She thought she'd hurt me, because she's so innocent she didn't understand."

James was staring at Ben, honest and steely-eyed. Carly was sitting on the curb, shaking with mortification. Stephen, having located his cigarette, was smoking quietly, analyzing Ben through dark blue eyes identical to James'.

Ben was the only real adult present, but damned if he felt like one. Sometimes this responsible parenting crap was a real pain in the ass. "Why did they say you were on your knees?" he asked Carly.

She looked up. "He put a cup of soda in his lap. I thought I'd squashed something, and he had to ice it. I was only trying to help."

Stephen laughed softly, and that sound echoed across the quiet corner of the parking lot. Three pairs of eyes glared at him.

Ben rubbed a hand down his face, feeling like the biggest idiot in the world, because he actually believed their story. James had probably edited a few details, for Carly's sake, but Ben couldn't fault him for it. Nor did he fool himself into thinking that youthful lust wouldn't win out eventually over restraint. "You two are going to be the death of me," he said with a sigh. "I thought Carly was accident-prone enough on her own."

"Is Nathan here?" James asked.

"He's inside, filing some paperwork. Why?"

"I was wondering if I could borrow him. I could use a lawyer."

The tension that had eased from Ben's shoulders returned, with reinforcements. "You in some kind of trouble?"

James eyed Ben warily. "Maybe. I guess they think I killed my dad."

# CHAPTER 17

After requesting that the slab in the Matthews' backyard be excavated, and turning in Olivia Fortune's bracelet to Grant, Sonny had a sit-down with Paula DeGrassi, bringing her up to speed on the federal case.

Ben and Carly had been released pending further investigation. With the new evidence linking Arlen Matthews to the SoCal murders, and to Olivia Fortune's death, Grant had decided to focus their efforts on him. He and Mitchell went to the Matthews residence to oversee the excavation.

Sonny had no choice but to divulge the truth about James, explaining that he had made the Christmas Eve phone call reporting Lisette's body.

She knew better than to air her concerns that the evidence against Arlen had been planted, reveal the details of their unfortunate biological connection, or confess that she may have been responsible for his death.

If James didn't tell either, the point would be moot. DeGrassi said she'd been aware of Arlen Matthews for years. Although none of the prostitutes he'd beaten up had pressed charges, he had an incredibly violent reputation. Any number of wronged women could have done the world a favor and taken him out.

Sonny was weaving a fine web of deception, one that might wrap her up and suffocate her, but she could see no other alternative. Revealing more at this juncture would only draw suspicion to Ben, James, or herself.

Complicating matters, Nathan Fortune had agreed to represent James. Sonny wasn't looking forward to meeting him across the interrogation table, considering what Ben had just gone through because of her.

She followed DeGrassi down the hall, every nerve in her body on edge.

In the interview room, Nathan was sitting next to James, looking windswept and elegant in navy trousers and a cream-colored sweater with maroon pinstripes. He could have just stepped off the pages of a cologne ad with a nautical theme.

"Ladies," he said pleasantly.

DeGrassi introduced herself to James, who shook her hand in sullen silence. Sonny studied him as she took her seat. He didn't look happy to see her.

Neither did Nathan. She supposed he didn't care for liars infiltrating his family's ranks. "Is my client under suspicion of committing a crime?" he asked.

"At this time we have no charges pending against him," DeGrassi hedged.

"Why is he here?"

"His father is a suspect in the murder of Lisette Bruebaker."

Nathan glanced at James, whose face registered neither relief nor surprise. Even so, the blank expression was telling. It was unusual for a seventeen-year-old boy to wear such an impenetrable mask. With a jerk of his chin, James consented to the interview.

"Did you see your father last night?"

He shifted in his chair. "Sure."

"What time?"

"Around midnight."

"Had he been drinking heavily?"

"As always."

"Did anything unusual happen?"

His blue eyes cut to Sonny and back. "Like what?"

"Late-night visitors...scuffles...accidents?"

Sonny couldn't help it. She closed her eyes and held her breath, waiting to be outed.

"No," James said. "When I left, he was asleep."

Relief washed over her, along with a measure of shame. She was amazed that he would cover for her, appalled that she would let him.

DeGrassi asked about Lisette, and in this, James told the truth. He described every detail of the morning her body was caught in the fishing net, omitting nothing, from his regurgitated Fruit Loops to his father's callous treatment of the remains. If anyone had been in doubt about what kind of man Arlen Matthews was, they weren't any longer.

"When did you last see Lisette alive?" DeGrassi asked.

"A few weeks ago, she was at my brother's."

"What happened?"

"We talked," he said shortly, fooling no one.

"You had sex?" DeGrassi interpreted.

"Just oral," he muttered.

"She performed oral sex on you? Then what?"

He shrugged. "Then nothing."

"Did you get her phone number? Arrange to meet again?"

"No. It was a one-time thing."

DeGrassi was speculative. "How do you know she felt the same way?"

Color stained his cheekbones. "She was kind of mad at me when she left. I said 'Carly' when I, uh— at the wrong moment."

"Who's Carly?"

"My girlfriend."

DeGrassi didn't mince words. "You said her name when you ejaculated into Lisette Bruebaker's mouth?"

James put a shaky hand over his face. "Yeah," he said, almost inaudibly. He glanced at Nathan. "This was before I started dating Carly, but Lisette knew I liked her. I think that's why she did...what she did. Anyway, when she left, she said, 'I'll tell Carly you said hi.' So she was threatening me, I guess, saying she was going to tell Carly about it, to embarrass me."

DeGrassi's brows lifted. "Did she?"

"Probably not. Carly didn't even know I existed back then. It wouldn't have meant anything to her."

"Did your father know about you and Lisette?"

"No. Why would he?"

"This incident occurred at your brother's house, correct?"

He followed her logic. "Yeah, but not in front of anyone. We were in the closet. Stephen didn't know, either."

"Do you meet a lot of girls at Stephen's?"

"Some," he admitted. "But it's not what you think. Stephen's girlfriend teases me. My dad called me queer all the time. I felt pressure, you know? To prove myself. Act like a man."

"Is that how you felt in the closet with Lisette? Like a man?"

"No. I felt like a jerk. That's why I didn't tell anyone."

DeGrassi studied his handsome face. "Do you like boys, too, James?"

James' eyes darkened. "No." He leaned back in his chair, distancing himself from the very idea. "Hell, no." As an afterthought, he turned to Nathan, aware that his attitude had been insulting. "No offense."

"None taken," Nathan replied amiably.

"Why do you think your dad accused you of that?"

James stared at the wall behind her head. "Maybe he wished I was queer, so he'd have an excuse to beat me up." He let out a harsh laugh. "Like he needed an excuse."

"He physically abused you?"

"Every day," he said, meeting her eyes.

"Sexually?"

James looked at Sonny. Her heart broke for him, but she couldn't offer him any words of comfort. DeGrassi had threatened her with bodily harm if she interfered. "He didn't touch me or anything like that. But he did other stuff that I would call sexual abuse."

"Like what?"

James studied his hands. "He made me watch, when he was with prostitutes. He made me partici- pate."

"He made you participate in sex with them?"

"No," he replied with a shudder. "I couldn't. He made me tie them up. I guess he thought that if I helped, I was just as guilty as he was."

"Tying up a woman for sex, if she consents, isn't a crime."

"Yeah, well, what he did to them should be, if it isn't." He put his head in his hands, humiliated to voice his father's atrocities.

"James, I know this is difficult for you," DeGrassi said, and gave him a moment. Then she asked, "Are you ready to continue?" When he nodded, DeGrassi brought out the photos of the previous victims. "Did your father ever have contact with these girls?"

James examined them carefully. "Not that I know of."

"Did you see any of them at Stephen's house?"

He shook his head. "No."

"What about Carly's mom? Did your dad ever meet her?"

"No. Our families didn't exactly travel in the same social circles."

"Are you sure you haven't seen the others?"

DeGrassi persisted. "Would you remember them if you had?"

"Yeah. Why wouldn't I?"

DeGrassi leveled with him. "We know what goes on at your brother's house. You said you meet girls there. Lisette was known to party. Do you like to party, too?"

He handed back the photos. "Are you asking if I do drugs? If I drink?"

She nodded.

"I've tried some stuff," he said, looking away again, out into space. No one in the room was surprised by that admission. A lot of troubled teenagers experimented with drugs and alcohol. Children of abusers were twice as likely to become addicts themselves. "But I found out something pretty quick."

"What's that?"

His gaze met hers, and in that moment, Sonny was convinced that he was speaking as a man, not a boy. "I duck blows a lot easier when I'm sober."

Sonny trudged up the steps to her apartment, in dire need of a long, hot shower. James' words had made an indelible impression on her, and the ugly crime scene had left her feeling as though an invisible film of smut coated her entire body.

Like most little girls without daddies, Sonora Vasquez had grown up believing her father was a grand champion, a golden hero, or a fairy tale prince.

Practicality came with age, but as a child, she'd often used fantasy as an escape. Later she would realize that her father was probably like the rest of Anita's loser boyfriends, a drug addict, an alcoholic, or a criminal. Even so, she'd imagined dozens of more palatable scenarios. Sometimes she dreamed he was a handsome Naval officer who'd never been aware of his daughter's existence. Other times, she would pretend he was a firefighter, an international businessman, or a jet pilot.

To be confronted with the monster who'd been her biological father was difficult. To be forced to explain his deviancies to strangers, to have participated in them—that was horrific. Sonny's heart ached for James, for the years he'd suffered under Arlen's rule.

There was probably no hope of salvaging any kind of relationship with either of her half-brothers or with Ben. She'd met them under false pretenses, had lied to, manipulated, and used them to suit her purposes.

Sonny felt as though she'd been robbed of the brothers she'd never known, the father she'd rather not have known, and the man she'd never known she wanted, all in one fell swoop.

Not only that, her career, the stronghold of her world, was on the rocks. She'd wanted to work for the FBI her entire life. In her favorite fantasy, her father had been a secret agent. Leland Grant had filled that missing piece of her heart quite nicely.

It would be a shame if she had to turn in her resignation when this assignment wrapped.

She put the key in the lock and opened the door, discarding items of clothing in her usual haphazard fashion as she made her way to the bedroom, removing her gun holster once she was there and placing it in her underwear drawer.

She stayed in the shower too long, plagued by recollections of the day and memories from the past. She felt Ben's strong hands on her body and Grant's disappointed gaze on her face, Mitchell's knuckles grazing her cheek and her stepfather's sweaty palm covering her mouth.

No amount of water could wash away her shame.

After she dried off, she dragged on her oldest pair of sweats and curled up in the dark atop the bed, exhausted, knowing sleep was beyond her reach. When the doorbell rang, she sat up and stared into the hallway, listening to the sound of traffic on the busy street below her living room window and watching shadows move across the wall.

She got up and walked to the door without thinking, without blinking, without turning on any interior lights.

Of course it was Ben. Grant would have called first.

"Come in," she murmured, making a shaky gesture with one hand.

He stepped inside and she closed the door behind him. They stood there in the stifling near-dark, neither of them saying a word.

"Wait here," she said, leaving him standing there. In the bedroom, she flipped on the light switch and threw open her underwear drawer. There among bits of cotton and lace, the leather of her shoulder holster, and a deadly glint of steel, she found the only piece of jewelry ever given to her by a man. Clutching it to her chest, she returned to the living room, back to Ben.

Taking him by the hand, she placed the necklace in the middle of his upturned palm.

"I didn't come for this," he said, jerking his hand away as soon as he realized what she was doing. In the muted light coming in from the doorway, he looked much the same as the first time she'd seen him: disturbingly handsome and irresistibly troubled, the wounded soul every woman longed to heal.

"Keep it," she said, crossing her arms over her chest.

After a moment's hesitation, he shoved the necklace into the front pocket of his jeans. "I guess I'm lucky it hasn't turned up at a crime scene with my fingerprints on it."

Considering the events of the past day, the accusation rocked her back on her heels. "Are you implying that I've planted evidence?"

"Of course not," he said, his eyes hard. "You'd never do anything unethical."

The sarcasm was impossible to miss. She'd anticipated his anger, but she hadn't expected his words to hurt so much. "I didn't put Lisette's hair in your bed, Ben."

"No," he agreed. "You did a lot of other things in my bed."

So that's how it was going to be. Fine. She clamped her mouth shut, determined to let him have his say. Sonny knew he hadn't come here to profess his undying love, and she could take whatever insults he dished out.

"You were watching me from the beginning, weren't you? You'd been following me. And Carly."

She stared down at her bare feet, refusing to look at him.

"You stood by while my daughter threw herself into the ocean. She could have drowned."

Her head shot up. "I didn't know what she was doing until it was too late to stop her. I risked my life—"

"You needed an in," he fired back. "You used her to get to me."

"No," she said. "That's not why I went in after her."

"Every move you made was calculated," he countered. "You knew I'd be more interested if you played hard to get. After so many years of surf groupies throwing themselves at me, you knew I wouldn't be able to resist your 'don't touch me there' act. Somehow you knew I'd love it if you pretended you were afraid to fuck."

"Ben—"

"Why were you watching me?" he interrupted, refusing to listen to any excuses. "How could I have been a suspect before Lisette went missing?"

After a moment's hesitation, she said, "Darrius O'Shea left a suicide note recanting his confession. The details weren't made available to the press."

Shock and pain flashed in his eyes as he processed that information. Being a suspect in Lisette's murder was bad, but being accused of killing his own wife was the ultimate insult. "I should have known what you were up to when you asked about Olivia," he said in a low growl. "You weren't jealous, or curious, or concerned. You weren't mad about what happened with Lisette. You were just investigating."

She couldn't argue with that.

"Was everything you said a lie?"

It wasn't easy, but she looked him straight in the eye and said, "Yes."

His face darkened with fury. "I guess that figures. For a woman who's terrified of cock, you couldn't seem to get enough of mine."

Resentment burned through her, heating her cheeks. "Don't flatter yourself, Ben. Getting close to you was part of my job."

He dropped his gaze to her lips. "Yeah, and you're so good at what you do. Did Grant get off on hearing about your undercover activities? I'll bet you gave him a blow by blow."

She drew back her arm and slapped him across the face. It was an instinctual act, pure fury, no fear, worlds apart from the times she'd lashed out at him before.

It still packed enough heat to snap his head to the side.

He touched his hand to his cheek then looked at his fingertips, almost as if he expected to see blood there. "What's the matter, Summer? I thought you liked being a federal whore."

"Sonny," she whispered, her palm stinging from the impact.

He looked around the dark room in confusion.

"My real name isn't Summer," she explained. "It's Sonny."

For some reason, that admission drove him over

the edge. In an unconscious imitation of the first time he tried to kiss her, he came forward, framing her chin with his hand and trapping her body against the wall. "I don't give a damn what your real name is. Do you think I'd believe anything that comes out of your lying mouth?"

The instant he said "mouth," she became aware of his hot gaze focused there, his large hand cupping her chin, his thumb pressing into her cheek. His body was hard and unyielding against hers, his chest rising and falling with every furious breath.

This time, it was he who closed the distance between them, lowering his mouth to hers. His kiss was rough and angry, meant to punish, not to please, but she welcomed it. She relished it. Slipping her arms around his neck and her tongue into his mouth, she moaned, digging her fingernails into his shoulders and begging for more.

Groaning, he moved his hands down to her bottom and lifted her up, fitting his erection into the notch of her thighs and pressing her back to the wall. She gasped, wrapping her legs around his waist as he plundered her mouth, kissing her hotly, hungrily, endlessly, possessing her so thoroughly she wanted to weep with pleasure.

It was too much and not enough. She tilted her hips forward, stroking herself along the ridge of his erection. Between her legs, she was already hot and swollen, pulsing with sensation. He shoved his hands into her sweatpants, making a low growl of satisfaction when he found her naked bottom.

They were both wearing too many clothes. He

stripped off her sweats, baring her from the waist down, and she tugged at his T-shirt, seeking heat against heat, skin against skin.

He tore his mouth from hers to yank his shirt over his head. "Tell me now if you don't want this."

In response, she removed her sweatshirt and tossed it aside.

His gaze raked over her nude form, lingered on the points of her breasts and the triangle of curls at the apex of her thighs. When he moistened his lips, she had to stifle the urge to put her hand between her legs, not to cover herself but to ease her ache.

Swallowing visibly, he jerked the buttons from the holes at the fly of his jeans, freeing his straining erection. While she watched, breathless with anticipation, he took a condom from his pocket and sheathed himself quickly.

"Tell me to stop," he warned, positioning her against the wall again.

"No," she said, all but begging him to come into her.

Still he waited, letting her feel the blunt tip of his erection at the cleft of her sex. "What do you want?"

She wrapped her legs around him. "You. In me."

Stalling no more, he plunged forward, slamming her back into the wall and impaling her on his thick, hard length. She was so wet he penetrated her easily, burying himself deep. With a strangled groan, he slid his hand over her bottom, touching the place their bodies were joined, tracing her with his fingertips.

"You feel so . . ." He sucked in a sharp breath and gritted his teeth, biting back the words he wanted to say. Moving his hands to her hips, he held her in place for his thrusts, withdrawing as far as he dared and driving back into her, rocking her against the wall, filling her so completely she thought she'd never be empty again.

Why did he have to be so amazing? With Ben, even a fast bang against the wall was a transcendent experience. It should have been hard and angry and impersonal. It wasn't. He was hard, all right, but sometime after they'd started kissing, he'd stopped being so angry, and the way he touched her was far from impersonal.

He paused, pinning her to the wall with the weight of his body and splaying his hands over her rib cage, framing her breasts. His roughened breath fanned her throat, sending shivers down her spine, and her nipples tingled with awareness.

The light coming in from the doorway fell upon both of them dispassionately, but the distorted glow from the street below her apartment painted streaks of color across her naked torso. Red hot brake lights washed over her skin.

She squirmed and tightened her legs around him, urging him on, so he dipped his head low and took the tip of her breast into his mouth, tugging gently. When she cried out, he picked up the rhythm, thrusting hard, his hands on her hips and his mouth on her breasts, assaulting her with the most exquisite friction and hot, delicious suction.

She was close, so close, but just before she exploded, he slowed, lifting his mouth from her breasts and tracing the line of her collarbone with his tongue.

"Are you going to tell me you love me again when you come?"

At first, the meaning of his words failed to register. She was so filled with him, caught up in sensation, teetering on the edge of climax, that she almost nodded, going along with anything he said. Love. Come. Yes.

Wait...what?

Her eyes flew open. His face was a handsome mask, devoid of emotion. Clearly, he was still angry with her, and intent on taking a measure of revenge by proving his mastery over her body. "You bastard," she panted. "I was faking."

He slid his hand between them, strumming his fingertips over her clitoris. "Like you're faking now?"

"Yes," she moaned, throwing her head back and biting down on her bottom lip, refusing to cry out his name as the orgasm rocketed through her. She gripped his shoulders, making crescents with her fingernails and feeling her inner muscles convulse around him as she came and came and came.

She was vaguely aware of him coming, too, pumping his hips and grinding into her, seeking the deepest possible penetration on his last, most powerful thrust. Then it was over, and he withdrew from her abruptly. Letting her slide down the wall, he stumbled away from her to dispose of the condom before she was steady on her feet.

Like a wet rag, she sank to the carpet amidst their discarded clothes.

He came back from the bathroom with his pants buttoned and his expression flat, appearing as cool and unruffled as if he'd just been discussing the weather forecast instead of fucking her against the wall.

Picking up his T-shirt and pulling it over his head, he said, "Give Grant my best," as he walked out the door.

# CHAPTER 18

When Ben got home, Carly and James were sitting at opposite ends of the couch, pretending to watch TV. If Carly's hair hadn't been mussed and James didn't have a pillow over his lap, Ben still wouldn't have bought it.

"Say good night, Carly," he said on his way to the den.

"That's what I was doing, Dad."

"Do it with words this time."

The den was a large room beyond the kitchen, in a dark, seldom-visited corner of the house. It was a miscellaneous space, part office, part storage room. Carly sometimes used the desk and computer for school projects, but she preferred her laptop and the comfort of her own room. The den also housed a collection of surfboards, trophies, and memorabilia. There were too many magazine articles and photo spreads to display, but Ben had framed a few classics, some of the most reckless moments of his life, caught forever, like death wishes frozen in time.

For all of those reasons, and more, the room was rarely used.

Nathan turned from the computer as Ben walked in. "Find out anything?"

Ben muttered a noncommittal reply and sank into the only other chair in the room, a black leather chaise lounge that looked like it belonged in a psychiatrist's office.

"Did she let you in?"

"Yeah."

"And?"

Groaning, Ben lay back and threw an arm over his face, shielding his eyes.

"You just had sex with her, didn't you?" Nathan's tone was scolding, and saturated with prurient interest. "How was it?"

Ben lifted his arm and quirked a puzzled brow.

"What?" Nathan asked innocently. "I'm gay, not dead."

"I know," he said, leaning back again. "It's just that you've never asked about stuff like that before."

Nathan pursed his lips together. "I wasn't curious about the bimbos you couldn't seem to get enough of in the nineties. And Olivia was your wife, so that was sort of off-limits, as far as casual discussion was concerned. But this is different. Special Agent Vasquez is pure intrigue."

"Not anymore," Ben lied.

"So dish details," Nathan prodded, not believing

him for a moment. "Did she handcuff you to the head-board?"

Ben gave him a wry smile. "You have a wild imagination."

"And you are ruining my tawdry perception of heterosexual relations," Nathan complained, smiling in return.

"No handcuffs," he said shortly, "but it was good." After finding out she'd been playing him from the beginning, Ben would have said she was as cold as ice. What they'd just done together proved the opposite was true.

If she'd been any hotter, they'd both have gone up in flames.

"What did you find out?" Ben asked, changing the subject.

Nathan turned to face the computer. "Ms. Vasquez has been on the FBI payroll for the past five years. She earned a degree in Criminal Justice and has attended the San Diego Police Academy, as well as the FBI Academy in Virginia."

Ben grunted, unsurprised to discover that she was well educated and expertly trained.

"You know that other name you gave me, Everett Moore?"

"Yeah. He doesn't exist, right?"

"Wrong. I had to bypass a few firewalls, but I found him in a criminal informational database for LA County Jail. About ten years ago he was doing time for rape. The underage victim is unlisted, of course."

Ben felt a strange hollowness spread through his chest.

"He was stabbed to death by a guy named Rodrigo Garcia."

"Garcia. Not Vasquez."

Nathan nodded. "I poked around in his file, too. Garcia is a model inmate at Santee Lakes Correctional Facility. His father is deceased, some Mexican national named Ramón Garcia, but his mother lives in East San Diego. Her name is Anita Vasquez."

Ben closed his eyes, hating her for lying to him about some things and telling the truth about others.

"Rodrigo Garcia has one sister, six years his junior. Sonora Mariela Vasquez."

"Sonny," he murmured, tasting the name on his lips.

Nathan turned to face him. "Hmm?"

"She goes by Sonny."

His brother gaped at him incredulously. "You're in love with her."

"Please," he scoffed, refusing to entertain such a ridiculous notion.

"It's written all over your face."

"That's not love, it's satisfaction," Ben said. "I just banged the hell out of her." Never mind that he'd never felt less satisfied. The sex had been phenomenal, but staying there and doing it again, going slow, taking his time... that would have been better.

"Whatever you say," Nathan chuckled, logging off.

"Tell me what happened with James."

"You know I can't."

"Nathan," he warned, doing a conscious imitation of their father, "this is my daughter we're talking about."

"No it isn't," Nathan replied, annoyed with Ben's intimidation tactics. "We're talking about a teenaged boy, and my client, a person to whom I have a legal and ethical obligation."

Ben wanted to press further, but knew his brother well enough not to bother. "Should I be worried?"

Nathan's smooth brow wrinkled. "Carly thinks she's in love with a kid whose father just turned up dead. Her best friend was also murdered, consequently. Yes, you should definitely be worried."

"You know what I mean."

"Carly is my niece, Ben. If she were in danger from James, don't you think I'd tell you?"

Ben rubbed a hand over his tired face. "What the hell am I supposed to do with him? Adopt him? Kick him out on the street? Send him to his brother's?"

"No. Don't send him there."

"Why not?"

"He's safer here. Trust me."

If anyone had ever told Ben that he'd be allowing his sixteen-year-old daughter's boyfriend to spend the night under his roof, even once, he'd have kicked their ass on principle. "And what about Carly?" he asked. "Where will she be safe?"

When her dad poked his head in to check on her, Carly pretended to be asleep. She made a little snuffling noise and turned her head to one side, letting her hair cascade across the pillow.

He shut the door quietly and moved on, walking down the hall to his own room.

She wanted to get up and sneak downstairs immediately, but she waited in the silent dark of her bedroom, ticking off endless minutes, her heart pounding with anticipation. When the walls seemed like they were closing in on her, threatening to suffocate her, she slipped out from beneath the covers and tiptoed across the hardwood floor.

At her bedroom door, she hesitated. The hallway was quiet and there was no sliver of light beneath her father's door. When he was awake, he checked in on her often, but when he wasn't, he slept like a log. She remembered climbing into her parents' bed one Christmas morning and jumping on the mattress, having a pillow fight with her mom, and opening several presents while her dad snored on.

She snuck across the hall and down the carpeted stairway, moving silently in her bare feet, feeling the delicious rush of blood through her veins. In the living room, she peeked over the edge of the couch to make sure James was sleeping. He was on his stomach, face making a dent in the soft feather pillow, one hand shoved down the front of his pants.

She smiled sadly, resisting the urge to ruffle his hair.

Earlier, when she'd been afraid James would be arrested for murder, she'd told him she loved him. She'd just blurted it out, right in front of everyone. The look on his face was one of total disbelief, as if he couldn't fathom why she would say such a thing.

It brought tears to her eyes, just thinking about it.

Being with James made her feel better, and hearing him tell her he loved her back warmed her insides, but she'd never been good about handling her emotions. Visions of Lisette's murder and her mother's bracelet made her head swim. Worrying about her dad, and James, and everything...

She just couldn't take it anymore.

Moving past the living room couch, she padded into the kitchen and felt her way down the black granite countertop as her eyes adjusted to the dark night. The butcher block was there in the corner, knife handles offering themselves up like saving graces.

Letting out the breath she'd been holding, she wrapped her hand around one and pulled, hearing it slide from its sheath with a soft *snick*.

The blade gleamed in the moonlight.

Pulse racing, she ducked into the guest bath, pulled the door closed, and turned on the light. In her reflection, her eyes were huge and her hair was wild. She looked like a deranged mental patient, fresh from the asylum.

Stifling a delirious giggle, she lowered herself to the bathroom floor and pulled her extra-large T-shirt over her head. Clad only in bikini panties, she stared down at her skinny body, looking for the best place to cut.

Everyone told her she was pretty. Carly didn't see what they saw. She was too tall and too thin, with flyaway hair and bones sticking out all over the place, her haughty attitude masking a thousand insecurities.

Her mother had been beautiful. She'd also been curvy and womanly, with an awesome pair of boobs and a butt her dad couldn't keep his hands off.

Carly looked down at her naked chest. She had cut herself here because it was one of the only places she had extra flesh. It also felt safer to nick this secret place, where no one would ever look, not even her dad.

Now that James had touched her breasts, and told her how much he liked them, she felt weird about cutting herself there. He would surely find out.

Where else could she do it? What places did boys not want to look, or try to touch? She frowned down at herself, experiencing a flurry of indecision. If she didn't make a cut, she'd have a long night to look forward to, awake and fraught with anxiety.

Raising the knife, she brought the blade toward her upper arm. It was winter, she rationalized, and she wouldn't be wearing any tank tops for a while.

The sharp sting was both shocking and comforting, painful and beautiful. Blood welled from the cut in jewel-bright beads, wet and red and luscious. Tears of relief fell down her cheeks and she closed her eyes, feeling the warm trickle, savoring the sweet release.

When she opened them again, James was standing over her. Groggily, she brought the T-shirt up to her chest and fumbled for the knife, but he'd already seen it.

He already had it.

Saying nothing, he rinsed the blade and set the knife aside, his hair sticking up all over the place, the muscles in his face tense. He sorted through the medicine cabinet, finding antibiotic ointment and bandages.

He cleaned up her cut and wrapped it carefully while she sat on the cold tile floor, her back against the wall, body shivering, mind numb.

"I won't do it again," she whispered, letting him help her up.

James didn't say he believed her, and he didn't promise everything would be all right. He just put her T-shirt back on and took her in his arms, stroking her hair, holding her close.

The next morning Sonny woke to the sound of an alarm. Reaching out with one hand, she turned it off with a weary groan.

She could've sworn she'd only just drifted off.

Assaulted by images of her wanton behavior with Ben last night, she punched the pillow beneath her head, wishing she'd told him to go to hell. How could she have let him use her that way? How could she have enjoyed it?

She covered her face with her hands and moaned, hating him for making her feel ashamed. Acting on impulse, sexually, was something she hadn't done since high school.

The way she'd behaved as a teenager was tragic, but not atypical. After the rape, she'd been removed from her mother's home. She no longer had Rigo. She'd never had a father. With equal parts self-loathing, self-pity, and self-destruction, she'd sought to fill that void with any boy who showed an interest.

At New Horizons Group Home, she'd been a very popular girl.

It wasn't until she'd gone to college that she'd learned how to respect, and protect, herself. But she'd never learned how to enjoy herself with men, until Ben.

Pushing aside a dozen painful memories, and even more regrets, she dragged herself out of bed and prepared to face the day. She'd overcome worse than this.

In time, she'd get over him, too.

Last night after Ben left, Grant had called and asked her to interview Stephen Matthews. She also had the unenviable task of breaking the news to him about his mother. Gabrielle Matthews' severely decomposed body had been found between cold layers of concrete in the Matthews' backyard, wrapped up in garbage bags and secured with duct tape.

Stephen lived with his girlfriend in a run-down duplex on the seedy edge of town. Sonny parked her rental car on the street and walked to the front door. As she approached, she could hear them arguing, so she paused to listen.

"I don't need to get a fucking job, you need to get a fucking job! I take care of the house, asshole! If you don't come up with some cash soon, I'm going to start throwing your shit out—"

A man's muttered retort was lost as the woman continued her shrill tirade.

Financial troubles, Sonny deduced with a wry smile. Perfect.

When Stephen's girlfriend, Rhoda, answered the door, she looked Sonny up and down, crossed her skinny arms over her flat chest, and said, "What do you want?"

Even if she'd been polite, Sonny would have disliked her on sight.

Rhoda had a mean, pretty face, ratty blond hair, and no figure to speak of. Her pupils were huge and her pale legs were covered with the kind of bruises Sonny associated with drug users and incredibly clumsy individuals. Dressed in cutoff jean shorts, with a long-sleeved flannel shirt knotted at her scrawny waist, she resembled a homeless anorexic. Someone should have told her the grunge look went out with heroin chic.

Rhoda Pegrine was trailer trash through and through. It took one to know one. While Sonny considered herself a credit to that dubious heritage, she knew intuitively that Rhoda embodied all of its negative stereotypes.

"I'm Special Agent Sonny Vasquez," she said. "I came to ask Stephen a few questions about his father."

Rhoda shoved a hand through her bleached hair. "Where's your credentials?"

Sonny showed her ID.

Behind Rhoda, Stephen approached, his air surprisingly protective for a boyfriend who'd just been thoroughly bawled out.

Rhoda let out an exaggerated sigh and let the door fall open. "Whatever," she said, pushing at Stephen's chest rudely before she passed by him, twitching her bony hips like an alley cat on the way to the couch.

As Sonny stepped inside, she gave Stephen a tight-lipped smile, for he truly discomfited her. With his prominent cheekbones and dark blue eyes, he had the Matthews good looks, although he did his best to hide them. His hair was lanky and overlong, he was too thin for his height, and he hadn't bothered to shave in a while.

Was this carbon copy of James more like Arlen on the inside?

She sank into the deep cushions of an old chenille recliner—the only place to sit besides the couch—that had been reupholstered liberally with duct tape. It was impossible to maintain a professional posture in a chair the consistency of marshmallow, so she gave up and leaned back, letting the cushions envelop her, folding her hands over her stomach.

She scanned the room, waiting for Stephen and Rhoda to get nervous enough to talk.

Sonny was no domestic goddess, but even she found Stephen and Rhoda's habitation offensively cluttered. Video games, DVDs, and CDs littered the floor. The coffee table's surface was a maze of crushed beer cans and cigarette butts. She couldn't see the kitchen from her vantage point, but she could smell it. If Rhoda's sole responsibility was to take care of the house, she was failing miserably.

Sonny moved her gaze to the strange pair, studying their body language. Stephen was nervous; he kept wiping his palms on the legs of his jeans. Rhoda, on the other hand, didn't seem the least bit concerned about Sonny's presence. She propped her skinny foot on the edge of the couch and resumed what Sonny supposed was her idea of a pedicure. She was painting intricate designs on her toenails with a black felt-tipped marker.

Sonny was familiar with the effects of crystal methamphetamines. Both Stephen and Rhoda were exhibiting classic signs of addiction, but while Rhoda was high as a kite, lost in her own mind, Stephen was sober, focused, and obviously in withdrawal.

He nudged Rhoda gently, aware that she was giving them away. "Why don't you offer the lady something to drink?"

Rhoda stared at him like he was the world's biggest moron. "We don't have anything in the fridge. What do you want me to offer her, tap water?"

Stephen's eyes darkened at her harsh tone but he didn't say anything more.

It wasn't difficult to understand the dynamic between these two. Like his brother, James, Stephen had probably been beaten and ridiculed his entire life. Children of abusers often chose a domestic partner who took up where the parent left off.

With her small stature and frail body, Rhoda wasn't a physical threat. But a person didn't have to be big to be a bully.

Sonny dug a twenty out of her pocket. Most struggling neighborhoods had liquor stores on every corner, and this area was no different. "Why don't you go buy us something, Rhoda? You can keep the change."

Rhoda regarded her suspiciously. "What do you want?"

"Just a bottle of water."

Rhoda didn't bother to ask what Stephen would have. After snatching the crisp bill from Sonny's hand, she shoved her tweaked-out toes into a pair of chunky-heeled sandals and was out the door in a blink.

"She'll be gone for hours," Stephen explained.

Sonny smiled. "Good."

He stared back at her through guarded eyes, the way a man looked at a woman he was alone with... and afraid of.

She felt her smile slip. Oh, Stephen, she thought, feeling her heart break for him a little bit. You and I are a lot alike. Grant sent her to do this interview because Stephen had been so sketchy and uncooperative at the police station. He thought Stephen would be more comfortable with a lone female. He wasn't.

To put Stephen at ease, she would have to move to another setting, one where he felt less closed in. "Do you have a backyard?" she asked.

"Yeah."

"I could use some fresh air."

He hesitated. "It's kind of cluttered out there. I usually sit on the front stoop."

She nodded, standing. "This will only take a few minutes."

Stephen led her out front and waited for her to take a seat before he hunkered down beside her, giving her plenty of space. Sonny took out her photographs of the victims. "Do you know any of these women?"

He looked them over, pausing only on the one of Lisette. "I don't think so."

Sonny pointed at Lisette's pretty face. "She and your little brother had oral sex in your closet."

"Really?" He studied it more closely, seeming impressed.

"She's dead now."

"Oh." The photo slipped from his trembling hands. "Is she the one from the net?"

"Yes. Are you sure you haven't seen the others?"

He shrugged. "Rhoda invites a lot of people over. Strangers. I don't pay that much attention to the girls."

Sonny arched a brow. "Are you more interested in the boys?"

A flush crept over his cheekbones. "No. I keep an eye on anyone who might cause trouble. Girls usually don't."

She believed him. Being wary of the opposite sex and repulsed by them were two separate issues; she was proof of that. She'd only asked because DeGrassi had posed a similar question to James, and it had made her wonder about the killer's profile. Strangulation was usually sexually motivated.

She thought of a question DeGrassi hadn't asked James. "Do you know any surfers? Someone Rhoda invites over, or a friend of your dad's?"

He looked doubtful. "My dad didn't have any friends. And surfers don't usually hang around with..."

"Meth addicts?"

His cheeks darkened further, but he inclined his head.

She cut to the chase. "James told us that your father sexually abused prostitutes on numerous occasions. Can you confirm that?"

He snuck a glance at her, his blue eyes swimming in the sun. "Yes."

"Do you think he killed these women?"

"I don't know," he said, returning the photos. He was silent for a moment, watching the steady flow of traffic on Harbor Drive. "I hope not, but I really don't know."

"Do you know who killed him?"

His mouth formed a thin, hard line. "No. I wish I did."

"Why?"

"So I could shake his hand."

Sonny took a deep breath, dreading the words she was about to say. Having little choice in the matter, she looked her half-brother in the eye and told him that his mother had been murdered, just like all of the young, vibrant women in the pictures she'd just shown him.


Ben felt like he hadn't been surfing in a week. Over the past couple of days, the physical activities he'd engaged in weren't quite as meditative as time on the water.

He'd wanted to talk to Carly the night before, but she'd been asleep by the time he finished his discussion with Nathan.

CRASH INTO ME    323

Now she was still asleep, as was James, snoring softly on the living room couch. Ben wandered around the house aimlessly for a while, checking every window and lock. Then he gave up, abandoned paranoia, and surrendered to the call of the waves.

JT was already out, standing at the edge of the water with an insulated mug in his hand. When Ben came up beside him, his lackadaisical friend greeted him with a complicated handshake and an engaging grin. JT didn't keep up with most current events, so he must not have heard about Lisette. Thank God.

"How is it?" Ben asked, nodding toward the surf.

"Better than yesterday," JT replied. "Way less eggy."

Ben grunted at the expression, which pretty much meant that the waves didn't suck.

"So what's up with that new wahine of yours?" JT asked. "She wax your stick?"

"No," he said, staring out at the ocean.

"Really? I thought you were in to her."

"Maybe she wasn't in to me."

JT laughed, taking another sip from his mug. Knowing him, it was laced with Kahlua. "Too bad. She was hot."

"You think so?" Ben wasn't surprised, exactly. JT thought most women were hot, and Summer certainly fit that description, but his friend's tastes had always run more toward young, empty-headed, and easy.

"Not like Olivia," he amended. "Kind of scary hot. Like she might throw you down and slap you around first." He shuddered a little, as if he had water in his ears. Then he gave Ben a sharp glance. "You didn't get cold feet, did you?"

"What do you mean?"

"You know what I mean, dude. Every time a good-looking chick walks by, you run the other way. It's embarrassing."

Ben wished he hadn't stopped to talk to JT. Even with a foggy head and bloodshot eyes, his friend saw him a little too clearly. He didn't want to talk about Summer—Sonny, he corrected silently, gritting his teeth. He didn't want to talk about anything. He just wanted to go out on the water and surf it all away.

"Seriously, man. Isn't it time you got back in the game?"

"What do you know about it?" he returned, his frayed nerves snapping. "Sleeping with every woman you meet isn't a game, it's a cop-out. You're the one who's afraid to commit, not me. You've never even had a real relationship!"

For a moment, JT actually looked offended. "You're right," he acknowledged with a stiff nod. "But we're talking about your issues, not mine. You can't live in the past, bro. Holding on to Olivia won't bring her back."

"*I'm* living in the past?" Ben sputtered, annoyed by his friend's sudden show of depth. "You haven't matured a day since your dad died. You've got no job, no girlfriend, no goals . . ."

JT's eyes darkened with anger. "You don't know shit about my goals," he said. "So what if I surf all day? You do, too! And maybe I see a lot of different women because I haven't found the right one yet."

Ben was struck speechless. He'd never seen JT this fired up before.

"What you had with Olivia was special," JT allowed, his tone quiet with intensity. "And you were lucky to find her. But she's been dead for three years now. If you let Summer go because you're still hung up on Olivia, then you're a fool."

It was on the tip of Ben's tongue to explain that the rift between Sonny and him was her fault, not his. She'd lied to him and used him, manipulated him and betrayed him. He kept his silence because the conversation was veering uncomfortably toward the chilling subject Nathan had brought up last night.

He was *not* in love with her.

"I'm not in love with her," he said out loud, his voice rising with panic.

A strange expression crossed JT's face. Then he threw back his head and laughed. "Whatever you say, dude. Now, are we going to stand here like a couple of old-timers, lying to each other about how good the waves were yesterday, or are we going to get out there and show these young fuckers how it's done?"

Ben went along with him, relieved that the tension between them had dissolved, but growing increasingly disturbed by his feelings for Sonny. When JT headed toward the lineup, Ben went the opposite direction, paddling out to a promising section of break that would have been heavily populated on a Saturday afternoon. At this hour, the ocean was wide open, and he wanted to be alone.

The Pacific was dishing out some of the same stuff

he'd seen on Christmas Eve, chest-high sets with perfect form, just about the best you could get this time of year. During heavy storm conditions, Ben saw double overheads every once in a while, but those were few and far between, and sometimes so powerful even he got pounded.

If he wanted big waves that were more or less manageable, he'd move to Hawaii. Days like this reminded him why he stayed in San Diego.

The first reason had always been Carly. He couldn't uproot her from the friends and family she'd known her entire life. When Olivia had been alive, he'd come and gone as he pleased, following where the surf (and the money) led him. As a single parent, he no longer had that luxury, and he was a better man for it.

He also stayed because he liked San Diego. Even when the waves were unimpressive, they were there, every day, like clockwork, and he'd come to appreciate constancy, to draw strength from and find comfort in stability. Ben had been everywhere, and he could honestly say that La Jolla, California, was the most beautiful place in the world. The weather was awesome, the sky was endless, and the views were breathtaking. Windansea Beach wasn't just ordinary surf-meets-turf, it boasted cliffs and tide pools, seals basking on rocks, waves crashing against the shore, and sand as smooth and soft as cream-colored silk.

The final answer, if he was soul-searching, was that he could no longer live as if tomorrow would never come. It had been great while it lasted, he'd had a swell run, but he just wasn't the same person. When

Olivia died, mortality hit him like a forty-foot crusher. Tow-in surfing was exhilarating, it was amazing, it was epic, and it was all-time. But it wasn't worth leaving Carly an orphan over.

Long before he'd had his fill, he swam in, shaking the water from his hair like a wet dog, striding across the beach with his board under one arm. He was glad no one bothered him for an autograph or approached him to gush. Obscurity was welcome.

Ben grabbed a shower in the poolroom and changed before making his way to the kitchen, stomach rumbling with hunger. When he saw his daughter, all of the restorative powers of exercise and ocean disappeared in the blink of an eye.

Carly was crying.

"What happened?" he asked, looking around for James. Blaming him was like second nature.

She scrunched up her face and sobbed.

He sat down and put his arm around her, feeling protective and paternal when she allowed the embrace.

"Where were you?" she asked shakily, her voice high-pitched with emotion.

Ben was at a complete loss. His whereabouts were never a mystery. When he was gone, he was always in the same place. "I went surfing. What's wrong?"

She shuddered, hiccuping against his chest. "I just thought...I don't know what I thought. I was worried."

He patted her back reassuringly. "I'm sorry, baby. I didn't even know you were awake."

Lifting her head, she focused her weepy, wet-lashed black eyes on him. "I couldn't bear it if you died."

His throat tightened. "Why would I die?"

"Mom did." She looked out the window behind him forlornly. "So did James' dad. And Lisette."

"Carly," he began, cringing a little. "About Lisette—"

She closed her eyes, as if anticipating a blow.

Ben found that he couldn't deal it. He couldn't tell her what happened. There were some things a father and daughter weren't meant to discuss, and this was one of them.

Or so he thought.

"You killed her," Carly whispered.

The words were so unexpected he wasn't sure he'd heard them. "What? I did what?"

Fresh tears squeezed out her eyes. "It's okay, Dad. I won't tell anyone. I'm sure it was an accident, and I know she, um, bothered you."

"You think I killed her?"

She was afraid to meet his eyes, but she did. "You didn't?"

Suddenly, he threw back his head and laughed, feeling lighter than air. His daughter thought he was a murderer! What a relief.

He hugged her so tight she squeaked in protest. "I thought *you* did."

Her jaw dropped. "Me? Why would I do it?"

He laughed and hugged her again. "I don't know. You have to admit you've been up and down lately. I thought you two got in a fight over what happened in my room, and you conked her over the head or something. Defending my honor."

"Defending your honor?" she sputtered. "I've been up and down? What, you think I'm a freaking psycho?"

"Yes. But you're my psycho." He dropped a kiss on her adorable nose.

"You didn't kill her," she said with a tentative smile.

"And neither did you," he returned, smiling back.

"So who did?" James asked with a yawn, standing at the doorway.

## CHAPTER 19

James looked from father to daughter, uncomfortable to have interrupted a private moment. He'd woken to the sound of Carly crying, and could not pretend, in good conscience, that he hadn't listened in on their conversation.

His question about Lisette echoed across the kitchen. Once out, he couldn't retract it. It just hung in the air, like a bad smell.

"Do you mind if I use the phone?" he asked, leaving the previous query unanswered. "I promised I'd call Stephen."

"Go ahead," Ben replied, pointing at the den. "There's a phone in there."

There was also one in the kitchen, right next to him, but James appreciated the privacy. Carly was looking at him like she'd lost her puppy, so he winked at her over Ben's shoulder as he walked by.

She gave him a wobbly smile that made his empty stomach flop like fresh catch.

Shivering with the memory of another arduous night, thinking about what she was doing in her bed upstairs, unable to sleep, unable to, er, relieve his tension, he ducked into the den and picked up the receiver, wondering if it was possible to die of acute horniness.

He shifted from one foot to the other, willing the ache in his groin to go away as he dialed the number.

" 'Lo?" Stephen answered, his voice barely registering on the sound scale.

Maybe it was James' imagination, but every year it seemed Rhoda got louder and Stephen got quieter. If she sucked up any more of his life force, Stephen would just plain disappear. "It's James," he said. "What's up?"

"Uh . . ."

"Any news about Dad?"

"Yeah. Maybe you should come by."

"What is it?"

"I don't know if I should say it over the phone—"

"Tell me."

Stephen hesitated for a moment. "They found Mom."

Elation lifted him. James felt a silly grin break across his face. "Yeah? Where is she? When can I see her?"

His brother made a strangled sound. At first, James couldn't place it. When he realized Stephen was trying to smother a sob, his stomach dropped to his shoes. "No," James said, denying the truth before it had even been spoken. "No," he repeated, an emptiness spreading through him, invading his soul.

"They found her in the backyard."

"No," he whispered, shaking his head back and forth.

Stephen's voice was thin and strained, but audible. Horribly, frighteningly audible. "They dug her up from under the patio."

"No, Stephen," he yelled into the phone, suddenly furious. "You're lying! Why are you lying? Sober the fuck up for once and tell me the fucking truth!"

Too wound up to listen to another word, James took the receiver from his ear and slammed it into the console, over and over again until the thing was smashed to bits.

"James," a quiet voice said from the doorway.

He looked up from the black plastic shards, hearing the sound of his own ragged breathing along with the echo of the mayhem he'd just created.

Ben was standing at the door, shielding Carly with his body. In James' fractured state of mind, he couldn't understand why Ben would do that. Then he saw the horrified expression on Carly's face, and felt a wetness dripping from his hands.

He glanced down stupidly, wondering where all the blood had come from.

"Fuck," he said, wrapping the tail of his shirt around his hand. Not only was he ruining their carpet, he was bleeding on borrowed clothes. "I'll buy you another one," he muttered, not sure if he was talking about the phone, the shirt, or the carpet.

"James," Carly said from behind Ben, her voice still raw from crying. "What's wrong?"

He stared at her, not remembering why she'd been upset. "It's my mom," he said. "They found her in the backyard." He sounded so calm, like a stranger was speaking for him. "She was under the concrete slab. Stephen and I helped my dad pour it out." He blinked, fragments of memory floating through his mind, pictures more vivid than the blood on his hands. "I still remember that day. My dad was in a weird mood. He was sober, for once, and didn't hit me all day. I can't remember another day like that. It was a nice day.

"We all worked together," he continued, "mixing the concrete, smoothing it over with trowels. Doing men's work. He said we did a good job." He laughed, looking from Ben to Carly, not really seeing them. "Can you believe that? We did a good fucking job, making my mother's grave."

Carly slipped around Ben and rushed forward, hugging James. He held her woodenly, not sure how she could cry when he couldn't.

"We need to take you to the emergency room," Ben said.

James took the T-shirt away from his hand. The cut could use a few stitches, but he'd had worse. "No. I have to go to Stephen's."

"James," Carly protested, her pretty face streaked with tears.

In that moment, he almost hated her. How dare she cry about anything, standing in her rich, perfect house, next to her handsome, perfect dad, wearing her expensive, perfect clothes, tears marring her lovely, perfect face? How dare she cry over his mother, when he felt nothing, had nothing, was nothing?

He set her aside. "It's fine, Carly. Just get away from me, okay?"

Her eyebrows drew together in confusion. "James, you're hurt. Why are you—"

"Look at me," he interrupted. "Look at my hands." Holding them up for her, he said, "Can't you see that I'm all fucked up? If I touch you, you'll get fucked up, too." To prove it, he put his hands on her shoulders and pushed her back, leaving bloody prints all over her pristine white T-shirt. "See?"

Ben strode forward and pulled Carly away from James. "Go put some shoes on. And get my keys."

Carly went, hugging her arms around herself.

James wanted to leave, too, but Ben was blocking the exit. "That's not going to stop bleeding on its own," he said. "Why don't you put some pressure on it?"

Annoyed, James put the bloody T-shirt back to his hand.

"No," Ben said. "Use your fingers. Like this." Taking James by the hand, he placed his thumb over the vein that was pumping blood to the injury.

James flinched, uncomfortable with Ben's touch.

Ben released him. "Put pressure on it with your fingers, like I showed you."

He complied, feeling the humiliating press of tears burning at the back of his eyelids. "I have to go," he insisted. "I can't be here right now. What if I had done that to Carly?" He jerked his chin at the demolished phone.

"It's a machine, James. It didn't feel a thing."

"She can't see me like this."

Ben assessed him with cool brown eyes. "She lost her mom, too. You think she'll consider you less of a man if she sees you cry?"

"I'm not a man," he whispered, feeling very small and infinitely vulnerable.

Ben put one hand on James' shoulder and guided him toward the door. "You've got a pretty good right hook, for a kid."

Sonny trudged up the stairs to her upper-floor apartment, a sense of hopelessness dogging her every step.

Stephen hadn't taken the news of his mother's death very well. She'd expected him to be more like James, stone-faced and silent, completely unable to show emotion. It wasn't that he'd broken down and sobbed. He'd just sat there, his red-rimmed eyes filling with tears, a wealth of sadness on his gauntly beautiful face.

She'd known better than to try to comfort him, or to ask any more questions. Leaving her card in his slack hand, she patted his shoulder once and walked away, fighting to hold her own tears at bay.

Hopefully, Rhoda would be selfish with that twenty-dollar bill and stay gone for a while. The last thing Stephen needed was her company. Or more drugs.

Sighing heavily, she turned the key in the lock and

opened the door. As soon as her eyes adjusted to the dim light, she went for her SIG, training it on the man sitting in her living room.

Grant didn't even flinch.

She leaned against the door, returning her gun to its holster and willing her heart to slow, rather than arrest. "You scared the shit out of me."

"I could have done a lot more than scare you."

Biting back a caustic response, she pushed the door shut behind her and ventured farther into the room. He was right, of course, and having him get the drop on her for the second time in as many days didn't bode well for her.

Had she lost her touch, along with her objectivity?

She trailed her fingertips along the island between the kitchen and living room, reluctant to start any difficult conversations. "You thirsty?"

He grunted a maybe. "What have you got?"

"Diet Coke," she said coyly, knowing he watched his waistline.

He shrugged, as if he wasn't secretly jonesing for one, so she popped the top off two cans and brought them to the awful retro coffee table, taking a seat in the dreadful vinyl chair.

"Who does your decorating?" he asked.

"*Design on a Dime.*"

Neither of them smiled at the halfhearted quip.

Grant took a sip of his drink and set it aside, his manner turning brusque. "Arlen Matthews' fingerprints are all over the duct tape and garbage bags he wrapped his wife in."

Sonny nodded, expecting as much.

"We also found fibers from the pillow slipcover in his lungs, and broken lamp shards with your finger-prints on them in his trash can."

She choked on a mouthful of Diet Coke.

Grant was only getting warmed up. "Yesterday, af-ter interviewing your new boy toy, I discovered that his daughter is dating the son of our current prime suspect. Do you know how fucking stupid I looked, learning details like those from Paula DeGrassi?"

"I'm sorry," she croaked.

"You'd better be. And you'd better start explain-ing now, before I haul your ass in for sexual miscon-duct, manipulating evidence, and who the fuck knows, maybe even murder!"

Whoa. She put her can down and her palms up. "I admit I hit Arlen Matthews over the head with a lamp. I knew James had reported Lisette's body, and that Arlen frequented prostitutes, so I went over there in disguise. Looking for clues."

Grant's eyes narrowed. "He made a move on you? You acted in self-defense?"

"Not exactly. He got a little ... fresh, and I overre-acted."

He muttered an expletive. "So you bashed him over the head, and then what? Shoved his face into the pillows?"

"No. James and I put him to bed. He was alive when I last saw him."

"You expect me to believe that?"

"It's the truth," she said, her stomach sinking.

"What about the bracelet?" he asked. "How in

the hell could evidence like that escape your attention?"

"It wasn't there," she admitted. "I swear to God, it wasn't there."

Grant studied her expression, his own revealing nothing. She wanted to tell him an even more disturbing truth, to confess that Arlen Matthews was her father. But the idea of saying those words aloud paralyzed her with fear. Grant would never believe she hadn't set up Matthews, or killed him on purpose, if he knew the man had abused her mother.

"DeGrassi doesn't like Matthews as the SoCal Stranger," he admitted. "MOs are different. Matthews killed his wife, no doubt about it, but the guy we're looking for is highly intelligent and extremely organized."

Sonny took a moment to breathe. This was going better than she'd hoped.

"I'd like to take another crack at Fortune," Grant said.

She gulped. Or not.

"He's smart enough to set up Matthews."

"No," she protested. "I realize that you think my attraction to him is getting in the way of the investigation, but I know he's not a killer."

"How? Because he has a cute smile and a hot bod?"

Sonny flushed. "Mitchell has a cute smile and a hot bod."

"So it's more than that," he said, waving his hand dismissively. "But sexual chemistry doesn't make him innocent. Guys like Fortune are experts at playing women."

She shook her head, wishing she could make him understand.

"What about Lisette Bruebaker? You know he was messing around with her, Sonny. And she was just a kid."

"A kid with a crush who crawled into his bed while he was sleeping. Nothing happened between them."

The corner of Grant's mouth tipped up, but the expression did not convey even an inkling of amusement. "Surely you must realize how deluded you sound." His eyes roved over her face. "Was he that good?"

Shame washed over her, and she looked away, her gaze landing on the narrow strip of wall between the couch and the entrance to the hallway. Her sweatpants and sweatshirt were still there, tangled in a pathetic little heap on the ground, because she'd never bothered to put them back on. Like a crazed sex fiend, savoring her sweet fix, she'd stayed naked in the dark for a long while after Ben left, her back against the wall and her hand between her legs, replaying the memory of their heated sexual encounter.

As if the outline of their entwined bodies had been burned into the wall, Grant leapt to his feet, gesturing angrily at her discarded clothes. "You were with him again last night? Have you lost your fucking mind?"

She groaned, covering her face with her hands. This was so humiliating.

Grant ranted and raved for a few minutes, which was so out of character for him that she couldn't help but stare. "I have to go back to Quantico," he said finally. "My daughter's been getting into trouble at school, partying instead of going to her classes, and my wife keeps complaining about how I'm never home." He turned and glared at her. "You're lucky this shit is happening during the holidays. If I could spare another agent, your ass would be on administrative suspension so goddamned fast."

Sonny gaped at him in amazement. He was actually going to let her stay on the case. "You won't regret this, Grant," she promised, giving him an impulsive hug.

His body stiffened in her arms. She didn't think he was uncomfortable with physical contact, or that he considered the display of affection inappropriate. He was merely surprised, because in the years they'd known each other, she'd always avoided his touch. She'd confided in him about her past and he'd been very conscientious about giving her the space she needed.

Only, now she didn't need it anymore.

Sonny smiled against his shoulder when he gave her back a few awkward pats. Although the embrace warmed a cold, lost place inside her, she took pity on him and let him go. The way he studied her, bewildered and concerned and stern all at once, reminded her of the way Ben looked at Carly.

Her eyes moistened with tears, and she had to laugh at her sudden sentimentality.

"I don't know what's gotten into you lately," he

said, shaking his head. "And don't think I'm giving you a free pass to play house with Ben Fortune. When this case wraps, you'll be up for review, and you'll be damned lucky if the board lets you keep your badge."

After driving him to get stitched up in the ER, and paying cash for the visit, despite James' protests, Ben took James to the medical examiner's office downtown.

James signed for the release of his parents' bodies, under Paula DeGrassi's express consent, and they referred him to a local funeral home that did low-cost cremations for the families of victims of violent crimes.

Arlen Matthews' remains would be "respectfully disposed of." James wasn't sure what that meant, and he didn't really care. Just as long as no iota of his father lingered behind on this planet, he was satisfied.

His mother's ashes would be ready for pickup tomorrow. He and Stephen planned to take out the boat and spread her remains at sea.

That chore completed, James was left with another, more daunting task: cleaning up the home his dad had mistreated for decades. He and Stephen were going to go cut a swath through the place with bleach and heavy-duty trash bags, throwing away anything that couldn't be sanitized. Despite the bad memories the house imbued, James decided he would sleep there tonight, away from Stephen and Rhoda and Carly and Ben, avoiding everyone who felt sorry for him or wanted to smother him or get rid of him or take a piece of him.

When Ben dropped him at Stephen's duplex, he jumped out of the SUV with a terse thanks, intent on a quick and painless escape.

Carly wouldn't let him off so easy. "Hang on a minute, James," she said, getting out and following him.

Summoning an insolent stance, he stopped at the front step to wait for her, noting that Ben had turned off the engine and covered his eyes with one hand, as if unable to watch his daughter's eminent destruction.

"What do you want?" James asked, annoyed with Ben for making him feel predictable, and with himself for needing Carly so badly it terrified him.

She crossed her arms under her breasts, a gesture that was both tentative and irresistible. "Just to say good-bye, I guess."

Her face was pinched with sadness. For the first time ever, she didn't look beautiful. And he loved her so much he was drowning in it.

"Do you mean good-bye for now, or good-bye forever?" he asked.

"Is that what you want?" she said, studying him from beneath sooty lashes. "Good-bye forever?"

Because he couldn't speak, he nodded, despair closing around him like commercial-grade netting.

"My mom's name was Olivia," she whispered. "I never got a chance to say good-bye."

Inside the Navigator, Ben rested his forehead

against the steering wheel. James focused on that image, instead of her words.

"What was your mom's name?"

He dragged his gaze back to Carly. "Gabrielle," he said, feeling the sudden rush of tears, hot and inevitable. His eyes filled and overflowed, but he was too proud to blink or brush the wetness away from his face.

She lifted a hand, as if to touch his cheek, but when he turned his head to the side, she let her arm drop, thinking better of it.

He didn't say anything else, just stared at her through burning, watery eyes, trying to memorize every detail of her appearance.

She'd thrown a hooded sweatshirt on before leaving the house. Unzipped, it hung open, revealing the edge of one red handprint, a visual representation of their ill-fated relationship. Born in blood. Doomed to fail.

Carly slipped the ring he'd given her off her finger, pressed it into his left palm, and closed his fist around it. Torturing him further, she lifted his knuckles to her lips and kissed them gently, her touch as innocent and sexual and exquisite as ever.

"I don't want this," he managed.

"Then throw it away," she said. "Like everything else."


Ben knew it was her before he opened the door. Before he disengaged the lock and turned off the security system. Before he looked through the peephole.

His body told him she was near.

He let the door fall open and leaned his shoulder against the jamb, having no intention of allowing her entrance. "I guess I should have been more direct last night. When I said 'Give Grant my best,' I actually meant, 'Tell Grant to fuck off.'"

Her pretty mouth twisted with annoyance. He still thought of her as Summer, but she didn't look the same to him anymore. Gone were the youthful attitude and softer, less severe expressions. Summer Moore had a certain vulnerability that the woman before him lacked. Special Agent Vasquez was like a block of ice.

Some of the black dye had washed out of her hair, leaving an odd mix of colors that resembled the remnants of a campfire.

Cold ashes and charred wood.

He still wanted to have sex with her. More than ever, strangely enough. He wanted to have her melting against him again, her eyes smoky and her mouth hot. He wouldn't mind playing out a few fantasies with the hard-as-nails secret agent side of her, either. Yeah, she could handcuff him to her headboard. Anytime.

"Is Carly here?"

Ben snapped out of his S&M daydream. "She's upstairs," he said, listening to a few dark chords of the gloomy Goth music that was emanating from her room. She'd been holed up in there for the past hour, playing the same breakup song over and over.

It was driving him insane.

"I'd like to talk to you about Olivia."

His blood chilled. "Then get a warrant for my arrest."

Something like hurt, or maybe even sympathy, darkened her beautiful eyes. "I don't think you killed her, Ben. I never did."

He thought he'd assuaged his anger, as well as his desire for her, last night. He was wrong on both counts. "Then what were you investigating?" he asked, giving her body an insultingly thorough perusal. "My stamina, or my technique?"

She crossed her arms over her breasts and looked away, her jaw tense with annoyance. Ben got the impression she was holding back a scathing retort, and he liked that. Her cheekbones were flushed and her eyes were flashing blue fire, and he liked that, too.

In jeans and a long-sleeved T-shirt, she didn't look like an FBI agent. It was her face that was different. She was closer to his own age than he had originally estimated, and about ten times more jaded.

It infuriated him that she'd deceived him so completely, and so easily.

"I think the killer is someone close to you," she said. "Someone who knew both Olivia and Lisette."

Ben felt some of the fight leave him, taking his indignation along with it. He didn't want to be a part of this. Any of this. For months after Olivia's death, he'd been plagued by nightmares. Every time he closed his eyes, he saw her face.

Now all he wanted was peace.

"What do I have to do?" he asked.

Hope leapt in her eyes, and he felt a matching twinge in his chest, an ache he was afraid to analyze. "Take me to Lisette's wake tomorrow morning. As your date."

"Your cover is blown," he argued.

"Who've you told?"

"No one," he said, running a hand through his hair. "But we're"—he gestured to the space between them, which all but crackled with animosity—"broken up."

She arched a fine brow. "So now we're back together."

Heat flared, low in his belly, as he was assaulted by images of how well they'd gotten back together against the wall in her apartment last night.

"Fine," he muttered, telling himself he was doing it for Olivia, for Carly, and even for Lisette. Not because he had any interest in spending time with Special Agent Sonora Vasquez, or getting wrapped up in her strong, slender arms again.

# CHAPTER 20

By dark, Stephen and James had cleared out most of the trash filling every square inch of the house that had been in the Matthews family for generations. Beneath the relentless squalor, buried under piles of filthy magazines, liquor bottles, and empty cigarette cartons, hidden below dirty dishes and dirtier clothes, there was a home.

A home their mother had kept tidy when she was alive. The linoleum floors were scuffed and scratched, but they both remembered when Gabrielle Matthews had mopped them with pine-scented disinfectant every Saturday afternoon. The drywall was damaged with holes and water stains, but still bore a few faded rectangular shapes, reminders of the framed photos and seascapes she used to have hanging there.

The furniture had never been expensive. Now

most of the chairs and couch cushions were riddled
with cigarette burns and stank of Arlen's fetid
breath. The stuff wasn't worth the hauling fee, let
alone reupholstering, so they broke it into pieces
with a sledgehammer, tearing fabric at the seams, ripping arms and legs, splintering wood.

When they were both hot and tired and dirty, and
Stephen figured James' hand was throbbing like a
son of a bitch, they silently agreed it was quitting
time.

With a little work and a lot of money, the place
could be fixed up to sell. They hadn't discussed it,
hadn't discussed anything, really, as they dragged
garbage bags into the backyard, studiously ignoring
the gaping hole in the earth. They just made the various grunts and shrugs working men had been using
to communicate since before the human race had
evolved to standing fully upright.

Being too worn-out to talk suited both of them
just fine.

Stephen hadn't had any meth in days. His body
was humming for it, taut as a wire, but he denied the
constant, sticky urge clinging to him like a thorn-
studded vine. Instead, he walked down the block to
the convenience store to get some suds.

He was tired of being ruled by dope, tired of wanting it, needing it, craving it. When he did get a fix, it
was never enough. He couldn't even get high anymore. The most he could achieve was a level at which
he could function as a normal person rather than an
asphalt scraping. Hell, he needed a little snort just to

sleep nowadays; otherwise he stayed awake, sweating, aching, panicking.

And since the whole point of speed was staying awake, using it to sleep totally defeated the purpose.

Besides, now he had James to take care of. Stephen was his legal guardian until he came of age. He couldn't stand the idea of his little brother getting caught up in his and Rhoda's addiction and dysfunction, or being a party to her perverted bedroom games.

For all his good intentions, Stephen was a drug addict, and it wasn't just a major personality flaw, it was a debilitating weakness. He needed something to take the edge off, so he grabbed a six-pack of mediocre beer, something strong but smooth, just in case James needed a little liquid comfort, too.

Stephen found his brother in the backyard, staring at the unearthed grave beside tree-trunk-sized chunks of concrete. He'd thrown most of the wood from the torn-up furniture into the hole, and they had the makings of a macabre campfire.

Stephen lit some old newspapers to get it started, then hunkered down on a concrete seat, setting the brown bag beside him. The liquor bottles clinked cheerfully, music to his ears. He popped the cap off one using the base of his cigarette lighter. "Want one?"

James glanced over at him absently, lost in thought. "Nah," he said, and went back to staring at the fire.

Stephen shrugged. "I know you don't drink, but I just thought, with your hand and all..."

James looked down at the bandage wrapped around his swollen knuckles.

"How'd you do it? Planting one on Carly's dad?"

The corner of James' mouth tilted up, just barely. "No. I demolished their cordless phone. One minute I was talking to you, the next I was bleeding all over their fancy carpet."

Stephen snorted, well able to imagine that scenario. His brother's words rang out in his ears, *Sober the fuck up for once and tell me the fucking truth!* He raised the bottle to his lips and took a long pull, his eyes burning.

"I broke up with her," James announced.

Stephen sputtered beer into the fire, where it made a loud hissing sound. "Are you out of your mind? Why?"

James focused on the flickering flames. "She was getting too clingy. Hanging all over me and stuff. You know how it is."

"Oh, yeah," he replied sarcastically. "It's so annoying when an unbelievably hot girl gives you a happy ending at the movies."

James stood, swiping the bottle from Stephen's hand. "I already told you she didn't do that," he said, taking a swig and making a grimace of distaste.

Stephen smiled and popped the top off another bottle. "What did she do?"

James sat down again. "Nothing."

"Yeah, right. And Rhoda's a virgin."

They fell into companionable silence, James drinking his beer like it was medicine. "I did it to her."

Stephen straightened. "*You* went down on *her* in

the theater? No wonder you had her panties in your pocket." He laughed, tipping his bottle up in salutation. "That's classic, man. Totally classic."

"I didn't go down on her," James said. "I just, you know, used my hand." He stared at his self-inflicted injury for a moment. "Fuck," he groaned, as something else occurred to him.

"What?"

"I can't even jack off now," he muttered.

Stephen laughed again, knowing his brother's problem all too well. "Sure you can. Just use your left."

James considered his left hand, wrapped around the neck of the bottle. "That works?"

"Yeah. It might take longer, but it's better than nothing."

"How do you know?"

"Remember that time a thresher latched onto my thumb? Motherfucker throbbed for weeks." He flexed his right hand, counting pale scars crisscrossing sun-dark skin.

"What about Rhoda? You guys don't—"

Stephen interrupted bitterly. "Oh, we do. I avoid her as much as possible, but she catches me sometimes. Afterwards, I feel as wrung out as one of Dad's hookers."

James closed his eyes, probably trying to dispel that mental image. "It's better to make a clean break. She'd hate me if she knew..."

"What Dad did?" Stephen finished for him.

He licked his lips nervously. "Yeah."

"She knows about Mom, right? You can't get any worse than that."

"That's just it, Stephen. Our father *killed* our mother. Threw her body in the backyard and poured concrete over it. I signed the grave! I fucking autographed it. How stupid could I be?"

Stephen could feel his brother's eyes on his face, and he struggled to keep the dirty, ugly truth buried inside him, where it had festered the past five years.

"You knew," James said, his voice faint with wonder.

Making a raw, feral sound, Stephen stood and threw his empty bottle at the house. It shattered into a thousand pieces.

James grabbed him by the front of the shirt. "You knew all along, and didn't do anything about it? What the hell is wrong with you?"

Shame coursed through him. Stephen had never hated himself more, but he lashed out at James, pushing him away with more force than necessary. James tripped over the rubble and fell to the ground, staring up at him, the agony of betrayal apparent in his eyes.

"I was sixteen, James. What was I supposed to do? Report it?" He dropped his voice and held his fist to his ear, as if placing a call. " 'Yes, Mr. Police Officer, I'd like you to check for my mom's body under the slab in the backyard, but don't tell my dad, because he'll kill me and my little brother.' Is that what I should have done?"

"Fuck you, you pussy," James spat, lifting himself

off the ground and brushing the dirt off his clothes. "I would have killed him. I should kill you."

"I was trying to protect you, you ungrateful little shit. Now I'm the pussy?" His gut twisted with resentment. "You're the one too scared to fuck your girlfriend."

James paled. "Shut up," he whispered.

Stephen clenched his jaw, instantly regretting his words. He ached to get high, to feel the chemical burn in his nostrils, the bitter taste in his mouth. "I'm sorry. I hate to see you give her up because you think you're not good enough for her."

James sank down in front of the fire again. "I'm not. God, I'm a mess, Stephen. I'll just mess her up, too."

"How? You going to tell her to drop out of school? Do drugs? Get pregnant?"

"No," he conceded. "But I can't keep my hands off her."

"Doesn't sound like she wants you to."

"Yeah, but she's only sixteen. And unlike Rhoda, she *is* a virgin."

Stephen smiled, relieved that they were talking about their troubles instead of pounding the hell out of each other. "Quit beating yourself up about it. You're not twisting her arm, pressuring her into anything. Are you?"

"Hell, no. She's pressuring me."

What a delicious conundrum, Stephen thought, to agonize over deflowering a sweet young thing with the face of an angel and a body that could tempt a saint. Most guys wouldn't think twice. He shook his head, finding James more principled than a seventeen-year-old boy ought to be. Of course, his little brother wasn't a typical teenager.

The age difference between Carly and James was minimal. Measuring in life experience, they were worlds apart. "There's no reason you can't be friends."

James gulped. "Friends?"

Stephen took the beer bottle from his brother's hands. "Sure. You can control yourself from jumping on her, right? So just be friends."

Stephen knew James didn't have any friends. He couldn't bring anyone over to the house, for obvious reasons, and Arlen had never let him go anywhere.

"Friends," he nodded, sounding pleased with the idea.

Stephen raised the bottle to his mouth, hiding a smile.

"About Mom," James began, after they were quiet a few moments, "I didn't mean what I said. I suspected him, too, especially after Lisette. If only I'd stood up to him, maybe some of those girls would still be alive. If only I had—"

Stephen hooked his left arm around James' neck. "No," he said, pulling his brother close in an embrace that was part headlock. "You couldn't have done anything but get killed, too. And you did stand up to him, in your own way. You told those cops everything, and that took a lot of guts. More than I had. Mom would've..." He cleared his throat, all but choking out the words. "Mom would've been proud."

It was all he could say. So he planted a hard kiss on top of James' head and kept him there, face pressed to his dirty T-shirt, while his shoulders shook with pent-up emotion.

The next morning, Sonny woke up with a tension headache and a knot in her stomach, exhausted after another restless night.

It was imperative that she find a break in the investigation. Grant had given her one last chance to redeem herself, and she didn't want to go back to Quantico empty-handed. She couldn't stand before a panel of stern faces at Internal Affairs with nothing. They could strip her title and make her a civilian. They might even bring her up on charges.

If she closed this case, her career would be in jeopardy. If she didn't, it would be over.

Groaning, she dragged herself out of bed and into the small bathroom, grimacing at her reflection in the mirror. Her hair looked like a tangled mass of scorched honey. Although it needed professional help in the worst way, she made do with another home dye job, this time choosing a nice, semi-permanent mahogany brown.

Lisette's wake would be an informal affair, so Sonny decided on a pair of tailored wool trousers and a soft blue sweater set. She knew she looked relentless, and too much like FBI, in head-to-toe black. For a touch of flair, she wore her sexiest shoes, a pair of sleek black heels, and underneath her clothes, her finest silk lingerie.

Not that anyone would see it.

She brushed her hair away from her face, securing it with a black velvet headband, and applied some makeup, using the tips Carly taught her. She took more time with her appearance than she ever had before, justifying that no one would believe a scrub like her could catch the eye of Ben Fortune. When she was satisfied that people wouldn't run from her screaming, she stepped back and studied her reflection.

She hardly recognized herself.

With black hair, she knew she'd looked a little scary, for the color had exaggerated her sharp cheekbones and strange blue eyes. As a blonde, she was attractive in an edgy sort of way. Being a brunette didn't exactly make her soft and sweet, but it did give her a certain girl-next-door prettiness that was completely at odds with her personality.

"Oh, God," she groaned, covering her face with her hands. "I don't even know who I am anymore."

Taking the disguise a step further, she slipped on Carly's silver cross necklace, telling herself she would give it back later, and undid a few buttons on her low-cut sweater, because she didn't want to look too angelic.

She rushed out of the apartment before she could change her mind, stashing her SIG and a pair of round-framed sunglasses in a black shoulder bag.

When Ben opened his front door, she almost forgot about her own appearance. He was wearing a dark blue pullover that hugged his biceps and a pair of loose-fitting black corduroys she wanted to snuggle up against. It wasn't as formal as the suit from Christmas Eve, but it was a step up from the surfer bohemian look he usually cultivated.

Carly peeked out from behind him. "Holy crap," she said. "Who did that to your hair? You look like a housewife."

Ben gave his daughter a warning stare.

"A really hot housewife," she clarified.

His gaze dropped to Sonny's breasts, then jerked back up.

Carly narrowed her catlike eyes. "What's with you two?" she asked, looking back and forth between them. "I thought you boned already."

Sonny felt her cheeks heat. Obviously, Ben hadn't told Carly she was an undercover agent, and neither had James. Good. Now she didn't have to worry about the outspoken girl throwing a tantrum and giving her away at Lisette's wake.

Ben cleared his throat. "At the risk of being redundant, Carly, I have to repeat that who, when, and how I ... bone ... is none of your business."

"Whatever," she muttered, brushing past him. She was wearing an eggplant-colored sack dress with bell sleeves and an abbreviated skirt. It was unique, stylish, and totally inappropriate for the occasion.

Nathan was hovering in the background as well, as handsome as a GQ model, with his precision haircut and tailored clothes. "Miss ... Moore," he said in greeting, his cool brown eyes skimming her outfit.

Immune to cleavage, he wasn't as easy to please as Ben.

She nodded at him, acknowledging a worthy adversary.

"Carly and Nathan are meeting us there," Ben explained, watching his daughter flounce away with trepidation.

Judging by the somber music she'd heard coming from Carly's room yesterday, and the almost indiscernible puffiness around her eyes today, the girl had split with James and was up to her old tricks.

Poor Ben.

He took her by the elbow and led her toward the SUV, as if she couldn't locate it on her own, parked right next to the curb in front of Nathan's shiny silver BMW. He also opened the door for her, a move she couldn't find fault with even though it was out of character for him. She guessed he was using formality to keep distance between them.

As if they needed more.

The anger he felt toward her was still there, reading loud and clear, but the attraction between them hadn't lessened. When he climbed behind the wheel, the roomy cab of the SUV seemed to shrink. She watched his hand on the gearshift and admired the muscles in his forearm. Beneath the fabric of his corduroy trousers, his right thigh was tense.

She took a deep breath, stifling the impulse to smooth her palm over his thigh, exploring the texture of his pants and the hard muscle beneath them.

"Are you cold?"

Catching his glance, she looked down and noticed the stiff points of her nipples, jutting at the delicate lace bra and thin blue sweater.

"I can turn the heat up."

"I'm fine," she said, face flaming.

Ignoring her, or just being contrary, he reached out to press a few buttons on the dash, getting so close she could almost taste him. He smelled good, too, like cool aftershave, clean water, and warm male skin.

She crossed her arms over her chest, forcibly reminding herself that she was here to do a job, not him. Losing focus again was out of the question. She couldn't afford to tremble at his touch or get breathless because of his proximity. There was too much at stake.

The Bruebakers lived near Mount Soledad, in one of the ritziest neighborhoods in La Jolla, a city that was already known for being a community of the elite. Ben's net worth was considerable, but with his modest house and casual style, he lived well below his means.

The Bruebakers didn't. They were loaded and it showed, from the marble statuary lining the cobblestone driveway to the gold-plated hardware on the front door.

Ben parked the SUV between his brother's pricey BMW and a vintage Rolls-Royce. Carly and Nathan strode toward the entryway like royalty, unfazed by the opulence. Sonny held on to Ben's arm, trying not to stare at the columned balustrade and enormous chandelier as they stepped into the busy foyer.

"Subtle, isn't it?" he said near her ear.

Hiding a smile, she looked past the small crowd,

watching Lisette's parents greet their guests. "Did you grow up in a place like this?"

"Not quite," he admitted.

Sonny wanted to ask more questions about his past, but Carly was already saying hello to Lisette's mother. The pained look on Sheila Bruebaker's face as she wrapped the girl in a warm embrace robbed Sonny of speech.

"I'm so glad you came," Sheila said, smoothing her hand over Carly's shining black hair.

It was easy to see where Lisette had gotten her good looks. Sheila was at least a decade younger than her husband, and at first glance, she was stunning. Her dark hair was expertly tousled, her tall, surgically enhanced figure trim, and her makeup flawless.

Upon closer inspection, the perfect façade was wearing a little thin. She had faint smudges under her eyes and fine lines around them. When her focus shifted from Carly to Ben, some of the misery faded from her face.

"Ben," she said, letting her lush red lips fall open in surprise. And a blatant sexual invitation. "It's good to see you."

He leaned in and brushed his mouth over her cheek, murmuring a few words about being sorry for her loss. "You remember my brother, Nathan," he said after he pulled away.

She blinked up at him. "Of course."

Ben placed his hand at the small of Sonny's back. "And this is . . . Summer."

Giving her a wan, dismissive smile, Sheila turned

and took a sip of the martini on the table behind her, its clear contents shimmering, her square-cut sapphire ring flashing. She moved with the serene precision of a person who had been mixing pills and booze, and at that moment, Sheila Bruebaker looked exactly like what she was: an aging trophy wife with too much money invested in plastic surgery and prescription drugs.

"Thanks for coming," her husband said, trying to cover for his wife's rudeness by shaking Sonny's hand. He needn't have bothered. Sheila's brittle exterior might have been fake, but her suffering was real, and heart-wrenching to witness.

Ben gave Tom Bruebaker a stiff nod and moved on, urging Sonny forward. Tom regarded Ben with similar distaste as he walked by. He was stout and silver-haired, a few years past his prime, so perhaps he begrudged Ben for catching the attention of his sultry younger wife.

And to think, Sonny hadn't been sure she was going to find out anything interesting at this get-together.

Nathan cast his brother an amused glance. "That could have gone worse."

Ben winced, tugging at the collar of his pullover shirt.

"Lisette's mom is a total nympho," Carly explained.

Sonny studied Ben's handsome profile, wondering if he'd slept with her. Maybe Tom Bruebaker had a good reason to be jealous.

Instead of asking, she tore her gaze away from him and studied her surroundings, wishing the thought of

Ben with another woman didn't make her insides twist. There were white candles and silver ribbons all over the room. On the baby grand piano, next to a window with a fabulous view of the bay, there was a framed portrait of Lisette and a large bouquet of white roses.

Seeing it, Carly's pretty face crumpled.

Nathan put his arm around her protectively, meeting Ben's gaze over the top of her head and letting him know he could handle a few tears. With obvious reluctance, Ben did his duty by showing Sonny around the room, his face pensive and his mouth hard.

Like most men, overt displays of emotion were not his style, but intuition told her how difficult the situation was for him. His concern for Carly was marked, and he must have felt guilty about what had passed between him and Lisette. The girl had fled the safety of his house—and the warmth of his bed, to put a finer point on it—right into the hands of a killer. Having Lisette's mother pant after him at her own daughter's wake was incredibly awkward.

Underneath all that, at a time like this, he must be missing Olivia desperately.

"Let's go outside," he said, so Sonny knew the ambience was getting to him. When she nodded, he took her by the hand and they strolled like lovers through the gardens flanking the side of the house, pausing on the west-facing lawn to take in the ocean air.

On a clear day, you could see all the way to Catalina Island from Mount Soledad. It was a crystal clear day.

He rubbed his thumb over her knuckles before he

released her hand, making her tingle with unexpected pleasure. "You know who you look like, with your hair that color?"

She touched the black velvet band on the top of her head, feeling self-conscious. "Winona Ryder?" she asked hopefully.

He laughed. "No. James."

Sonny felt the blood drain from her face.

"You're much prettier than he is, of course," he said, backpedaling. "Not that he isn't handsome. Carly seems to think so anyway."

She found his discomfort oddly amusing. It must have felt weird for him to compare a woman he'd been intimate with to a skinny teenaged boy. "I guess we *should* look alike. He's my brother."

Now she'd shocked him. "Are you serious?"

"Yes," she said, fumbling around in her handbag. "You remember how I told you I didn't know who my real father was?"

He nodded.

"Now I know." Finding her sunglasses, she covered her eyes. "Surprise."

"Are you sure?"

"Unfortunately, yes. I showed a picture of him to my mother."

He studied her carefully, his face showing a hint of distrust.

She deserved it, but that didn't make his suspicion any easier to bear. "Not everything I told you was a lie," she whispered.

He cupped her chin in the palm of his hand, forcing

her to look at him. "What did you tell the truth about?"

She bit down on her lower lip, feeling the hot press of tears behind her eyes. "All the important stuff."

As if she hadn't just bared her soul to him, he stared back at her in silence, his gaze cool, assessing, unresponsive. She disentangled herself from his grasp and turned to leave, clutching her handbag beneath one arm like a lifeline, needing to put some distance between them before she broke down completely.

"Don't," he said softly, reaching out to grasp her wrist. "It doesn't have to be this way."

"What way?"

He lifted her sunglasses, exposing her emotionally. She knew love was brimming in her eyes, and coursing down her cheeks, but she couldn't look away. "Apart," he said, brushing his thumb over the tears on her face.

Held captive by his touch, paralyzed by the intensity of her longing, she stayed motionless while he pressed his lips to hers. In contrast to their sincere conversation, his kiss felt contrived, technically proficient but devoid of all feeling.

She blinked up at him in confusion when he lifted his head. He wasn't drowning in her sweetness, lost in her eyes. He wasn't even looking at her.

Following Ben's gaze, she saw Tom Bruebaker standing at a polite distance, staring out at the sea. Perhaps he was uncomfortable with having interrupted their private moment, because he turned and left without saying a word.

Sonny backed up a step, feeling betrayed. Ben

hadn't kissed her because he wanted to. He'd done it for Tom's benefit. "What was that all about?" she asked, glancing at Tom's retreating form.

Ben shoved his hands into his pockets. "You want everyone to think we're dating."

"That was more proprietary than affectionate," she pointed out.

"I guess I'm not as clever with deception as you are."

She wiped the tears from her cheeks, embarrassed that she'd been so caught up in him, while he was just playing a part. "Does he hate you because you slept with Sheila?"

His eyes cut back to her. "You must be joking," he said flatly.

"I never joke."

His gaze cruised over her face, as if he could solve the mystery of her existence by analyzing its components. "I don't know why he hates me. Maybe because his wife makes a fool of herself, trying to get his attention."

"I could have sworn she was trying to get *your* attention."

He shrugged, as if the difference were negligible.

Sonny examined his insouciant expression. He was hiding something from her, and she was going to find out what. "That lame kiss you just gave me was like an ownership stamp. Why do want Tom to know I'm yours?"

His mouth tensed, causing the tiny, crescent-shaped scar above it to stand out in harsh relief. "He slept with Olivia."

Her jaw dropped open. "No," she breathed. "Why?"

"I told you why. I was a selfish bastard. She did it to hurt me."

Sonny felt a pang inside her own chest, aching for him, and for herself. It was so painful to hear him talk about his wife. "Why did she pick him?"

"Probably because of Sheila," he admitted. "Tom and I went in together on several business ventures, so we'd all known one another a long time. Olivia didn't like her."

She nodded. Tom Bruebaker owned a hugely successful corporation that manufactured everything from sunglasses to sportswear. Ben had been part of a very lucrative marketing campaign in the early stages of his career.

"Why didn't you tell the police about her affair?" she asked, her mind reeling.

"It wasn't an affair, it was one isolated incident," he said through clenched teeth. "And it was none of their goddamned business."

"They would have questioned him in connection with Olivia's death, Ben," she said, struggling to keep her voice low. "You impeded the investigation."

"He was out of the country at the time," he replied, "so he couldn't have done it. Besides, he's hardly the forceful type, despite being a financial heavyweight. He lets Sheila walk all over him. I still can't believe he had the balls to fuck my wife."

"Did you argue with him about it?"

"No. Olivia cried and begged and—" He broke off, shoving a hand through his dark hair. "Goddamn it!

I put this behind me years ago. I don't want to talk about it anymore."

"Okay," she said, taking a calming breath. Tom Bruebaker had been thoroughly investigated by local police and wasn't considered a suspect in Lisette's murder. Sonny couldn't imagine Sheila putting the cord around her own daughter's neck, either. Sheila seemed obsessed with Ben, though, and that raised red flags.

Sonny had been looking for a suspect with connections to Lisette and Olivia. Both of the Bruebakers fit the bill.

"I'm going to poke around inside the house," she decided. "You can be my lookout."

# CHAPTER 21

Sheila and Tom Bruebaker shared a bedroom suite that was at least twice the size of Sonny's current living space at Neptune Apartments.

After observing the estranged couple for several hours, she was surprised they didn't keep separate bedrooms. Or live in separate houses, for that matter. The perfectly coiffed pair had hardly spoken two words to each other the entire afternoon.

While Ben stood sentry at the top of the stairs, Sonny thumbed through boxes of photos and keepsakes, looked into linen closets and peeked behind furniture, pushed aside hanging fur coats and reached into satin-lined pockets.

She found a lot of loose pharmaceuticals and stray tubes of lipstick, confirming what she'd already suspected, that Sheila was fond of pills and flashy colors. Her closet was overflowing with designer dresses and shopping bags.

Something was missing, but Sonny couldn't think what. Sheila appeared to own everything a material girl could dream of.

Moving on, because she knew she had only a few moments, she rifled through Tom Bruebaker's belongings, which were meager in comparison to his wife's. He was neat and orderly, like Ben, and she didn't expect to find anything of note in his dresser drawers. Men tended to tuck away their secrets in the study or at the office, preferring a more personal space than a shared bedroom.

On a hunch, she continued down the hall, taking a quick glance at Ben's back before she ducked into the next room. In this gorgeously decorated guest suite, she located Sheila Bruebaker's holy grail: the shoe closet.

Her eyes widened with appreciation. Sonny wasn't a fashionista by any means, but what woman's heart didn't beat a little faster when presented with such a glittering array of footwear? There must be a thousand pairs, all the outrageously expensive kind, made by designers whose names Sonny probably couldn't even pronounce.

Before she had a chance to process the sheer magnificence of the collection, Ben rushed into the room and pushed her inside the closet. "They're coming," he said in a low voice, tightening his arm around her waist as he pulled the door shut behind them.

The closet went pitch black.

"Why didn't you stall them?" she whispered back.

"I panicked," he admitted.

Sonny stifled a groan. Most of the guests had departed, including Carly and Nathan, so the Bruebakers would be very surprised to find a few stragglers hanging out in an upstairs closet. Ben was supposed to act as though he'd been looking for Carly.

From beyond the closet door, she heard a muffled voice. "What are you doing in here?" It was Tom Bruebaker.

Behind hers, Ben's body stilled. Sonny held her breath.

"I thought I saw someone..." This from Sheila.

"You liar," he growled, his voice dripping with menace and increasing in volume. Sheila made a small cry of distress. "Who were you meeting?"

The closet door was the old-fashioned kind with a keyhole. A tiny sliver of daylight poured in. Ben's body was taut, like a tiger ready to pounce, so she clutched his arm in warning and whispered, "Wait."

Bending her head, she peered through the keyhole.

Tom Bruebaker was holding his wife down on the guest bed, his hand partially covering her mouth. "Are you issuing invitations for sex at your own daughter's funeral?" he asked. "Is that how low you've sunk?"

Sheila bit down on the fleshy pad of his thumb.

Wincing, he jerked back his hand, drawing his arm up as if to slap her. Sheila glared up at him, her eyes glowing with spite, daring him to follow through.

He didn't.

Sonny let out a slow breath and placed her hand

on Ben's knee, signaling for him to stay calm. She was aware of his body pressed intimately against hers, his groin against her bottom. The position was made all the more provocative with her bent so far forward.

He tried to back up a step and give her some room, but the closet was so littered with boxes and loose shoes that he almost stumbled. Tightening his hands on her hips, he steadied himself instead of sending them both crashing to the floor.

She had to bite her cheek to keep from laughing at the absurdity of the situation. Because there was nothing funny about Tom and Sheila's dysfunctional relationship, she remained quiet, sinking into a kneeling position in front of the keyhole.

Ben was still too close for comfort, and if she turned her head, her mouth would be level with the fly of his pants, but that couldn't be helped.

"I saw his number on your cell phone," Tom continued, breathing hard. "There were three missed calls the night Lisette disappeared. Is that why she's gone, Sheila? You were out boinking Ben Fortune while our daughter was being murdered?"

Sheila stared up at him in bleary-eyed confusion. "I didn't know he called me."

Tom let out a harsh laugh. "Are you so wasted you can't even remember who you've been screwing?"

She pushed at his chest, but he didn't budge. "We haven't been screwing, you idiot. Ben hasn't so much as looked at another woman since Olivia."

"Oh, yeah? He was doing more than looking at

that little Italian girl. Or whatever she is. They were all over each other on the back lawn."

She stopped struggling and raised her brows. "Really? I can't imagine what he sees in her. She looked so coarse, with that dark complexion and unfortunate hair."

Sonny ground her teeth together.

"You're jealous," Tom remarked.

Sheila's lush mouth thinned with anger. "I wish I was having an affair with him, just so I could throw it in your face."

"Who is it, then?" Tom asked, holding his hand over her throat. "I know you've been with someone, in this very room. Yesterday there was sand in the bed."

"Go to hell," she spat.

"Did you pick up a stranger on the beach again?"

Sheila bucked and clawed, almost dislodging her husband. He grabbed her flailing arms and pinned her wrists to the mattress. "It's none of your business if I screw Ben Fortune, one of his surfing buddies, or the entire West Coast," she panted. "You were with Jennifer the weekend Lisette went missing, after promising to go away with me!"

He loosened his grip on her, empathy softening his expression. "No. I only said that because I saw Ben's number in your directory."

Her lipstick-smeared lips trembled and tears squeezed out her eyes, leaving dark rivulets of mascara on her face. "I hurt so much," she whispered. "Every few seconds I think about my—" Her voice caught on a sob. "My little baby. And I want to die. Oh, God, I wish I'd died with her."

Tom stared down at her in silence, his chin unsteady.

"I don't want to hurt anymore," she said, tears streaming from her eyes. "Please, Tom. I don't want to hurt like this anymore."

Letting out a defeated groan, Tom lowered his head to his wife and kissed her, his mouth made sloppy by grief and his motions stilted with pain. Sheila didn't stop crying, but she kissed him back, and when he let her wrists go she moaned softly, arching her back and running her clawlike fingers through his thick silver hair.

In the next instant, he was reaching beneath her skirt, tearing off her panties, and she was wrapping her legs around him, urging him on. He fumbled with his zipper, reared back, and thrust inside her. It wasn't the most tender coupling Sonny could imagine, or the most aesthetically pleasing sight, but at least they were making love instead of hate, and holding their misery at bay for a few fleeting moments.

Sonny pulled her gaze away from the keyhole, realizing that she was gawking at the spectacle. Feeling mildly ashamed of herself for enjoying the show, she stood up, aware of her body brushing against the legs of Ben's corduroys as she straightened.

Returning to their initial positions created another problem. With the fly of his pants fitted snugly against her bottom, the growing pressure was difficult to ignore. Especially considering what was going on beyond the closet door.

"What are they doing?" he whispered, resting his hand on her hip, his warm breath fanning her ear.

She squeezed her eyes shut and swallowed dryly, another wave of heat washing over her. In the bedroom, the mattress creaked and moaned. Sheila was a panter—wouldn't you know it?—and as Tom grunted and heaved on top of her she grew louder and louder, gasping "Uh! Uh! Uh!" with each rhythmic thrust.

"Oh," Ben said, getting the picture.

After what seemed like an eternity, the noisy couple quieted.

"Are they done?"

Sonny bent forward to look. And jerked her head back up abruptly, eyes scalded by the scene. Tom Bruebaker was pretty adventurous, for an older guy.

"Well?" he asked.

She shook her head, cheeks burning. It was depraved, of course, to get turned on in a situation like this. But the front of Ben's body was pressed to the back of hers, and it was dark, and there was nothing to look at or think about or listen to . . . except hot, dirty sex.

Either he was picking up on her vibe or the ambience was getting to him, too, because he was fully aroused. The length of his erection felt like a branding iron against her bottom. Desire pulsed between her legs, as thick and heavy as warm honey.

She shifted, trying to ease her discomfort.

"Don't," he warned quietly.

She clenched her hands into fists, wanting to push her bottom against him, to take his hand and put it everywhere she hurt, to cover his fingertips with hers while he touched her aching nipples and stroked her sensitive cleft.

Torturing him, and herself, she bent to look through the keyhole again.

After being trapped in the closet, listening to the Bruebakers get it on for an infernal amount of time, Ben should have felt relieved to be free. Tom finally got up and left Sheila, passed out from drink and sexual satisfaction, in the guest room bed.

Ben and Sonny were able to sneak away, undetected.

The distance from the Bruebakers' swank mansion to his house was short. He knew better than to pull into the small public parking lot off Nautilus, the one facing Shores Beach, but that was what he did.

He couldn't go home like this, leaving so many things between them unresolved. She hadn't spoken a word since they got in the SUV. Neither had he.

Cutting the engine, he rested his forearm on the steering wheel and stared out at the Pacific. It was early-afternoon glass—smooth sets, perfect fetch, excellent conditions.

He arched a glance at Sonny, in no mood for surfing, for once. Avoiding his gaze, she crossed her arms over her breasts. Her pale eyes glittered in the sun, and her chest rose and fell with each soft breath.

She was still aroused. So was he.

His reaction had nothing to do with the Bruebakers' sexfest. The last thing he wanted to picture—or hear—

was Tom giving it to Sheila. He supposed it was the danger of being caught, the tawdriness of the encounter, and the unintentional voyeurism. Not to mention the tempting proximity of her mouth and the feel of her tight little ass against his hard-on.

"You called Sheila three times the night Lisette disappeared?" she asked.

"Yeah."

"Why?"

"To tell her what happened."

Her gaze cut to his, dropped down to the front of his pants, and skittered away. "Did you talk to her?"

"I couldn't get through."

When she moistened her lips, he almost groaned aloud. "I can't do this," she said, looking him straight in the eye.

"Do what?"

"You know what," she whispered.

He shifted, stretching out in his seat, but it didn't help. The breeze coming in from the open windows wasn't exactly cooling his ardor, either.

"I have too much to lose. Maybe everything."

The way she said those words, and the wistful tone of her voice, made one point very clear to him. He knew law enforcement officials had rigid standards for professionalism. Despite what her boss had implied the day he caught them in bed together, she hadn't been sleeping with him for information.

"Grant was covering for you," he said, straightening. "Won't he continue to?" She kept her eyes downcast, revealing nothing, and he felt some of the pain of her betrayal ease away. "I won't tell," he promised. "No one has to know about us."

She smiled sadly, shaking her head.

"That son of a bitch bodybuilder will," he guessed, remembering Grant's muscle-bound sidekick. "Why does he have it out for you?"

"I beat him up a few times," she said, sniffling.

He returned her smile. "So you'll be in trouble when you go back to ... where do you live?"

"I rent an apartment in Richmond. But I'm hardly ever there."

Ben was a world traveler, but he'd never been to Virginia. As far as he knew, the surfing was no good there. "Maybe you'll get fired, and have to move back here."

She slanted a puzzled glance his way.

Right. What was he thinking? He didn't want to get involved with a woman like her. She was too volatile, too physical, too willing to put her life on the line. Taking risks was her job. She was ... exactly like he used to be.

He studied her prim headband and cute little sweater, wishing the circumstances were different. In the demure outfit, she looked somewhere between fierce and adorable. And like always, he couldn't tear his eyes away. "If you're going to get fired anyway," he said, releasing his seat belt, "you might as well make it worth your while."

When he reached across her lap to do the same for her, she sucked in a sharp breath. "I don't want to be your latest diversion, Ben," she said, stilling his hand. "A temporary, meaningless replacement for Olivia."

He stared at his hand on her hip, feeling a dark storm of emotions wage inside him. He couldn't lie and say he hadn't thought of Olivia today. Being at Lisette's wake had brought back a thousand memories, some painful, most bittersweet.

He was finally letting go of her, and that hurt almost as much as losing her the first time.

"I'm not looking for a replacement for Olivia," he admitted. "What I've always wanted is to have her back."

Her eyes filled with tears, and she tried to push away from him.

"Wait," he said. "If I had the choice, right now, to have her in my arms or to hold on to you, I'd choose you." He cleared his throat, feeling anger and sadness building there. "And I hate you for that. I hate you for taking her away from me."

Her mouth softened with understanding. She lifted her hand to the nape of his neck and threaded her fingers through the short hair there, soothing him, enflaming him. One touch from her and his body was on instant alert, as ready as he'd been in the Bruebakers' closet. He didn't want this good-bye to mean too much but he couldn't bear for it to mean too little, so when he lowered his head to kiss her, he tried to hold his desire in check.

When he swept his tongue over her bottom lip, she made an urgent sound and opened her mouth, not just allowing his entry but actively seeking it. She tasted so good he wanted to fall upon her like a savage beast. Impeded more by bucket seats than self-control, he pulled her into his lap, fumbling with a lever that moved the steering wheel back a few inches.

She squirmed on him, her bottom teasing his erection, and he groaned into her mouth. He was so intent on penetration, with his tongue sinking deep and his hands moving beneath her clothes, that he could hardly concentrate on giving her pleasure. If he could have unzipped his fly and buried himself in her then and there, he would have, but in the meantime, her breasts were a delightful distraction.

It took very little effort to tug down the front of her sweater and push aside the lacy cups of her bra. Her breasts popped free, exquisite and caramel-tipped. Mesmerized, he took one pale brown nub into his mouth, then the other, bathing her nipples with his tongue until they were as wet and stiff as beach pebbles.

She moaned and put his hand between her legs, pressing hard.

Outside the open window on his left side, seagulls chattered noisily and human voices carried on the wind.

Ben lifted his head, panting. The beach was quiet but not deserted. A small crowd was the norm during winter break. "Get in the back," he said in a low voice.

Her eyes were smoky and her mouth wet. She nibbled on her lower lip for a moment, deliberating.

"The windows are tinted," he added, helping her off his lap.

The back of his SUV had an extra stretch of space he used to house his surfboards. The conditions weren't always stellar at Windansca, so he often took short trips up and down the coast. Right now the aisle was clear of equipment, and although it would be a tight squeeze, he thought they could manage. Urgency dictated that he try, at any rate. His cock had been throbbing for what seemed like hours.

By the time he got his long legs untangled and climbed into the back of the SUV, she had already solved the mystery of how they were going to proceed. On her hands and knees, she undid her zipper and lowered her pants, exposing her sweetly rounded bottom, covered only by a pair of very brief, very sheer, blue panties.

Giving him a hot, hesitant glance over her shoulder, she dropped those, too.

Ben was floored by the erotic sight. He knew how aroused she was; he could smell her tangy scent and see the proof on her glistening slit. He wanted to have that moisture on his bare cock, to test it with his fingertips and taste it on his lips.

Wracked by lust, he stared at her, frozen in place.

"Take off your shirt," she said.

God, he loved it when she bossed him around. He pulled the shirt over his head and tossed it aside, enjoying the feel of her eyes on his naked skin. He wasn't cold, but his muscles were tense with longing, his nipples tight and hard.

She moistened her lips. He wanted her mouth on him, too, but her gaze dropped to his distended fly and she said, "Hurry," ruining him for foreplay. He didn't know why the pressure had escalated to such an agonizing degree, but if he didn't get a condom on right now he was going to come, with or without her.

With trembling hands, he took the package out of his wallet and unzipped his fly. She was watching him intently, arching her spine in anticipation, and even the process of stretching latex over taut skin, a sensation that was always more awkward than pleasurable, threatened to send him off.

He positioned himself behind her, slipping the tip of his cock between the plump folds of her sex. She made a breathy little sound and backed into him, wanting more, and he couldn't help but push forward, all the way to the hilt, plunging deep into her sleek heat.

"Oh!" she gasped, digging her nails into his upper thigh.

He closed his eyes, savoring the unparalleled ecstasy of being inside her. She was so smooth and slick, he gritted his teeth against the urge to start pumping.

For most of his adult life, Ben had been as selfish in the bedroom as he had been everywhere else. He'd learned more about pleasing a woman during his brief marriage than in too many years of indiscriminate sex.

He regretted that he'd never taken his time with Sonny and probably never would. Doing her hard against a wall and taking her from behind in the back of his truck didn't exactly showcase his level of maturity.

The least he could do, this last time, was get her off first.

He flattened his palm over her belly, his heart knocking hard against his ribs, his breath rasping against the back of her neck. She jerked and moaned, trying to move, but he held her in place, knowing he had only a few moments before he exploded. Stomach muscles quivering under the effort of restraint, he reached up with one hand and down with the other, brushing his fingertips over her stiff nipples and parting the damp curls at the top of her sex.

A few quick strokes and she was flying apart, crying out as her snug sheath gripped him like a silky fist.

"Oh, fuck," he groaned, unable to stay still a second longer. Moving his hands to her hips, he drew back and lunged forward, thrusting into her again and again. He was locked in, driving hard and deep, riding the wave of her orgasm as his own slammed into him. It hit like a white hot crusher, closing out on the back of his skull and washing over his entire body, rushing from the base of his balls to the tip of his cock.

When it was over, he collapsed on her back, his legs quaking as if he'd just come in from a marathon session.

She didn't complain about his weight, but he slid off her, vaguely aware that while he was struggling to recover, she was setting her clothes to rights. Embarrassed by how roughly he'd handled her, he got rid of the condom and jerked up his pants, casting a guilty look toward the front windshield to make sure no one had caught a glimpse of them.

He considered apologizing, because he knew she'd been honest about her past. Underneath her tough-girl exterior, she wasn't that experienced with men.

"I have to get home," she said. "I've got a meeting with Grant."

He stared back at her for a moment, disliking her carefully composed expression. "You're lying."

Her brows rose. "Why would I bother?"

"Because you're going to do something danger-ous, and you don't want me to worry."

"Why would you worry?" she asked lightly. "You hate me."

Anger flared in his belly. Those words had been closer to a confession of love than hate, and she damned well knew it. "If you think you know who murdered my wife," he said, gripping her upper arms, "I want you to tell me."

Her cool blue gaze met his. "Why would I do that?"

*So I can protect you,* he wanted to shout. *So I can do for you what I couldn't do for her.* "So I can kill him," he said, because he wanted to do that, too.

She laughed in his face. Her gaiety was forced, but it still made him furious. "Ben," she said, cupping her hand over his cheek. "Catching bad guys is what I'm good at. Why don't you stick with what you're good at?" Slowly, insolently, she rubbed her thumb across his mouth, tracing the scar he'd had, compli-ments of a surfboard fin, since he was seventeen.

By implying that he was just another dumb surfer with a soft head and a hard dick, she was trying to make him mad, and it worked. But what really got to him was the feeling of helplessness. She would do whatever she wanted, no matter what he said.

He pulled away from her and climbed back behind the wheel, driving her home in silence. After he dropped her off, he watched her ascend the stairs to her apartment, wondering if he'd ever see her again. At that moment, he decided karma was a real bitch.

Now he knew exactly how Olivia must have felt every time he walked away.

# CHAPTER 22

James approached Carly's front door, a lump in his throat and a package under one arm. Taking a deep breath, he raised his left hand, the one that wasn't covered with angry red scabs and ugly black sutures, to knock.

Ben answered the door, his face set in criticism. "Yeah?"

James cleared his throat. "Is Carly home?"

"Yes."

They stared each other down for a moment.

"Can I see her?"

Ben widened his stance and crossed his arms over his chest. The movement emphasized the breadth of his shoulders and the size of his biceps. James felt puny in comparison, as he was assuredly meant to. "What for?"

He paused, searching for the right words. "To apologize for yesterday," he said, glancing back at his dad's old blue junker. Stephen was slouched in the passenger seat, offering nothing by way of encouragement. "And to, uh, give her back the watch she gave me. It's too expensive, and ..." He started to say that he wasn't worth such a gift, but that sounded pathetic. "And I wanted to ask if she would go with me to distribute my mom's ashes." There, that was better. Still pathetic, but more to the point.

Ben considered him for a moment. "Do you remember how you felt when I dragged Carly across the parking lot by the arm? When you said I was hurting her?"

James nodded miserably.

"That's how I felt yesterday. Do you get me?"

"Yessir," he replied. He held out the box containing the watch he'd never worn. "Just give this back to her for me, and I won't bother her anymore."

The watch was probably worth more than the truck James was driving, but Ben didn't bother to take it from him. "Carly," he yelled, turning toward the stairs. "James is here." With that, he cast an averse glance over his shoulder and walked away. It wasn't a good-luck wish, but it was better than getting a door slammed in his face.

Carly came down the stairs, looking so fantastically beautiful that James' heart threatened to burst from his chest. Her black eyes flashed with defiance and her hair bounced jauntily with each step. She was wearing jeans and a faded T-shirt with gold lettering across the front. TRIUMPH, it said. Even James knew it was some kind of motorcycle, but that detail paled in comparison to the way her breasts moved beneath the soft cotton.

On the last few steps she slowed down, sticking her hands into her pockets and hunching her slim shoulders in a way that was irresistibly tentative. A silky strip of midriff was visible between the hem of her T-shirt and the low waistband of her jeans. Less than an inch of taut, smooth skin, more than enough to send his pulse skyrocketing.

He jerked his gaze from her belly to her face. She stopped in the entryway, waiting for him to speak.

All the words he'd practiced on the way over, everything he'd imagined saying while he lay in bed awake last night, every carefully constructed explanation flew from his mind in that moment, and he could only stare at her.

Incredibly, he felt the burn of tears behind his eyes. He'd cried a little last night, but it had been a painful, awkward release, as if his heart wanted to keep the agony locked away inside, holding him prisoner. Now, in front of the one person he wanted to be strong for, he was breaking down like a baby.

She pulled the door shut behind her. "James?"

He shook his head, unable to reply. He desperately tried to deny his emotions, to hold it together, to keep the tears from falling.

He wasn't up to that task, either.

She took the box from his trembling hands and set it aside. Then she put her arms around his neck, let him bury his face in her shoulder, and held him there while he cried.

• • •

Ben had misgivings about letting Carly go with James and his hoodlum brother to scatter his mother's ashes, but the poor kid was so emotionally wrecked that Ben couldn't help but feel sorry for him, and Carly was brimming with renewed love.

Trying to keep those two apart at this stage would only encourage a disaster of Shakespearean proportions.

Maybe he was being naïve, but he didn't think Carly could get into too much trouble on a boat in broad daylight with Stephen "chaperoning." He made sure her cell phone was charged and told her to get home before dark. When he reminded her to take a sweater, he grimaced, sure he was turning into his mother.

If he was honest, Ben would have to admit his attitude toward James had changed. He didn't hate Carly's boyfriend anymore, or pity him, or think he was trash. Begrudgingly, he'd actually come to like him.

"Ugh," he muttered, shuddering with distaste. He needed to go surfing.

Instead of walking outside, he climbed the stairs to his bedroom. What Sonny had said about the killer having a connection to Olivia and Lisette had been bothering him, niggling at the corner of his mind. Like his complex feelings for the elusive special agent, he didn't think a few hours on the water would solve this problem.

Frowning, he crossed the room, moving toward

the sliding glass doors facing the ocean, drawn inexorably to the Pacific.

After Olivia had been murdered, Ben had considered selling this house, and the decision to stay had been a difficult one. Her death had been so tragic, so pointless, so impossible to make sense of. O'Shea's confession had brought no closure, no relief. The police had called the incident a home invasion murder. A random act of violence.

Moving had seemed like the only option in those first few weeks. He and Carly had stayed with Nathan and at his parents' house more often than in their own home. He'd been like a zombie during that time, the only extended period of his life, since the age of ten, that he hadn't given in to the lure of the waves. He hadn't deserved it.

Surfing had always been more than a job to him. It had been his religion, his drug, his ever-faithful panacea, curing what ailed him without the pesky hangover or drunken misbehavior. Quitting had been the ultimate punishment, and he'd earned every minute of it for letting Olivia die.

A month after the funeral, Carly returned to school and Ben went home for what he thought would be the last time. He'd wanted to memorize every detail, to remember how Olivia had looked in every room. He wanted to see her in the living room, laughing as she put up Carly's homemade Christmas ornaments. He wanted to revisit the kitchen, to run his hand along the granite countertops she'd selected. He wanted to lie down in the bed where they'd slept together every night. He wanted to say good-bye.

The instant he walked through the door, he was assaulted by images more horrific than sentimental, from the nightmare morning he found her dead. Stomach lurching with nausea, eyes brimming with tears, he rushed through the house and ran outside, desperate to escape the overwhelming sadness.

He hadn't been able to. On the sand below the steps at the base of the cliff, he'd fallen to his knees and sobbed like a madman. It had been the only time he'd broken down completely. Holding his grief inside had been painful, but this uncontrollable outburst had been worse. Cathartic, perhaps, but an agony to experience.

James' reaction to his mother's death reminded Ben of that feeling, one he still wasn't comfortable reliving.

After a long while, eyes burning and throat raw, hands buried deep in damp sand, he came to grips with himself. And had some kind of epiphany. Leaving his home, abandoning his profession, denying what his soul needed to carry on...it was wrong.

He wanted to stay in the house he'd loved Olivia in. That Carly had grown up in. His wife may have been taken from him, but no one could steal his home, his past, his memories.

Ben remembered staring out at Windansea Beach and noticing the wave conditions for the first time since Olivia died. He didn't go back to the ocean that day, but he knew without a doubt it was where he belonged. He'd always known.

Surfing had been his downfall and his salvation.

Looking out at the same scene today, standing in

front of the sliding glass doors in his upstairs bed-room, he still felt the same way.

He'd made some major changes over the past three years, to his house and to himself. He'd had a security system installed. The bedroom and master bath had been remodeled because they reminded him too much of Olivia, but the west-facing wall remained the same.

Open to the ocean. Visible from the beach.

He rarely bothered to close the heavy curtains. He liked the view. It was one of the main reasons he'd bought the house.

Now he couldn't help but think someone had been looking *in*.

James was having trouble driving. He'd taken the bandage off his hand, and the swelling had gone down, so his injury wasn't bothering him. The problem was that every time he shifted gears, the back of his right arm brushed Carly's left breast, and he had a sneaking suspicion she wasn't wearing a bra.

She was squashed between him and Stephen, strad-dling the gearshift console because the pickup truck had a narrow bench seat. When he put the truck in reverse, to back out of her driveway, he practically had to place the stick right up against her crotch.

He glanced across the cab at Stephen, who only smirked and pulled his hat down over his eyes, slouching in his seat like Arlen had.

Thankfully, it was a short trip from Carly's house to the harbor. James parked in the free lot, like always, although it was a half mile from there to the dock. They walked the distance in silence, the sound of their footsteps absorbed by the wooden planks on the causeway.

After they boarded *Destiny* James took her all the way around San Diego Bay. It was a glorious, sunny afternoon, and there were plenty of other day-trippers milling about, but he noticed very little about the weather or the sea, other than those details necessary to navigate. He was torn between fuzzy-edged memories of his mother—patched together and soft from use, like a faded quilt—and the vibrant temptation of Carly Fortune in the flesh.

They went to Crystal Cove, his mother's favorite place, to spread the ashes. For a split second, he was struck by a memory of the nightmare he'd had a week ago, and he imagined that he saw a dark, ominous shape swimming underwater. When he blinked, it was gone, and there was just Carly, holding his hand.

"You do it," he said, transferring the urn to Stephen. "You've got more experience with ashes."

Stephen smiled around his cigarette, although the joke wasn't worth it.

Before he took off the lid, Carly placed a kiss on the top of the urn, and a few of her tears splashed there, too. James and Stephen followed her lead, kissing the urn as if it were their mother's golden cheek. When it was time, Stephen overturned its contents, and they watched the ocean absorb what was left of Gabrielle Matthews.

Stephen put his arm around James' shoulders, and

Carly pressed her face into the front of his shirt. James just held her, stroking his hand down her back, watching the sun dip toward the horizon and feeling the comforting lean of his brother beside him.

"Why don't you let me out at the wharf?" Stephen suggested. "I'll catch up with you guys later."

Stephen's intention was probably to give James some time alone with Carly, but he may also have been thinking about getting high. It hadn't escaped James' attention that Stephen had been clean lately, and struggling to stay that way. If he was looking to score a bag of dope, it would be an easy enough task at America's Cup Harbor.

Hoping to find his brother sober, and safe, when they returned, James dropped him off at the closest dock and said good-bye.

"Let's not go back just yet," Carly murmured, her lips against his neck. They had about an hour before sunset, and James knew of many private hideaways where they could be alone.

He also knew what would happen if they were.

Telling himself he could always keep going, that they didn't have to stop, he took them on another loop around the bay. Of course, they found the perfect spot, hidden in a rocky, sun-drenched cove, so he lowered anchor and brought an old, scratchy blanket out from belowdecks. They sat together for a while, watching the sun dip low on the horizon and letting the gentle pitch and sway of the waves lull them into a drowsy sensual reverie.

James wasn't sure if he reached for her first, or if she started touching him. It just seemed as though one moment they were holding hands, side by side, the next they were holding each other. When he kissed her, he felt her lips tremble. His hand slipped under her T-shirt and she moaned, arching her back, giving herself to him.

Most of the times they'd been together, Carly had been the sexual aggressor. This time, he couldn't allow her to bear the brunt of the responsibility for their actions. He'd known exactly what he was doing when he'd dropped anchor, gone into the cab to get the blanket, and checked his wallet for the condom he'd been keeping there.

If he was going to lay her down on an old wool blanket atop the tar-soaked planks of *Destiny,* a surface that had seen a hundred thousand gallons of fish blood, seawater, sweat, and tears, he wasn't going to pretend it was all her idea.

"Your tits have been driving me crazy all day," he said against her mouth, cupping their delicate weight in his hands.

"Why?" she asked.

"I thought you weren't wearing a bra. I could see the shape of your nipples."

She gasped, because he was tracing their shape now, brushing his thumbs over the distended tips that were poking against the lacy fabric of her bra.

Emboldened by his words, she ran her hand up his thigh. In the past, he hadn't let her touch him because he'd known his control would disintegrate. Today, he must have left his control, and his conscience, on the mainland, because he guided her hand directly to the danger zone and initiated a stage four emergency.

Catching her bottom lip between her teeth, she squeezed his hardened flesh experimentally, watching him through half-lidded eyes.

The pleasure was so intense it almost blinded him.

"James," she said, "I want—"

He stilled her hand. "I know."

Pulling her T-shirt over her head, he tossed it aside. She returned the favor, tearing his shirt in the process, ripping buttons from holes as she pushed it off his shoulders.

The top of his head nearly came off with it.

Panting, she pressed her lips to his, running her hands all over him, exploring the muscles in his arms and back. He knew he didn't have the kind of body girls swooned over, but the way she was touching him made him feel like he did.

"Now," she whispered, rolling away from him to kick off her jeans.

With a low groan, he unzipped his own, and she reached for him, putting her hand down the front of his pants.

Her mouth formed a soft O of wonder as she curled her fingers around him.

He was lost in a visual, sexual trance, mesmerized by her hand, moving up and down on him; her body, exquisitely revealed by a few triangles of cream-colored lace; her skin, dusky gold in the waning light; and her lips, soft and moist and pursed in concentration.

Making a strangled sound, he thrust his tongue into her mouth again and slid his hand over her taut belly, into her panties. "Oh, God," he gasped, feeling her heat.

"What's wrong?"

"Uh—" He was beyond ordinary communication skills. "Carly—"

"Let me," she said, and in that moment, he would have allowed her anything. Smiling, she unclasped her bra and let it fall. Stripped her tiny panties down her slim hips.

"Oh my God," he repeated. Her naked body was the most beautiful thing he'd ever seen.

"You'd better have a condom," she warned.

"Wait," he heard himself say, but when she lay back on the wool blanket, he positioned himself over her, digging the condom out of his pocket. "You're not ready."

"Yes I am," she countered, wrapping her long, sleek legs around him.

He made quick work of the condom, wishing it were fashioned out of something strong enough to slow him down. Like titanium-lined neoprene.

James knew, even if Carly didn't, that they were moving too fast. He'd meant to touch her first, to take his time, to be sweet and tender and gentle, but she was writhing with impatience, and he was out of his mind with desire. Unable to hold himself back, he thrust inside her, taking her virginity with very little fanfare and absolutely no finesse.

Carly cried out, her body tensing under his.

James lifted his head to look at her face. It was pinched with pain. "Did I hurt you?" he managed, his voice raw.

She nodded, tears flooding her eyes.

His gut clenched with regret, and he tried to withdraw. It was a valiant effort, and he moved back slightly, but the friction was too much for him. His hips jerked forward again involuntarily.

She clutched her hands at his shoulders. "James, stop," she sobbed, hitting him with her fists. "It hurts. Take it out."

He pulled away from her and rolled onto his back, chest heaving. "I'm sorry," he gasped, cursing himself for being so clumsy. "I'm going to die now," he added, wallowing in the agony of sexual frustration.

Carly smiled. "Maybe we should try again."

"I can't."

"You look like you can."

"I mean I can't stop again. So we better not."

She pouted gorgeously, because that's what she did when things weren't going her way. "But, James, I'm all ..."

"What?"

"Itchy and aching."

He opened his eyes, let them slide over her lithe body. "I can probably help you out with that."

She gave his penis a questionable look, and he laughed. It hurt to laugh, so he stopped. "With my mouth," he clarified.

"Oh," she said, a soft blush of color on her cheeks. "No," she decided, biting down on her lower lip.

"Why not?" He stared at the apex of her thighs eagerly.

Suddenly shy, she covered herself with her hand. "Because."

He was beguiled by her modesty. "Why?"

"I think I bled a little bit."

He sat up and took her hand away. "Let me see." He stroked her with the tips of his fingers, barely touching her, then pulled his hand back to look at it. Her moisture was there, and a tinge of pink. "Yeah," he said in wonder, smiling slightly. "You did." Without thinking, he licked the tips of his fingers, and heard her sharp intake of breath.

Puzzled, he drew his eyes up to her face. She was flushed and lushly dark-eyed, her dusky nipples jutting forth, her respiration coming in short, soft pants. Not sure what had caused her reaction, he touched his slick fingers to her and brought them up to his mouth again.

"Why are you doing that?" she asked, spreading her legs a little more.

"I want to taste you."

She moaned, throwing her head back and resting her hands behind her, palms facedown on the deck. He skimmed his fingertips over her, very lightly, and she moved her hips against his hand, yearning. At the same time, he bent his head to her and wet her nipple with his tongue. She whimpered, so he did the same with the other nipple, watching the sun and breeze dry them, then doing it all over again.

When he thought she was almost to the point of climax, judging by the breathy sounds she was making, he moved his mouth down her body. He quickly discovered it wasn't as difficult to please her as he'd imagined. He just put his tongue where he thought he should and laved that spot, like he'd done with her nipple.

She clutched at his hair, holding him there, so it must have been the right place, and then he was sure, because she stiffened and shook and screamed his name.

After she was finished, she lay back on the blanket, eyes closed, murmuring something unintelligible. She was dewy with perspiration, languid with release, holding a hand over her quivering belly.

James lifted his head, very proud of himself.

"Do it again," she said, raising herself up on her elbows.

"Again? I don't think you can. Give yourself a chance to rest."

She laughed. "No, I mean, come inside me again. For you."

He was still aching with need, but he felt strangely satisfied, to have fulfilled her so thoroughly. "You don't have to."

"I want to." She pulled him back on top of her. "Tell me what to do."

He was reluctant to hurt her again, to ruin everything pleasurable she'd just experienced, but he couldn't make himself say no. "Put your knees up."

"Like this?"

"Yeah. Oh, God, yeah. Tell me if it hurts," he grated, going slower this time, sliding in inch by inch.

"Ooh," she said, squeezing her eyes shut.

"Does it hurt?"

"Not as much as before."

He made himself say it. "Do you want me to stop?"

"No," she said, taking a calming breath. "Keep going."

He held himself very still. "Are you sure?"

She nodded, smiling hesitantly. Placing a soft kiss on his lips, she tilted her hips up, encouraging him.

He groaned, surging forward, trying not to go too fast or too hard or too deep. Despite his preoccupation, it took only a few shallow strokes before he was gasping, shuddering, collapsing, and burying his head in the wild tangle of black hair at the curve of her neck.

After it was over, he lay sprawled on top of her, sweating like crazy and panting like a dog, too wrecked to move.

"If I'd known it was going to be over that fast I might have let you finish the first time," she teased, running her fingers through his damp hair.

"Sorry," he said, smiling back at her shyly.

"Don't be," she whispered. "I love you."

Tears came to his eyes, so he buried his face in her hair again. "I love you, too, Carly," he replied, shifting his weight to one side and wrapping his arms around her, never wanting to let her go. "God, I love you, too."

# CHAPTER 23

Sonny should have asked one of DeGrassi's staff members, or even Special Agent Mitchell, to accompany her on the return trip to the Bruebaker residence.

Instead, she went alone. She'd always preferred flying solo. She was good at watching her own back, being responsible for only herself, and taking calculated risks without having to worry about endangering someone else.

She didn't need any more liabilities.

A uniformed servant led the way to Tom Bruebaker's home office. He did a double-take when he saw her standing in the doorway.

The maid frowned. "Is everything all right, señor?"

"Of course," he said, leaning back in his chair.

After offering them both coffee, and showing Sonny to her seat, the maid quietly departed.

Tom Bruebaker wasn't a fool. He set aside his discomfort at having an undercover agent posing as a guest at his daughter's funeral and processed the ramifications of her presence. "Does Ben know who you are?" he asked, reading her card.

She gave him a tight smile. "I'm not at liberty to discuss the details of the case."

"What's to stop me from picking up the phone and calling him?"

"Nothing." She folded her hands across her lap, confident he wouldn't.

His eyes narrowed. "What do you want?"

"I want to know about your relationship with Olivia Fortune."

He looked away, stalling for time, his fingertips drumming a nervous rhythm across the surface of his desk.

"Did you sleep with her?" she persisted.

He met her gaze. "No."

Sonny arched a brow. He appeared to be telling the truth. "Why does Ben think you did?"

"I have no idea," he replied flatly. An obvious lie.

"Mr. Bruebaker," she chided, "I'm investigating the death of your daughter—"

"Really? It looked to me like you were investigating Ben Fortune's tonsils."

"Tell me what you know about his wife," she offered, ignoring the insolence, "and I'll tell you what I know about yours."

It was a good bluff, and he bought it. She'd known

he would be weak where Sheila was concerned, and felt a twinge of shame, to have obtained that information so amorally. "Olivia and I were friends," he began. "Nothing more. She visited me one morning while Ben was out of town. In tears. Inconsolable." He paused for a moment, as if disturbed by the memory of her distress. "She'd been angry with him, and gone with another man to get even. She regretted acting so impetuously, and wanted my advice."

"Why yours?"

His mouth twisted with bitterness. "Sheila has... betrayed me a number of times, and I've always taken her back. Olivia wanted to know how to make it right. What to tell him."

"What did you recommend?"

"I told her to confess to the affair," he admitted. "Ben was a terrible husband and he needed a wake-up call."

"Why did she say it was you she'd been with?"

He shrugged, not because he didn't know, but because he was uncomfortable with the answer. "I'm... older. Not a match for him physically."

"And the other man was?"

"I suppose so. Olivia was certain there would be bloodshed if she told Ben the truth."

Sonny felt her stomach clench with apprehension. Ben wasn't a fighter by nature, but neither was he a good candidate for the cuckold. She pictured his fierce expression this afternoon as he said he wanted to kill the man who'd hurt Olivia.

She didn't doubt he would try, if given half a chance.

"You don't know his name?" she asked.

"No. It was someone close to him, that's all I know. She said Ben could never find out because it would destroy both relationships. Their marriage, and—"

"It couldn't have been Nathan," she thought aloud.

"Nathan?" Tom let out a humorless chuckle. "No. I believe it was a friend of Ben's. A surfing buddy, if you will."

Sonny's blood ran cold. Sheila had used those exact same words this afternoon, after Tom had accused her of picking up a stranger on the beach. She'd said she could sleep with anyone she pleased, including Ben's surfing buddies.

And who else could she have meant but his free-wheeling, soul-surfing, lady-loving friend, JT Carver?

There was a noisy little dive within walking distance of America's Cup Harbor, a popular local joint by the name of Fishbone.

Although he rarely ventured into the bar scene on his own, Stephen went there to waste a few hours of his time. The place was rustic, the mugs were frosty, and the microbrew was expensive. Fishermen were always welcome, even penny-ante dope dealers like him.

Stephen generally stayed away because of the women.

Not that he didn't like them. He did, from a safe distance. In San Diego, a guy couldn't turn around in a crowded place without bumping into some damned pretty ones. There were a couple of good-looking girls sitting next to him at the bar right now.

They scared the hell out of him.

He wasn't sure why, but women tended to approach him when he went out. Maybe because he kept to himself and didn't try to hit on them or act clever. He knew better than to think he could impress anyone.

There was a guy across the bar who had been employing the opposite tactic. He was witty and charming in that modest way everyone liked. *Self-effacing*, he thought the term was. Bullshit, Stephen called it.

The guy must have said something funny, because the small crowd of ladies he'd been chatting up burst into another round of giggles.

Stephen didn't understand how the guy did it; but then, he didn't know much about women. He'd lived with Rhoda for the past three years and never come close to solving any of her screwed-up emotional equations. This morning, when he'd gone to retrieve his belongings at the duplex, she'd been totally off the wall. He told her he'd paid the rent for January but wouldn't be back, and she'd come at him with teeth and claws.

Christ, it had ended badly. Had he expected it to go any other way?

Now he was a free agent, alone in a bar for the first time since turning twenty-one a year and a half ago. Any red-blooded man in his situation would be interested in talking to either of the two girls next to him. They had already introduced themselves and seemed . . . friendly.

He stifled the urge to flee.

Instead, he lifted his mug and drank deep. He wished he could think about his mom without being blindsided by guilt and shame and sadness, but he couldn't. The beer helped. A little dope would have done better.

Stephen knew he was weak. James had always been the strong one. And the smart one, and the handsome one. His little brother was going to be somebody. Now that their parents were gone, Stephen's sole purpose in life was to make sure James succeeded.

So while he waited for *Destiny* to come back to the mainland, he sipped his beer, responding only when asked a question and paying more attention to the guy across the bar than the girls who were right beside him.

Then it finally hit him. He knew the guy. Damn, drugs had messed up his head. Sometimes he felt as though he'd been walking around in a fog for the past few years.

The guy across the bar was JT Carver. Stephen didn't remember meeting him, and wasn't sure how he knew his name. Maybe he'd sold pot to him a couple of times. By the looks of the dancing bears on the front of his T-shirt, he was still a stoner.

What Stephen did recall, very clearly, was that JT was a surfer. And a john.

Unless he was mistaken, at one time or another, he'd seen JT Carver out on the beach at night, trolling for whores.

Stephen hunched over a little more, not wishing to

be recognized. He didn't know why, but JT struck him as a cagey bastard. Stephen had grown up cautious, always hiding out and dodging blows, so it was second nature for him to avoid shady characters.

After spending his formative years under the rule of Arlen Matthews, Stephen knew a dangerous man when he saw one.

"We're staying at the Sheraton," the girl sitting next to him said. She was blond and petite and a lot curvier than Rhoda, which he liked.

"That's nice," he said. He'd never been in a motel room in his life.

A crease formed between her brows, and he realized that he was supposed to read something more into her comment.

"Do you have any friends around here?" she asked.

"No."

She giggled, exchanging a glace with the other girl, who wasn't quite as pretty as the first one was, and tucking a strand of hair behind her ear. "Well, if you want to come along with us, we're heading over there."

He looked back and forth between them. "To do what?"

She giggled again, whispered something in her friend's ear, and they both dissolved in laughter. "To hang out," she explained. "You know. Party."

"I don't have any pot," he said, figuring that was what they were after.

"We do," she replied with a smile.

A shiver of awareness passed through his body.

Were they inviting him back to their motel room for...? Good God.

Across the bar, JT Carver was paying his tab, preparing to leave.

"Sorry," he muttered, rising to his feet. "I have something else to do."


Sonny sent Grant a quick text as she drove down to America's Cup Harbor. JT rented a slip on Shelter Island, and she wanted to get there before anyone else did.

She hadn't told Tom Bruebaker she suspected JT of sleeping with Olivia—or with Sheila, for that matter—but he might put two and two together. God forbid he bury the hatchet and call Ben. She'd never be able to question JT if the disgruntled husbands showed up.

When she arrived, it was just past sunset and the sidewalk traffic along the marina was steady. Shelter Island was a patrolled, gated community, and it cost a lot of money to tenant here. Gleaming yachts sat alongside smaller, more modest recreational crafts and sport fishers.

Most of the owners didn't live aboard.

JT's houseboat, *Captain Trips,* floated quietly in a far corner, windows dark. The slap of water against the hull and the faint cacophony of distant voices were the only sounds.

It took her less than five minutes to break in.

The place was neat as a pin and ruthlessly organized—necessary, perhaps, with such limited space, but not what she'd expected from a party boy like him. She also found things she did expect, champagne and candlesticks, condoms and soft-core porn. Nothing terribly kinky. Just your average arsenal for seduction.

In his closet he had casual, expensive sportswear, vintage T-shirts, and designer jeans. He must be independently wealthy, because he also owned a lot of high-tech gadgets, an impressive collection of surfboards, and a top-quality, titanium-lined wetsuit.

Heart pounding with excitement, Sonny worked faster, sorting through a significant array of masculine beauty products and rifling through closed drawers.

There was one nondescript cardboard box hidden beneath a pair of sweatpants in the bottom drawer. Sonny pulled out the box and took off the lid. Inside, there was a dirty green trucker hat and a pair of old sunglasses.

"Oh my God," she whispered. These things had belonged to Arlen.

Scrambling to her feet, she dug her cell phone out of her purse to alert Grant. And heard the click of a revolver in the entryway behind her.

Making a split-second decision, she let the phone fall to the carpet and slipped her hand into her jacket, going for her gun.

"I wouldn't do that if I were you," he warned.

She paused, fingers touching metal. If she ducked down as she drew her weapon, there was a good chance he'd miss.

"This is a .38," JT explained. "At this range it

would blow a hole through you the size of a water-melon."

Keeping her hand where it was, she tilted her head to look at him.

He smiled at her, coldly handsome without the charming, sleepy-eyed façade. "Remove your weapon and take out the clip."

It occurred to her that not only did JT know she was carrying, he knew *what* she was carrying. He'd been in her apartment. Feeling sick with unease, she slid her SIG out of the holster and let the clip drop.

"Good," he said, nodding. "Toss that on the bed."

"Backup is on the way," she said, hoping it was true. "Any minute, there'll be feds and local police crawling all over the place."

"Then we'd best get going," he said.

She turned to face him, moving slow. His eyes were cool and his hands were steady, but she knew he was afraid to approach her. As well he should be.

"Do you have a pair of cuffs in your purse?" he asked, studying her warily.

"If you think I'm going to make this easy for you—"

"Do it or they'll never find Carly."

Her stomach lurched. "Where is she?"

JT's mouth twisted with impatience. "We aren't negotiating, bitch, we're leaving. Now take those cuffs out and put them on your wrists or I'll just shoot you now and be on my way."

It was highly inadvisable to let a perp take her to another location. Her best chance at survival was to scuffle with him, even to risk taking a bullet in an attempt to break free.

Because she had Carly to consider, she removed the handcuffs from her purse.

"Make them tight," he said.

Gritting her teeth, she secured her own wrists. She didn't know how he'd snuck up on her, because she hadn't heard a sound, and the boat had never shifted under his weight. If she made it out of this situation alive, and she wasn't sure she deserved to after this rookie mistake, she would never leave her back to a door again.

Stephen watched JT and the woman from a distance. They were walking away from Shelter Island Marina, and in the deepening gloom, he couldn't see her very clearly.

Something about her was familiar.

He hesitated, glancing back at the houseboat. It appeared as though JT had forgotten to lock up on his way out. The woman wasn't struggling or showing any signs of distress, and JT was leading her toward other people, not away from them.

If Stephen followed them, he might not see anything more interesting than a moonlit walk or a romantic dinner, and what he really wanted to do was snoop through JT's belongings. He waited until the couple was out of sight before he stepped from the shadows, hurrying across the concrete pathway and slipping onto *Captain Trips*.

He was afraid to turn on the lights, so he had to

wait for his eyes to adjust. Heart pounding a mile a
minute, he stood inside someone else's home, a silent
intruder. After an indescribable length of time, the
gleaming surfaces and clean lines took shape.

Stephen gulped, more nervous than ever. This was
the kind of place where one stray fingerprint would
be noticed. He had to be careful not to touch anything.

Hands sweating, pulse racing, he moved from
room to room, hoping his boots didn't leave scuff
marks on the polished hardwood. A quick glance
told him what was out of place. In the bedroom,
there was a clip on the ground and a gun on the bed.

Next to the clip lay a woman's handbag. It was lying on one side, its contents spilled across the carpet.

"Damn," he whispered, knowing he'd made the
wrong decision. He should have followed them.

Wiping his palms on the legs of his jeans, he
reached down to pick up a single white business card.
Flipping it over, he saw a familiar name.

Special Agent Sonora Vasquez.

"Damn!" he repeated. The woman who took off
with JT was that blue-eyed FBI agent, the one who'd
treated him kindly. She'd made him uncomfortable—
all women did—but he'd felt an instant connection
with her. A kinship.

His eyes moved past the card, to an empty shoe box
near the foot of the bed. Inside, barely discernible in
the approaching dark, was one of his dad's old trucker
caps and a pair of dirty sunglasses. The lenses glinted
wickedly in the meager light.

Stephen sucked in a sharp breath. And felt his vision narrow.

Arlen may have deserved killing, but none of those girls had. He could still see their pretty faces, smiling up at him from their photos.

"You murdering motherfucker," he muttered, picking up the gun. He didn't know how to use it, but it felt good in his hands. It felt damned good. He scooped up the clip and jammed it into the chamber, surprised when it easily clicked into place.

He was locked and loaded. Ready to go.

And when he heard a voice behind him, a man busting through the door, he was so geared up for violence, he whirled around and pulled the trigger.

# CHAPTER 24

JT draped a T-shirt over her wrists, hiding the cuffs, and stuffed his gun in the pocket of his jacket. He led her down the causeway with the muzzle pressed against her spine, a chilly reminder that he meant business.

To the casual passerby, they were a cozy couple taking a quiet stroll.

As they approached Fisherman's Wharf, she felt another surge of panic. At dusk, the docks were quiet, but when one last boat cruised into the harbor, she knew it was *Destiny*. Carly and James were safe inside, oblivious to the danger, snuggling close as they came in from their stolen afternoon at sea.

JT had lied. Not only had Sonny allowed herself to be captured, she'd given him an opportunity to use her as leverage.

"Don't start resisting now," he clucked, reading

her body language. "It will hardly do them any good."

"Eat shit and die," she returned in a bored tone, deliberately relaxing her shoulders. If there was any time to fight, it was at this very moment, before James and Carly got involved. Twisting her body toward him, she swung her cuffed hands up, catching him under the chin.

He staggered back a step, stunned.

Encouraged by the small victory, she struck again, aiming a roundhouse kick at JT's right hand, the one holding the gun. With amazingly fast reflexes, he caught her ankle before her foot connected and jerked her off balance.

Having no way to break her fall, she landed hard on her back. Pain jolted down her spine and the wind rushed out of her lungs.

He looked around to make sure there were no witnesses, keeping the gun in his pocket pointed down at her. "Get up."

She rolled to one side, gasping for air.

He kicked her in the ribs. Pain exploded upon impact, sharp and exquisite. She would have cried out if she could have drawn breath.

"Get up," he repeated, pulling her by the arm.

She couldn't walk and he couldn't make her, so he dragged her useless body the last twenty feet, coming to a stop in front of *Destiny* as she docked. Not bothering to wait for James or Carly to greet him, he shoved Sonny aboard, digging the muzzle of his gun into the tender spot in her side.

Sucking in a desperate lungful of air, finally, brought another bolt of agony.

Inside the cab of the boat, James was behind the wheel with Carly at his side, leaning her head on his shoulder and ruffling a hand through his hair. When she saw Sonny and JT, she let out a little yelp.

JT took the gun out of his pocket and placed it against Sonny's temple. "I need to go to Mexico."

James put his body in front of Carly's.

JT ground the muzzle against Sonny's head. "Cooperate, and no one will get hurt."

James' dark gaze moved from the gun to Sonny's face. She tried to blank her expression, hiding the pain, but he saw the evidence in her labored breathing and bowed back. Obviously, someone had already been hurt. "Let Carly out and I'll take you anywhere you want to go."

JT didn't appreciate James' attempt at negotiation any more than he had appreciated hers. He took the gun away from her temple, preparing to point it at James.

In a last-ditch effort to save them, and herself, Sonny drove her elbow into JT's midsection. It was a direct hit, and although she had the element of surprise on her side, he retaliated faster than she could follow up. With little more than an annoyed grunt, he backhanded her, sending her sprawling across the deck.

Her head rocked back against the planks so hard she saw dark flashes.

"As I was saying," JT continued, rubbing his belly with his free hand and holding the gun on James with the other. "Cooperate. Keep your mouths shut. And take me to Mexico."

Sonny squeezed her eyes closed, reeling from the blow.

"Carly doesn't need to be here," James insisted.

"Oh, but she does," JT countered. "I think she needs to be here most of all."

"Why?" James asked, fear making his voice quake.

"Because she has to learn a lesson. One that is overdue, judging by your lovesick face and torn shirt. It seems she's a slut, just like her mother."

Sonny forced her eyes open. James had a jacket over his shirt, both of which were open down the front, exposing a strip of lean midsection. His face was flat, but his stance indicated a barely restrained fury.

"You..." Carly stuttered. Her skin was ashen and her eyes huge. James tightened his grip on her arm, as if afraid she might lunge forward. "You killed my mom."

"Yes," JT admitted, sounding bored. Seeing a length of rope at his feet, he kicked it toward James. "Tie her up," he said, waving the gun in Carly's general direction. "I don't need another she-cat clawing at me."

Having little choice in the matter, James picked up the rope, darting a glance at Sonny as he did so. From the ground, she looked back at him, her wrists cuffed and her head swirling with nausea, unable to offer him any type of assistance.

James knew the score as well as she did. The options were to die now or die later. Eyes downcast, he tied the rope around Carly's wrists, choosing to die later.

When Ben flipped on the bedroom light, Stephen Matthews was standing there, pointing a gun at him. It made a clicking sound as he pulled the trigger.

Ben froze, anticipating the explosion. He'd always thought images from his entire life would flash before his eyes at the moment of his death.

Only one did. Carly's face.

"God*damn,* man," Stephen said, lowering the weapon. "I almost shot you."

Ben let out a slow breath. Apparently, the kid hadn't meant to give him a heart attack. Or to attempt murder. "Where's my daughter?"

Stephen frowned at the gun in his hand, probably wondering why it hadn't gone off. "She's on the boat with James," he said, inspecting the weapon. At his feet, there was a black leather handbag and some miscellaneous female items.

Recognizing them, Ben's heartbeat began to thunder in his ears. He'd come to talk to JT, figuring he'd been the scumbag sleeping with Sheila. His friend had absolutely no discretion when it came to women. Now, seeing Stephen Matthews here with Sonny's purse—and her gun—it occurred to him that JT had been up to more than adultery.

Quite a bit more.

"You'd better call the cops," Stephen said.

Ben already had his cell phone out.

"I think the guy who lives here killed my dad.

Probably all those women, too. I just saw him take off with an FBI agent."

"Was she all right?" Ben asked, dialing 911 with trembling fingers.

"I think so. He might have had a gun on her. I couldn't see."

She was alive. Thank God, she was still alive.

"Emergency services," an operator answered. "Please hold."

Ben took the phone away from his ear, staring down at it in dismay. "Fuck," he yelled, his blood pressure skyrocketing. He turned his attention back to Stephen. "Where did they go?"

"Toward the wharf," Stephen said. His blue eyes widened. "You don't think he'd go after Carly and James, do you?"

They both scrambled outside, looking past the edge of Shelter Island to catch a glimpse of America's Cup Harbor. While they stood there, Ben with the phone pressed to his ear, listening to elevator music, a lone boat moved away in the distance, heading south.

"Holy Christ," Stephen exclaimed. "That's *Destiny.*"

Not Carly, Ben's mind screamed. Please, not Carly. He searched the marina frantically, looking for a security guard, a uniformed officer, a man with an operating boat they could hijack. Anything. Anyone. But the place was deserted.

A soft rock instrumental continued to flow from the receiver into his ear. "Fuck!" he yelled again, not knowing which direction to run for help.

"I can hotwire this son of a bitch," Stephen decided, stepping back inside *Captain Trips*. Ben followed eagerly, relieved to be in the company of a petty criminal.

As it turned out, there was no need to resort to extreme measures. JT had left the keys on the dash. "Thank you, Jesus," Stephen said, kissing the key ring and fumbling for the proper key to fit the ignition. Before the operator responded to Ben's emergency call, *Captain Trips* was out cruising.

It took almost ten minutes of stammered explanations and department transfers for Ben to get though to Special Agent in Charge Leland Grant.

"The Coast Guard is on its way," Grant promised. "I'm working on air support. You have to back off now. I don't want him to know he's being followed."

Up ahead of them, *Destiny* chugged along, tiny in the distance, the length between the two boats seemingly insurmountable.

"Can't this thing go any faster?" Ben complained, ignoring Grant.

"I'm doing my best," Stephen replied.

"Turn around now," Grant repeated. "Let us do our job."

"He wants us to back off," Ben said to Stephen.

"Fuck that," was the kid's succinct answer.

Ben nodded. His sentiments exactly.


"This is a midshipman's knot," James whispered in her ear. "Looks tight, but if I give it three good tugs, you'll be free."

Carly was careful not to nod or make any verbal

reply. JT's hands were busy with Summer, but his eyes were on her. James was only able to get a few words in by hiding his mouth behind her hair as he bound her wrists.

"I love you," he added before he stood.

Tears filled her eyes.

JT strung Summer up like fresh catch, securing the chain between her handcuffs to a hook on the mast. With her arms extended over her head, she was stretched taut, barely able to touch the deck with her tiptoes.

It looked painful. Carly would have hung her head and cried, but Summer stayed quiet, her breathing steady, almost meditative, her eyes flashing dull blue fire.

There was something different about her, something a little scary. Carly was both afraid to analyze the change and glad for it. Having another helpless, hysterical female on board wouldn't have done them any good.

Carly couldn't believe JT had killed her mom. She wanted to throw herself at him, to slap him and hit him and claw at his face. But her arms were pulled behind her back, rendering her motionless. Useless.

JT kept his gun against James' ear while he navigated *Destiny* through the fog. Carly felt like a trapped bird, her heart hammering in her chest, her pulse fluttering against the coarse rope at her wrists. Her frantic mind searched for a possible escape route, but she couldn't find any way out. She could only see flashes of her mother, images from the past mixed with the reality of the present, Summer's stoic endurance and James' inscrutable face.

They hadn't gone far when JT asked James to cut the engine—and the lights. When James complied, JT moved the gun away from his head. For a long, restless moment, *Destiny* floated on dark, calm waters. The glow from the dash illuminated his face from below, casting jagged shadows above his brows and making him appear twice as sinister.

Carly held her breath, waiting for all hell to break loose.

Keeping his gaze on James, JT ran the muzzle of his gun down Summer's front, popping open a few buttons on her blue sweater. Summer closed her eyes and held herself perfectly still, refusing to give him the satisfaction of struggling.

"You have nice tits for a butchy chick," he murmured, pursing his lips.

Carly turned her head away from the disturbing scene, horrified by the idea that JT had touched her mother the same way. She hated herself for being cowardly, but she wanted to cover her ears and close her eyes, to curl up in a little ball and wish it all away.

"Leave her alone," James growled.

JT smiled, pleased to have angered him. "Or what?"

"You know what. If you want to hurt someone, why don't you try me?"

Carly didn't like that suggestion, and neither did Summer. She kicked out, jerking her body forward, trying to dislodge herself from the hook she was hanging on. It was an exercise in futility, and it amused JT to watch her flail.

"Okay, pretty boy," he said, turning to James. "I'll try you."

James blanched but he didn't argue. "Away from them," he stipulated.

JT laughed. There wasn't a place on the boat they couldn't be seen from the cab, but he waved his gun in a conceding gesture. "After you."

That's when Carly knew JT was going to kill him. Tears blurred her vision as she watched JT follow the boy she loved, the one who thought he was giving her a chance to live by sacrificing himself, through the cabin door.

On his way out, JT directed the gun toward Carly. "Don't move," he said, "or I'll kill you next."

James paused in the doorway, his throat working convulsively. She thought he wanted to say good-bye, but he only shook his head and kept going, as if the sight of her might weaken his resolve. Carly wanted to tell him how much she loved him, but when she opened her mouth, the only sound that came out was a strangled sob.

As soon as JT walked out on deck, Carly found her mettle. She tugged on the binding at her wrists, intent on freeing herself and following. The ropes didn't budge.

"Help me," Summer whispered, casting a nervous glance up front. "Come over here and get down on your knees."

Tears streaming down her face, Carly scrambled over to the mast, kneeling before Summer like a worshipper of an Eastern religion. Summer's heels dug into her back, hurting her, but Carly was glad to be of use. In a matter of seconds, the woman unhooked herself and fell forward, careening headfirst into the dash.

Stifling a whimper of dismay, Carly leapt to her feet, searching for the dark shapes of men at the bow. James was standing with his back to JT, ready to be executed.

Carly screamed.

Hearing her, JT turned his head toward the cab. James, seeing the opening, turned to fight.

His fist connected with JT's chin.

Growling in pain, JT swung the gun at James, catching him hard across the left temple. Carly cried out again, tugging on the ropes around her wrists. They cut into her skin, stretching taut. She looked to the other woman for help.

Summer must have been hurting more than she let on, because she was still bent across the dash, breathing hard. Her hands were bone white and her lips a cold, chalky gray. "Don't go out there," she rasped.

Disregarding Summer's warning as soon as it was issued, Carly ran out to help James. He was lying in a crumpled heap on the deck, a dark pool of blood seeping across the planks beneath his head. His eyes were closed and his body motionless.

"No!" she cried, wanting to drop to her knees beside him and weep. Instead, she narrowed her eyes on JT, seething. Driven wild by fear and grief, she lowered her head and ran toward him at full speed. Surprised by her sudden, armless attack, JT side-stepped at the last second, and Carly went sprawling over the edge.

She hit the water with a shocking *slap*. It enveloped her like an icy blanket, wrapping her in its inky depths. The temperature was so cold her heart almost stopped beating. Pinpricks of pain broke out over her skin, like a thousand tiny needles.

She jerked against the ropes, kicking furiously, feeling the stiff fibers cut into her skin. With her arms tied behind her back, the cold was the least of her worries.

James heard the splash as Carly went overboard. The sound was muffled by the pounding in his ears, or maybe it was just blood rushing into them. His head throbbed and his scalp was gushing like a gutted thresher.

He didn't know how, or why, but he was conscious, and alive.

JT walked by him, probably to get back to putting his creepy hands all over Summer, or Special Agent Vasquez, whatever her name was. There was an awful ruckus in the cab. James didn't like it, but he had other fish to fry.

Dragging himself forward, his movements slow as molasses, he pulled his uncooperative body to the starboard side, where Carly had gone over.

He could see bubbles on the surface. He blinked, staving off another wave of unconsciousness, feeling blood trickle down his neck. He wouldn't be much good to Carly if he passed out the instant he hit the water. On the other hand, if he waited longer, he wouldn't be any good to her at all.

With a low groan, he heaved his body over the rail.

The first contact with cold water was a shock to his tender skull. He couldn't help but cry out in pain, sending a flurry of bubbles to the surface. White spots flashed behind his eyes, and he almost inhaled a lungful of seawater in his panic. Fortunately, he broke through the surface and sucked in air, clearing his head.

The water was alarmingly cold. Menacingly black. More bubbles appeared on the rippled surface, giving him a surge of hope. Praying for strength, and lucidity, he took another deep breath and dove down. The pressure was agonizing; his ears felt like they were going to explode. Salt water stung his eyes and cut into his scalp.

Somehow he found her. He knew she was still alive because he could feel movement in her body as he slipped his arm around her waist and pulled her toward the surface.

They came up together, panting.

"I can't get my hands free," she choked.

"I'll do it." Fumbling at her wrists, he tugged on the end of the knot. His fingers were so clumsy it took several tries to release her, and when he was done, he felt exhausted, as if he'd been wrestling sharks.

Speaking of sharks...

He eyed the dark water with trepidation, aware

that his scalp was bleeding profusely. The contrast between warm blood and cold sea was marked.

Carly frowned at him, rubbing her sore wrists. Her wet hair was clinging to her cheeks and neck, and he could see her breath, puffing out in the crisp night air.

"Why did you jump overboard?" he said in a low voice, glancing back at *Destiny*. He couldn't make out JT, but he was having trouble focusing. "Jesus Christ, Carly, that was..." He swallowed back his nausea. "That was..."

"Stupid?" she finished for him.

Treading water, he stared at her, trying to keep her in his sights. His limbs felt heavy, as if his clothes were weighted with bricks.

"James?"

Her voice sounded so far away. Although he struggled to stay there with her, the dark water lapped up over his head, beckoning him to oblivion.

Sonny slammed her hands against the dash, desperate to bring some feeling back to the useless appendages. There was a utility knife hanging by a scabbard above the dash. If she could just wrap her fingers around it...

On the deck, Carly launched herself at JT. A bold move, and a stupid one, but desperate times called for desperate measures. Unfortunately, JT had the devil's own luck.

The girl missed him and fell overboard. To her certain death.

Sonny slammed her hands down again, tears of panic and frustration scalding her eyes. If she didn't get out of these cuffs, she couldn't help Carly. Or James. And to get out of the cuffs, she had to defeat JT.

Her fingertips tingled but it wasn't enough. Her hands wouldn't work and her rib cage was on fire, burning with every intake of breath. She couldn't pull the knife from the scabbard—or maintain a grip on it, in any case.

"What's this?" JT asked, coming into the cab. Pushing her aside with humiliating ease, he pulled the short knife from the leather sheath and looked at its wicked blade. "I was going to save the cutting for Carly."

Staring at the serrated edge, Sonny backed away slowly, moistening her dry lips.

He tucked the gun into the back of his jeans, then tested the blade's sharpness with his fingertip. "Ouch," he said with a grin.

Outside, there was another splash. James!

JT flinched at the sound. "That sneaky son of a bitch," he murmured, looking out into the dark and clucking his tongue in appreciation. "Well, now they'll both drown."

Sonny flexed her fingers, feeling blood returning to her cuffed hands. The pain was fierce and she smiled, relishing it. Carly and James were alive, God willing, and although they couldn't climb aboard, or swim back to land, they could tread water until help arrived.

Which would be soon, as long as Grant had sent someone to look for her.

Now was the time to stall rather than fight. She retreated until her back hit the wood siding at the edge of the cab. "Did you have an affair with Olivia?"

"Yes," he said, his cold eyes sweeping down her body once again. "And unlike you, she was a luscious piece." He reached out and grabbed the chain between her wrists, holding her hands out of play while he touched the blade to her cheek. "Not that I won't enjoy having you screaming and begging beneath me."

She laughed at the idea, but it hurt so much she stopped. "What about Sheila?"

He studied her face, not amused by her bravado. "I may have"—he slid the tip of the knife down her chest—"thrown her a bone."

Sonny focused on regulating her breathing. Every time she inhaled, she felt a sharp stab in her side. He may have bruised a few ribs when he kicked her. "Did she pretend you were Ben the whole time you were in bed together," she panted, "or only when she came?"

JT's eyes returned to hers. With a deft movement, he sliced her sweater in half, exposing her bra. "You're a ballsy little bitch," he murmured, nodding his approval. "It will be a pleasure to break you."

Sonny drew in another shallow breath. JT was planning to rape and torture her before he killed her. It was her worst nightmare, but she would endure him. And when the time came, she would overpower him.

"Ben is your best friend," she said as he traced the edge of her bra with the tip of his knife. "Why did you kill Olivia? How could you do that to him?"

"She was a cheating whore. I did it *for* him."

Another piece of the puzzle clicked into place, something she should have considered before. "Did you lie to the police for him, too? Claiming to be his alibi?"

"Of course." He slid the blade down her stomach, skimming over her flesh. "Those fools took forever to find O'Shea."

"How did you know he'd confess?"

"I didn't," he admitted. "That was just a stroke of luck."

"What about the others? What did they do to deserve being brutally murdered?"

"Worthless sluts," he said with a sigh. "I did the world a favor."

"You'll never get away with this," she gasped, struggling for air. She didn't have to feign her fear.

He shrugged. "It hardly matters. I knew it was over for me the minute I saw you standing in my bedroom."

"You won't make it out alive."

He cut away the front of her trousers, nicking her hip. "Neither will you."

# CHAPTER 25

One moment they were punching it through the increasing fog, catching up with *Destiny*, and the next she was gone.

"What happened?" Ben asked, searching the horizon.

"He cut the lights," Stephen said, reaching up to do the same. In an instant, they were cloaked in darkness.

Fear gripped him. "Why?"

"Either he realized he was being followed, or he stopped to..."

Ben's chest tightened like a vise. "Go faster."

"I can't. In these conditions, we'd be right on top of them before I had a chance to react."

Ben tried to stay calm, but it was impossible. He couldn't bear the thought of Carly in danger. "I'm going out on deck," he said, figuring he could see better from there.

"Good idea."

Adrenaline rushing through his veins, he walked to the bow, eyes straining to see through the mist. When he caught up with JT, he was going to fucking kill him. Beat the hell out of him first. Then wrap his fingers around his throat and squeeze.

So intent was he on vengeance, he almost missed them. The fog was patchy, intermittent, but between the breaks he caught a glimpse. "Up ahead," he shouted to Stephen, who nodded and changed direction slightly, making a beeline toward *Destiny*.

In its cab, Ben could see the vague outline of two figures, locked in struggle. From their respective heights he knew it was JT and Sonny.

No one else was visible. Where was Carly?

It felt as though *Captain Trips* was moving in slow motion. Christ, he could swim faster than this!

The sound of splashing alerted him to his daughter's location. About twenty feet away from *Destiny*, there were two dark heads bobbing on the surface of the water. When he saw them, tears of relief sprung into his eyes. "Carly!" he shouted, leaning out over the rail.

"Daddy," she cried back. "Help me!"

Ben didn't hesitate. Carly needed him. There was no other choice to make. Taking a second to flip off his shoes, he leapt onto the railing and dove into the dark Pacific. The water was bracingly cold. Life-affirming. He reached her in a few sure strokes.

"It's James," she panted, her breath puffing out in

front of her. In the moonlight, her eyes were black with fright. "I can't hold him up."

James was in the crook of her arm, unconscious. Rivulets of watery blood streaked down his ghostly-pale face. "Give him to me," he ordered, shoving his forearm under James' chin. The boy's body was limp and his skin was icy. "Can you swim?" Ben asked Carly. If he had to, he'd drop James to save her. In a heartbeat.

No way would he let his daughter go under. No way.

"I think I'm okay," she said, teeth chattering.

"Are you hurt?"

"No, Daddy, I'm just cold."

Ben looked over his shoulder, keeping James' head above the surface as he treaded water. JT and Sonny were out of his line of sight. While he watched, Stephen edged *Captain Trips* as close as he could to *Destiny*. Jumping distance, as a matter of fact.

"That crazy bastard," he breathed, starting to swim. With his back to the boats, he couldn't see what Stephen was doing, but he didn't have to. He knew the kid was climbing onto the railing and hopping the gap. Acting a fool.

Risking his neck for a woman he didn't even know.

Tears burned Ben's eyes again, but he didn't have time for them. He had to get Carly and James out of the water before he could help Stephen.

Ben knew JT was stronger than Sonny. He could probably strangle her in a matter of moments. Perhaps her FBI training had kept her alive this long, but JT wouldn't continue to toy with her now.

Ben pushed that thought aside and focused on the task at hand, swimming as fast as he could. James wasn't big, but he was heavy. Ben didn't know how Carly had held him up at all. She reached *Captain Trips* before he did, climbing the aluminum ladder leading to the deck.

Getting James up the ladder was difficult. With Carly's help, he managed, bracing his weight on one arm and wrapping the other around James' midsection. When James' back hit the deck, none too gently, he began to sputter and cough.

Carly burst out crying.

Ben put James on his side, and Carly cradled the boy's head lovingly while he vomited sea water all over her lap.

"I think he'll be all right," he said with a grimace, glancing toward *Destiny*.

"No," she said, grabbing Ben's wrist. "Don't go over there."

Ben would do anything in the world for Carly. Anything but this.

Taking her face in his hands, he planted a kiss in the middle of her forehead. "I love you, baby, but I have to," he said, and rose to his feet.

When he heard the gunshot, he knew he was too late.


JT dragged her to the cabin floor to cut away the rest of her clothes, so intent on terrorizing her he didn't hear the commotion outside.

"Please don't hurt me," she cried out suddenly,

trying to cover the sound. "I'll do anything you want. Please don't kill me."

He smiled, delighted to hear her beg. "You'll do anything I want anyway."

"Yes," she agreed, sobbing. "Anything you like. Whatever you say. Please."

He pursed his mouth, deliberating.

Stephen Matthews exploded through the cabin door before JT could make up his mind. "Get off her," he said, pointing Sonny's SIG Sauer 9mm at JT.

She hoped to God he knew how to use it.

JT straightened slowly. "I don't think you have the balls to shoot me, junkie."

Stephen clenched his jaw, but his aim didn't waver. "Try me."

JT switched the knife to his left hand. The blade glinted in the dim light. Sonny knew JT would go for his gun. With his body turned toward Stephen, she could see the .38 in the waistband of his jeans.

Just inches from her reach.

He went for it at the same time she did. And Stephen pulled the trigger, hitting JT dead-on, straight through the chest.

Sonny screamed as the bullet tore into him. She couldn't help it. Like JT, she hadn't been sure Stephen would go through with it, and the noise was incredibly loud. Feeling the full force of the impact, she recoiled as if the bullet had struck her.

The pistol's report echoed across the sea, drowning out all other sound.

JT fell back against the wooden siding, arms akimbo, eyes glazed. Stephen must have hit him in the heart, because the wound hardly even bled. A perfect kill shot.

Making sure, she raised her fingers to JT's neck, feeling for a pulse. There was nothing. "He's dead," she said, lifting her gaze to Stephen's.

Her half-brother lowered the weapon. "I killed him?"

She nodded.

His face went green. "I guess I didn't want to shake his hand after all," he said, swallowing. With a final glance at the neat hole in JT's chest, he set the pistol on the dash, staggered out toward the railing, and was violently ill.

Shaken to the core, Sonny crawled out from underneath JT's dead body. Sitting with her back to the wall, she drew her knees up protectively and brought the tatters of her clothes together with trembling hands. She didn't feel sick, but she'd never been particularly squeamish. She didn't feel anything, other than aches and pains. She was just...numb.

Stephen was leaning over the rail, still retching, when Ben appeared in the doorway of the cabin, soaking wet. Puddles formed beneath his feet and steam rose from his clothes. He glanced at JT, making sure he was dead before he kneeled before her. He must be cold, like she was, but the concern in his eyes warmed her more than any blanket could have.

"Carly and James?" she whispered.

"They're safe."

He looked down at her cuffed wrists. Very gently, he reached out and cupped her chin, turning her head to one side to study her face. "Did he hurt you?"

"Not much," she said, giving him a wobbly smile. It wouldn't stay in place. "He didn't get the chance."

Ben squinted at JT, as if he wanted him to die a few more times. Along with anger, she saw relief on his face, and a trace of regret. "I should have known you wouldn't need me to play your knight in shining armor."

Tears filled her eyes. He was wrong. She needed him desperately. With an inarticulate cry, she leaned forward, putting her head against his chest as he wrapped his arms around her.

No longer numb, she pressed her face to his neck and wept. She cried for Rigo and for her mother, for lost chances and broken dreams. And then she cried for herself. "I love you," she said, unable to hold her feelings back.

His body tensed. "I love you, too."

She lifted her head, staring up at him in teary-eyed wonder. "Are you saying that because you thought I was going to die?"

He smiled. "No. What about you? Do you mean it this time?"

"Yes," she said, sniffling. "But I meant it last time."

Blinking away his own emotions, he cupped his hand behind her neck and brought her head back to his chest. "I know," he said, holding her there, cherished and safe, sheltered in the strength of his arms.


Sonny opened her eyes, aware of a man's presence in the small room. Grant's face wavered into focus, concern etched on his features.

"I didn't mean to wake you."

Sonny glanced at the clock beside the hospital bed. Several hours had gone by since they'd returned to the mainland. In the minutes following JT's death, local and federal investigation units had converged on the scene. The Coast Guard's rescue helicopter had been deemed unnecessary, but James was rushed to Scripps Hospital in a snazzy-looking Harbor Police powerboat. Carly insisting on accompanying him, so Ben had gone with her, casting Sonny an apologetic glance over his shoulder.

Stephen had wanted to go, too, but because he'd been the one to pull the trigger, he hadn't been allowed to leave the scene of the crime.

Sonny had debriefed Staff Sergeant Paula DeGrassi, explaining that Stephen had been acting in self-defense and giving her sworn statement. After speaking with Grant via satellite phone, Sonny had excused herself politely, taken a few steps away from the crowd of officers aboard *Destiny*, and collapsed in an untidy heap on the deck.

Apparently, she'd needed more than air. According to the nice doctors at Scripps, she had two fractured ribs and suffered some internal bruising. She'd been poked and prodded, her midsection wrapped up tight as a drum. One of those pokes must have included a dose of pain medication, because sometime between then and now, she'd closed her eyes, and Grant had arrived from Virginia.

"Sorry," she murmured, wincing at the pull in her sore ribs as she straightened.

"For what? Getting hurt?"

She nodded, although she'd been apologizing for falling asleep, as ridiculous as that seemed. "It's nothing," she said, minimizing her injury. "You didn't have to come back."

Hurt registered on his face. "What kind of boss would I be if I didn't care about the welfare of my agents?"

Tears filled her eyes, because the relationship between them went deeper than employer–employee. He was the closest thing to a father she'd ever had, and they both knew it. "Sorry," she said again, this time for getting sentimental.

He cleared his throat, not unaffected by the exchange. "Homicide found a pile of evidence in JT's locker on Shelter Island. Photos of the victims, personal items, electrical cord..."

Sonny nodded. She hadn't doubted JT's guilt for an instant.

"It's better than a signed confession," he said gruffly. "Good work."

Coming from a tight-lipped taskmaster like Grant, it was fine praise indeed. She fairly glowed with pride.

"About your review..."

The warm fuzzies left as quickly as they'd come.

"I'm thinking we'll postpone it for now," he continued, surprising her. "You haven't taken any leave time in a while, and with your injuries, I recommend you do so. Six months down the road, or a year, when this whole thing blows over..."

She frowned at him. "You're not turning me in to Internal Affairs?"

His expression was deliberately blank. "For what?"

"And Mitchell?" she asked, caution warring with giddiness. "Will he talk?"

"Leave Special Agent Mitchell to me," Grant replied, eyes narrow.

Gratitude washed over her. "Thank you," she said, reaching out to grab the front of his shirt. Ignoring the pain in her side, she pulled him close for an impulsive hug. "Thank you so much."

While he tolerated her embrace, only a little less stiffly than he had before, she noticed the outline of another figure standing in the hall.

Grant lifted his head, following her gaze.

Instead of coming in, Ben hesitated outside the doorway, a gift-store bouquet of flowers in one hand and a wary expression on his handsome face.

As Grant straightened, he looked back and forth between them, understanding and acceptance in his intelligent gray eyes. Sometimes he knew her better than she knew herself. "You aren't going to be working with me much longer, are you?"

Tears welled up again. "No," she whispered.

If he was disappointed, he didn't show it. Maybe this was what he'd hoped for her all along. To love herself, and someone else, enough to want to live past the age of thirty. "DeGrassi's looking for an FBI liaison to San Diego Homicide."

She swallowed. "You would approve of the transfer?"

He nodded slowly. When she leaned forward to hug him again, he held up a hand. "Please. Your young man already wants to rip me to shreds."

Laughter bubbled from her throat. She was so happy, her ribs didn't even hurt. With one last good-bye and a respectful nod at Ben, Grant was gone.

"Can I come in?" Ben asked.

Sonny leaned back against the pillows. "Of course," she said, making a murmur of thanks when he set the bouquet on the nightstand. "How's James?"

"Fine," he said with a snort. "Eating pudding."

"And Carly?"

"Won't leave his side."

She smiled at his affronted tone. After Carly's near-death experience, Ben probably wanted to hold his daughter close, but Carly was more interested in making eyes at James. *Her* knight in shining armor. "What about Stephen? Is he still here?"

"Yes," Ben said, running a hand through his disheveled hair. "He's in the lobby, shivering. They offered him a sedative but he wouldn't take it. I think he's detoxing."

Sonny wondered how long her half-brother's sobriety would last. Getting clean was a hard row to hoe alone. "Maybe you could sponsor him."

"You mean, pay for rehab?"

"That would be nice, but he might be too proud to accept your money. It wouldn't cost anything to take him to a few meetings."

Ben appeared to consider the idea, and although he didn't make any promises, neither did he refuse outright. "You didn't tell me you were hurt," he said, changing the subject.

"Bumps and bruises," she claimed.

He didn't believe her for a second. "I've had

broken ribs before. You won't be able to take care of yourself."

"Are you offering to nurse me back to health?" She'd been playing coy, but when he nodded, his eyes dark with intensity, her heart swelled with love for him. "It just so happens that I have some leave time," she said. "I've been thinking I'd like to laze about on the beach for a few weeks, admire your cutback."

He wasn't fooled by her lighthearted banter. "Is that all we have? A few weeks?"

"Actually, I—"

"Never mind," he interrupted. "It doesn't matter."

She blinked in confusion. "It doesn't?"

"Not really," he said, meeting her eyes. "After Olivia died, I'd have given anything to have one more day, one more hour, one more *minute* with her. I don't want to make the same mistake with you."

Warmth tingled in her belly. "Are you sure?"

He took her by the hand, rubbing his thumb over her knuckles. "Yes. I don't like the idea of you risking your life, but I can't ask you to give up your job. I couldn't give up mine. So we'll work around it. I'll visit you in Virginia whenever I can."

"You would do that?"

"Of course."

She stared down at their entwined hands, her body humming with anxiety. Putting her heart on the line was the scariest thing she'd ever done. "I'm going to request a transfer."

"You...what?"

"I'm leaving my position at VICAP," she clarified. "No more undercover work."

"Why?"

Taking a deep breath, she said, "I guess I found out some risks aren't worth taking. Not when I have so much to lose."

His brown eyes softened with understanding. With his dark hair hopelessly rumpled and worry lines creasing his forehead, he was still the handsomest man she'd ever seen. When her vision blurred, she blamed it on the medication. It also must have been responsible for her clogged throat, the heavy *lub-dub* of her heartbeat, and the swelling in her chest.

Because neither of them was able to speak, she reached out to him, lifting her hand to his face. He sank to his knees at her bedside, giving her easier access, and wrapped one arm around her, very gingerly. She threaded her fingers through his hair and brought him closer to her, grabbing handfuls of happiness and holding it tight.

# CHAPTER 26

Sonny pulled into the parking lot at Neptune Apartments, exhausted from the red-eye flight but giddy with anticipation.

Over the past few weeks, she'd slept too little and worked too much. Her lovely plans to recuperate on the beach, lazing about in the warm sun and admiring Ben's cutback, had been thwarted by cold, hard reality. As soon as she was cleared to fly, she'd been whisked back to Quantico. Wrapping up a serial murder case was a meticulous, time-consuming process, and because of her involvement with every step of the investigation, her input was essential. Requesting a transfer to San Diego, giving notice to her landlord, and tying up the loose ends of her old life were also tasks that required hours of attention.

Now that she was free, unencumbered by the past and finished with her position at VICAP, she should feel as light as the ocean breeze that rifled through her hair as she walked toward Windansea Beach. Instead, she was stiff-limbed and awkward, her palms clammy and her pulse racing. Anxiety curled up in her belly like a lead ball.

Ben didn't know she was coming.

It wasn't as though she hadn't talked to him on the phone every night before she went to sleep. He'd told her how Carly was doing and given her updates on her half-brothers. James had enrolled in La Jolla Shores High School and Stephen had been staying clean, working on the *Destiny* and attending NA meetings.

Over the phone, things between them had been... friendly. Heated, even. But they hadn't exchanged an "I love you" since that last tumultuous evening together.

The press had had a field day covering the case, and John Thomas Carver became America's favorite new monster. He might have enjoyed the attention if he'd lived. Every detail of his past was exposed, including his father's drug overdose and his mother's sordid lifestyle.

Although JT rarely spoke of his mother, he'd given Ben the impression that Cheryl Carver, better known as Cherry, had been a B-movie actress. She was actually a porn star who'd been strangled by her boyfriend when JT was fourteen. Perhaps her death had been his breaking point, or maybe that time came years before, during the incident that had precipitated JT's transfer from his mother's care. When her house was raided for drugs, two uniformed officers found her ten-year-old son unconscious, tied to a bed, naked but for lipstick smudges and candle drippings. Apparently, a couple of Cherry's doped-up girlfriends had made a game of him, and after they grew bored, they left him there, used up and forgotten.

The history of childhood abuse, and JT's failure to maintain healthy relationships with women as an adult, were the only indications of his darker nature. On the outside, he was a party boy who lived the good life. No one suspected him of violence, including Ben. JT had hid his true self behind a very handsome, very charming façade.

Along with various trinkets and mementoes from his victims, JT kept a journal of the killings. The accounts were rich in description but completely devoid of emotion. He seemed to believe he was doing the world a favor by eliminating "predatory females." The only person, besides his late father, he claimed to care about was Ben, who didn't appreciate "the gift" JT had given him by murdering Olivia. Darrius O'Shea and Arlen Matthews had been nothing more than "convenient sacrifices for a greater cause."

After the story broke, one of O'Shea's comrades came forward with another sad tale. During his final tour of duty, O'Shea had been involved in a mission that had gone terribly wrong. An innocent had been gunned down. The veteran said he'd always wondered if O'Shea confessed to a crime he didn't commit because he felt so guilty about the one he did.

Sonny wished she could have stayed in California and ridden out the aftermath of the scandal with

Ben. His face had been all over the newspapers once again. He'd insisted on attending JT's funeral, and the photos of him at the grave site were on every front page.

Now, three weeks later, the frenzy had finally died down.

She knew he'd be out on the water. It was another glorious winter day, sunny and cool, and judging by the number of wetsuits dotting the blue horizon, the surf was up. When she spotted Ben, her heart jumped. Weak-kneed and dry-mouthed, she watched him from the shore.

At first, he didn't notice her. He was as steadfast as always, single-minded in his focus, unswerving in his intensity. But, to her surprise, his concentration broke, and he glanced toward her.

Her pulse pounded, rushing through her veins.

She told herself not to get too excited when he came out of the water. They hadn't discussed future plans. He hadn't made her any promises. Now that he'd had time to reflect, he might not want to have anything more to do with her.

As he dropped his surfboard in the sand, she swallowed dryly. "Hey, stranger," she said in a hoarse voice.

All of her second thoughts evaporated like mist when he took her in his arms and he swept her off her feet. This was a man who knew what he wanted. This was real. Salt water soaked through her T-shirt and jeans everywhere her body touched his. His shoulders were hard as granite beneath her hands and his neck was cool and moist against her trembling lips.

"You're getting me all wet," she mumbled, deliriously happy to be here with him. He was squeezing her breathless, and she loved it.

He stepped back to look at her, drinking in her appearance. Smiling, he cupped his hand around her chin and rubbed his thumb over her cheek. "Are you here to stay?"

She blushed and nodded, covering his hand with hers. For the first time in her life, she wished she was beautiful. The dye had kind of ruined her hair, so she'd had it cropped short. At least it was back to its natural color.

"I'll have to take you inside and warm you up," he said, his eyes moving from her face to the front of her body, which was indecently revealed by her wet T-shirt.

She flushed again, but not with embarrassment. "I don't expect us to just...take up where we left off," she stuttered, feeling foolish. Thirty seconds in his presence, and she was already getting all hot and bothered. "I mean, our emotions were running high that night, so if you didn't mean what you said..."

He tore his gaze from her chest, nonplussed. Then his expression cleared. "Oh, I meant it," he asserted, daring her to dispute him. "I love you."

Her heart melted. "I love you, too," she said, tears pricking her eyes.

The corner of his mouth tipped up. "Does this mean we can go back to my place and get you out of those wet clothes?"

When she said yes, he took her in his arms again, wrapping her in a tight embrace. Laughter welled up inside her, overflowing. He kissed her tears away and tasted the happiness on her lips, smiling against her mouth, sharing her joy.

It was a perfect day.

## ABOUT THE AUTHOR

Jill Sorenson's family moved from a small town in Kansas to a suburb of San Diego when she was twelve. In the past twenty years, she hasn't lost her appreciation for sunny weather, her fascination with the Pacific Ocean, or her love for Southern California culture. She still lives in San Diego with her husband, Chris, and their two children. Jill is happily working on her next novel.